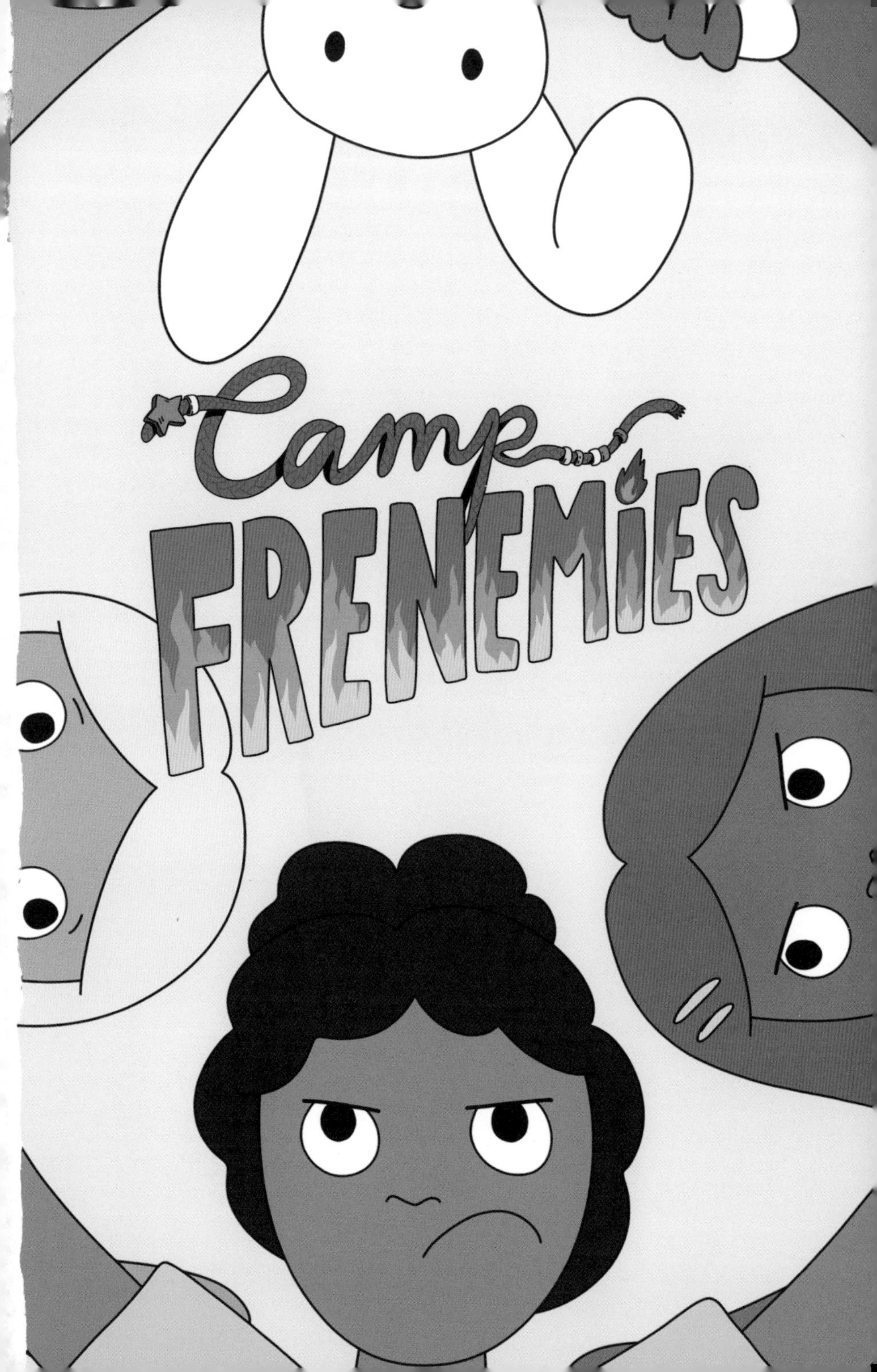
Camp
FRENEMIES

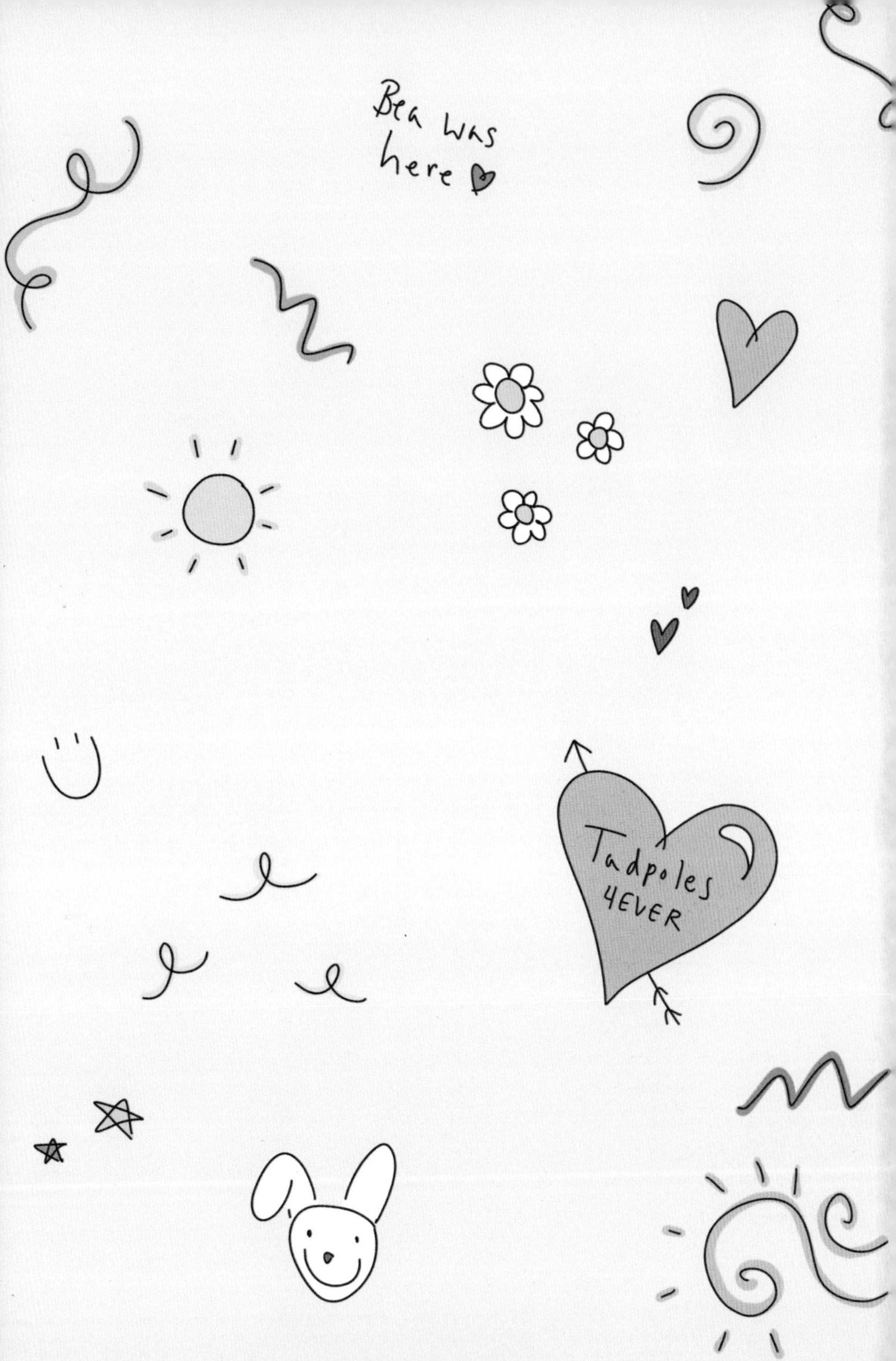
Bea was here
Tadpoles 4EVER

Camp FRENEMIES

LIZ MONTAGUE

RANDOM HOUSE STUDIO
NEW YORK

TO JENN AND ERIN,

MY FIRST CAMP FRIENDS

All rights reserved. Published in the United States by Random House Studio, an imprint of Random House Children's Books, a division of Penguin Random House LLC, New York. Random House Studio with colophon is a registered trademark of Penguin Random House LLC. RH Graphic with the book design is a trademark of Penguin Random House LLC.

Visit us on the Web! rhcbooks.com

Educators and librarians, for a variety of teaching tools, visit us at RHTeachersLibrarians.com

Library of Congress Cataloging-in-Publication Data is available upon request.

ISBN 978-0-593-80623-4 (hardcover) · ISBN 978-0-593-80625-8 (paperback)
ISBN 978-0-593-80624-1 (ebook)

The text of this book is set in Maybe an Artist.
The artist used an XPPEN tablet display and Adobe Photoshop to render the illustrations in this book.
Interior design by Jules Buckley and Sylvia Bi

MANUFACTURED IN CHINA
10 9 8 7 6 5 4 3 2 1
First Edition

I have *Love*
in me the likes
of which you can <u>scarcely</u>
<u>imagine</u> and **Rage**
the likes of which you
would <u>**not**</u> believe.
If I cannot satisfy the
one, I will indulge
the <u>**other.**</u>

—Mary Shelley

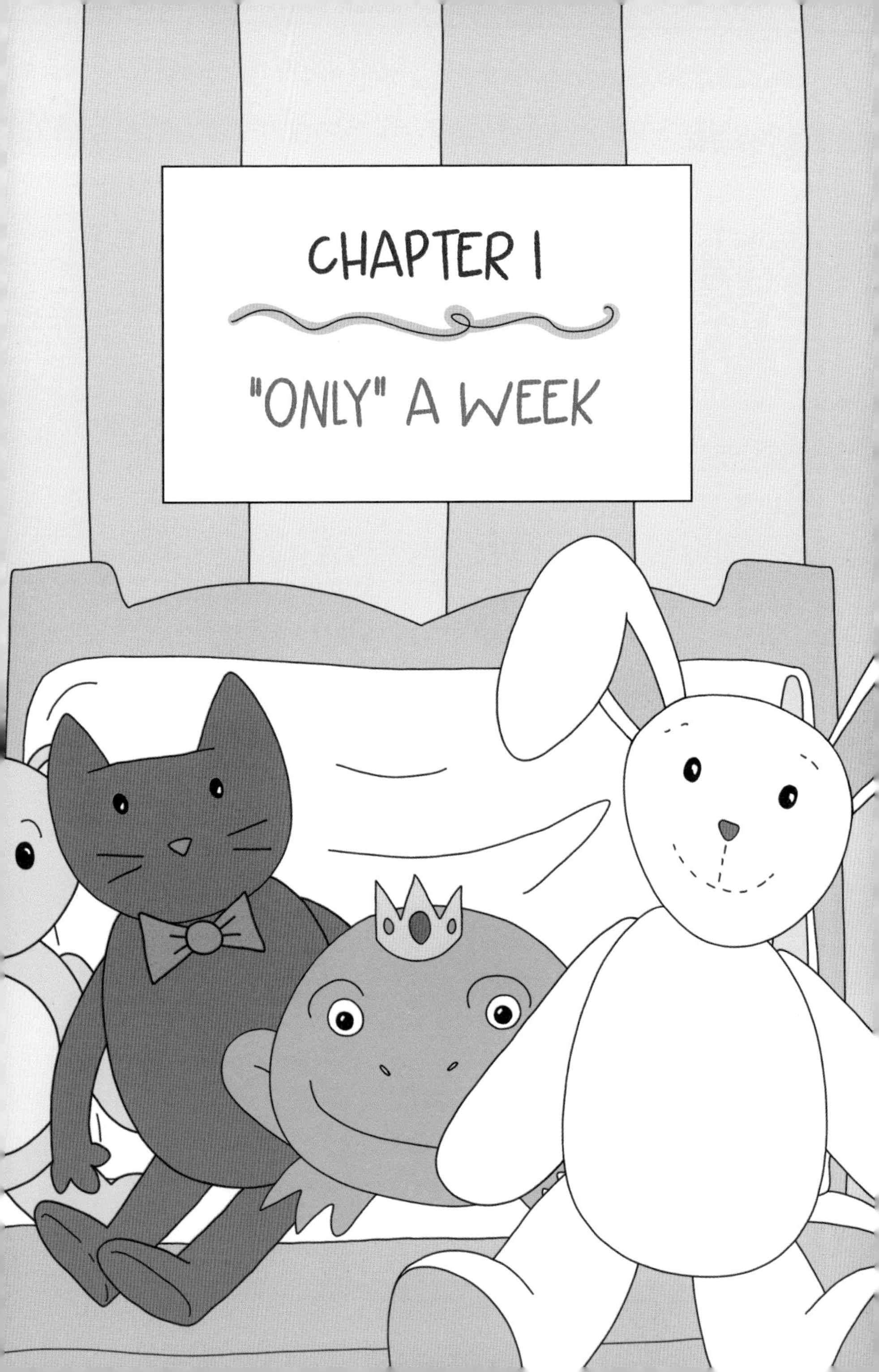
CHAPTER 1
"ONLY" A WEEK

Never again?

Yes, Beatrice.
Never again.

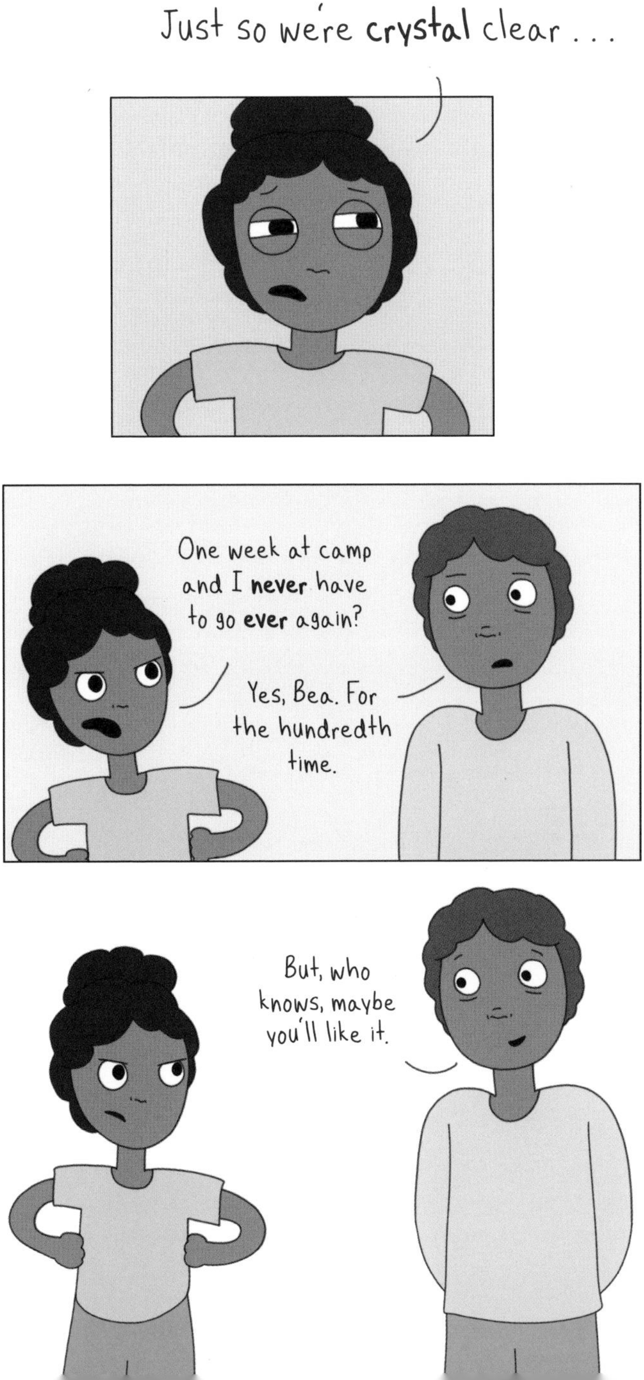
Just so we're **crystal** clear . . .
One week at camp and I **never** have to go **ever** again?
Yes, Bea. For the hundredth time.
But, who knows, maybe you'll like it.

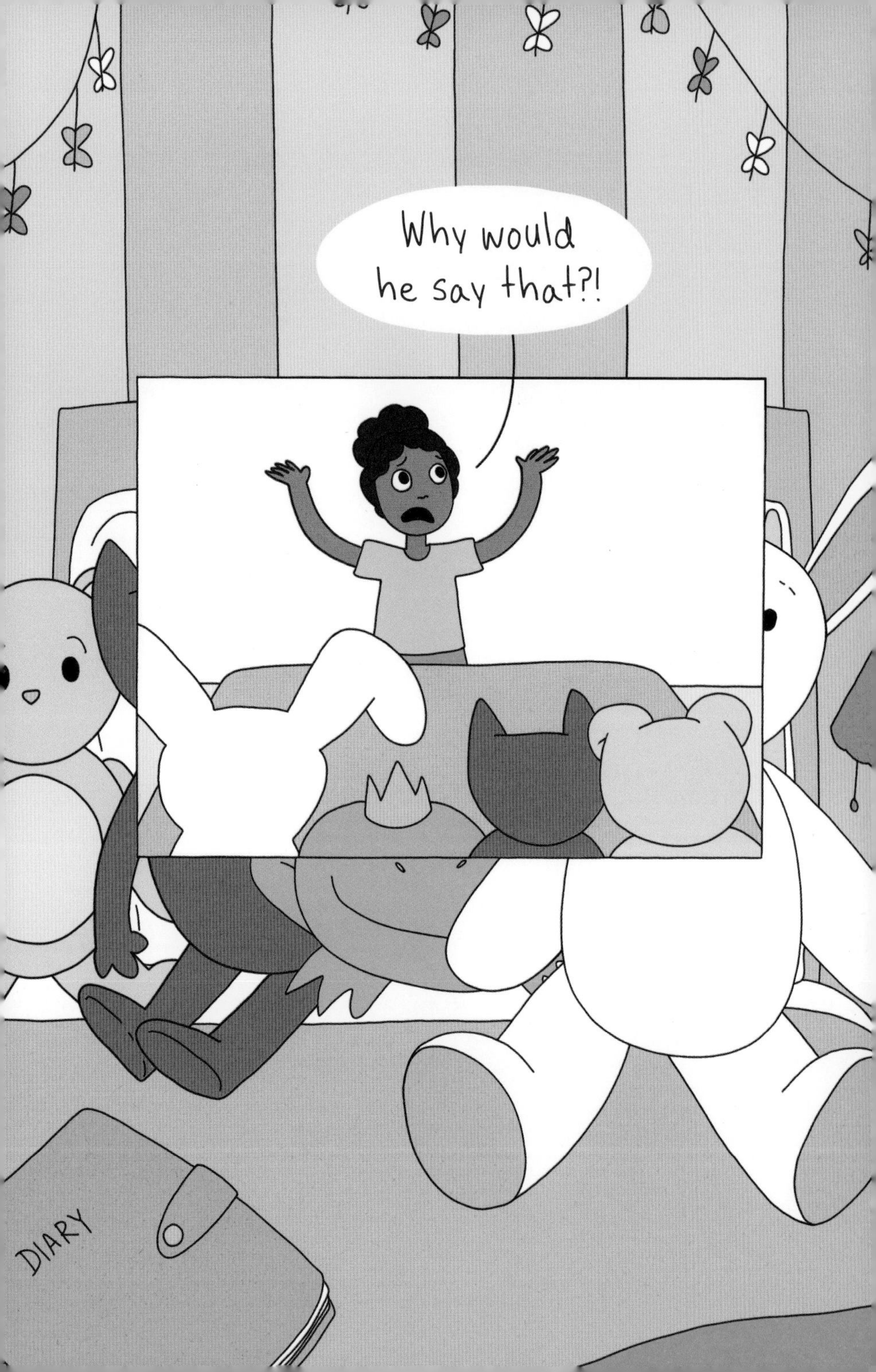
Why would he say that?!
DIARY

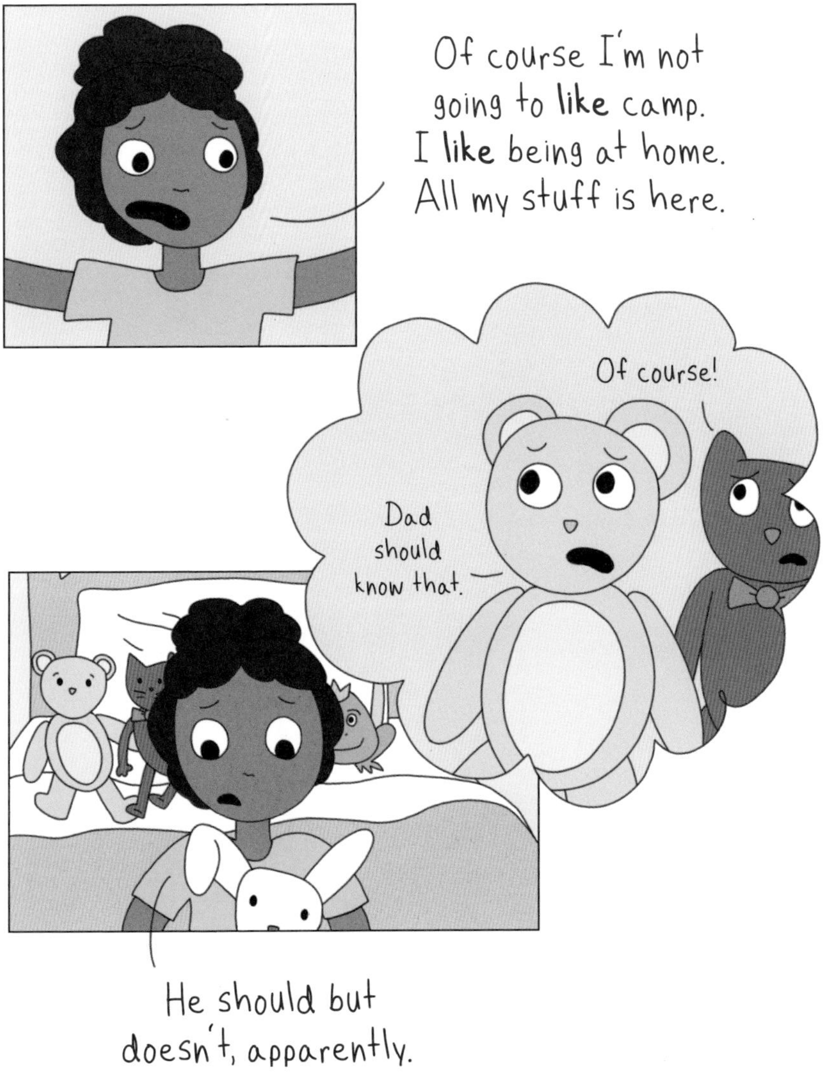
Of course I'm not going to **like** camp. I **like** being at home. All my stuff is here.
Dad should know that.
Of course!
He should but doesn't, apparently.

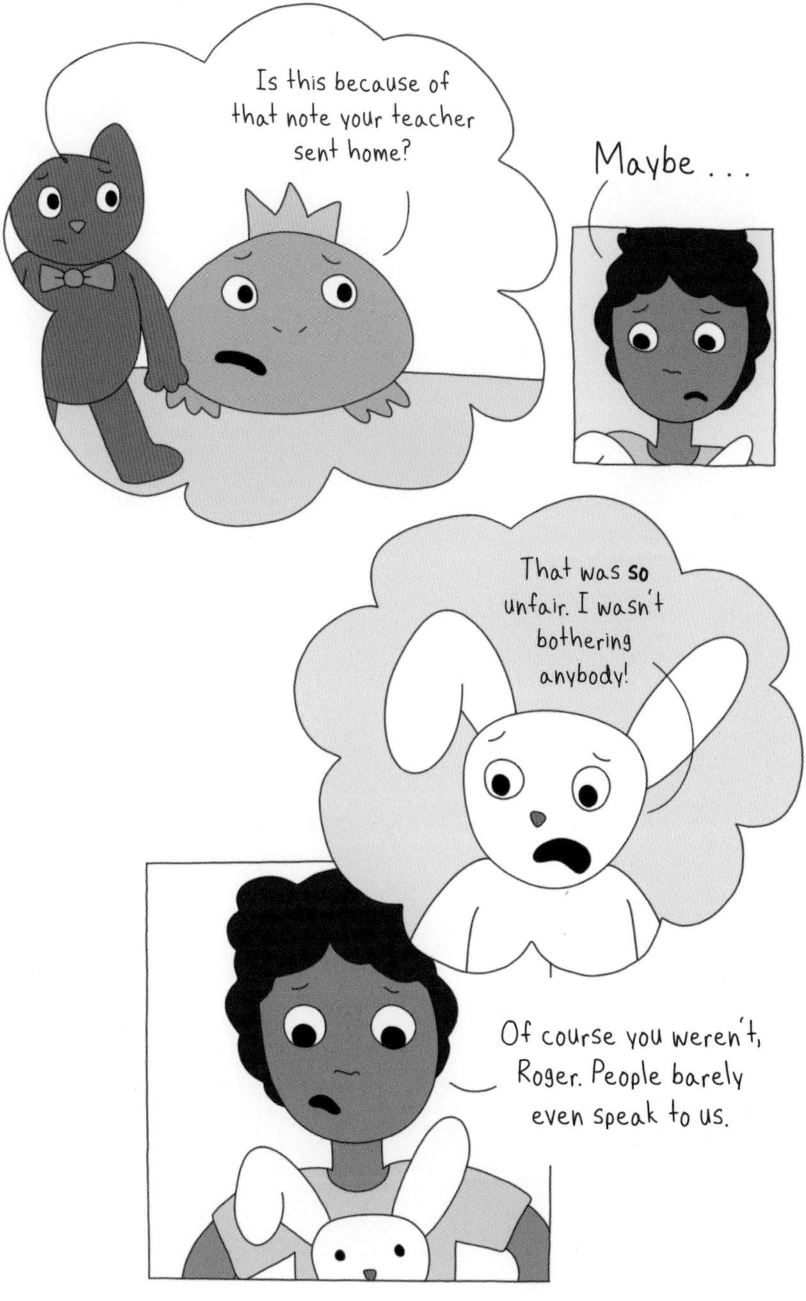

Is this because of that note your teacher sent home?
Maybe . . .
That was **so** unfair. I wasn't bothering anybody!
Of course you weren't, Roger. People barely even speak to us.

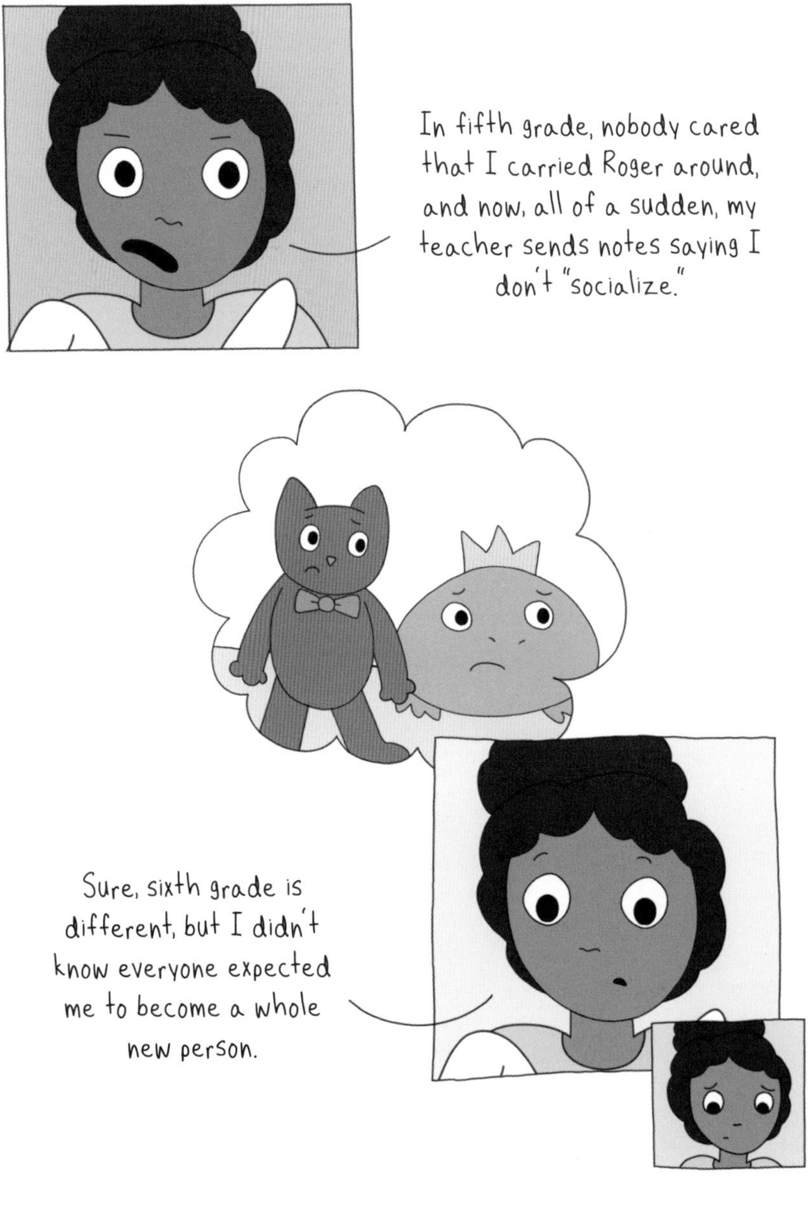
In fifth grade, nobody cared that I carried Roger around, and now, all of a sudden, my teacher sends notes saying I don't "socialize."
Sure, sixth grade is different, but I didn't know everyone expected me to become a whole new person.

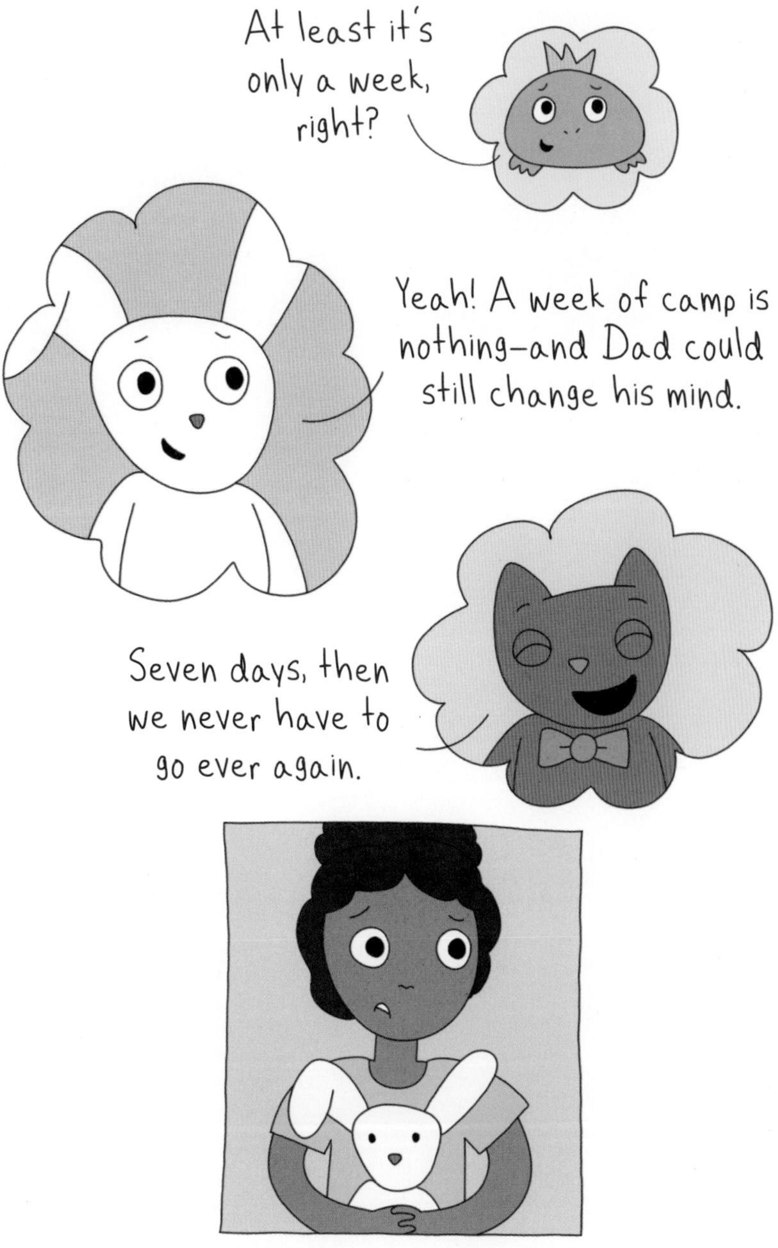
At least it's only a week, right?
Yeah! A week of camp is nothing–and Dad could still change his mind.
Seven days, then we never have to go ever again.

CHAPTER 2

FIRST DAY (UNFORTUNATELY)

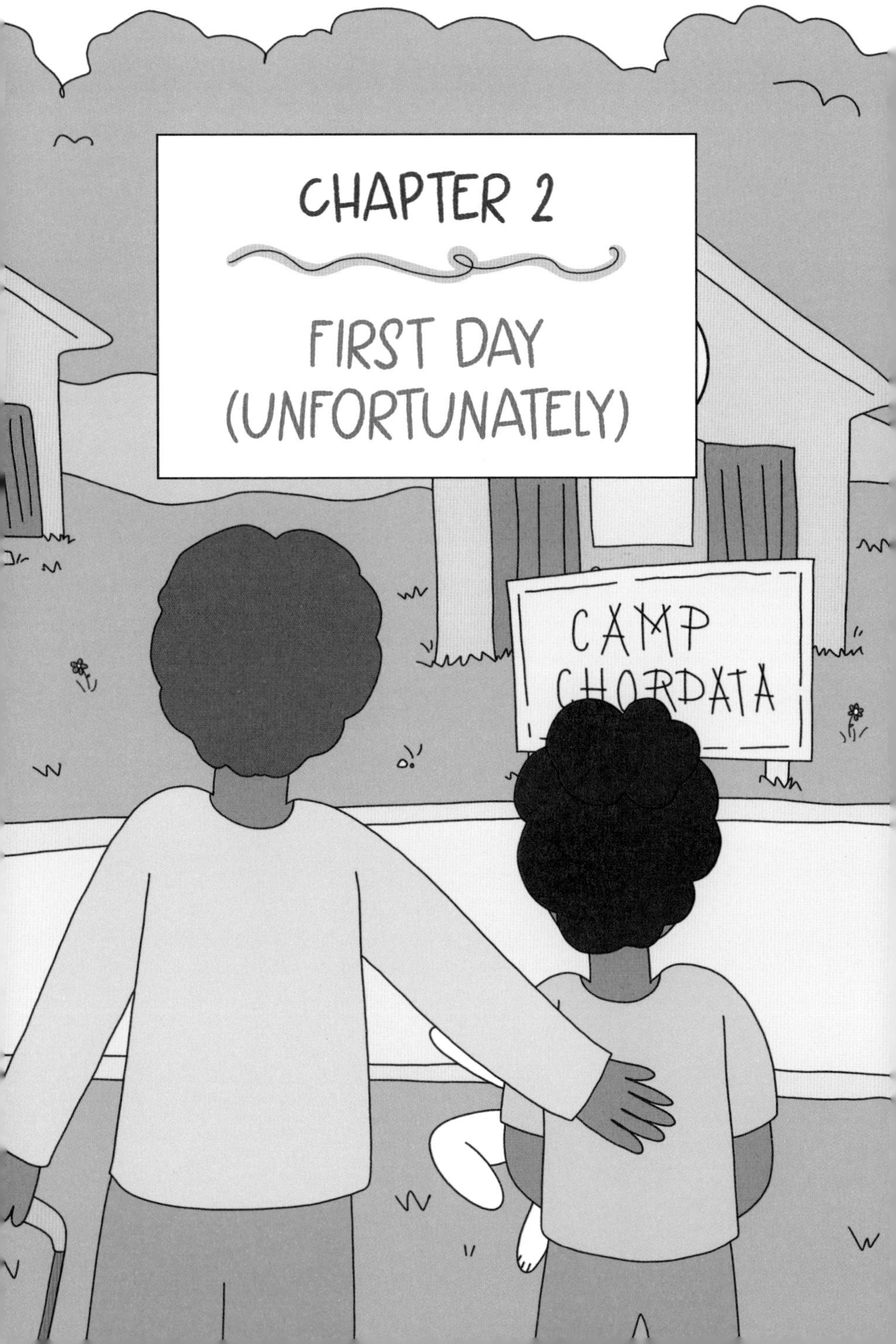
CAMP CHORDATA

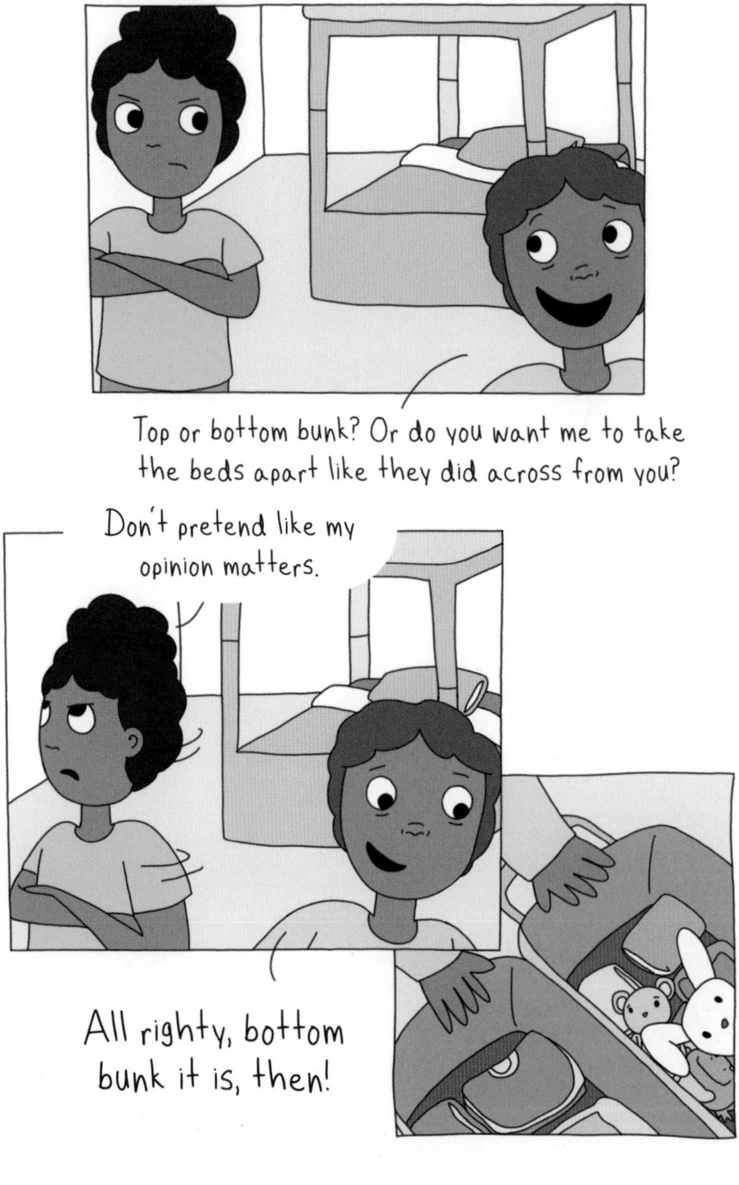

Top or bottom bunk? Or do you want me to take the beds apart like they did across from you?
Don't pretend like my opinion matters.
All righty, bottom bunk it is, then!

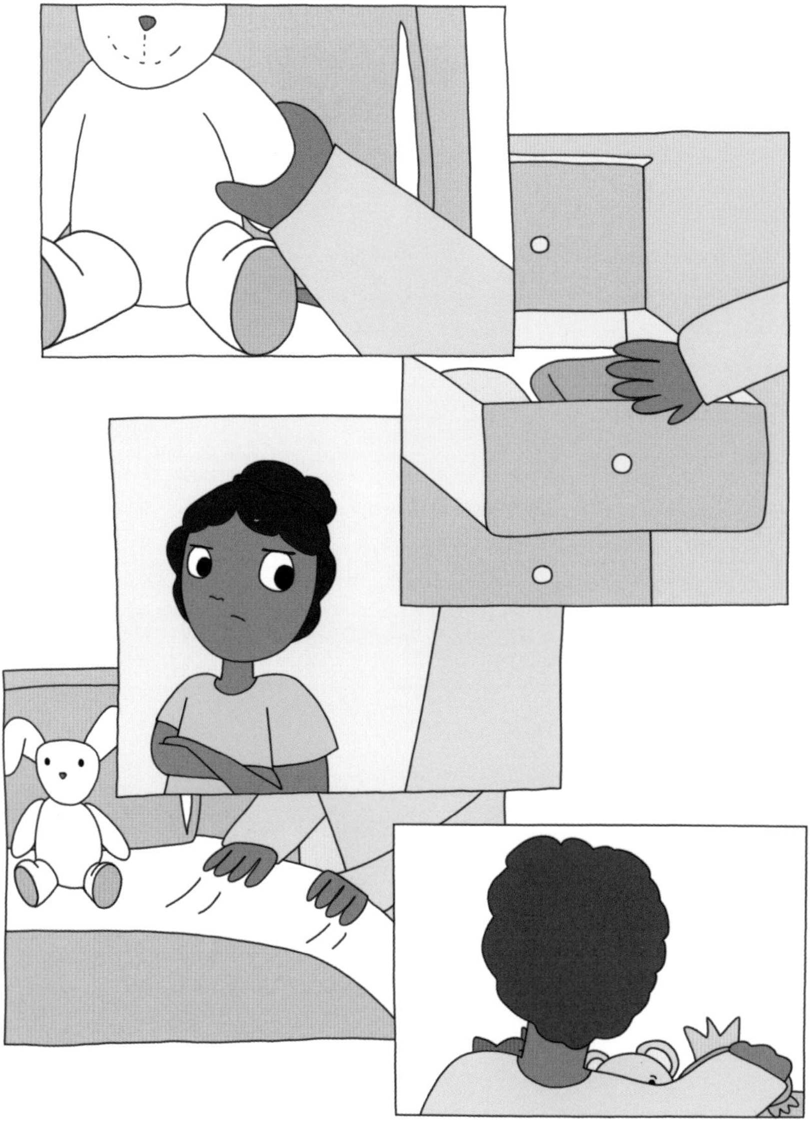

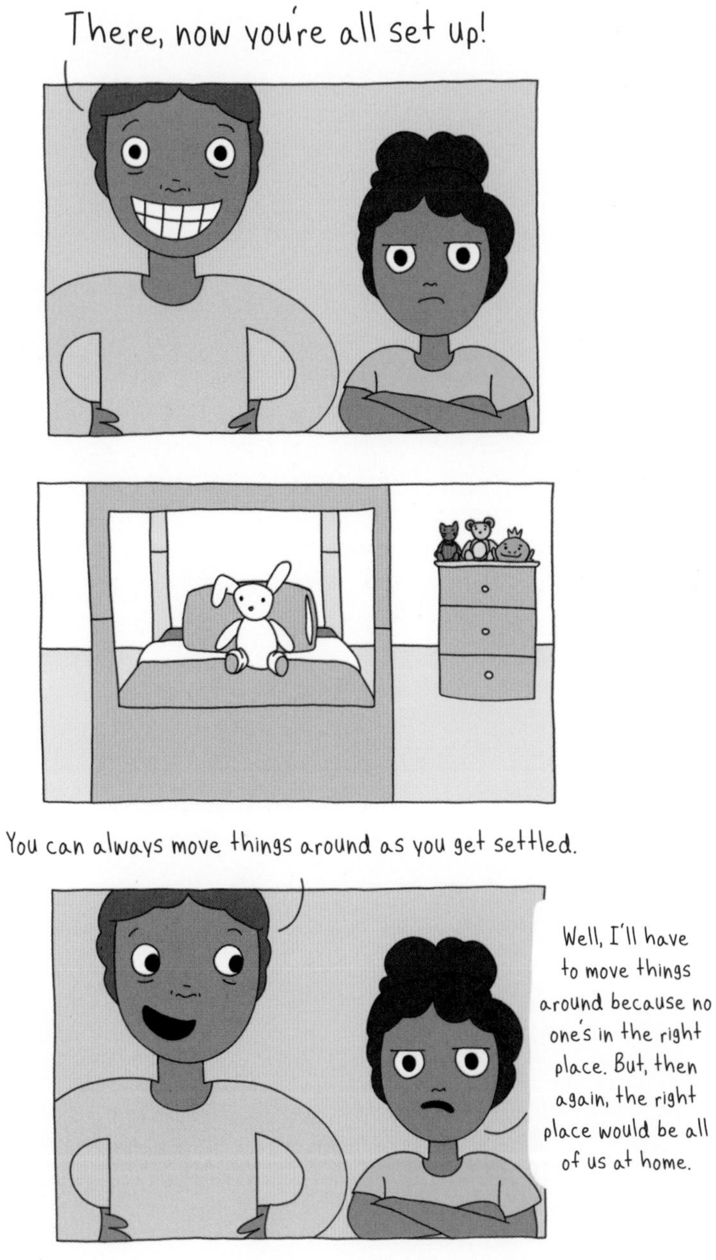
There, now you're all set up!
You can always move things around as you get settled.
Well, I'll have to move things around because no one's in the right place. But, then again, the right place would be all of us at home.

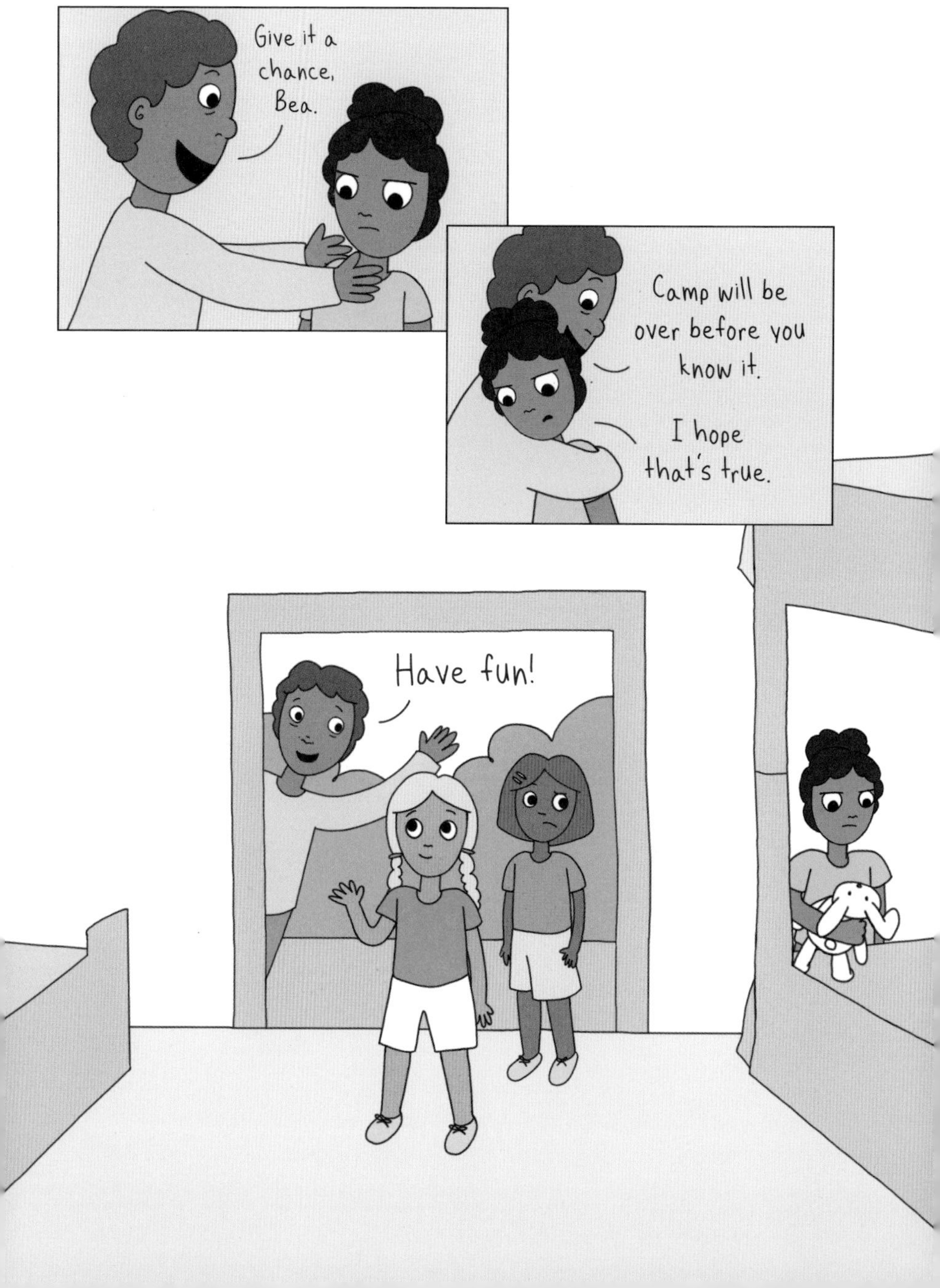
Give it a chance, Bea.
Camp will be over before you know it.
I hope that's true.
Have fun!

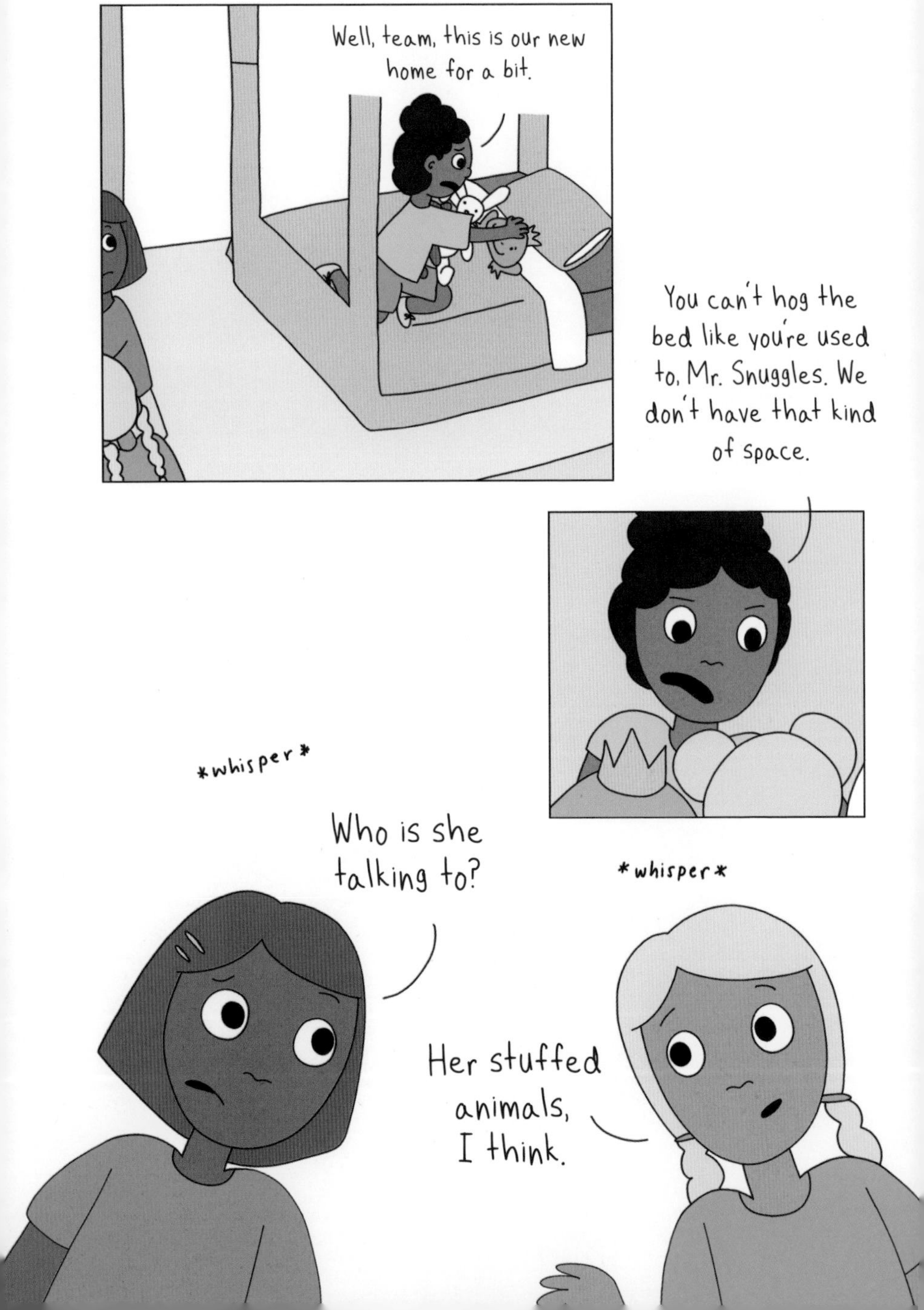
Well, team, this is our new home for a bit.
You can't hog the bed like you're used to, Mr. Snuggles. We don't have that kind of space.
whisper
Who is she talking to?
whisper
Her stuffed animals, I think.

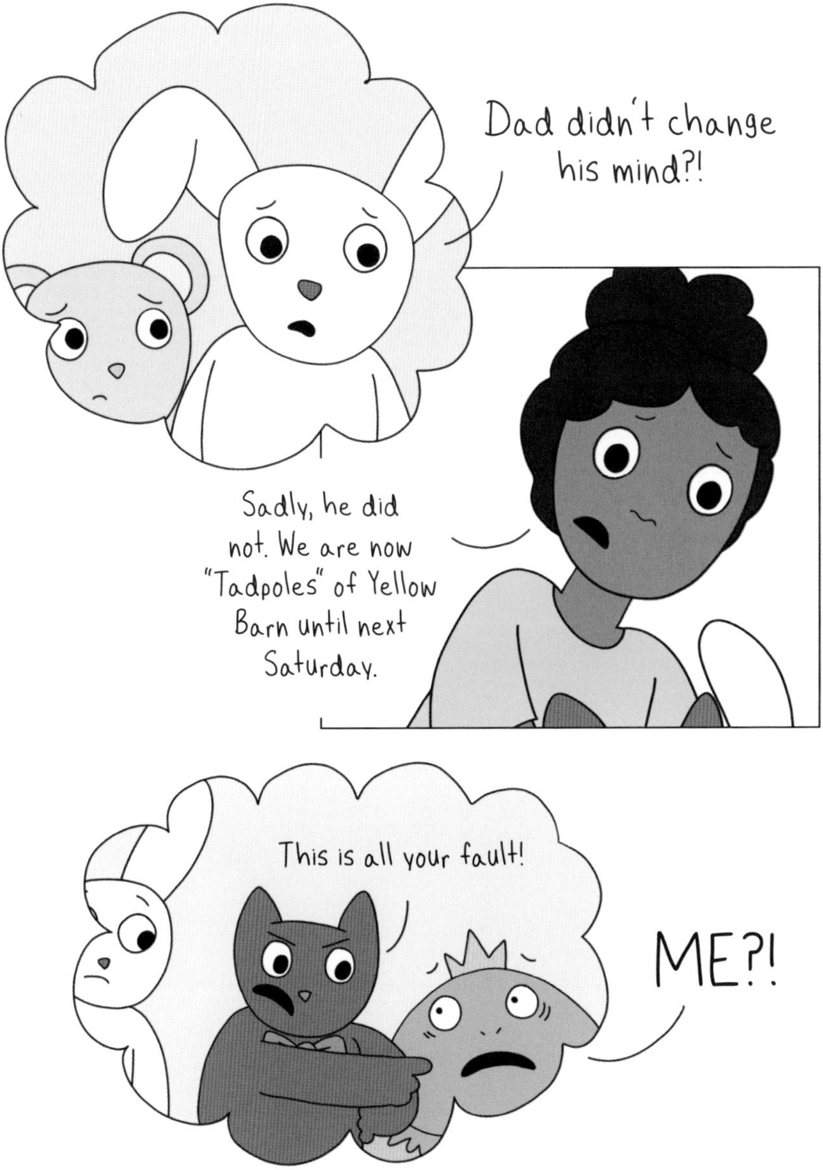
Dad didn't change his mind?!
Sadly, he did not. We are now "Tadpoles" of Yellow Barn until next Saturday.
This is all your fault!
ME?!

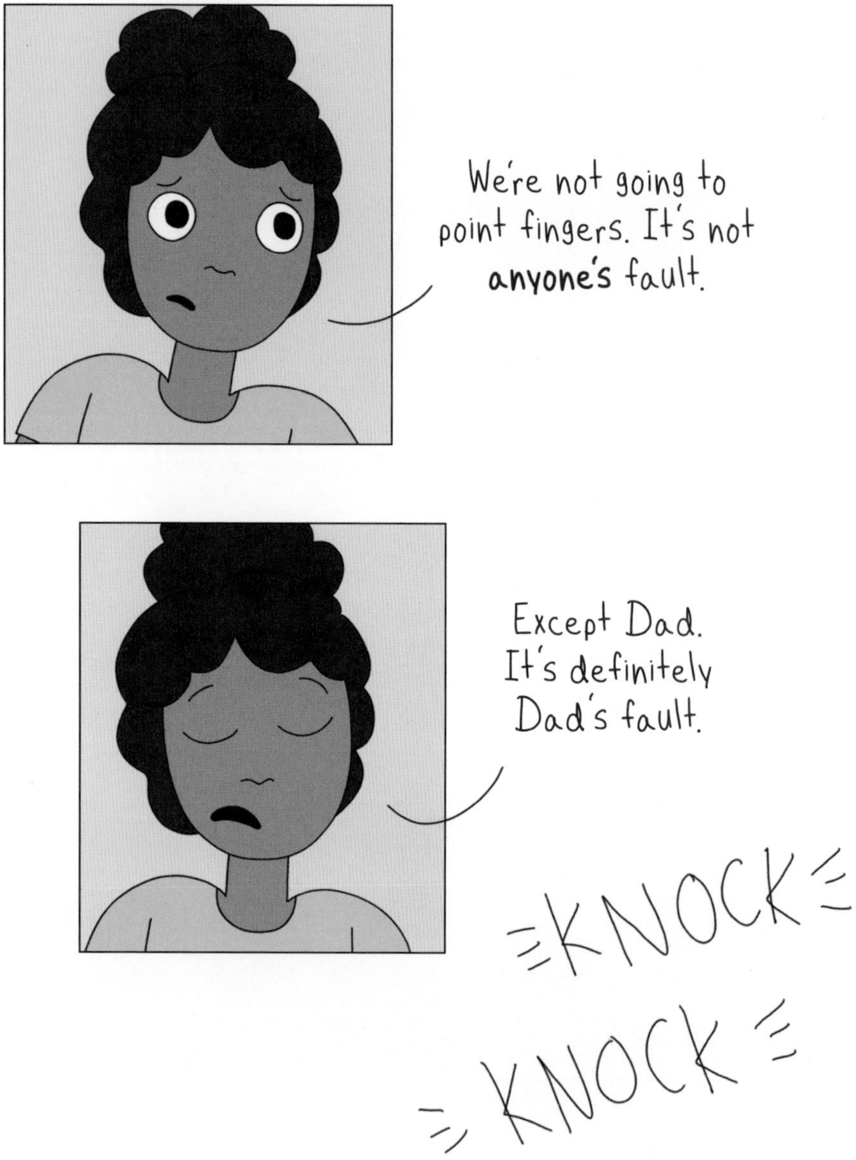
We're not going to point fingers. It's not **anyone's** fault.
Except Dad. It's definitely Dad's fault.
KNOCK
KNOCK

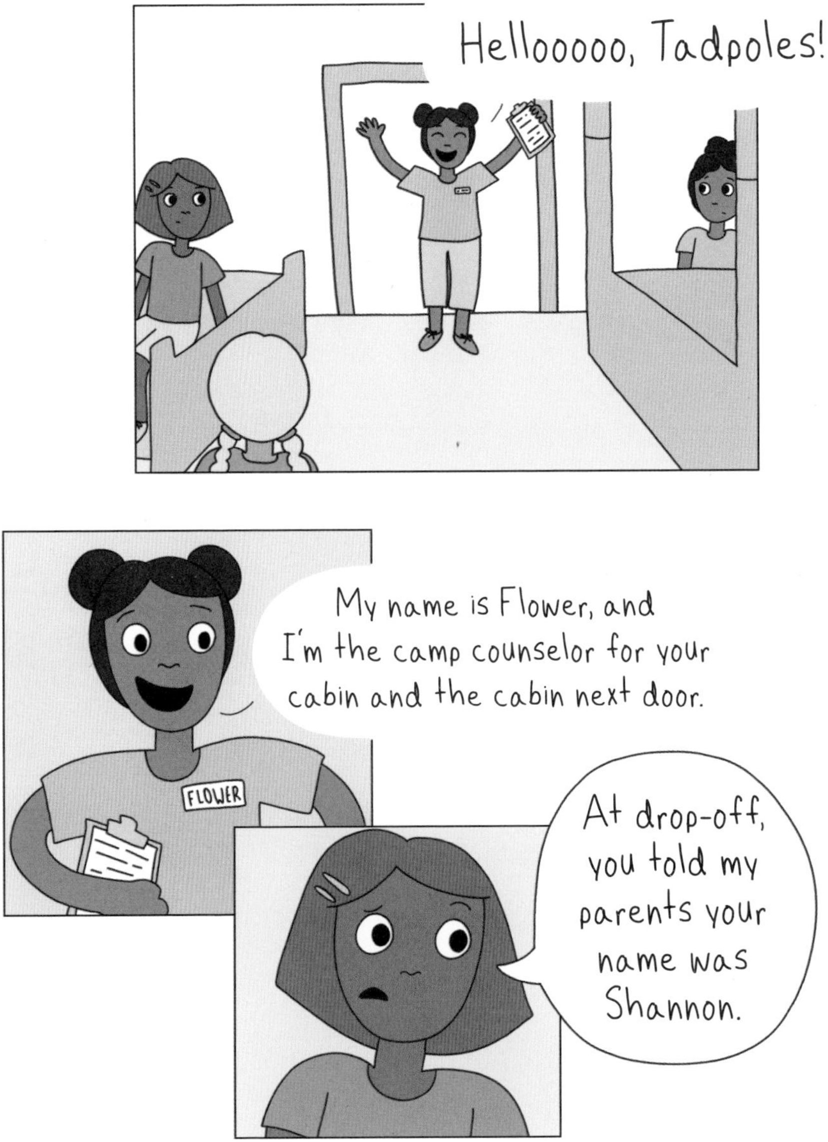
Hellooooo, Tadpoles!
My name is Flower, and I'm the camp counselor for your cabin and the cabin next door.
FLOWER
At drop-off, you told my parents your name was Shannon.

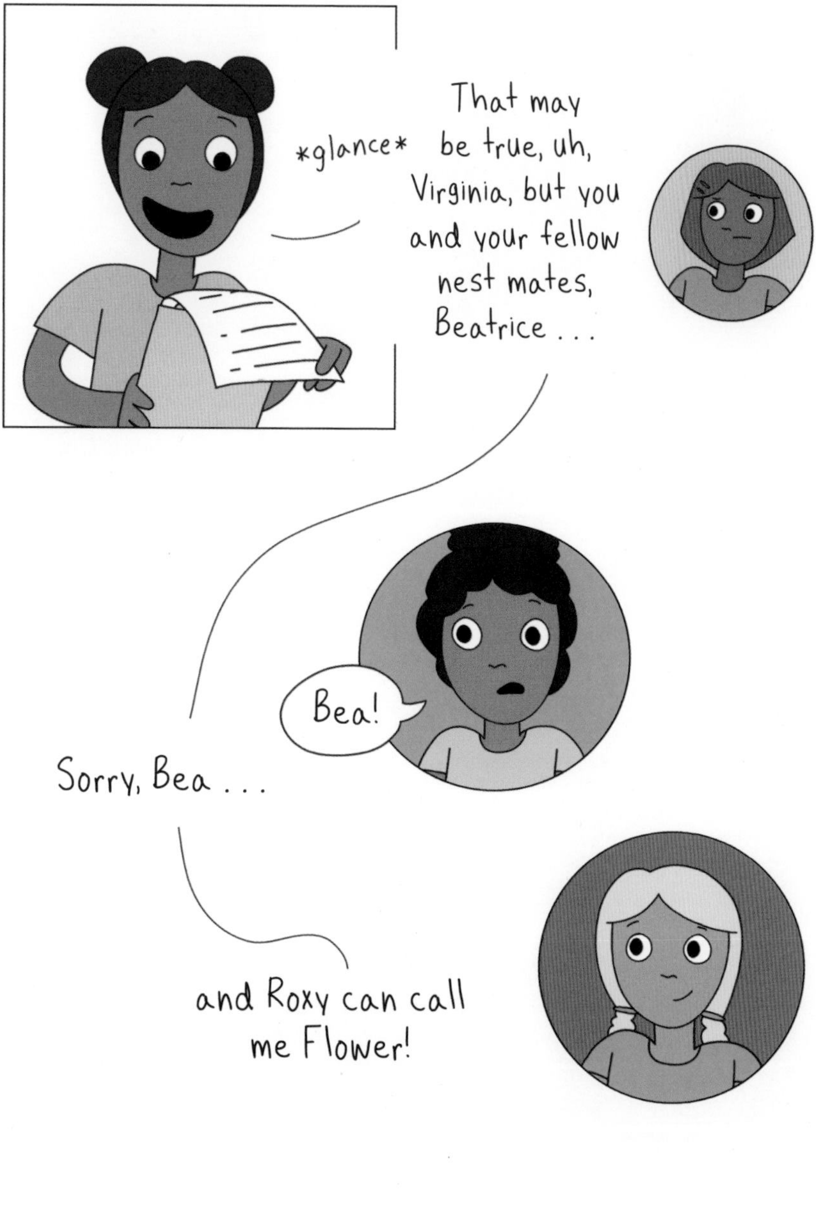
glance
That may be true, uh, Virginia, but you and your fellow nest mates, Beatrice . . .
Bea!
Sorry, Bea . . .
and Roxy can call me Flower!

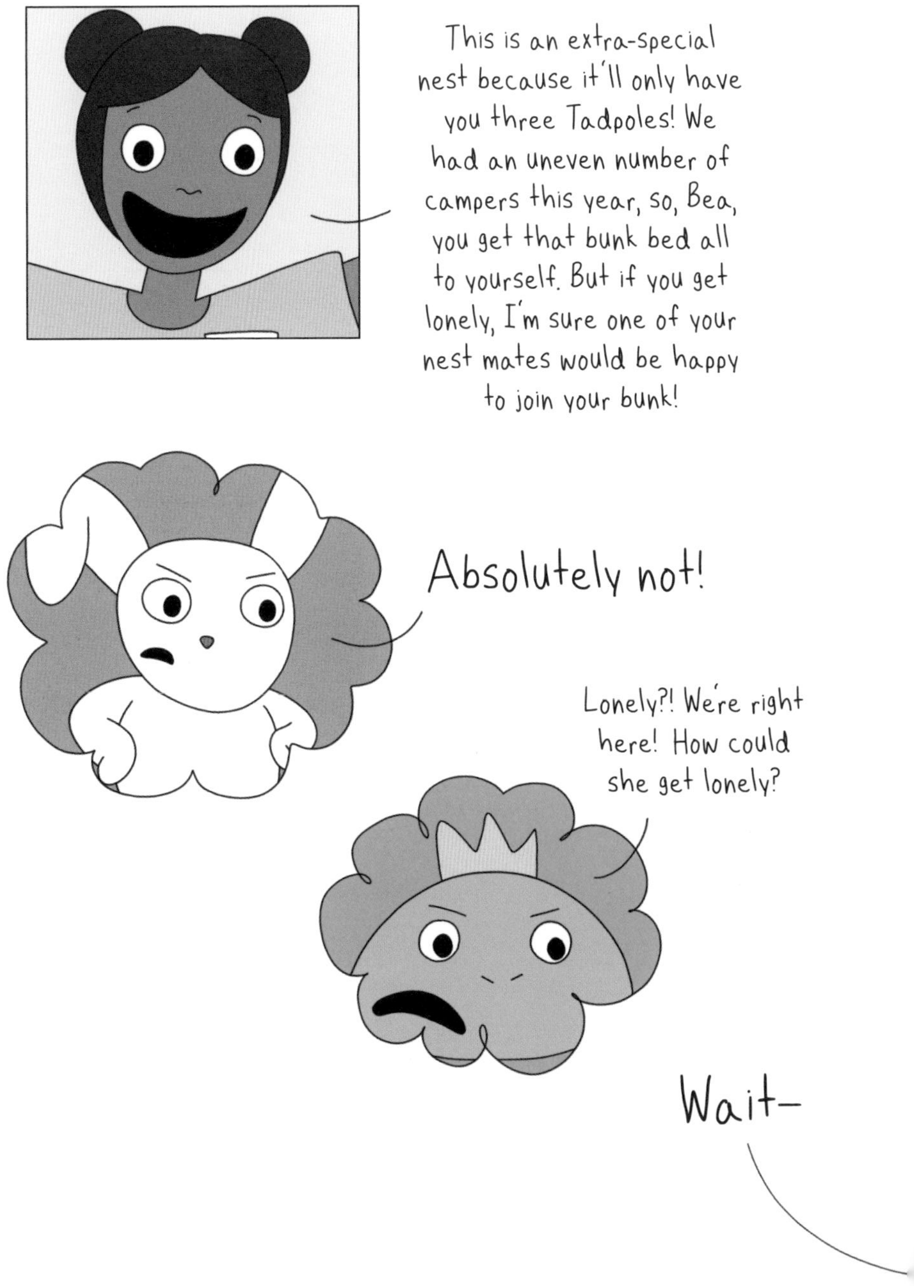
This is an extra-special nest because it'll only have you three Tadpoles! We had an uneven number of campers this year, so, Bea, you get that bunk bed all to yourself. But if you get lonely, I'm sure one of your nest mates would be happy to join your bunk!
Absolutely not!
Lonely?! We're right here! How could she get lonely?
Wait–

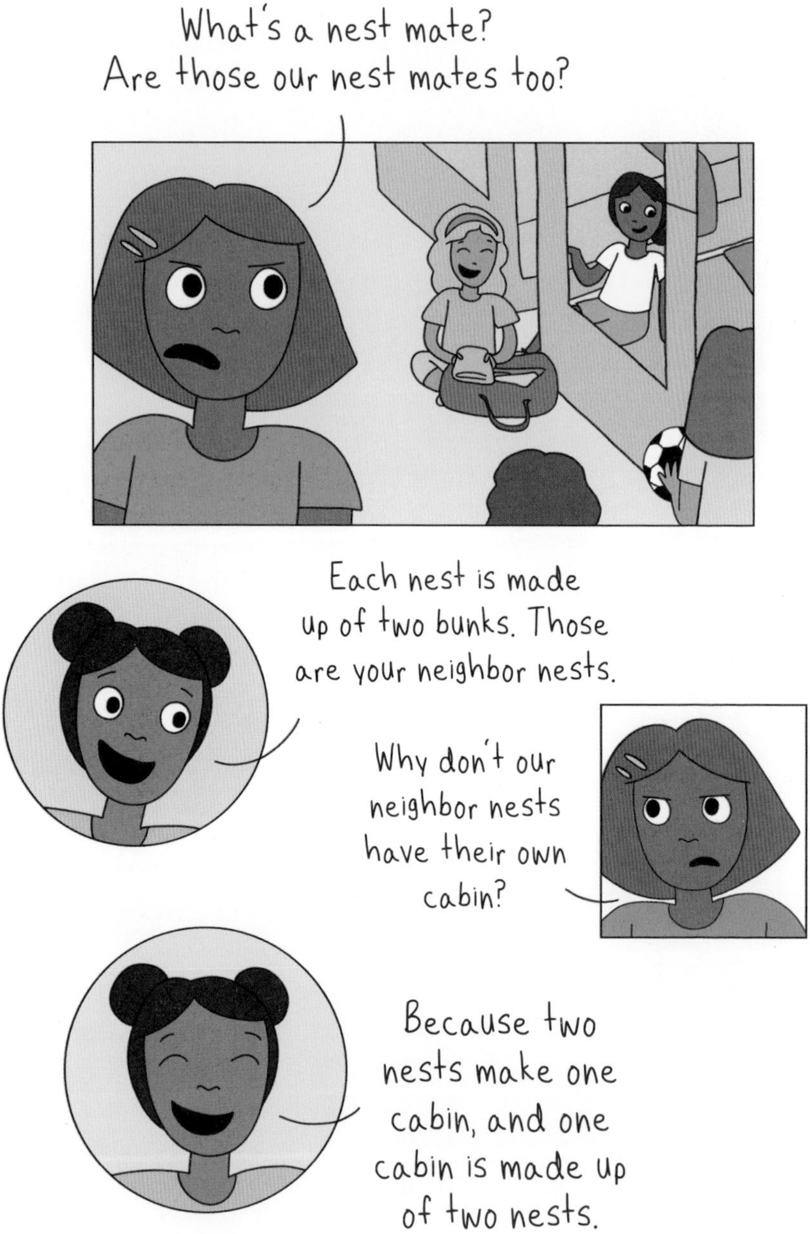
What's a nest mate?
Are those our nest mates too?
Each nest is made up of two bunks. Those are your neighbor nests.
Why don't our neighbor nests have their own cabin?
Because two nests make one cabin, and one cabin is made up of two nests.

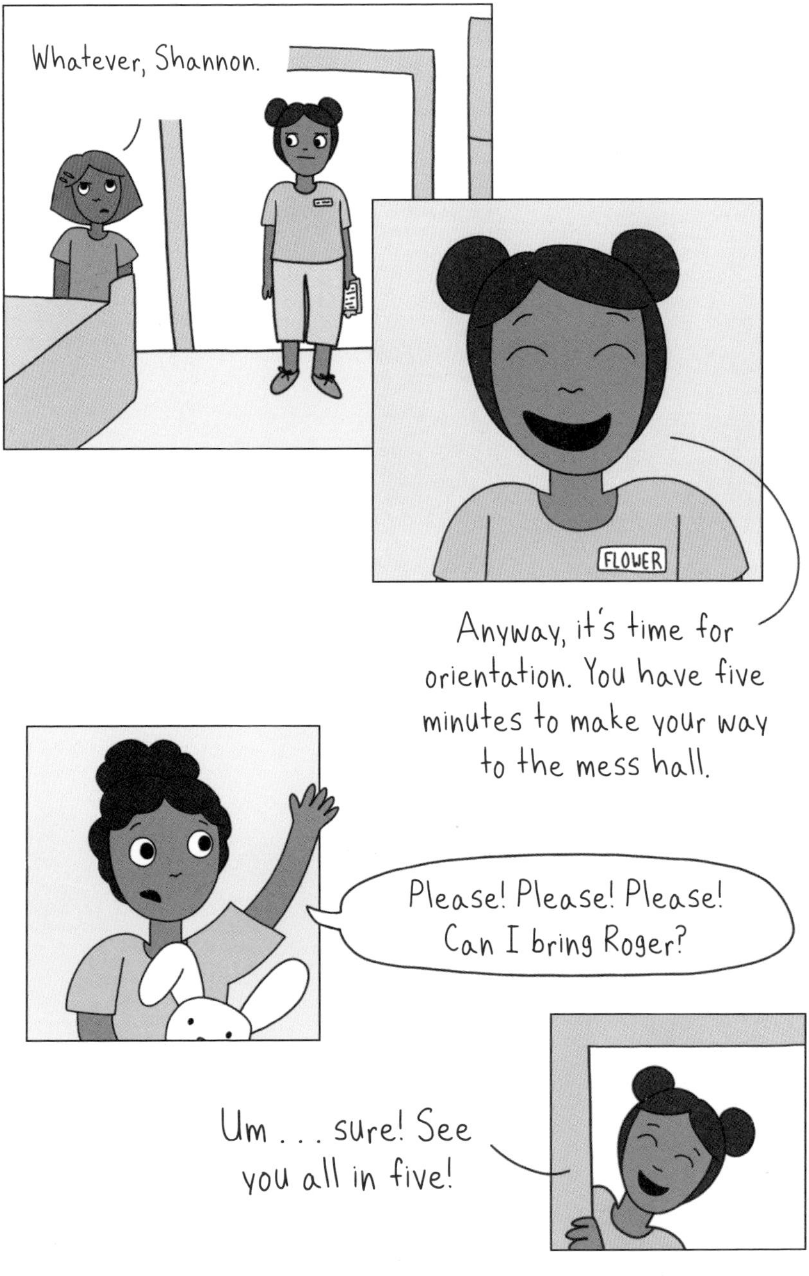
Whatever, Shannon.
FLOWER
Anyway, it's time for orientation. You have five minutes to make your way to the mess hall.
Please! Please! Please! Can I bring Roger?
Um . . . sure! See you all in five!

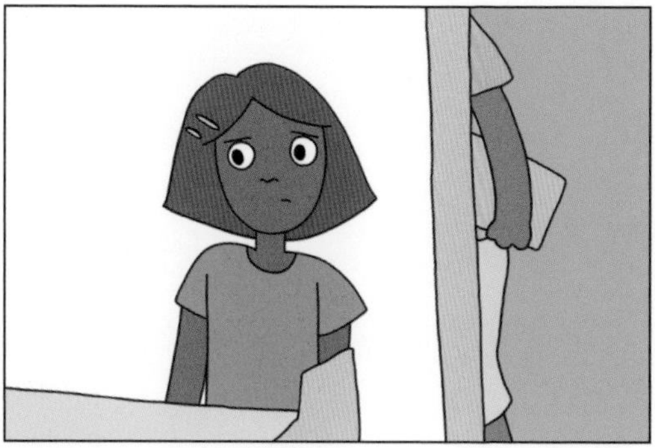

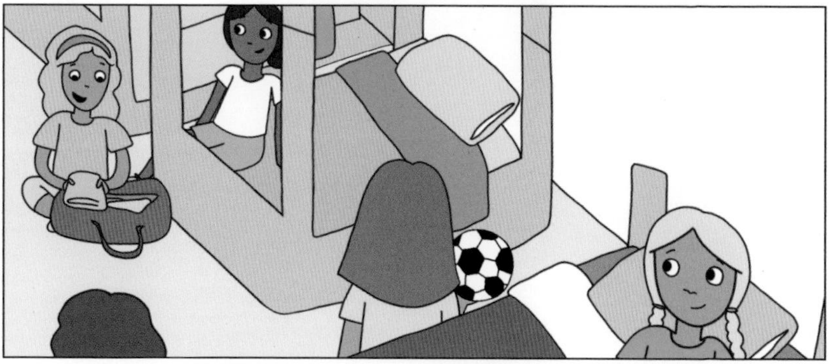

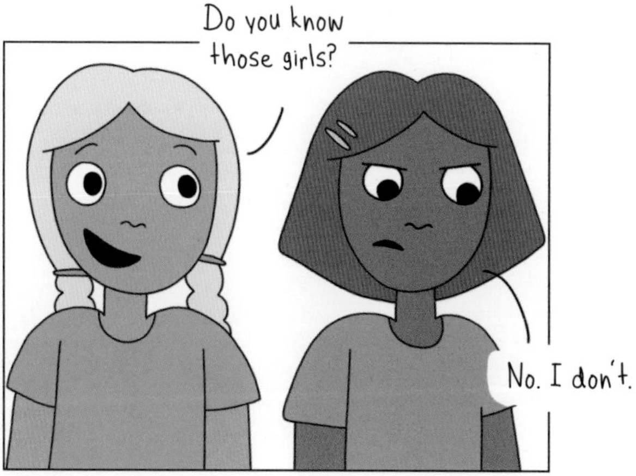
Do you know those girls?
No. I don't.

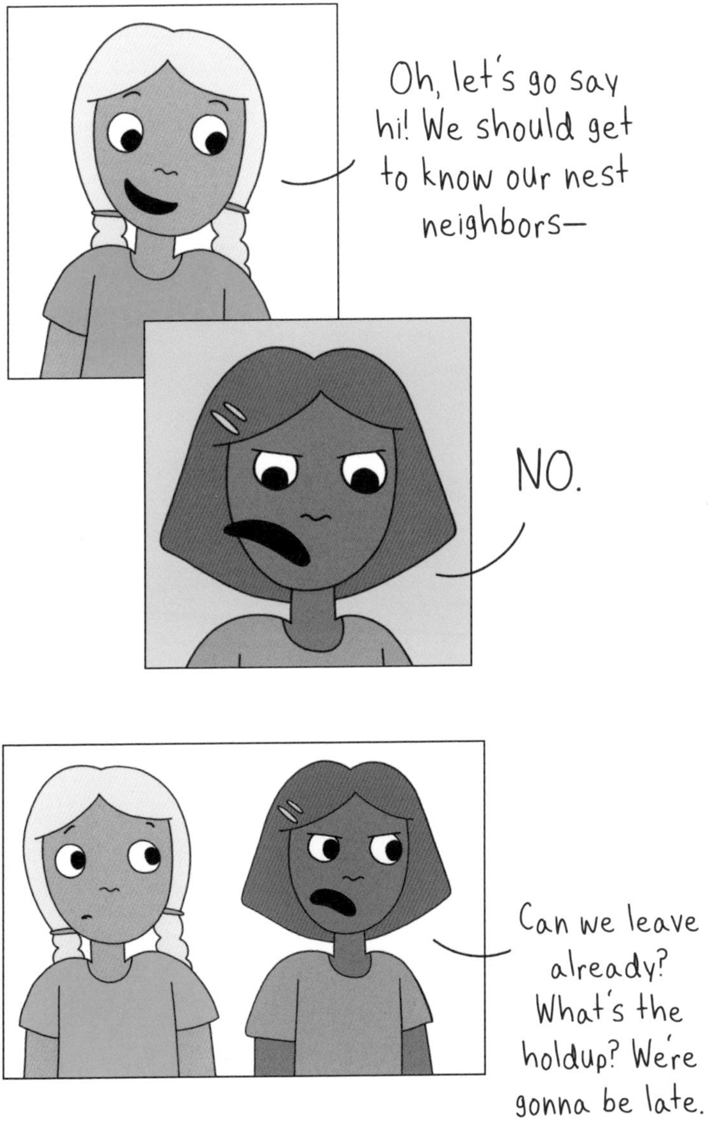
Oh, let's go say hi! We should get to know our nest neighbors—
NO.
Can we leave already? What's the holdup? We're gonna be late.

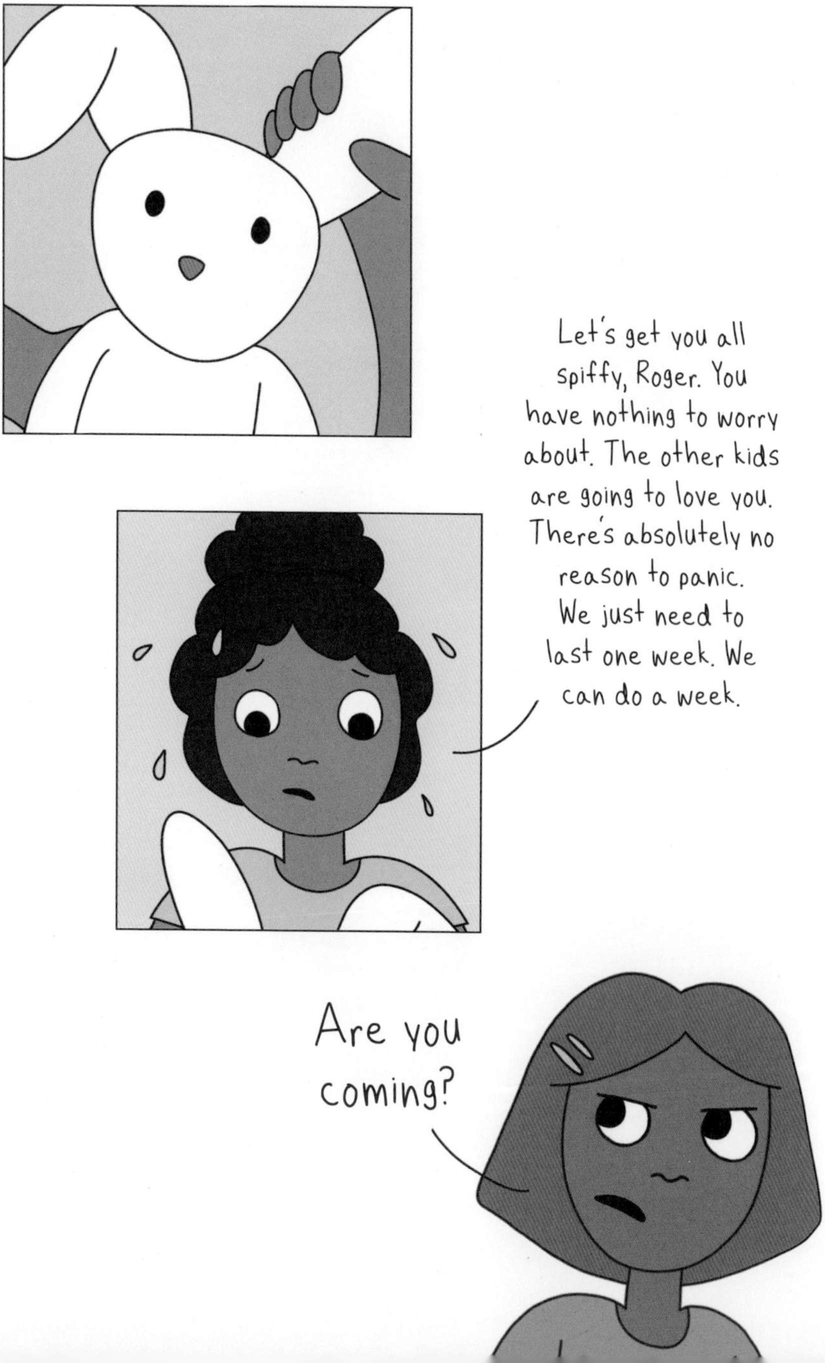
Let's get you all spiffy, Roger. You have nothing to worry about. The other kids are going to love you. There's absolutely no reason to panic. We just need to last one week. We can do a week.
Are you coming?

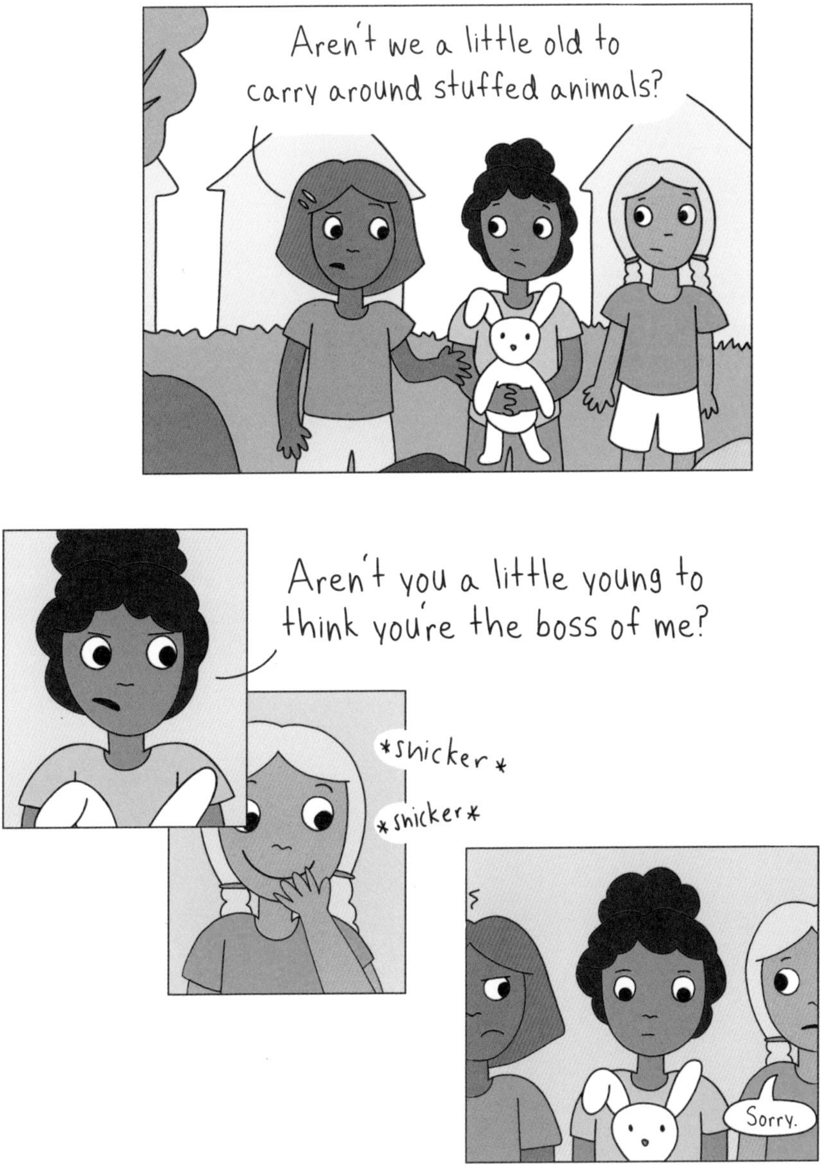
Aren't we a little old to carry around stuffed animals?
Aren't you a little young to think you're the boss of me?
snicker
snicker
Sorry.

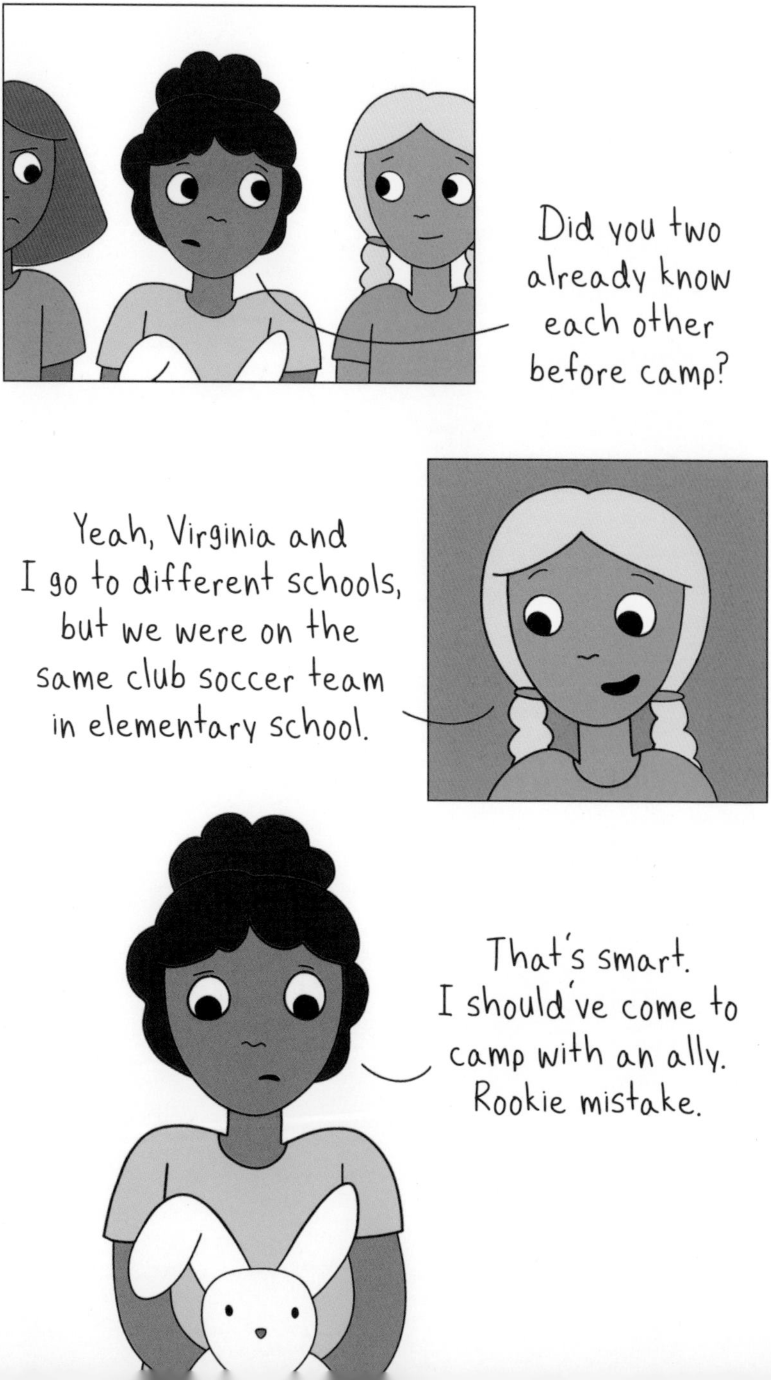
Did you two already know each other before camp?
Yeah, Virginia and I go to different schools, but we were on the same club soccer team in elementary school.
That's smart. I should've come to camp with an ally. Rookie mistake.

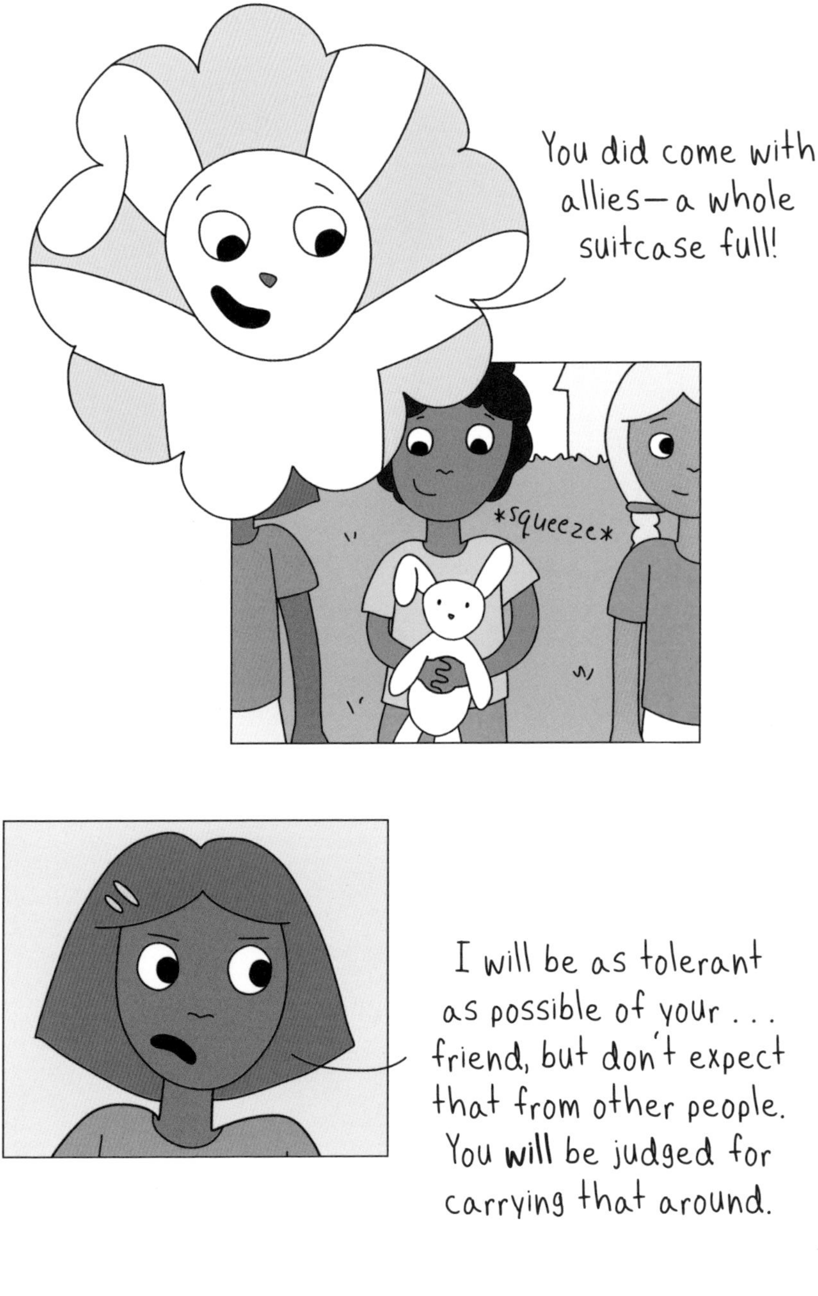
You did come with allies—a whole suitcase full!
squeeze
I will be as tolerant as possible of your . . . friend, but don't expect that from other people. You **will** be judged for carrying that around.

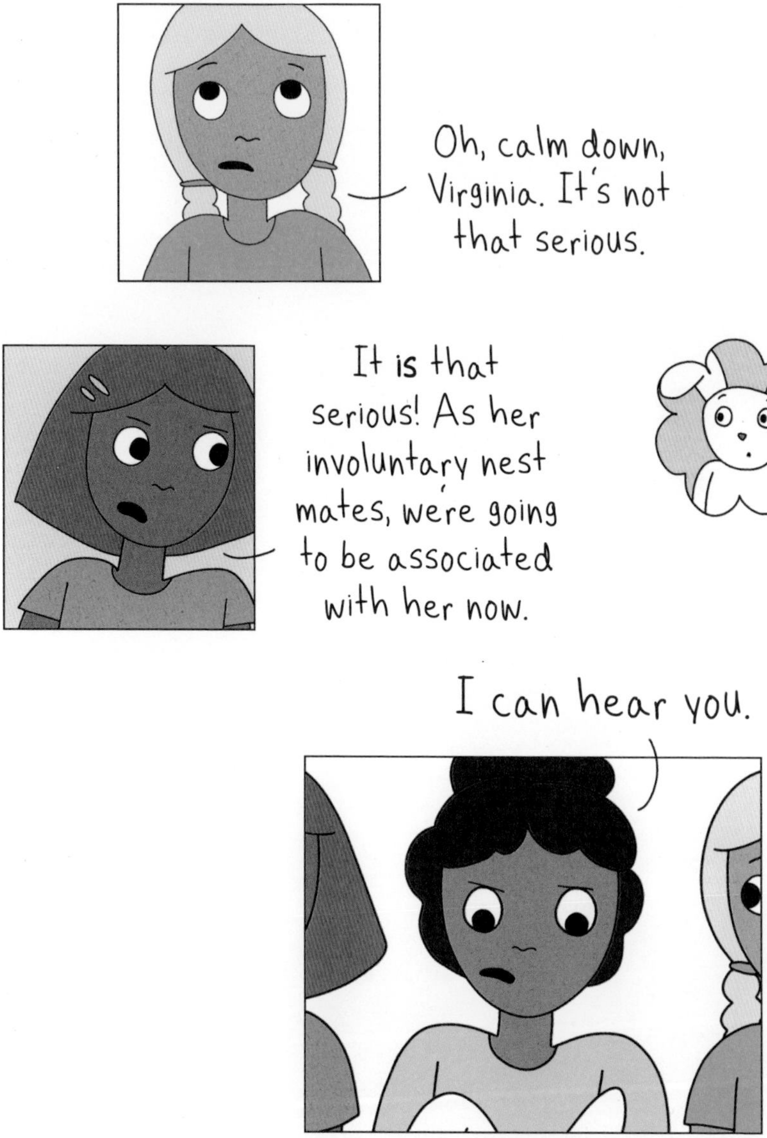
Oh, calm down, Virginia. It's not that serious.
It **is** that serious! As her involuntary nest mates, we're going to be associated with her now.
I can hear you.

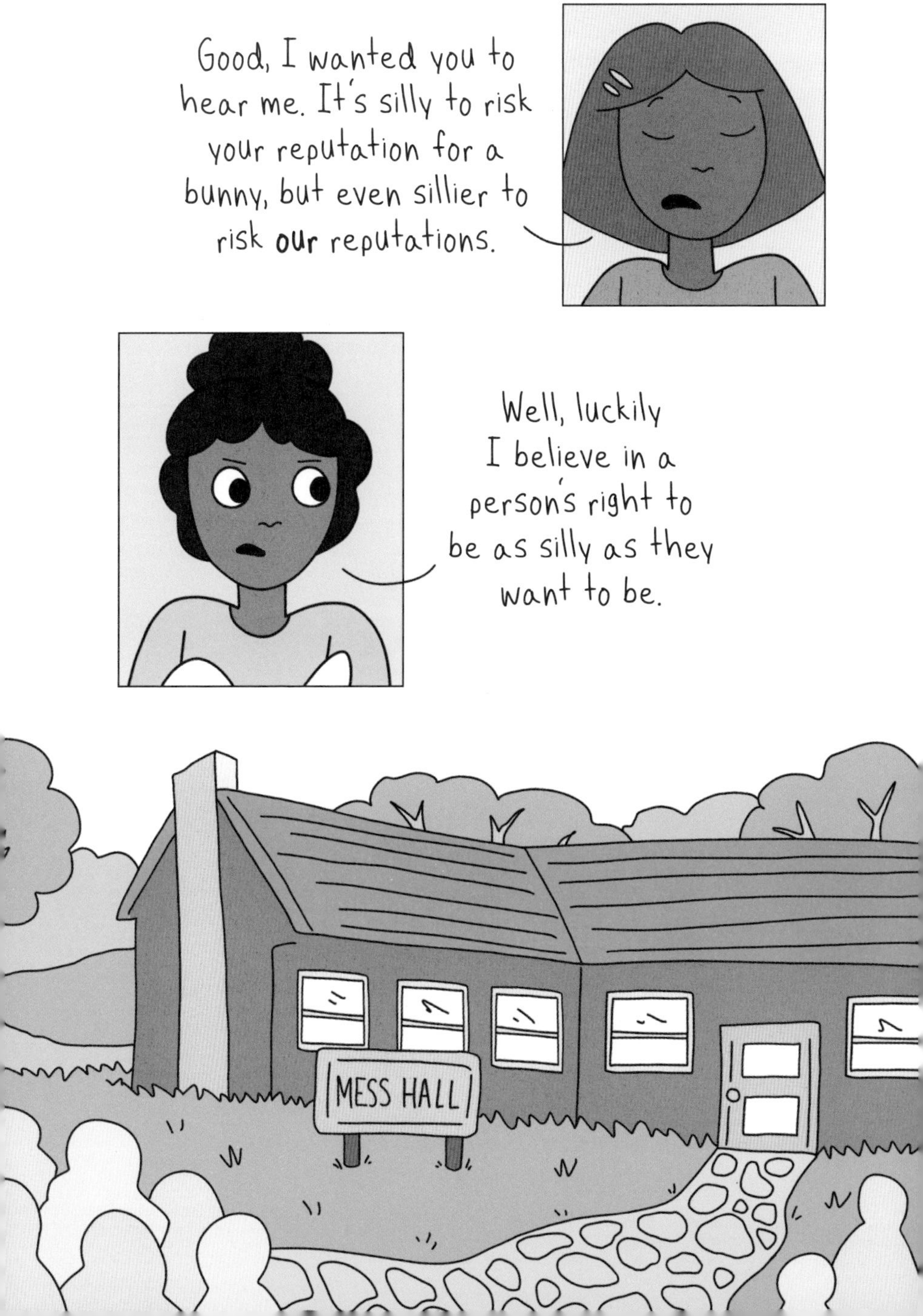
Good, I wanted you to hear me. It's silly to risk your reputation for a bunny, but even sillier to risk **our** reputations.
Well, luckily I believe in a person's right to be as silly as they want to be.
MESS HALL

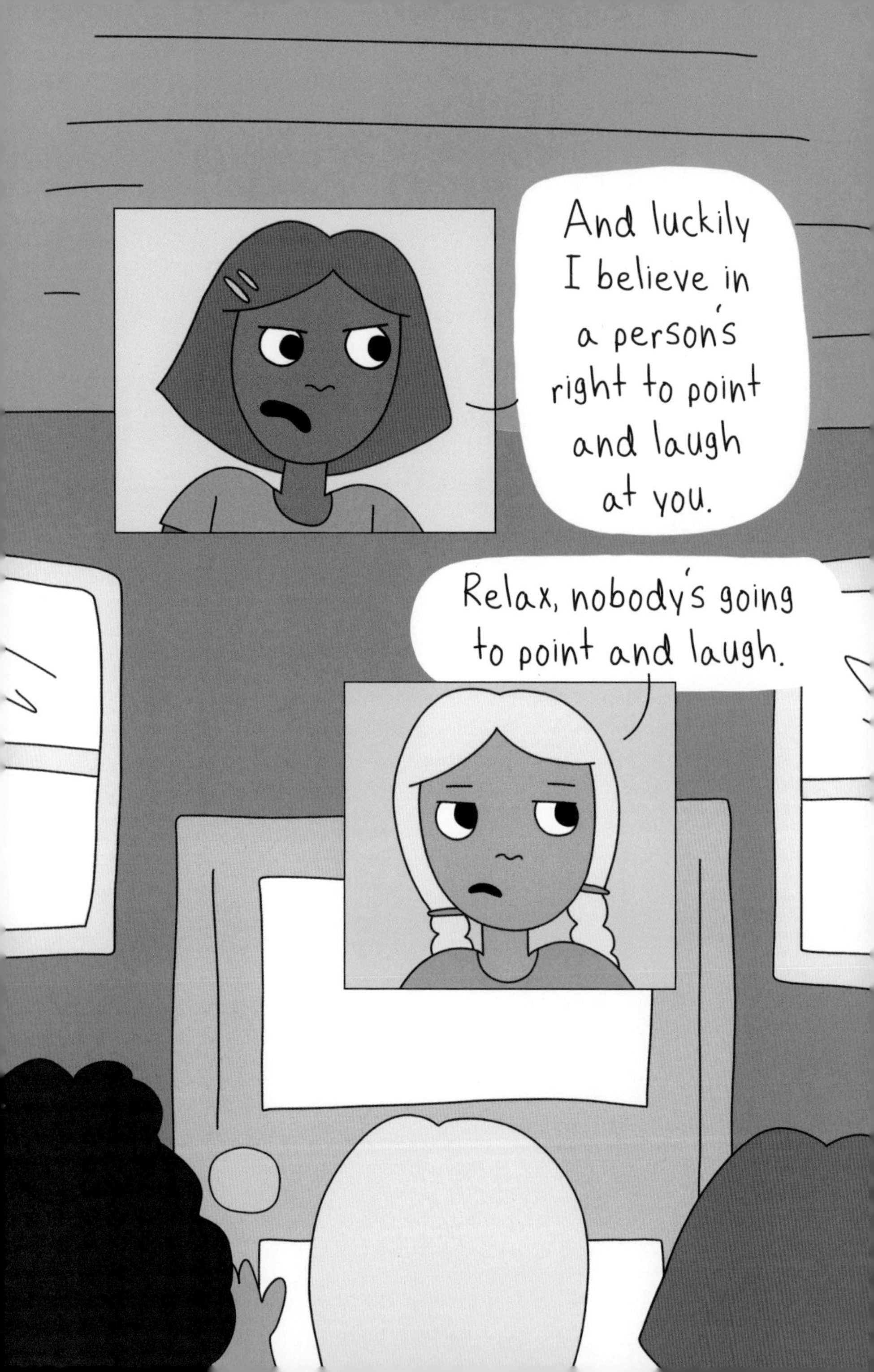
And luckily I believe in a person's right to point and laugh at you.
Relax, nobody's going to point and laugh.

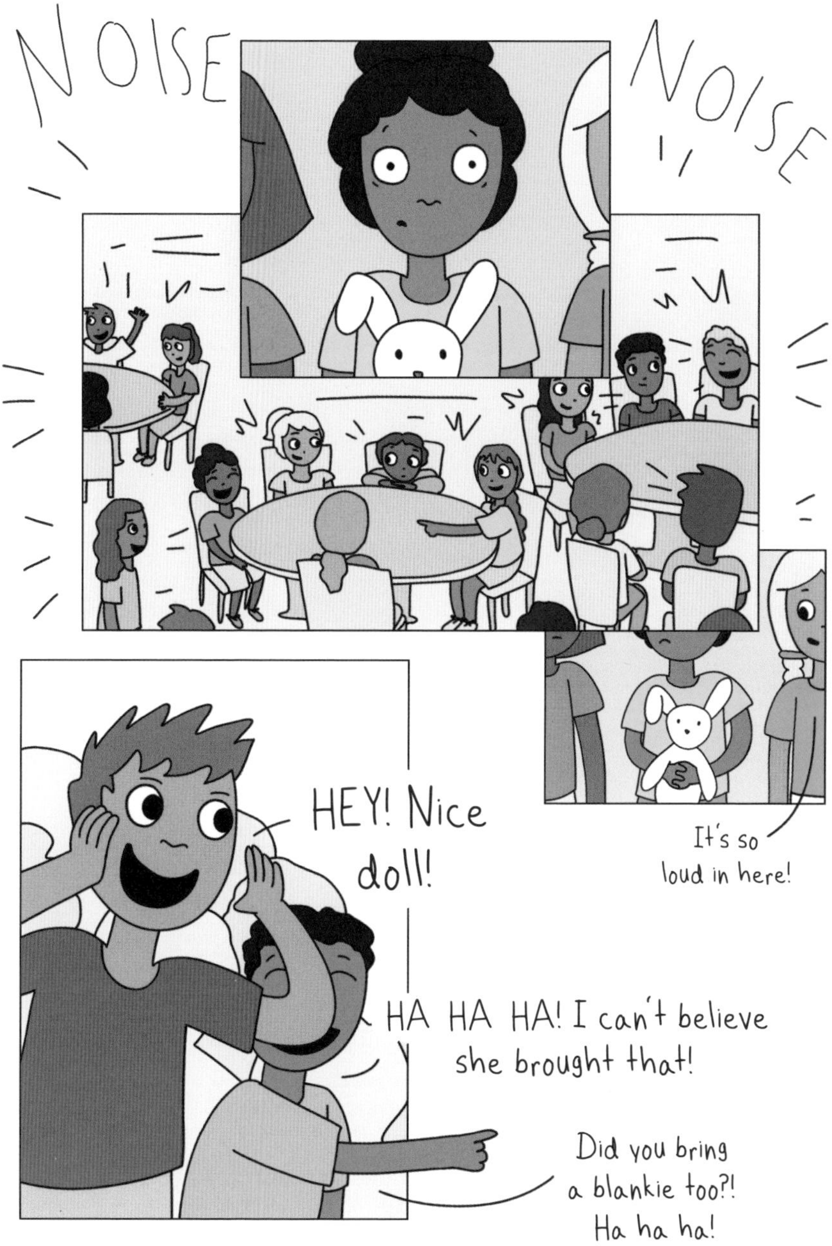
NOISE
NOISE
It's so loud in here!
HEY! Nice doll!
HA HA HA! I can't believe she brought that!
Did you bring a blankie too?! Ha ha ha!

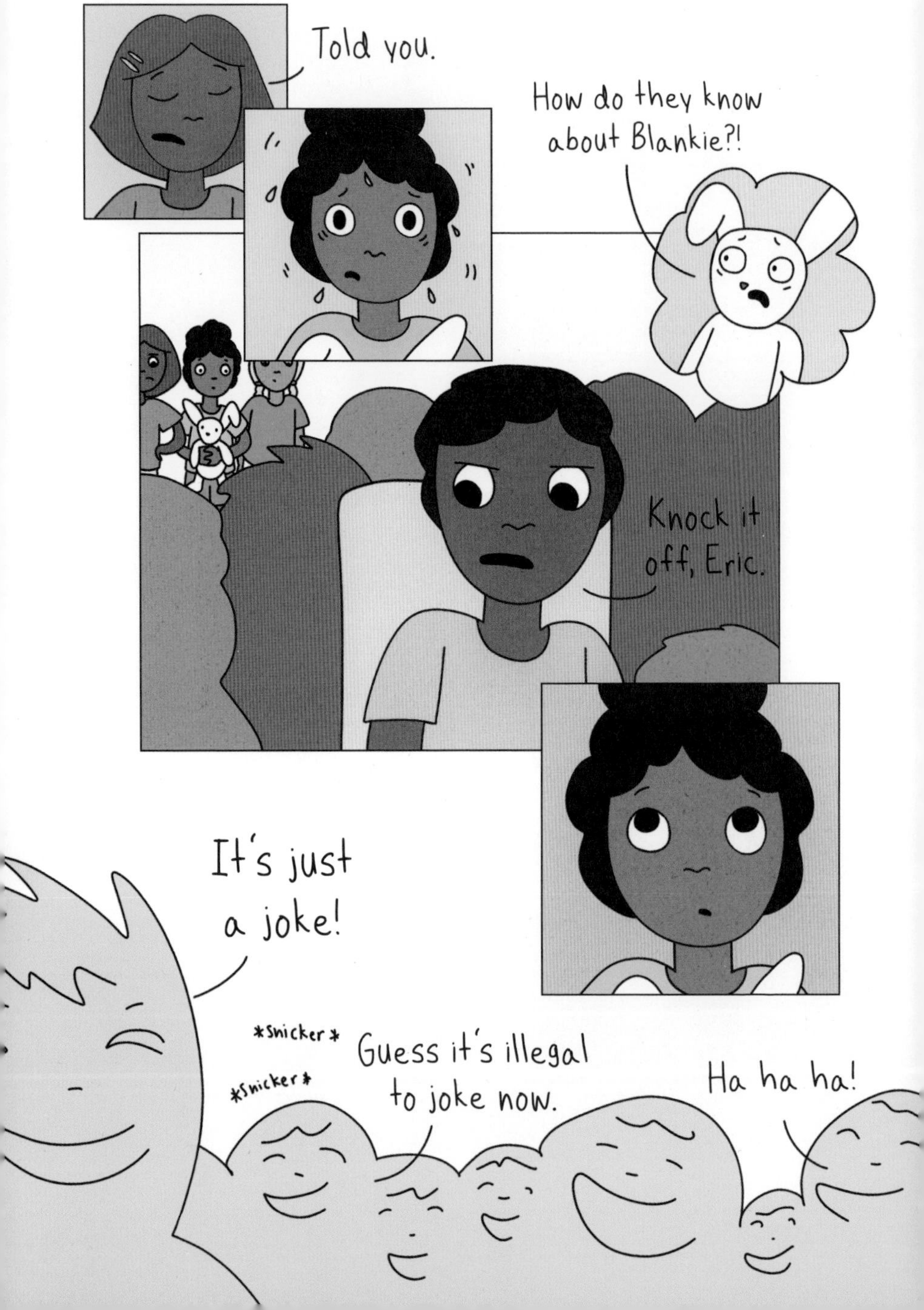
Told you.
How do they know about Blankie?!
Knock it off, Eric.
It's just a joke!
snicker
snicker
Guess it's illegal to joke now.
Ha ha ha!

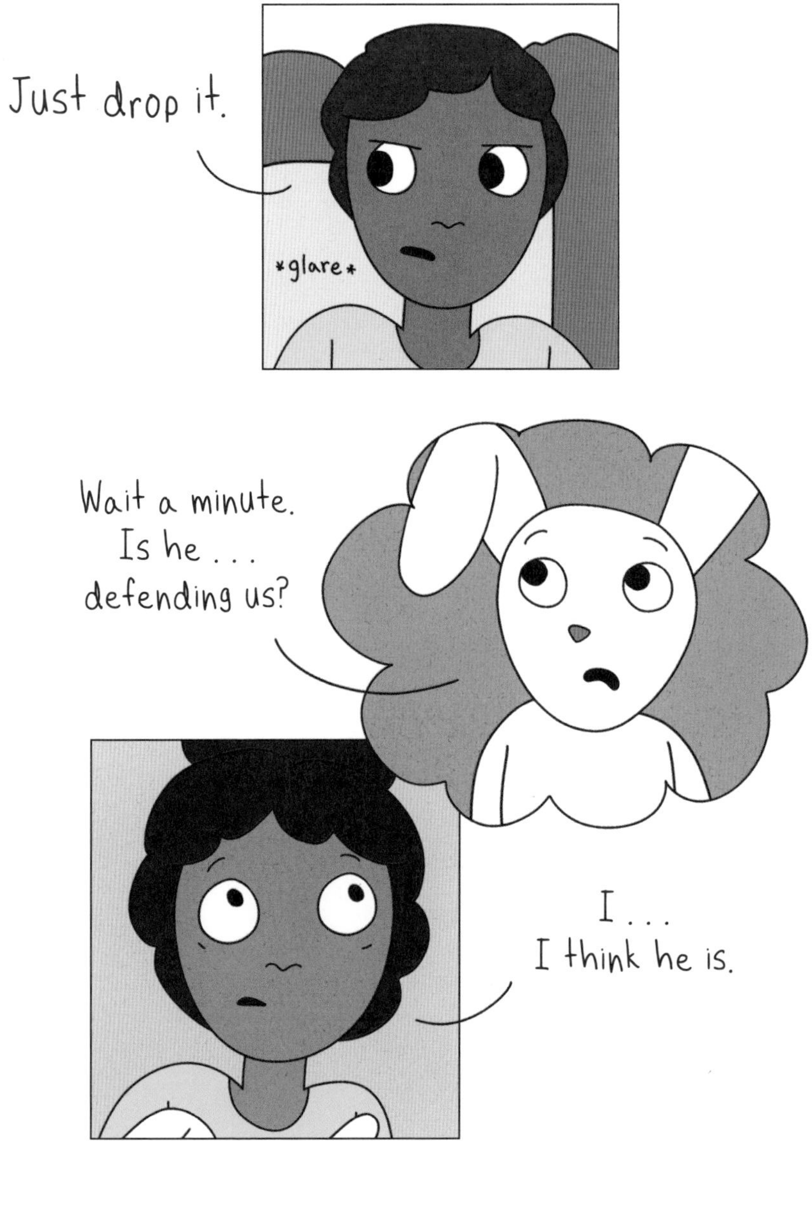
Just drop it.
glare
Wait a minute. Is he . . . defending us?
I . . . I think he is.

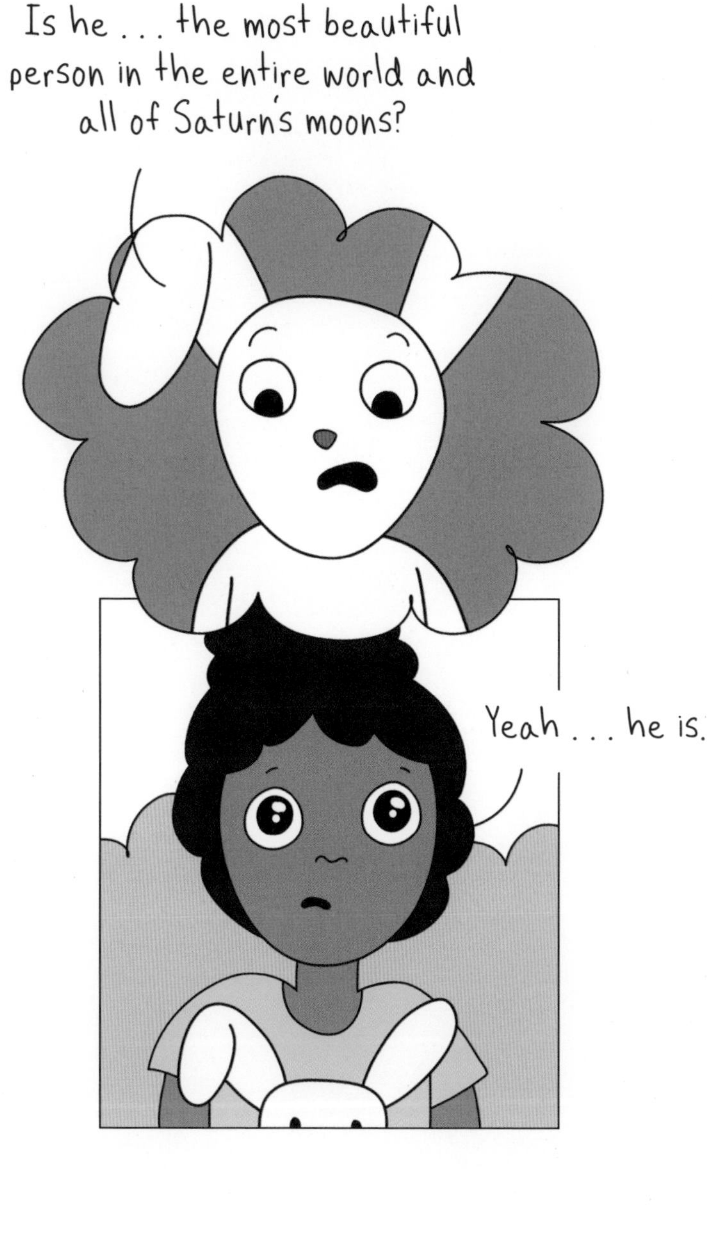
Is he . . . the most beautiful person in the entire world and all of Saturn's moons?
Yeah . . . he is.

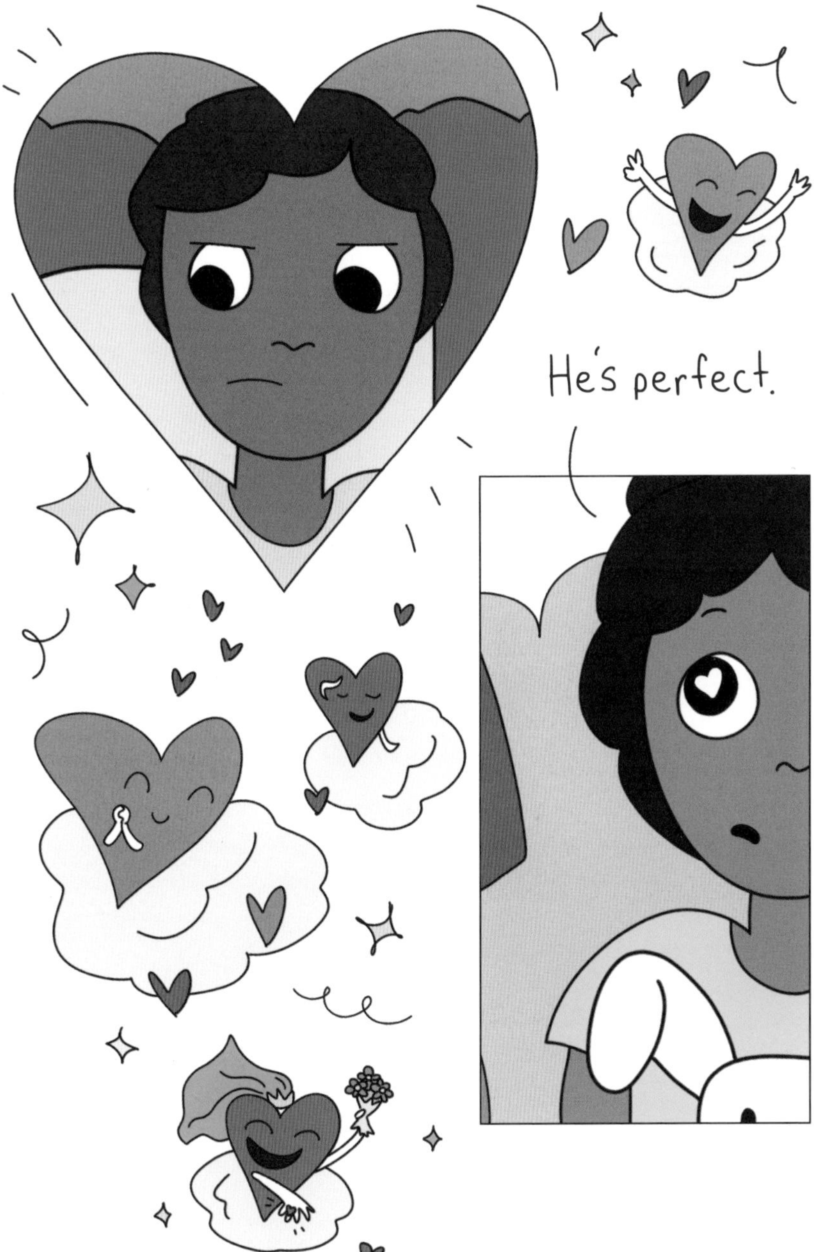
He's perfect.

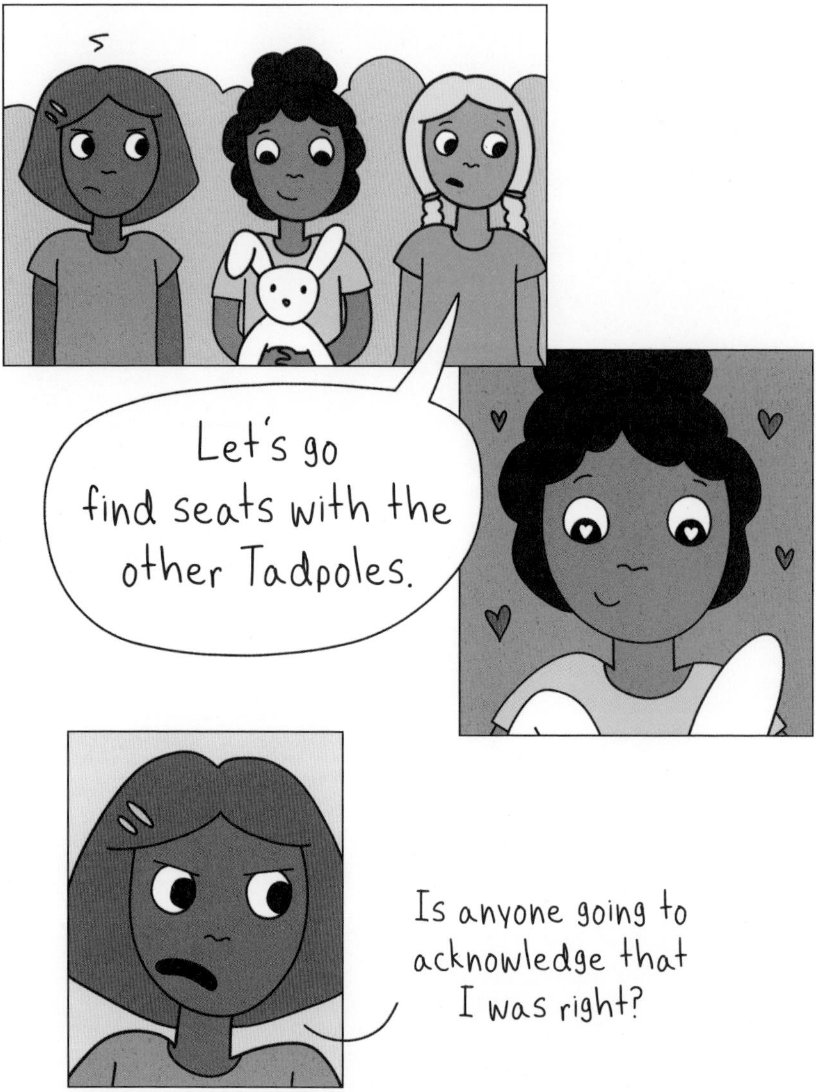
Let's go find seats with the other Tadpoles.
Is anyone going to acknowledge that I was right?

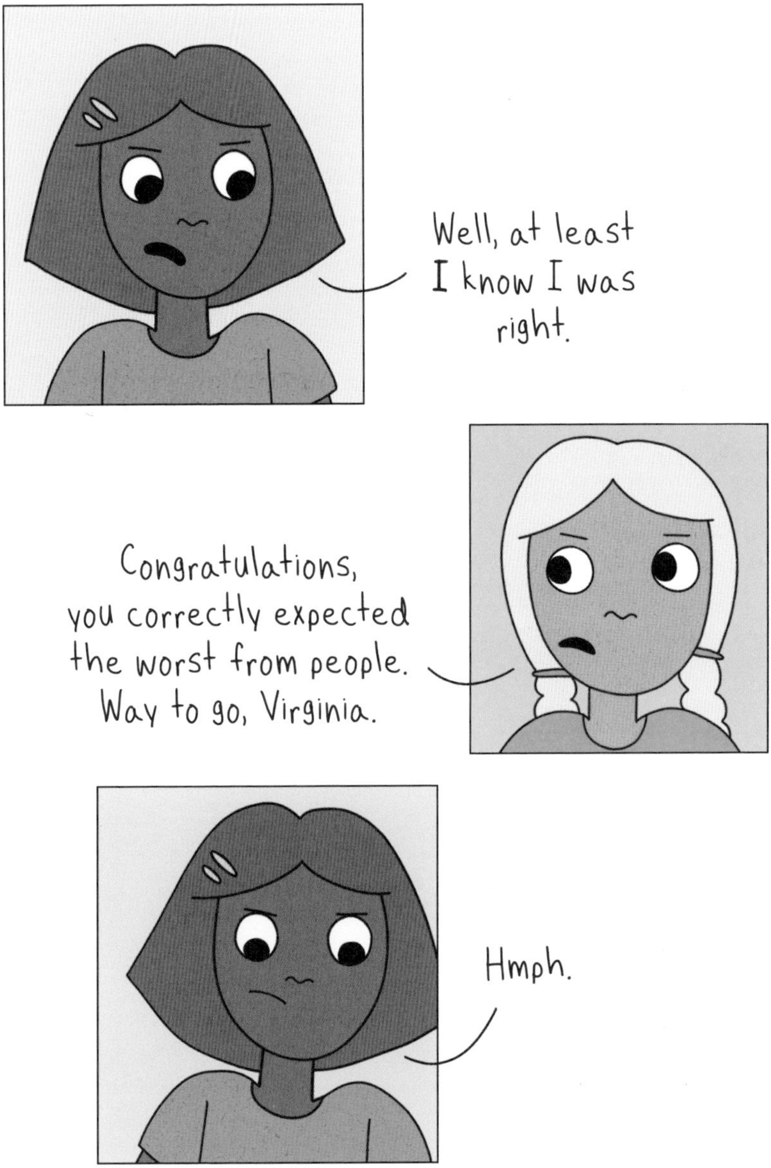
Well, at least I know I was right.
Congratulations, you correctly expected the worst from people. Way to go, Virginia.
Hmph.

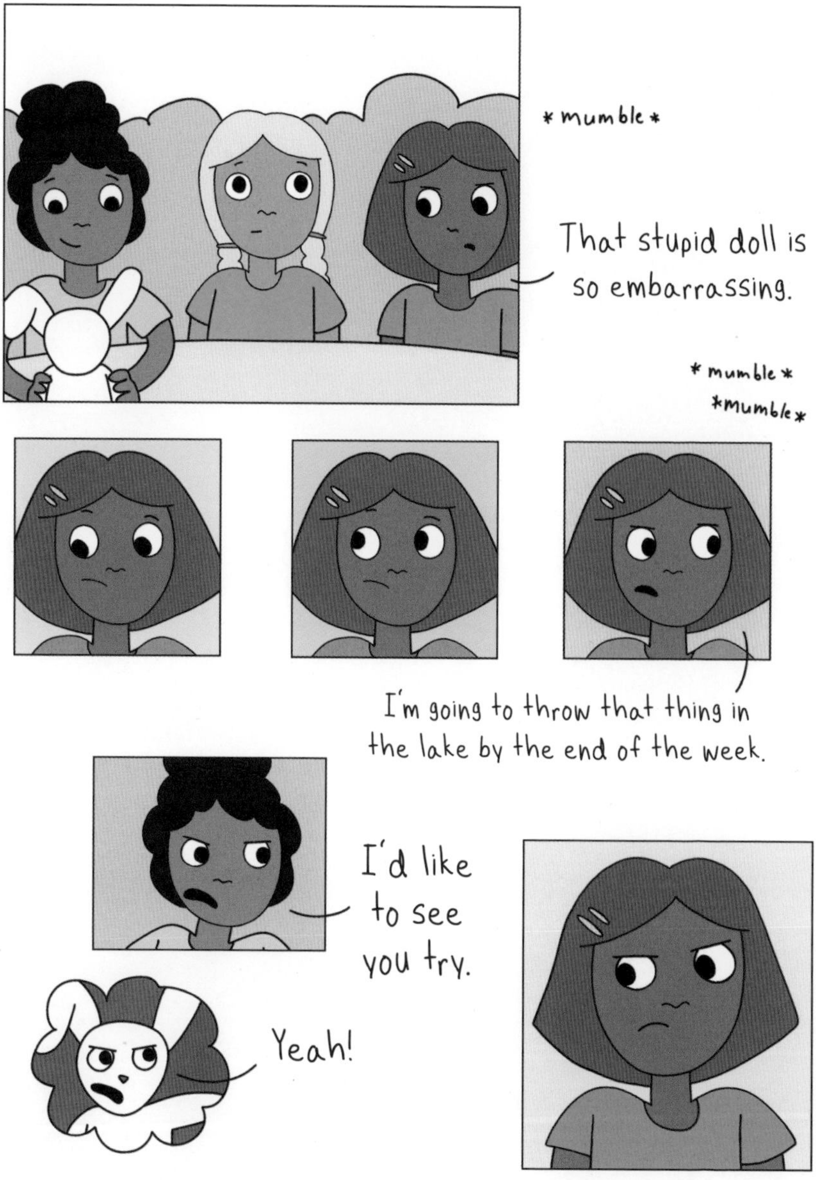
mumble
That stupid doll is so embarrassing.
mumble
mumble
I'm going to throw that thing in the lake by the end of the week.
I'd like to see you try.
Yeah!

Welcome, Minnows and Tadpoles! Camp Chordata is so excited to have you! You have many adventures and new friendships ahead of you.

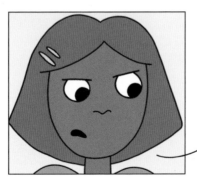

Not likely.

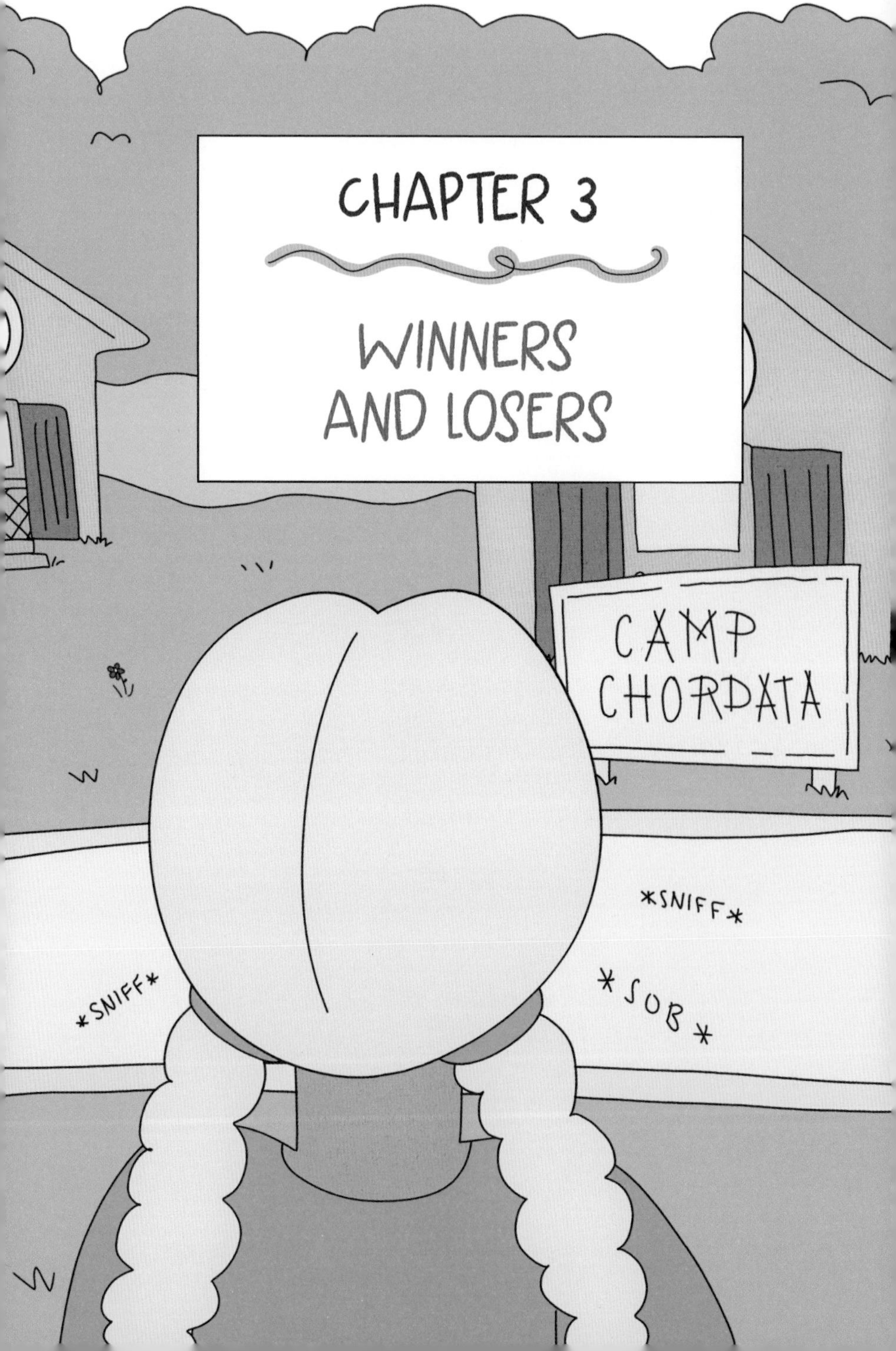
CHAPTER 3
WINNERS AND LOSERS
CAMP CHORDATA
SNIFF
SNIFF
SOB

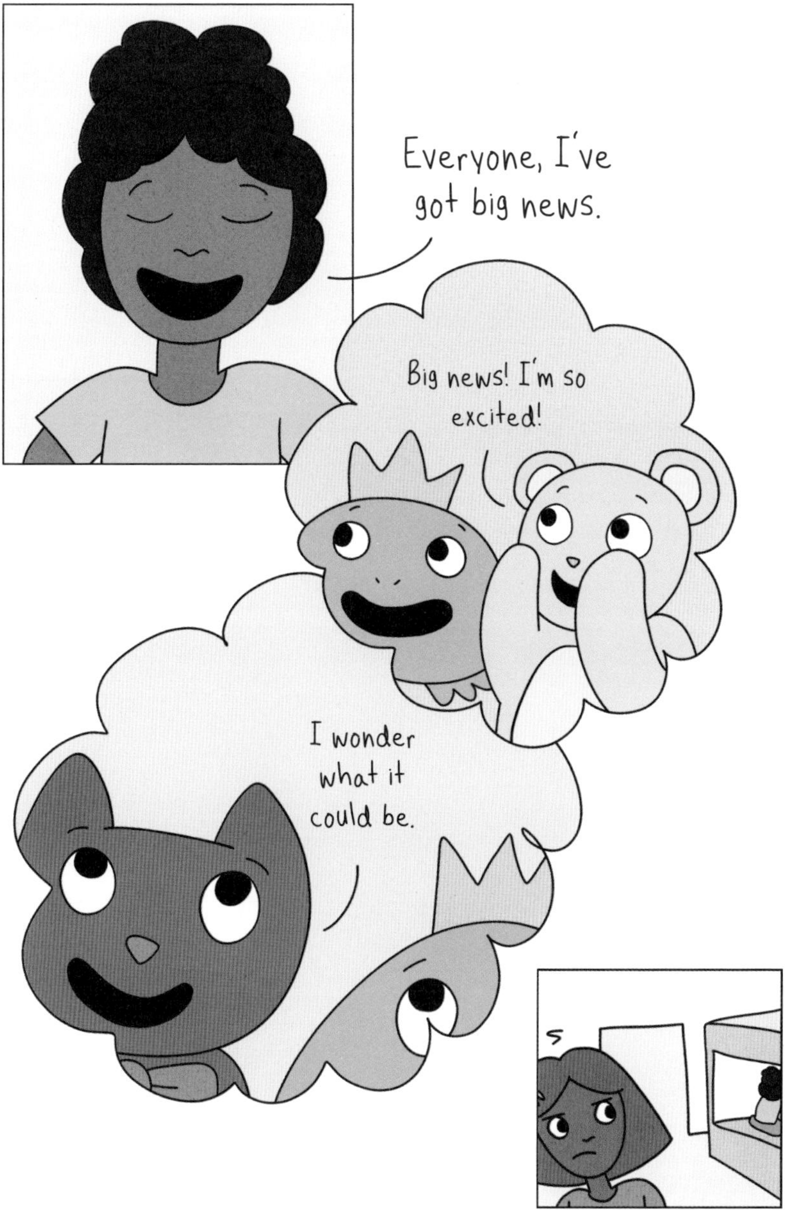
Everyone, I've got big news.
Big news! I'm so excited!
I wonder what it could be.

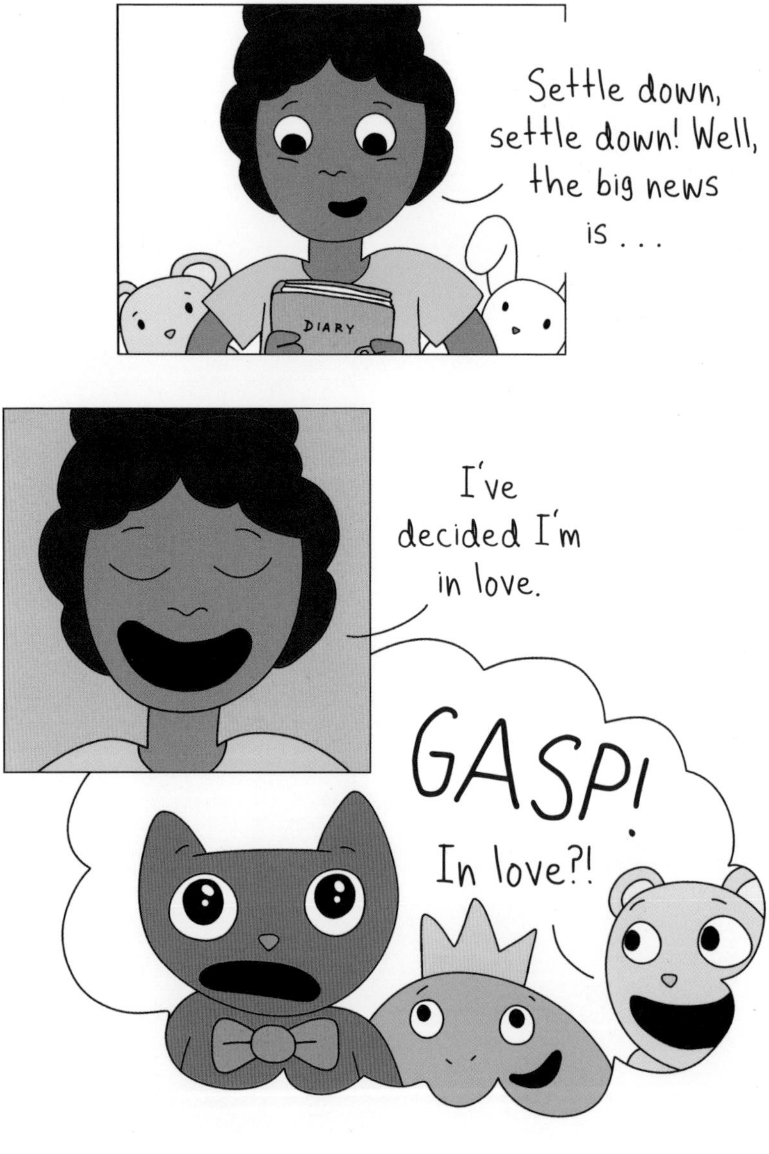
Settle down, settle down! Well, the big news is . . .
DIARY
I've decided I'm in love.
GASP!
In love?!

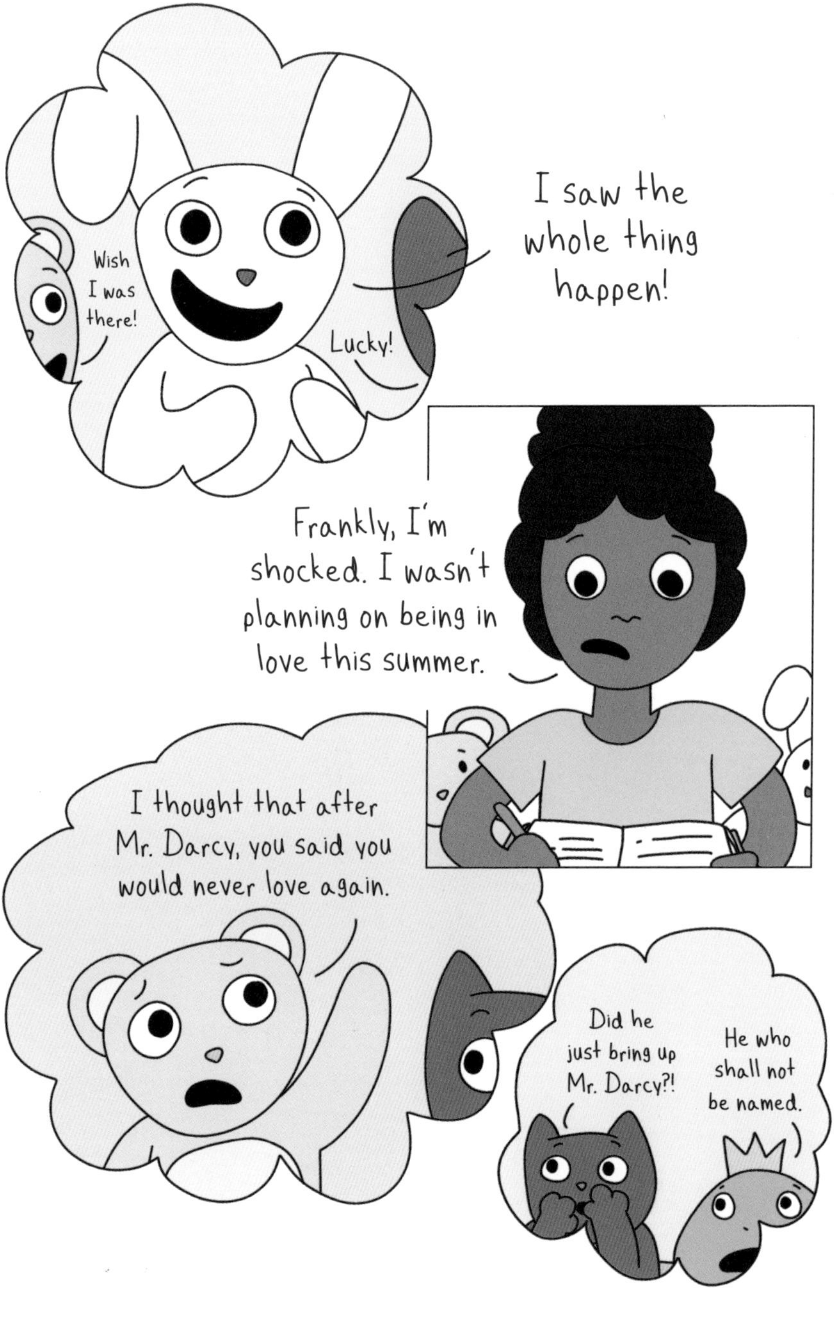
Wish I was there!
I saw the whole thing happen!
Lucky!
Frankly, I'm shocked. I wasn't planning on being in love this summer.
I thought that after Mr. Darcy, you said you would never love again.
Did he just bring up Mr. Darcy?!
He who shall not be named.

Before I left for camp, I got to the end of that movie, and Mr. Darcy ended up not being so bad after all.

That doesn't matter, though. Mr. Darcy is a fictional character. He's not real.

But luckily the boy who told Eric to knock it off is.

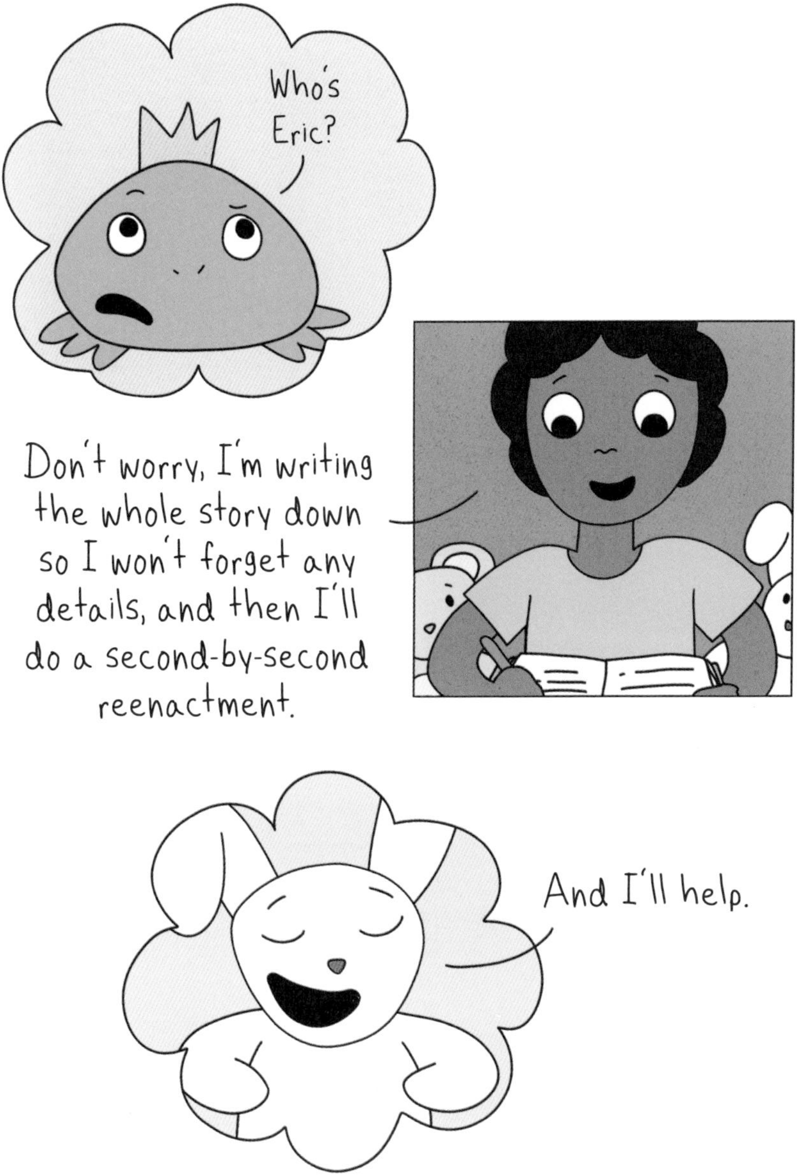
Who's Eric?
Don't worry, I'm writing the whole story down so I won't forget any details, and then I'll do a second-by-second reenactment.
And I'll help.

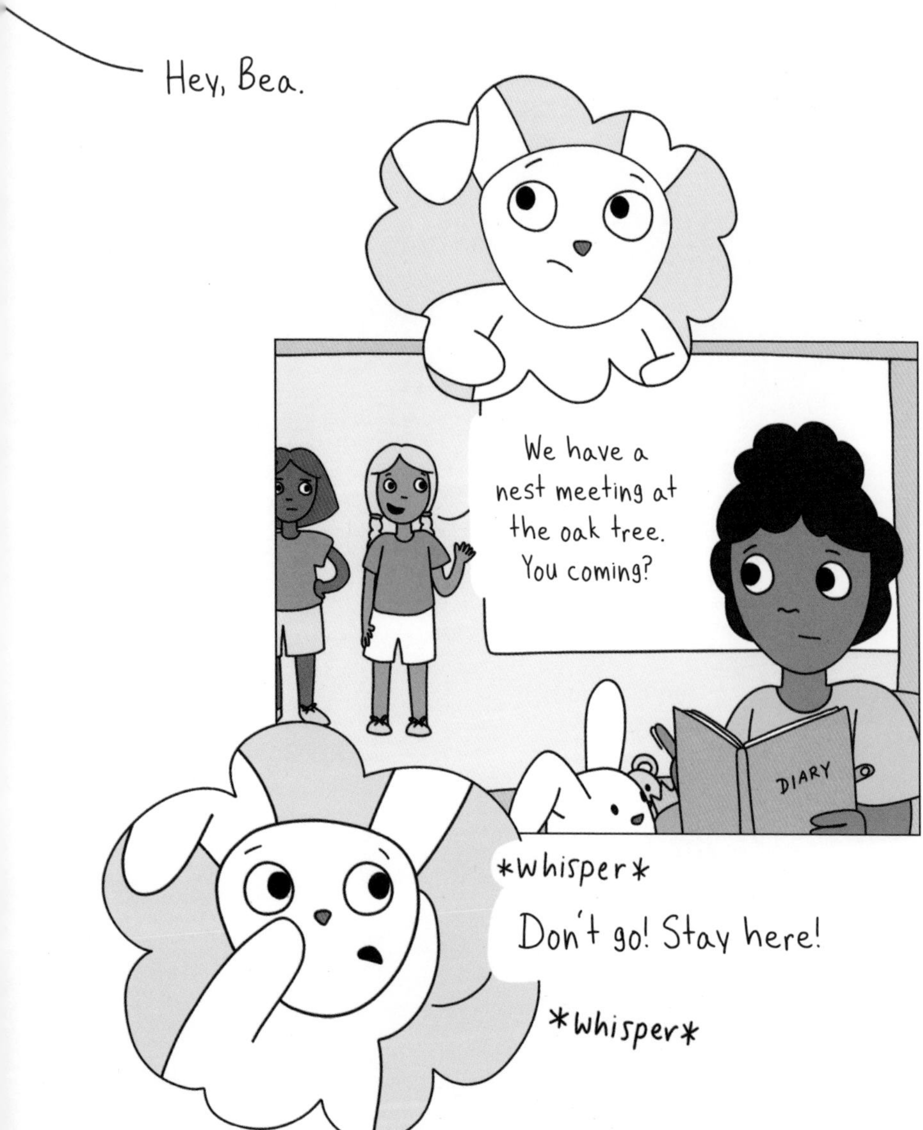
Hey, Bea.
We have a nest meeting at the oak tree. You coming?
DIARY
whisper
Don't go! Stay here!
whisper

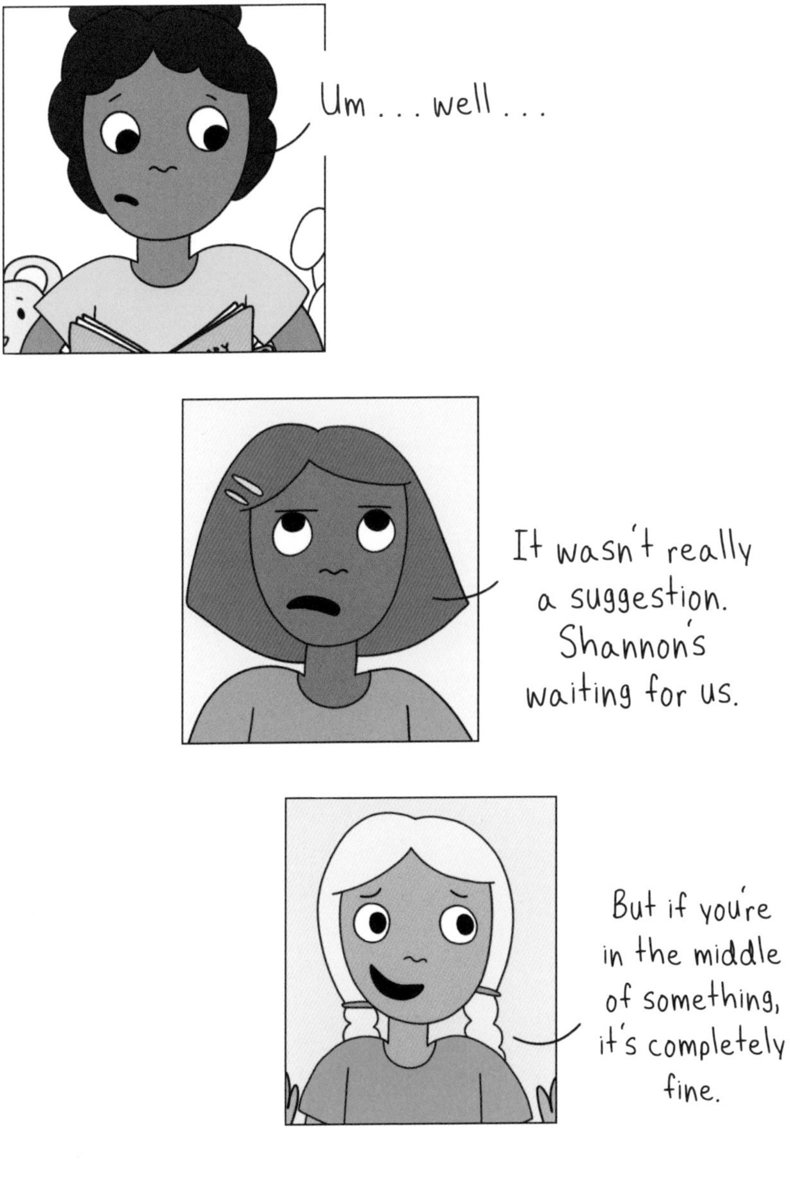
Um . . . well . . .
It wasn't really a suggestion. Shannon's waiting for us.
But if you're in the middle of something, it's completely fine.

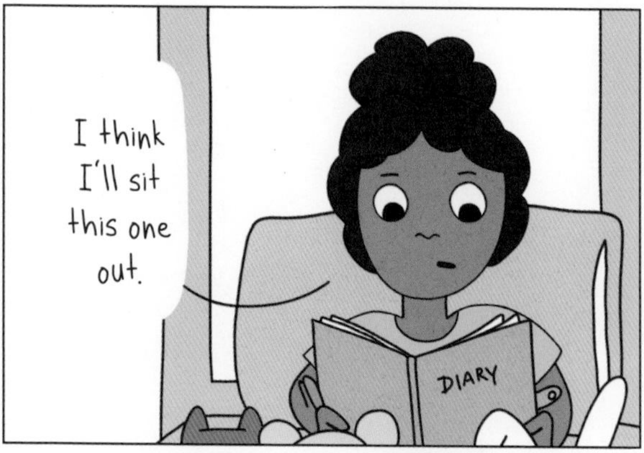
I think I'll sit this one out.
DIARY

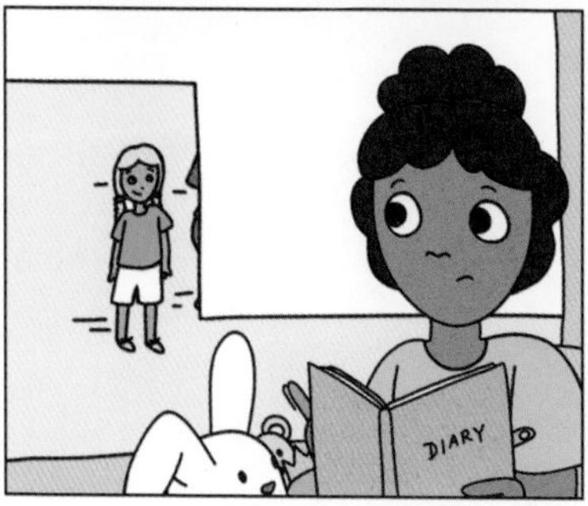
DIARY

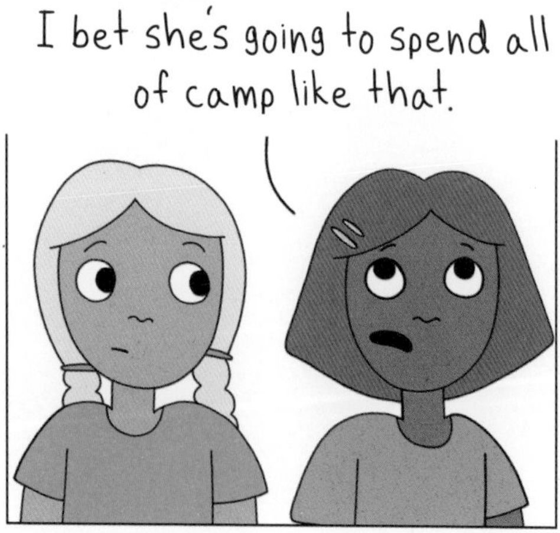
I bet she's going to spend all of camp like that.

MY TADPOLES HAVE ASSEMBLED!

Today we will be working on grit, strategy, teamwork, and more through an ancient and time-tested ritual.

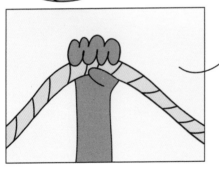

Tug-of-war!

Do we have to?

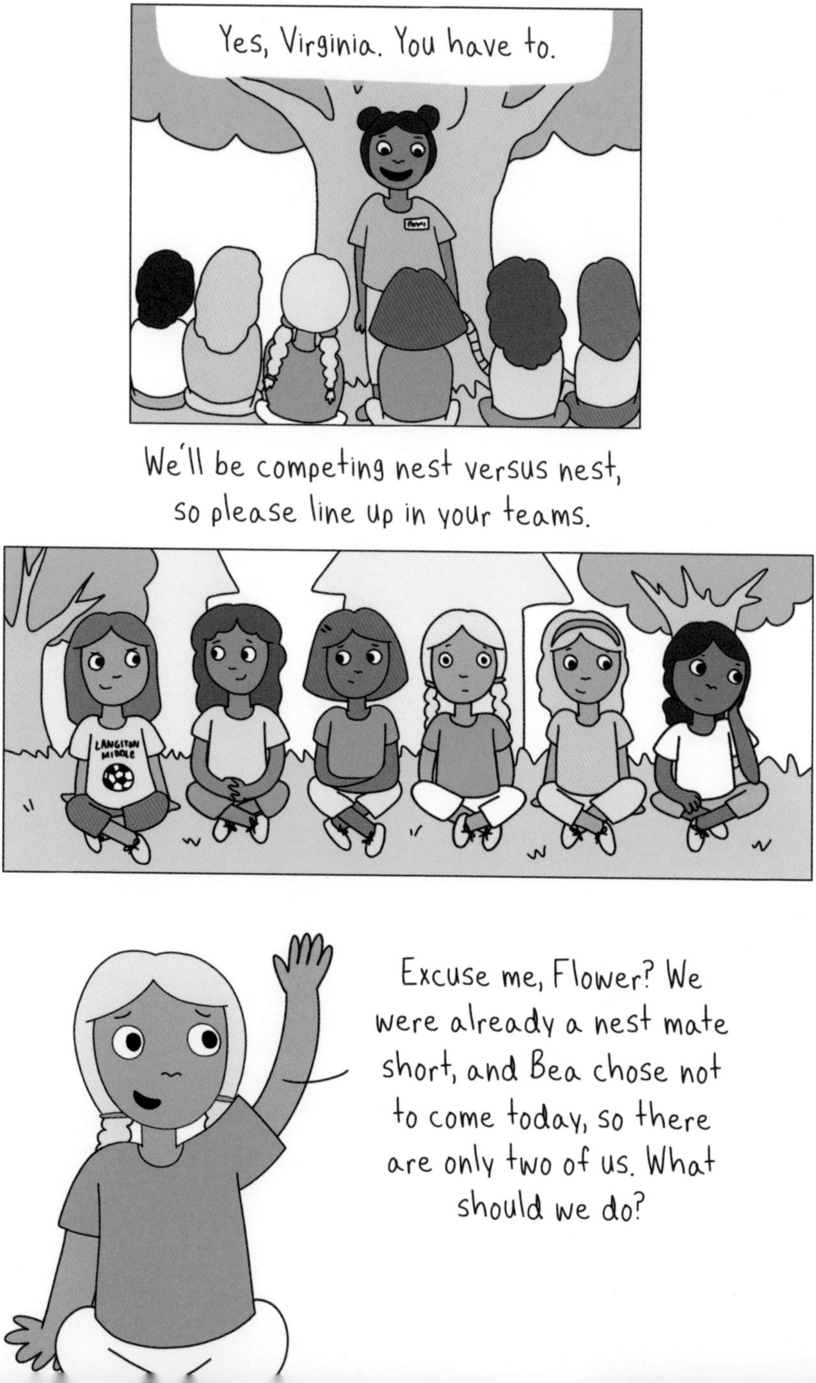
Yes, Virginia. You have to.
We'll be competing nest versus nest, so please line up in your teams.
LANGITON MIDDLE
Excuse me, Flower? We were already a nest mate short, and Bea chose not to come today, so there are only two of us. What should we do?

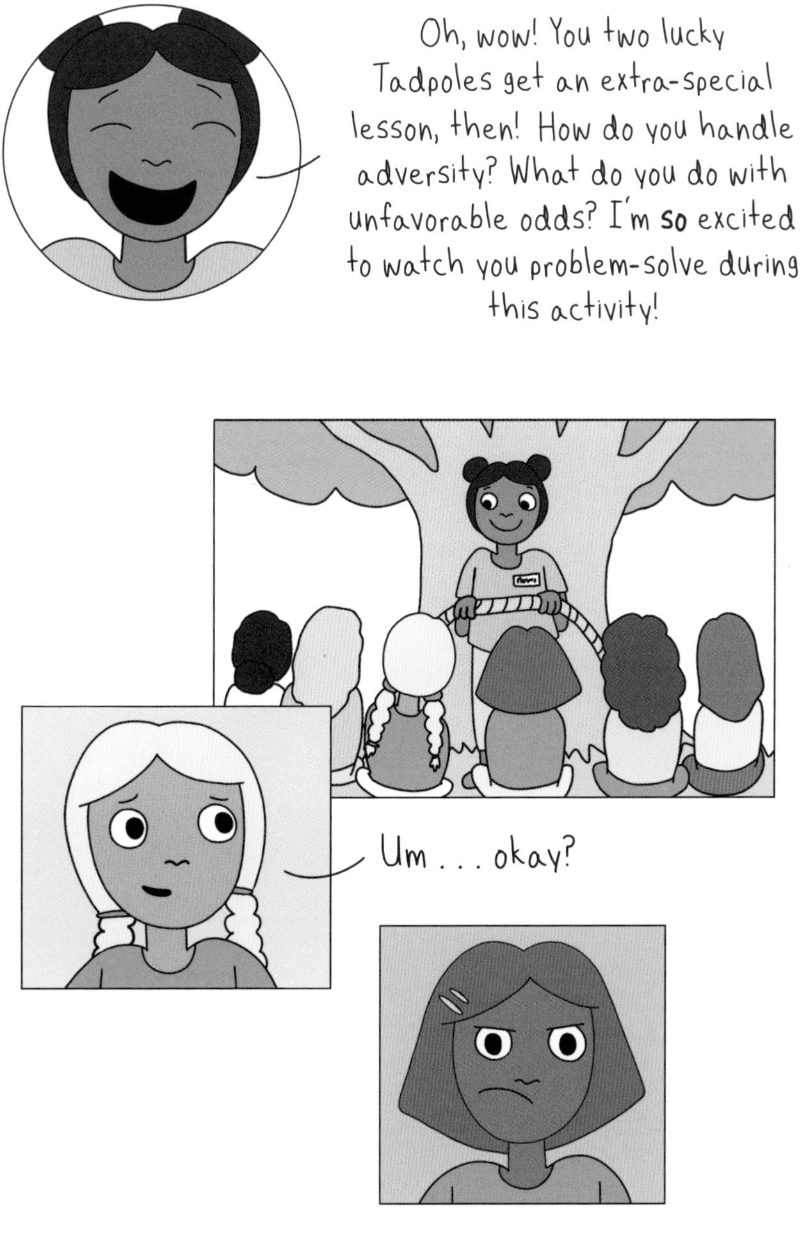
Oh, wow! You two lucky Tadpoles get an extra-special lesson, then! How do you handle adversity? What do you do with unfavorable odds? I'm **so** excited to watch you problem-solve during this activity!
Um . . . okay?

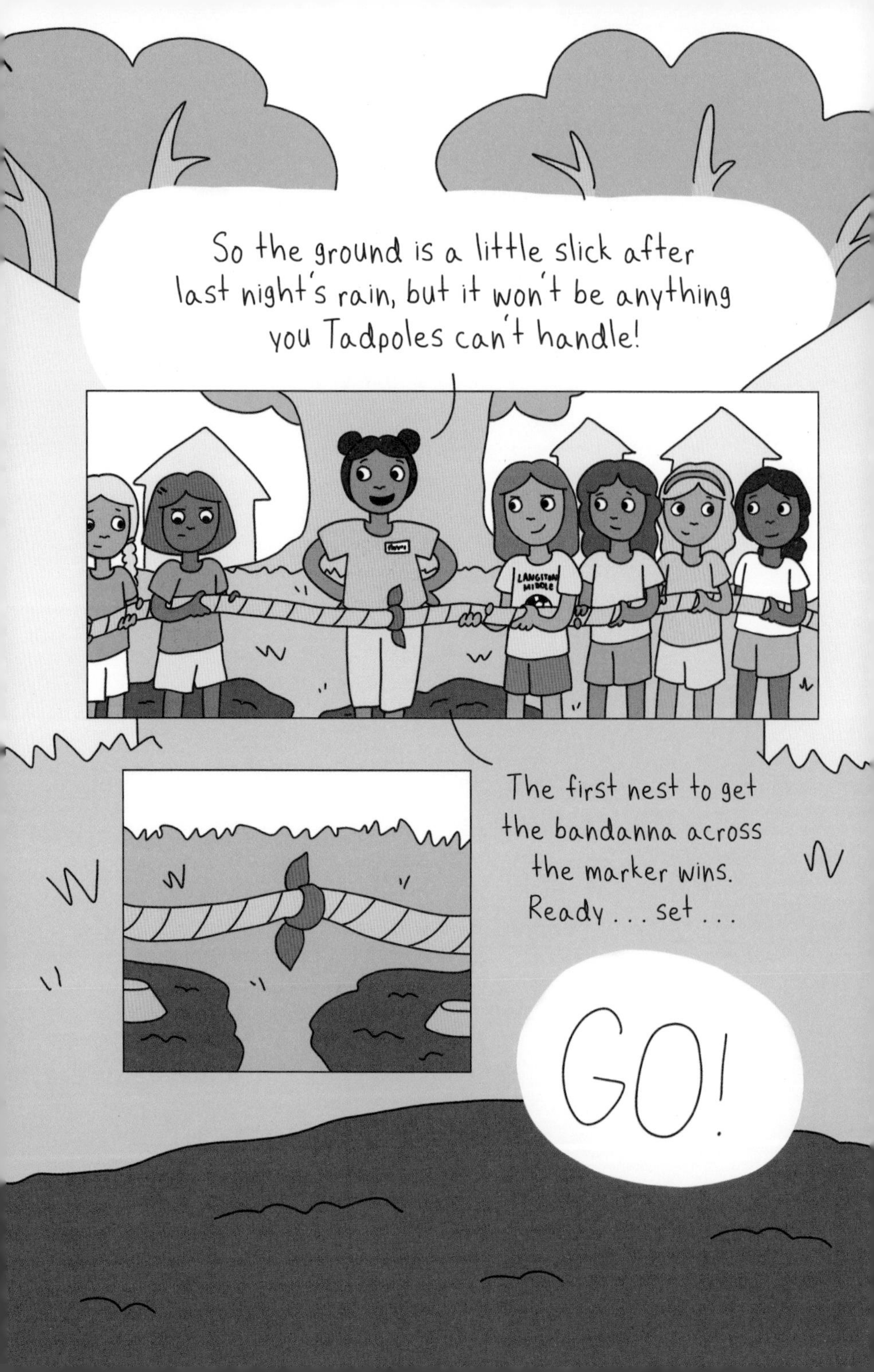
So the ground is a little slick after last night's rain, but it won't be anything you Tadpoles can't handle!
The first nest to get the bandanna across the marker wins.
Ready . . . set . . .
GO!

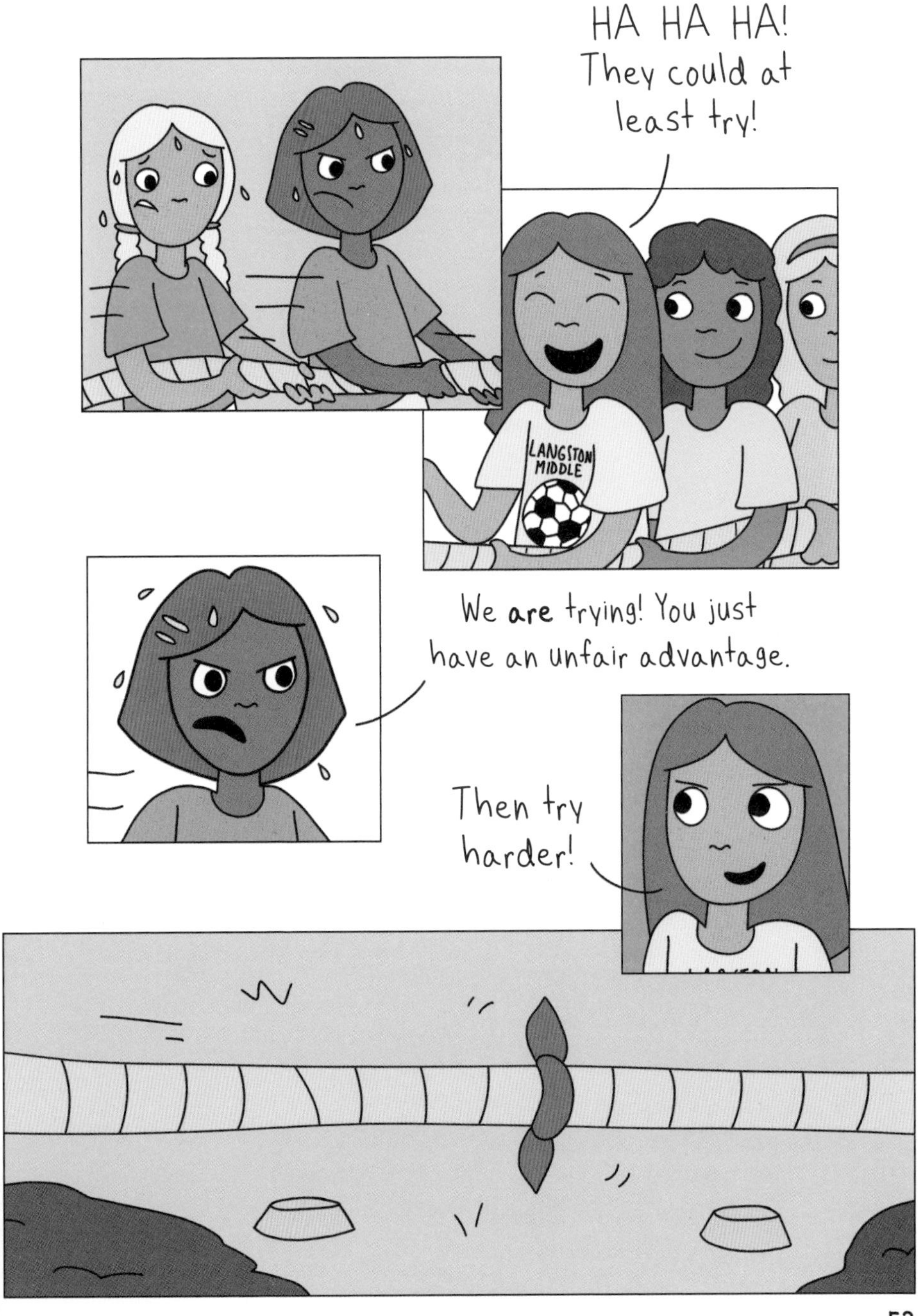
HA HA HA! They could at least try!
LANGSTON MIDDLE
We **are** trying! You just have an unfair advantage.
Then try harder!

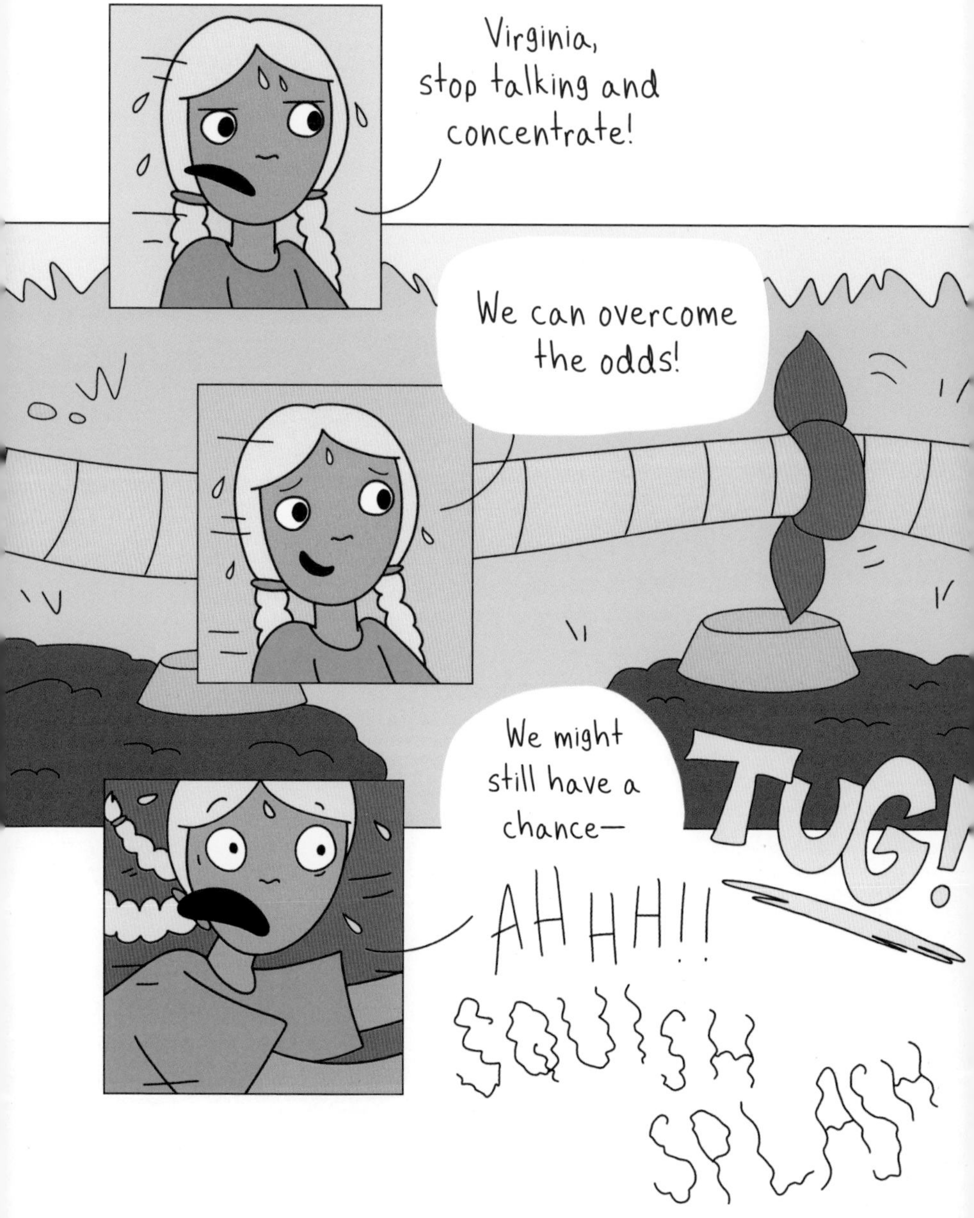
Virginia, stop talking and concentrate!
We can overcome the odds!
OoW
We might still have a chance—
TUG!
AHHH!!
SQUISH
SPLASH

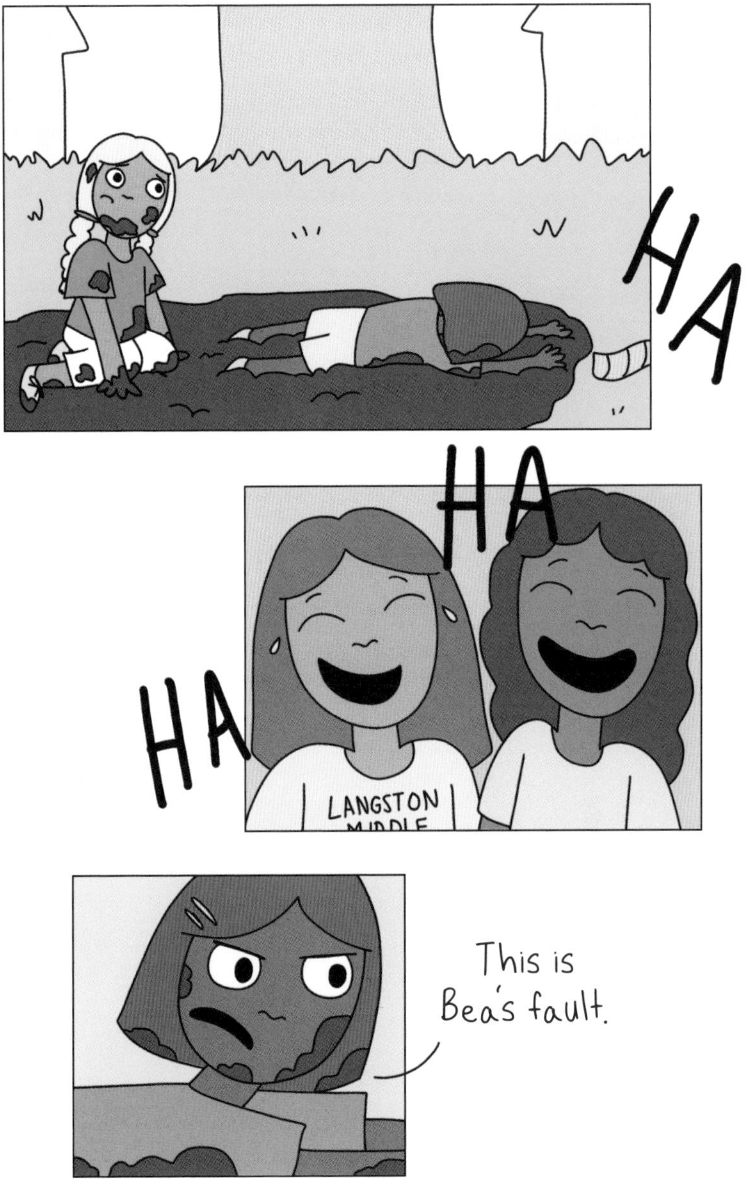
HA
HA
HA
HA
LANGSTON
This is Bea's fault.

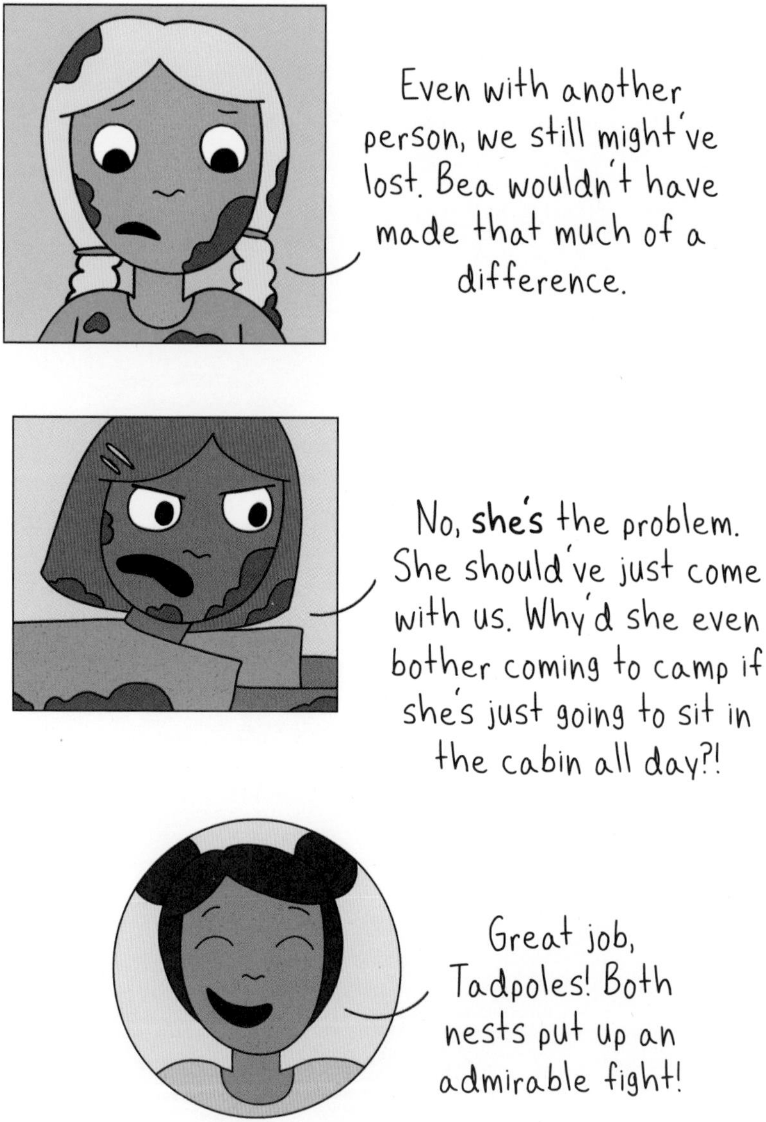
Even with another person, we still might've lost. Bea wouldn't have made that much of a difference.
No, **she's** the problem. She should've just come with us. Why'd she even bother coming to camp if she's just going to sit in the cabin all day?!
Great job, Tadpoles! Both nests put up an admirable fight!

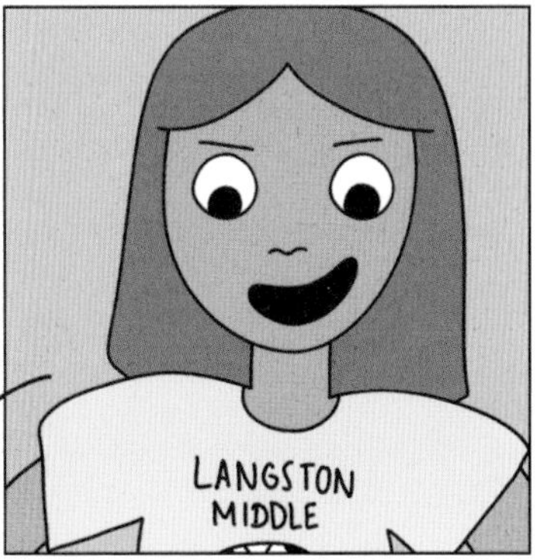
LANGSTON
MIDDLE

But clearly the
better nest won.

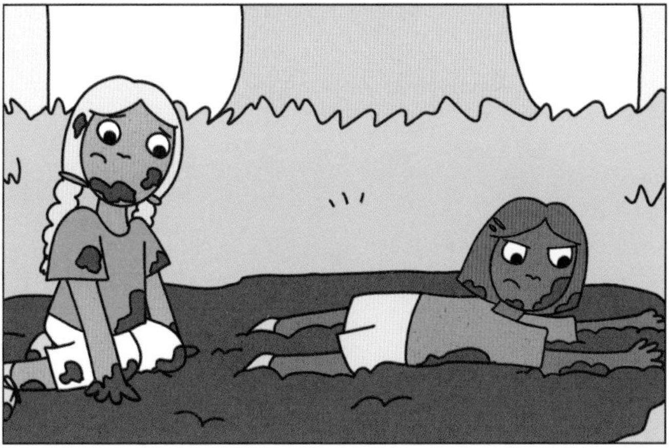

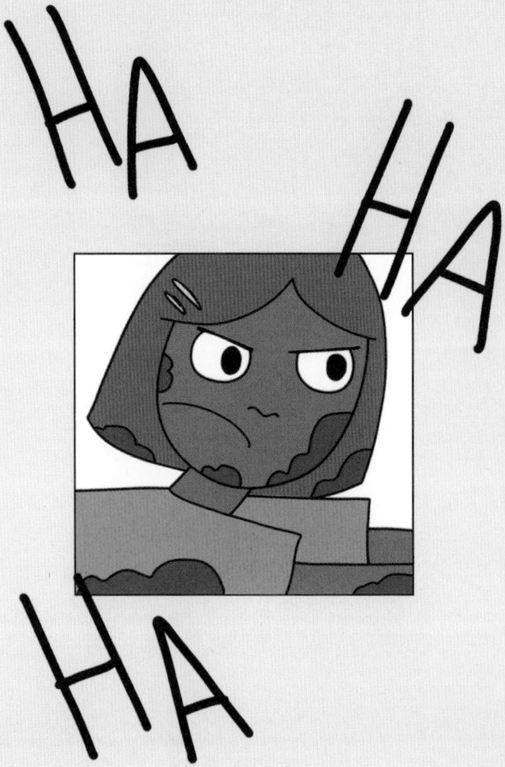
HA
HA
HA

CHAPTER 4

VIRGINIA'S VENGEANCE

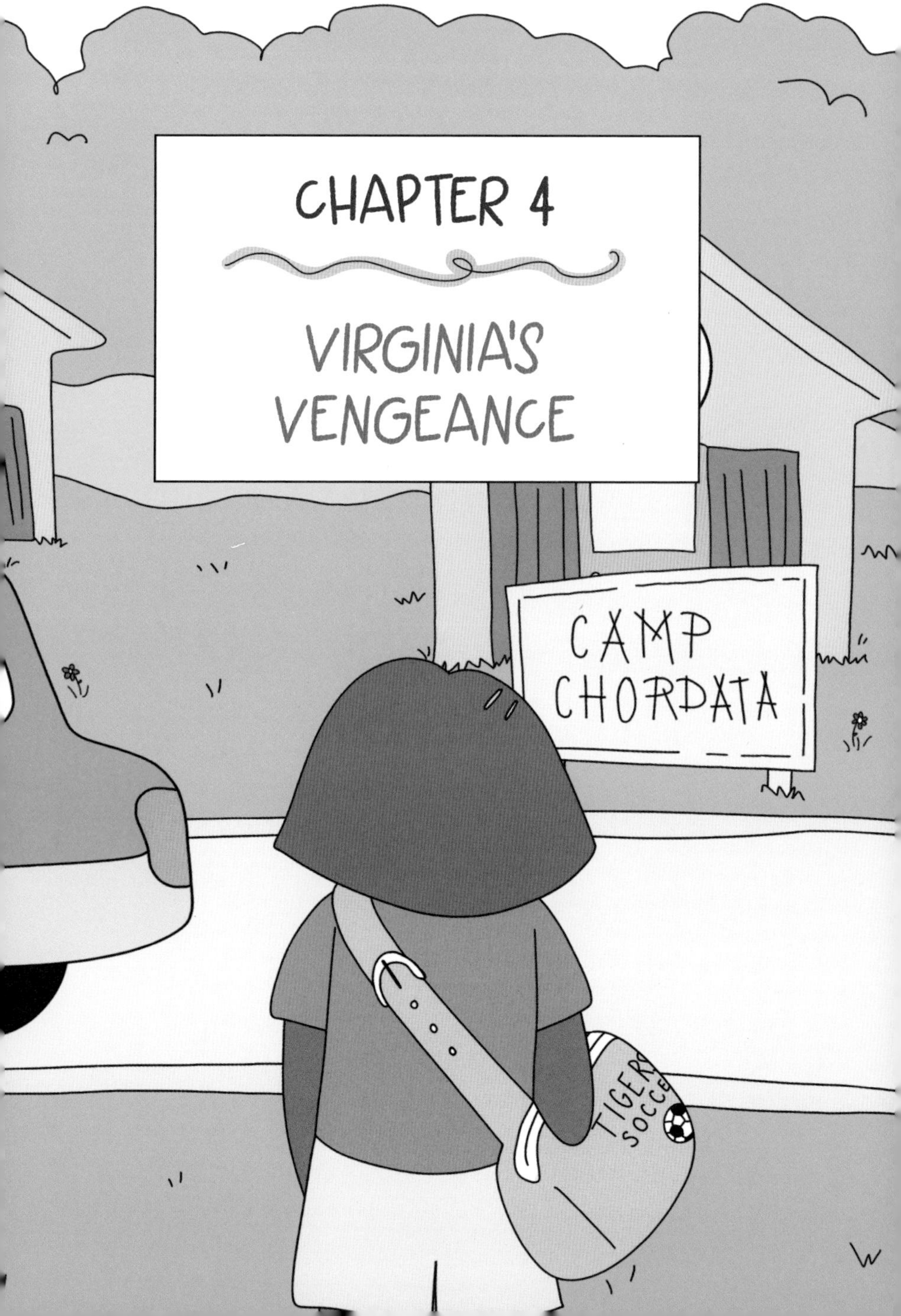
CAMP
CHORDATA

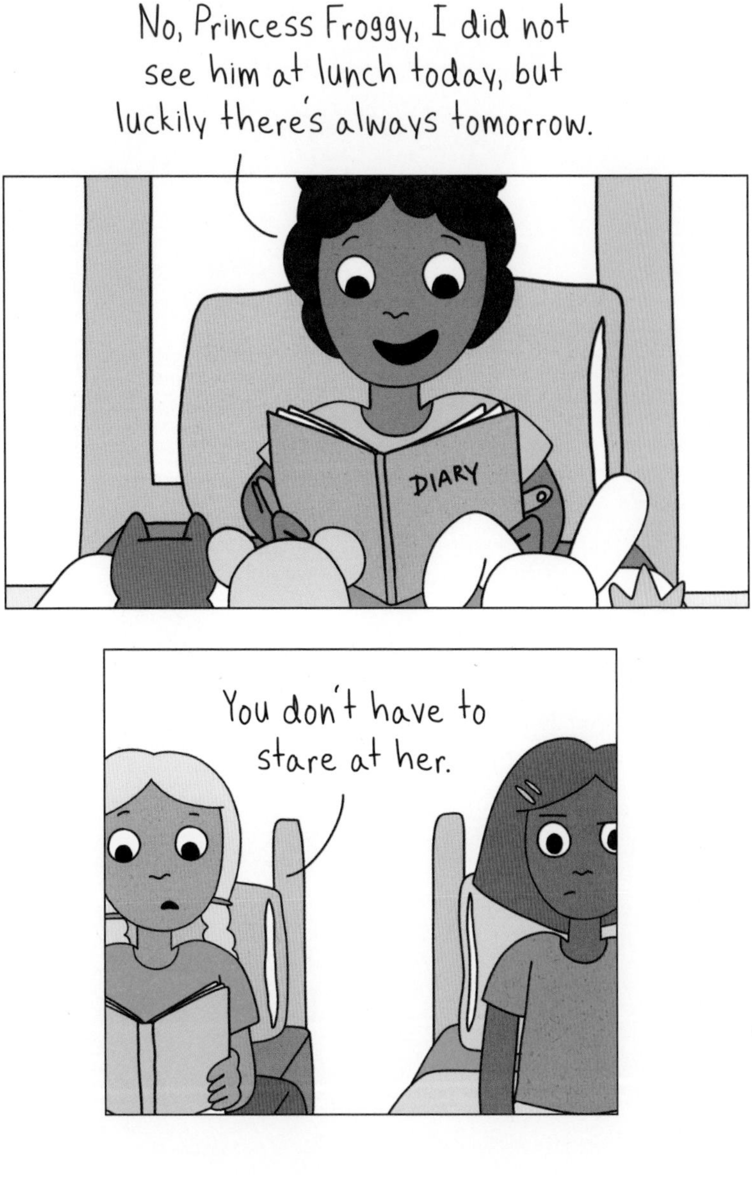
No, Princess Froggy, I did not see him at lunch today, but luckily there's always tomorrow.
DIARY
You don't have to stare at her.

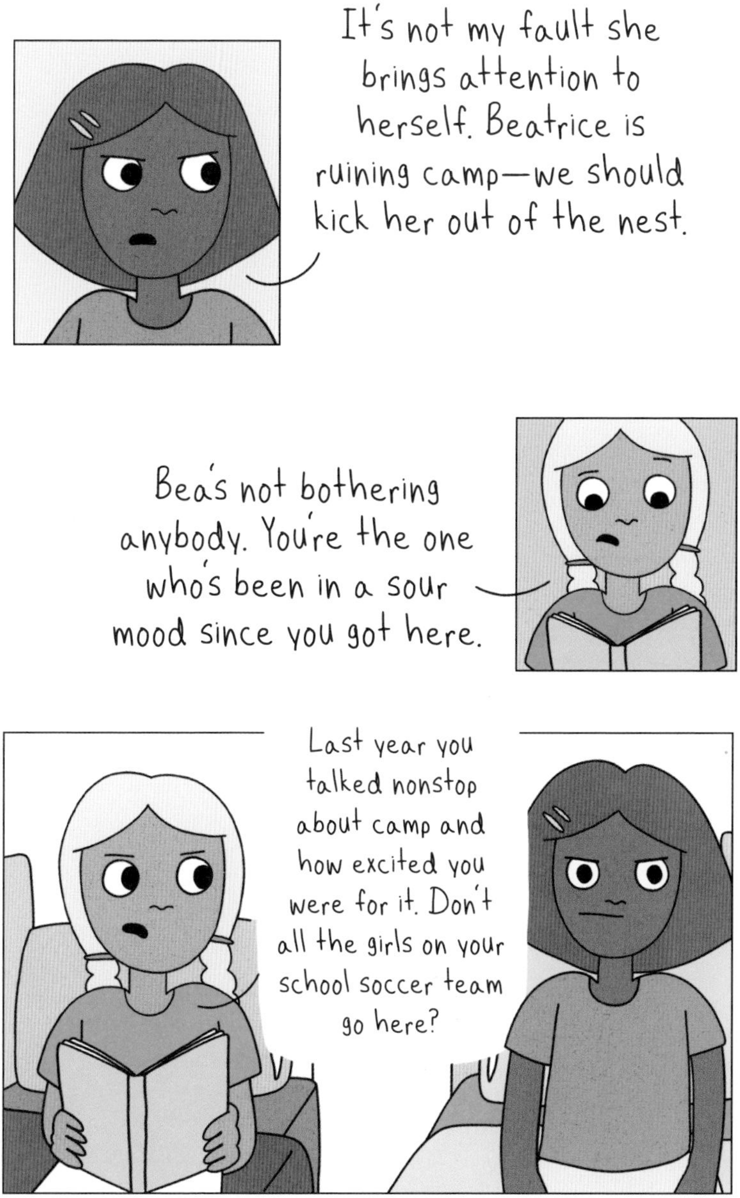
It's not my fault she brings attention to herself. Beatrice is ruining camp—we should kick her out of the nest.
Bea's not bothering anybody. You're the one who's been in a sour mood since you got here.
Last year you talked nonstop about camp and how excited you were for it. Don't all the girls on your school soccer team go here?

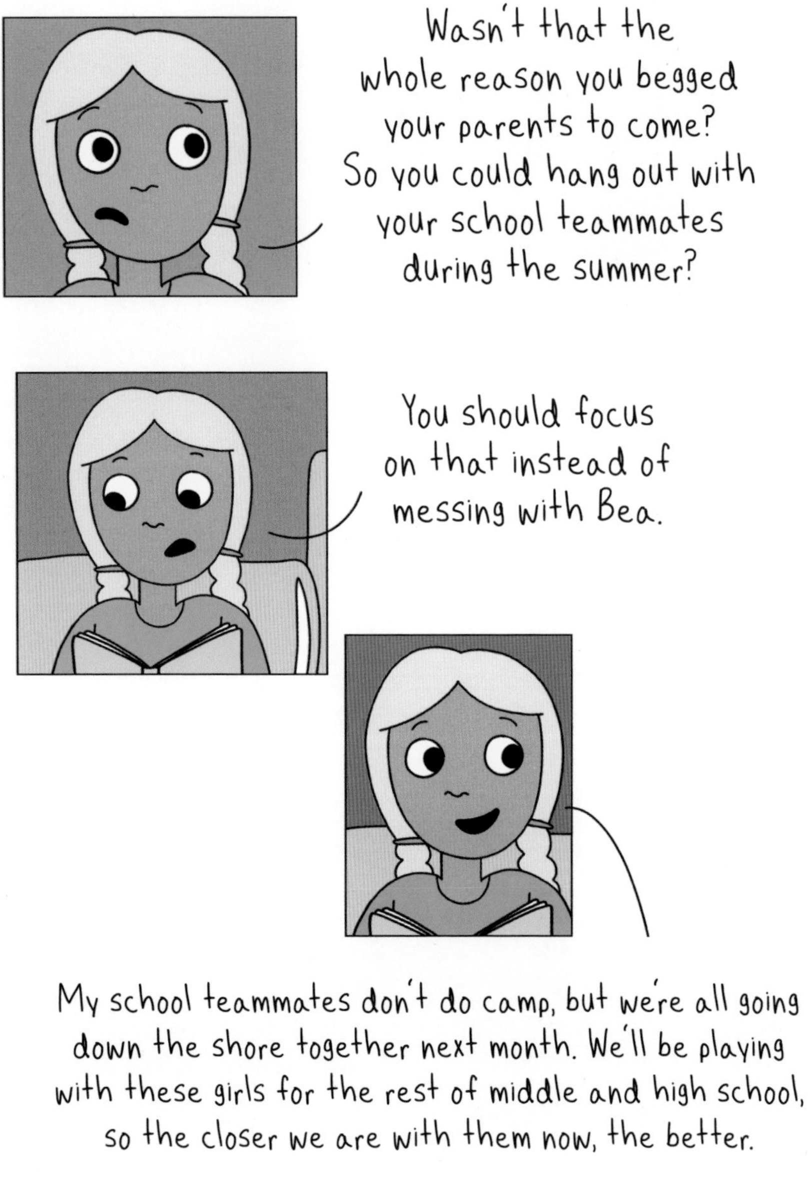
Wasn't that the whole reason you begged your parents to come? So you could hang out with your school teammates during the summer?
You should focus on that instead of messing with Bea.
My school teammates don't do camp, but we're all going down the shore together next month. We'll be playing with these girls for the rest of middle and high school, so the closer we are with them now, the better.

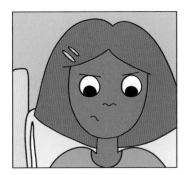

sniff

Wait—are you crying?!

What's wrong?

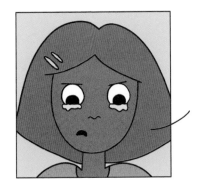

Yes, Roxy, I **am** crying. I **did** beg to come here, and yes, all the Langston Middle soccer girls **do** go to camp here.

But no, I do **not** need to hang out with them.

Because they're not my teammates. I didn't make my school soccer team.

Virginia, I'm so sorry—

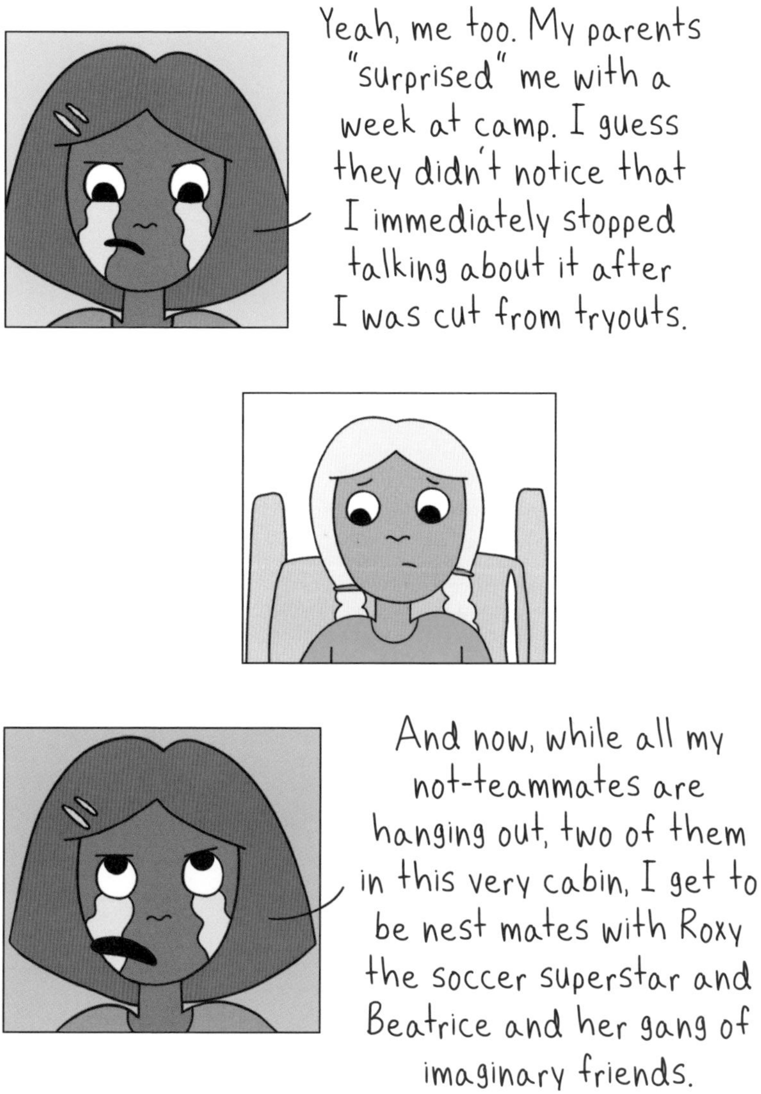
Yeah, me too. My parents "surprised" me with a week at camp. I guess they didn't notice that I immediately stopped talking about it after I was cut from tryouts.
And now, while all my not-teammates are hanging out, two of them in this very cabin, I get to be nest mates with Roxy the soccer superstar and Beatrice and her gang of imaginary friends.

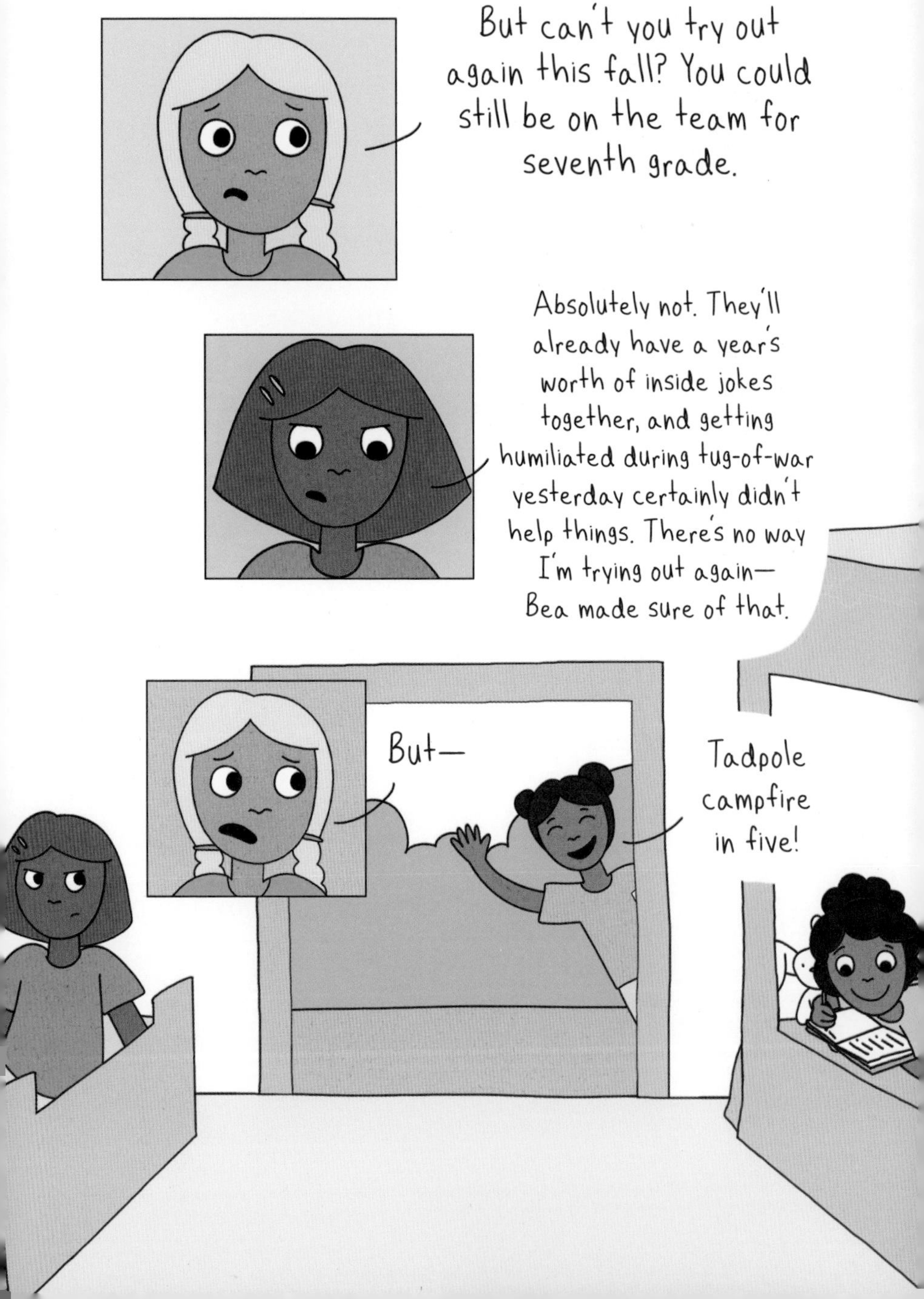
But can't you try out again this fall? You could still be on the team for seventh grade.
Absolutely not. They'll already have a year's worth of inside jokes together, and getting humiliated during tug-of-war yesterday certainly didn't help things. There's no way I'm trying out again— Bea made sure of that.
But—
Tadpole campfire in five!

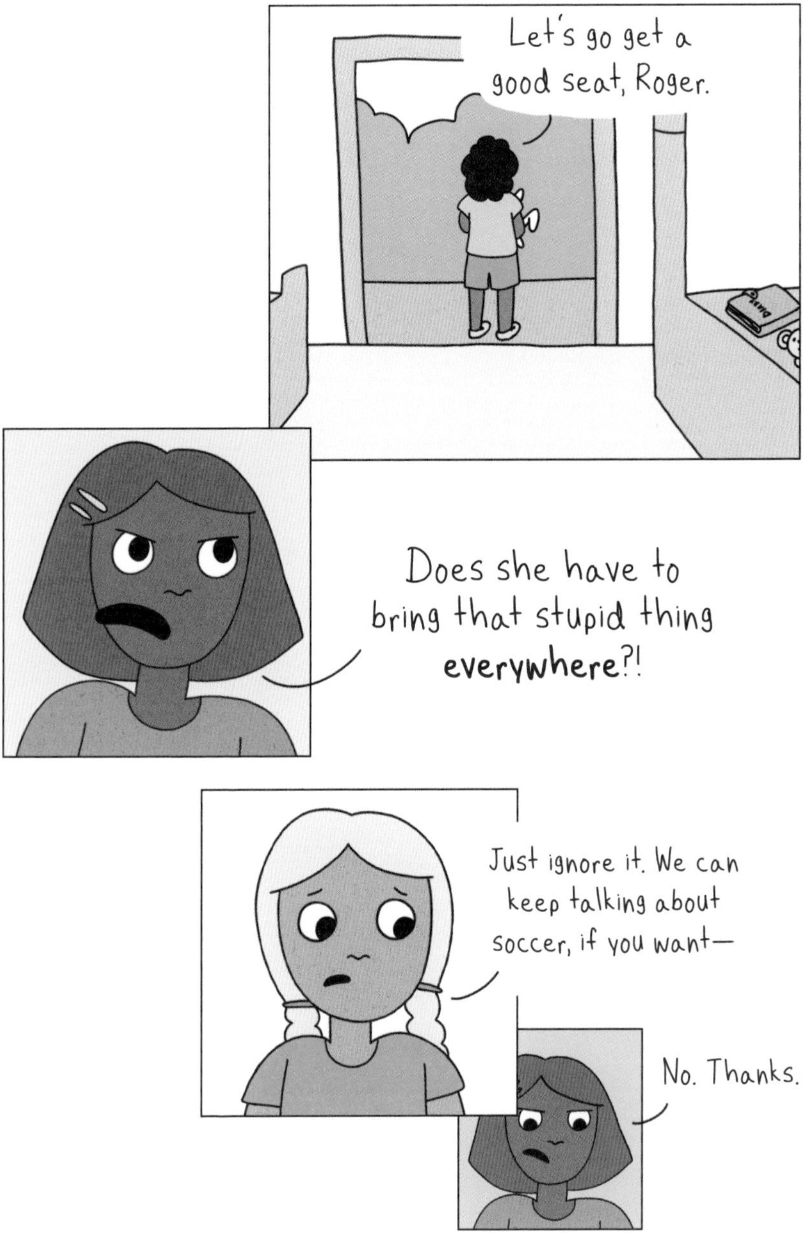
Let's go get a good seat, Roger.
Does she have to bring that stupid thing **everywhere**?!
Just ignore it. We can keep talking about soccer, if you want—
No. Thanks.

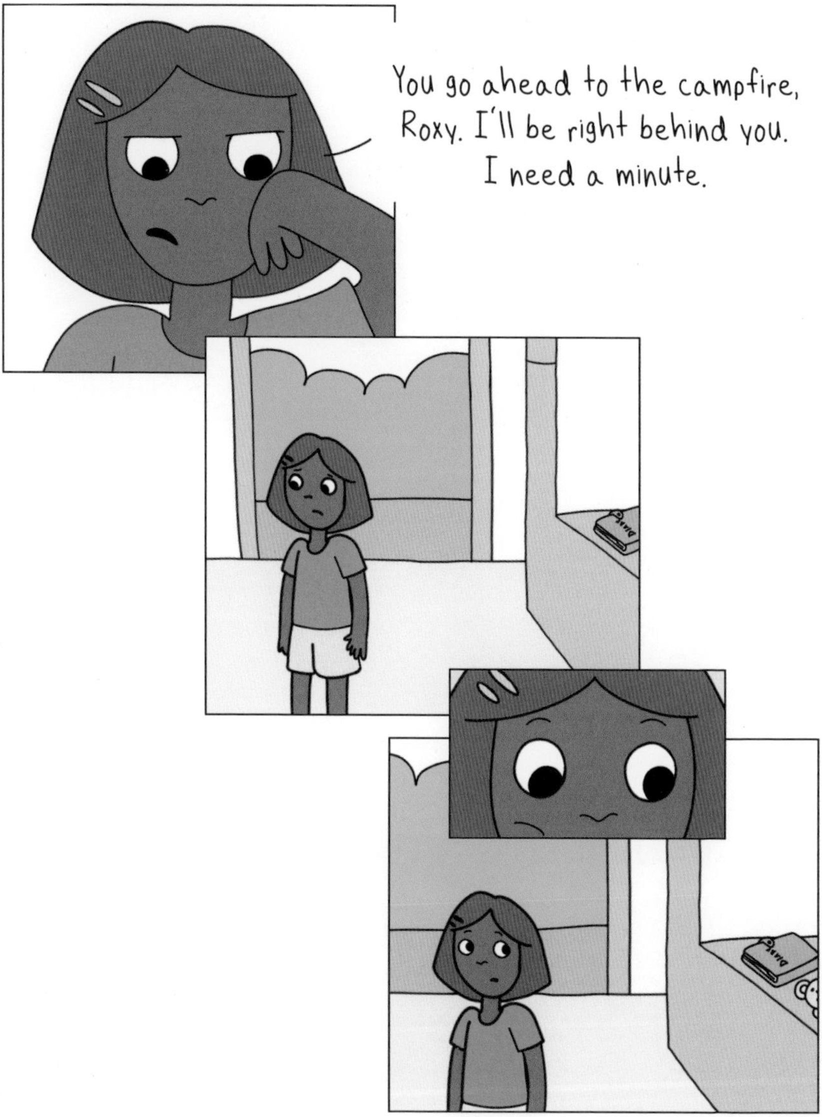
You go ahead to the campfire, Roxy. I'll be right behind you. I need a minute.

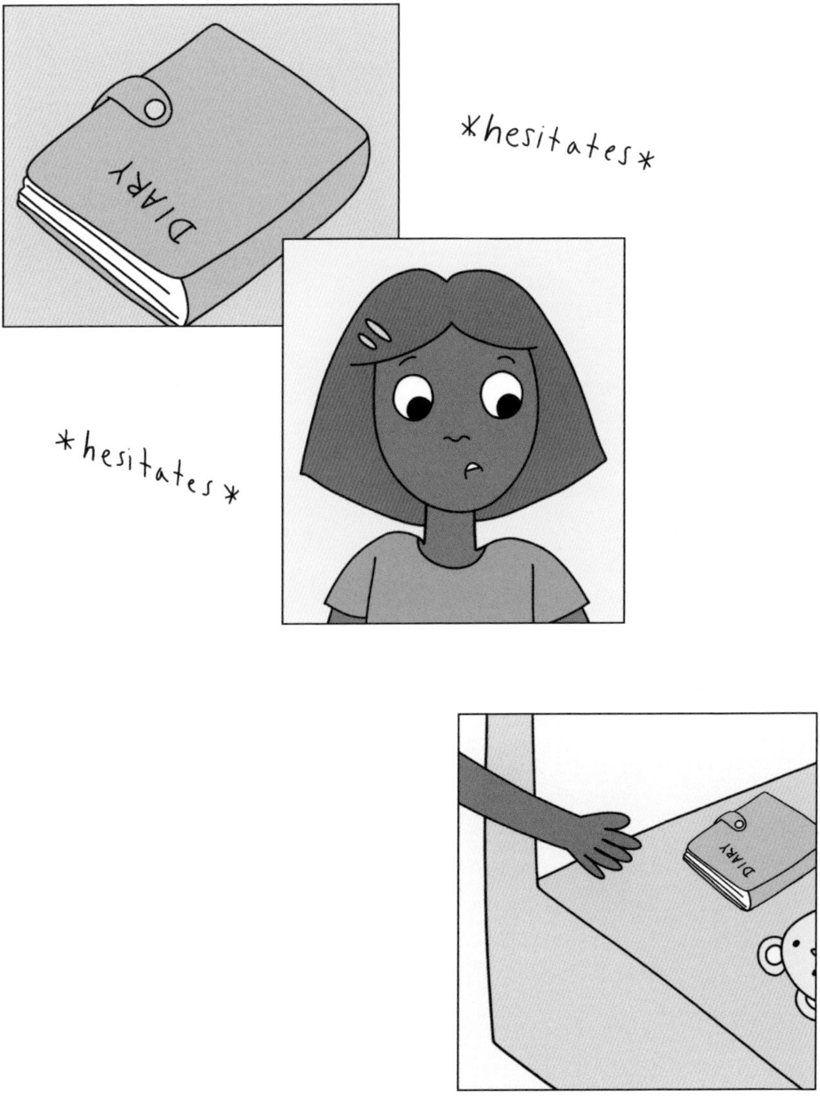
DIARY
hesitates
hesitates
DIARY

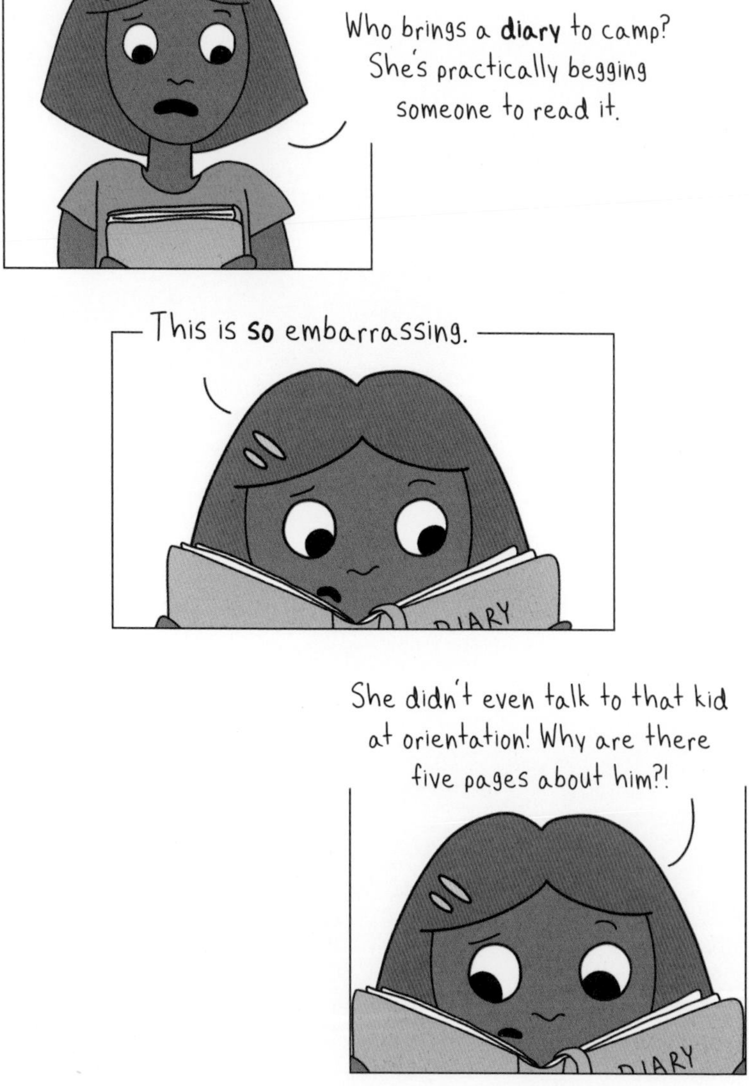
Who brings a **diary** to camp? She's practically begging someone to read it.
This is **so** embarrassing.
DIARY
She didn't even talk to that kid at orientation! Why are there five pages about him?!
DIARY

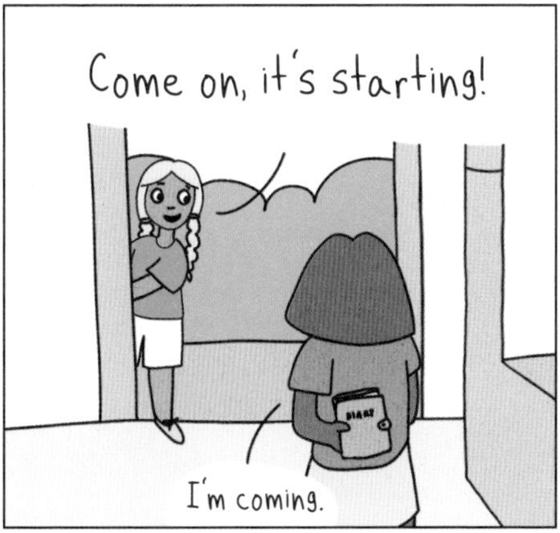
Come on, it's starting!
I'm coming.

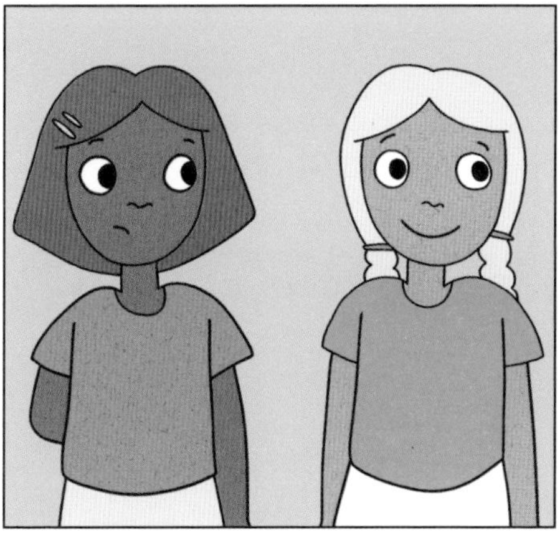

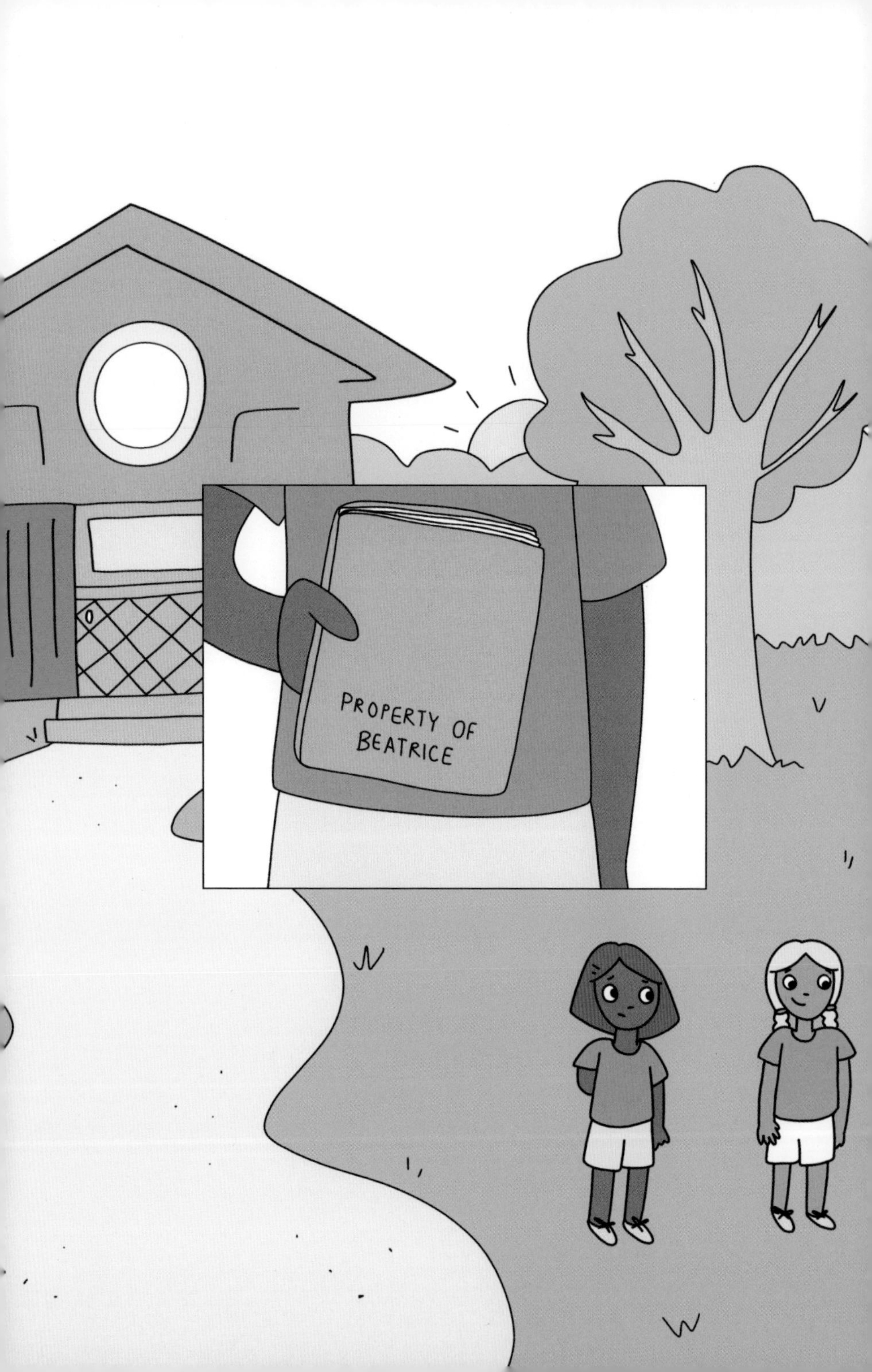
PROPERTY OF
BEATRICE

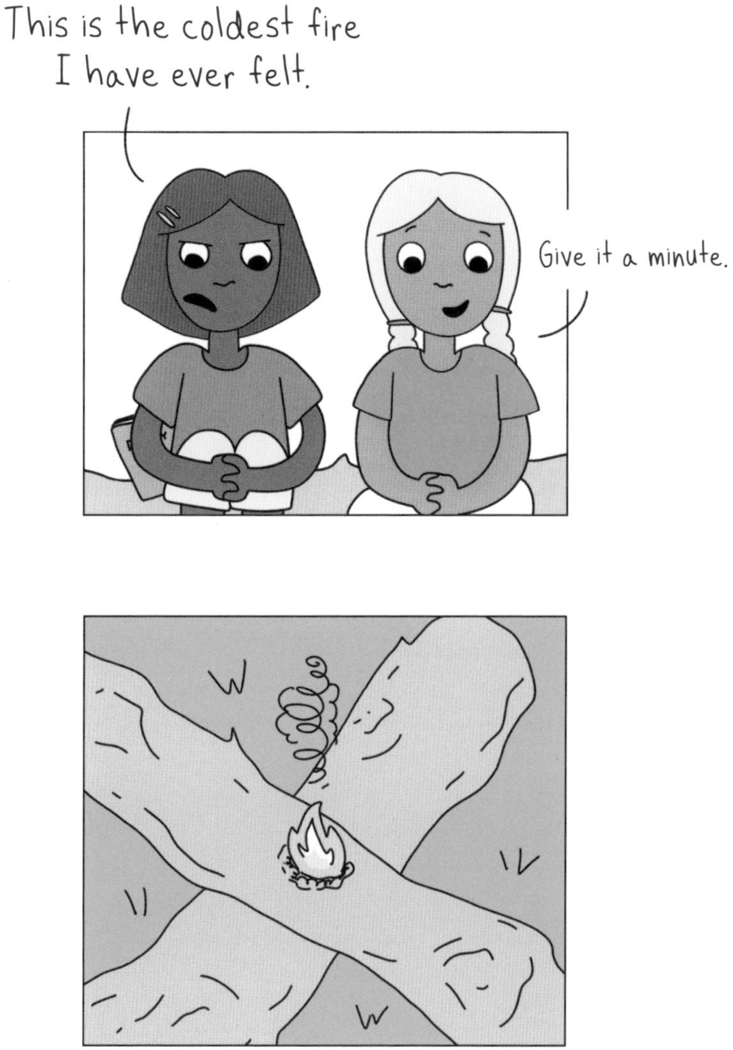
This is the coldest fire I have ever felt.
Give it a minute.

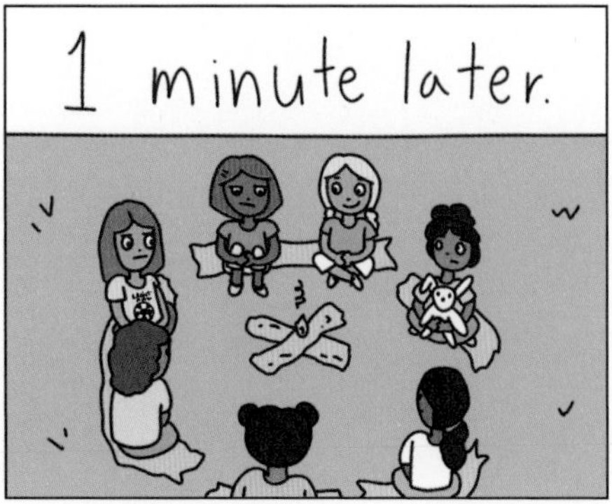
1 minute later.

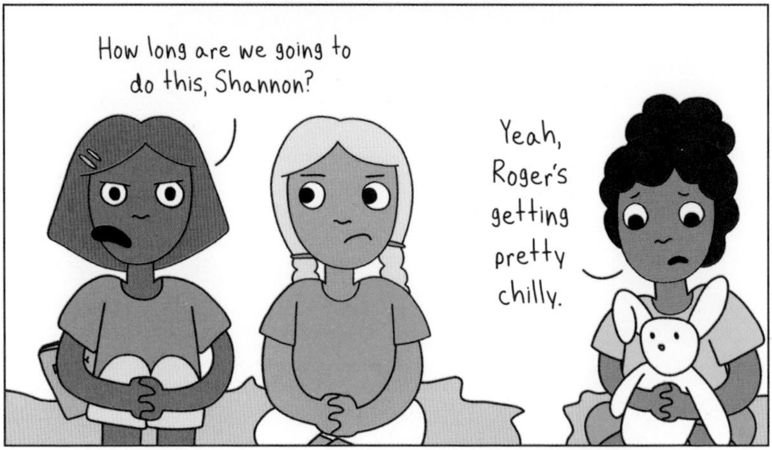
How long are we going to do this, Shannon?
Yeah, Roger's getting pretty chilly.

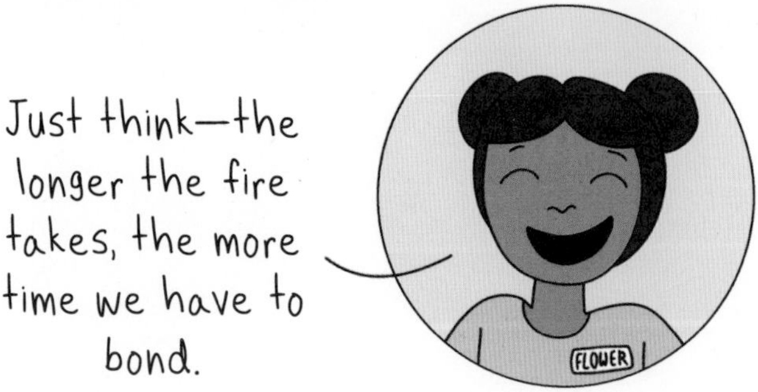
Just think—the longer the fire takes, the more time we have to bond.
FLOWER

silence

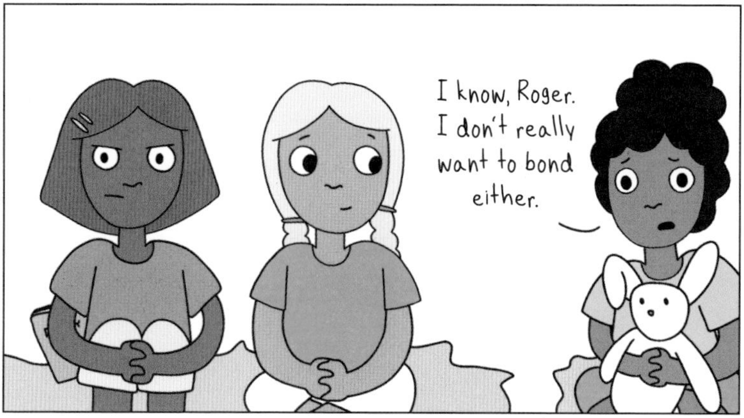
I know, Roger. I don't really want to bond either.

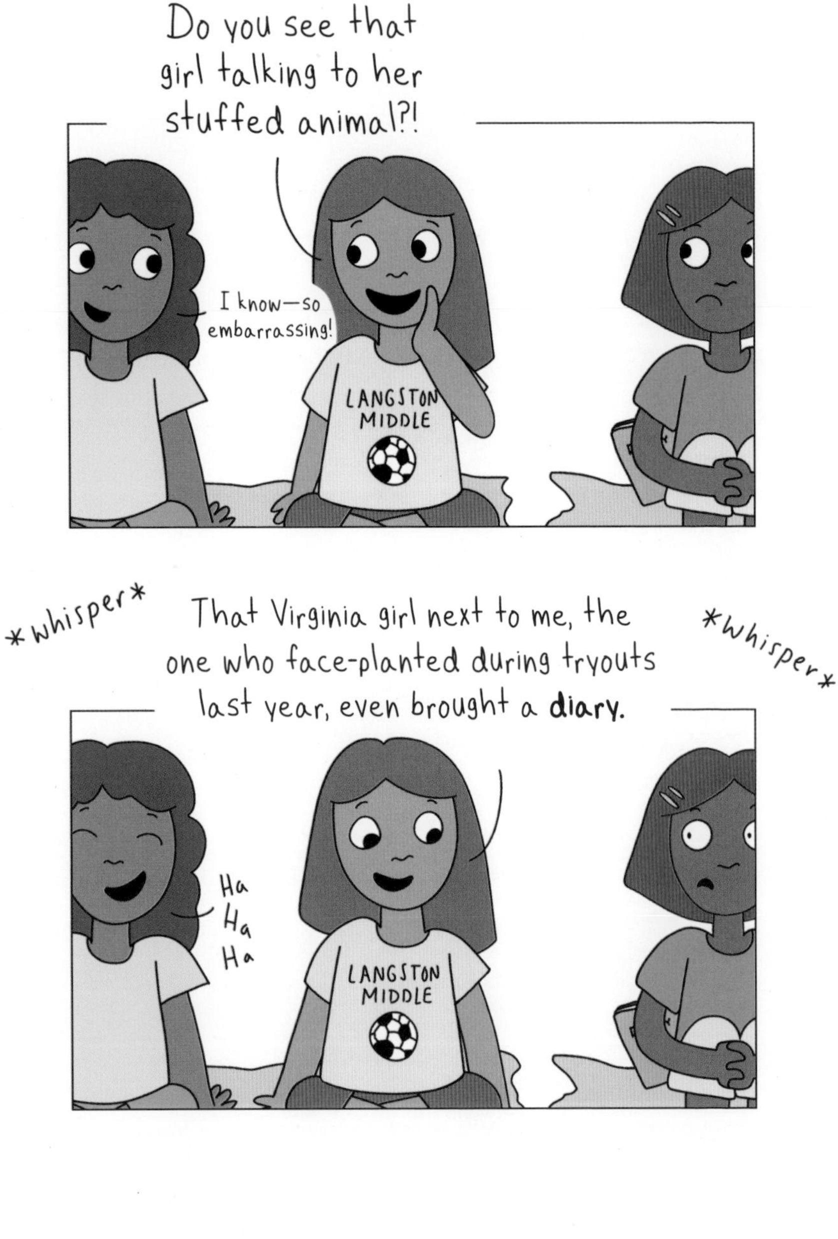
Do you see that girl talking to her stuffed animal?!
I know—so embarrassing!
whisper
That Virginia girl next to me, the one who face-planted during tryouts last year, even brought a **diary**.
whisper
Ha Ha Ha
LANGSTON MIDDLE
LANGSTON MIDDLE

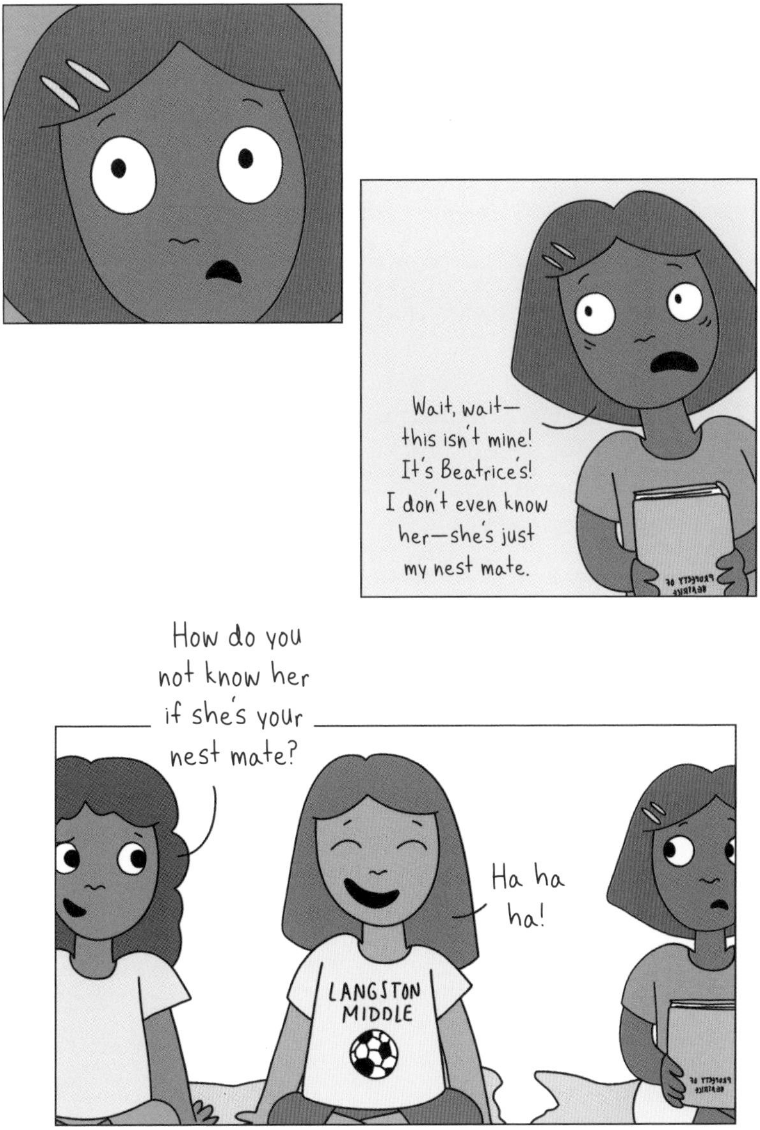
Wait, wait— this isn't mine! It's Beatrice's! I don't even know her—she's just my nest mate.
How do you not know her if she's your nest mate?
Ha ha ha!
LANGSTON MIDDLE

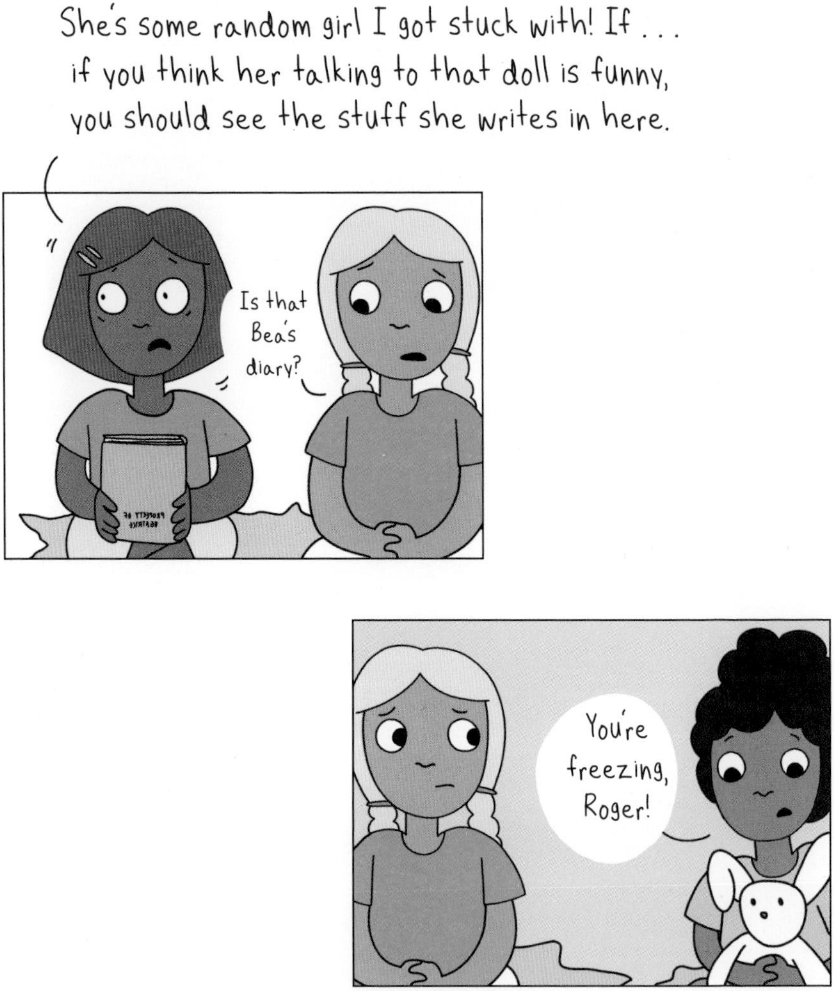
She's some random girl I got stuck with! If . . . if you think her talking to that doll is funny, you should see the stuff she writes in here.
Is that Bea's diary?
You're freezing, Roger!

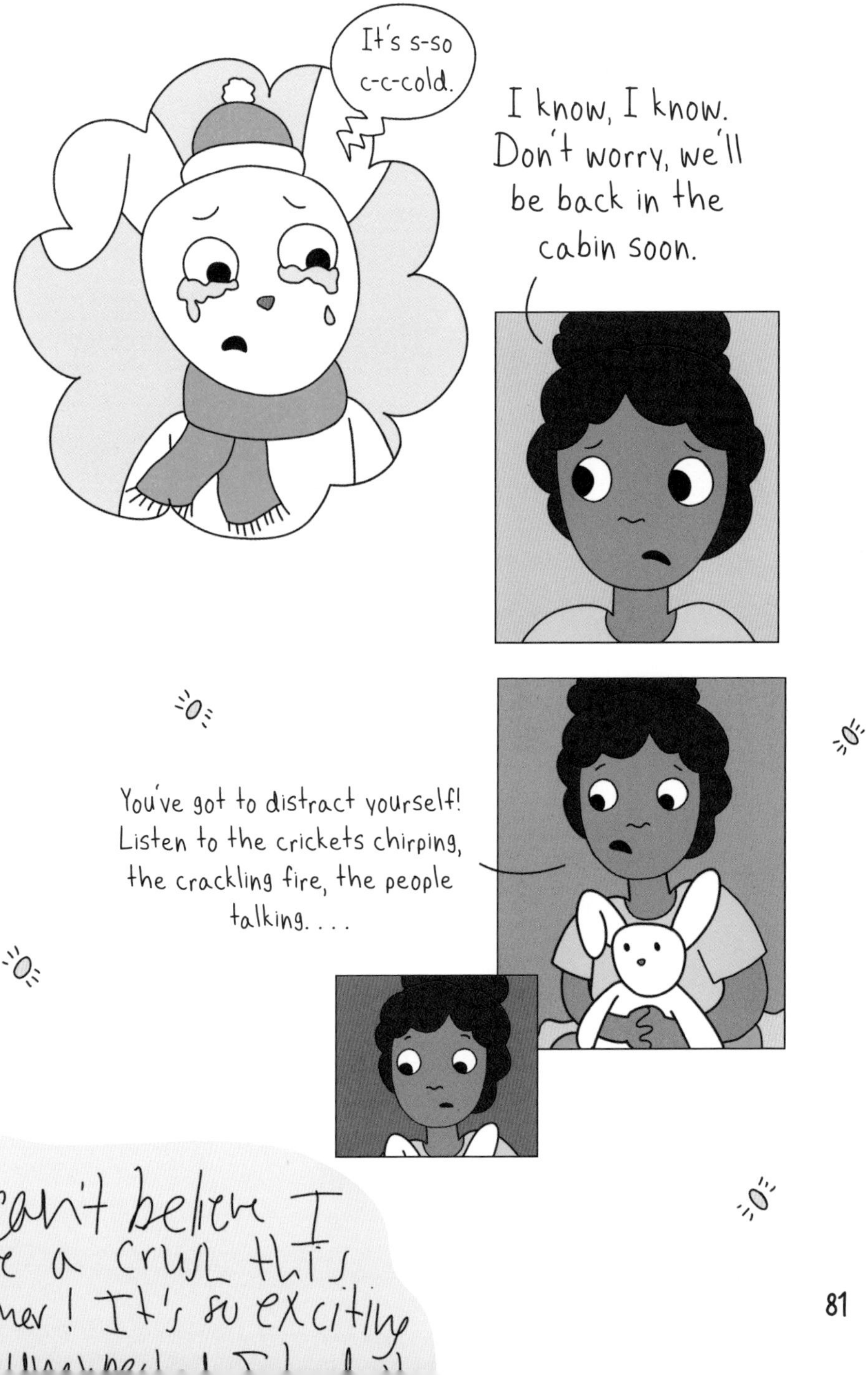
It's s-so c-c-cold.
I know, I know. Don't worry, we'll be back in the cabin soon.
You've got to distract yourself! Listen to the crickets chirping, the crackling fire, the people talking. . . .
can't believe I
a crush this
It's so exciting

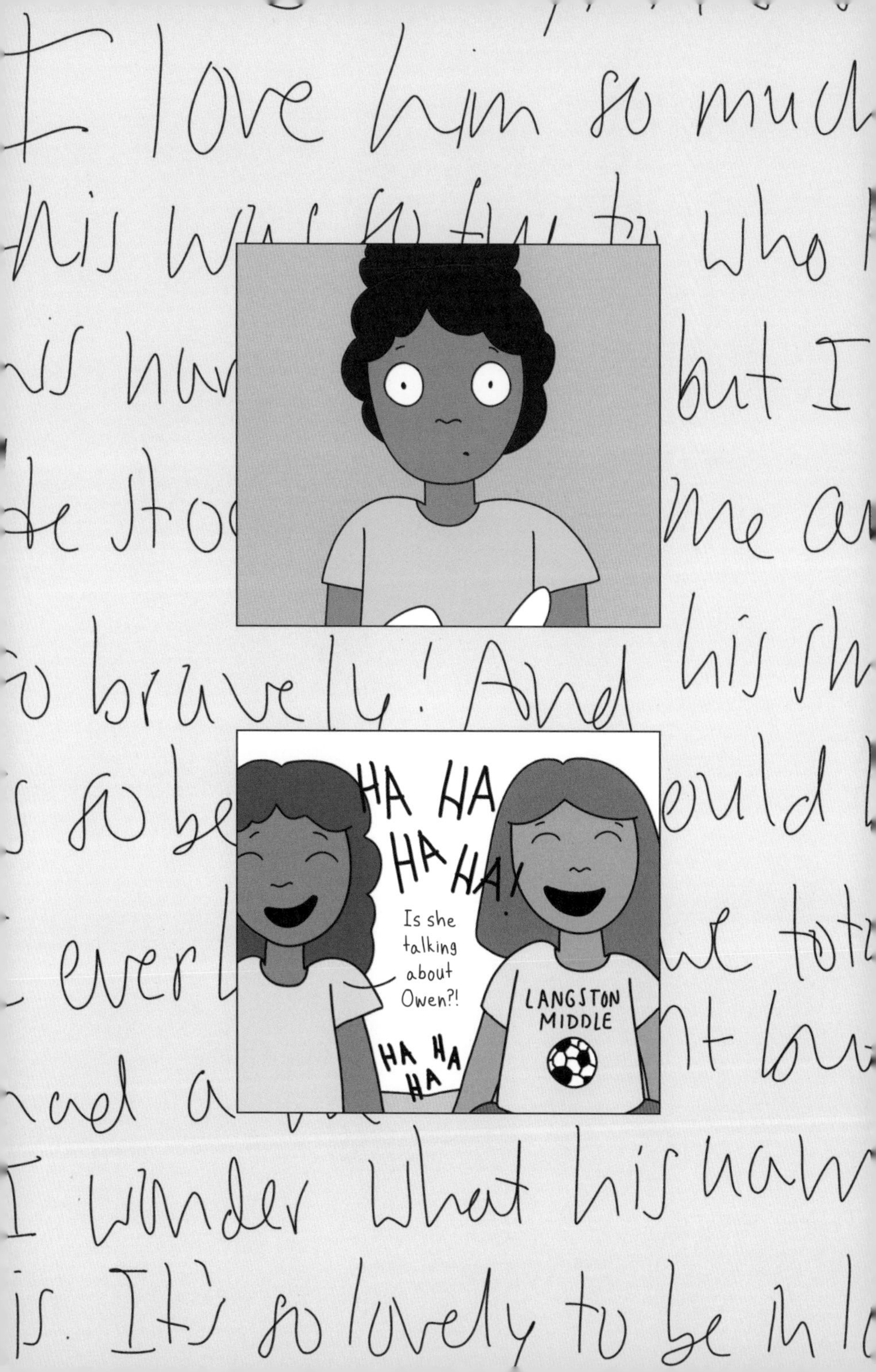
I love him so much
but I
bravely! And
HA HA
HA HA!
Is she talking about Owen?!
HA HA HA
LANGSTON MIDDLE
I wonder what his
It's so lovely to be

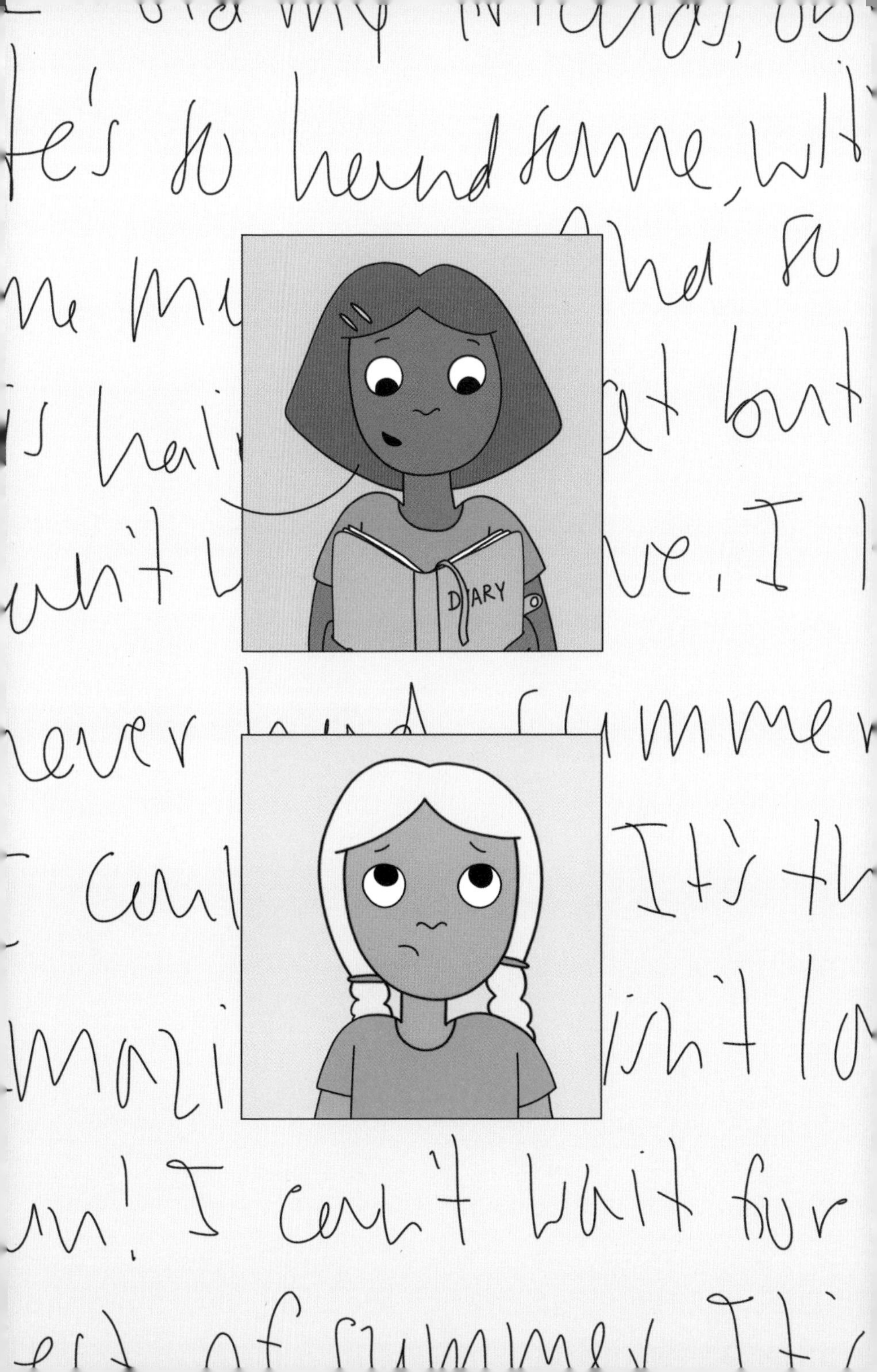
He's so handsome,
DIARY
I can't wait for

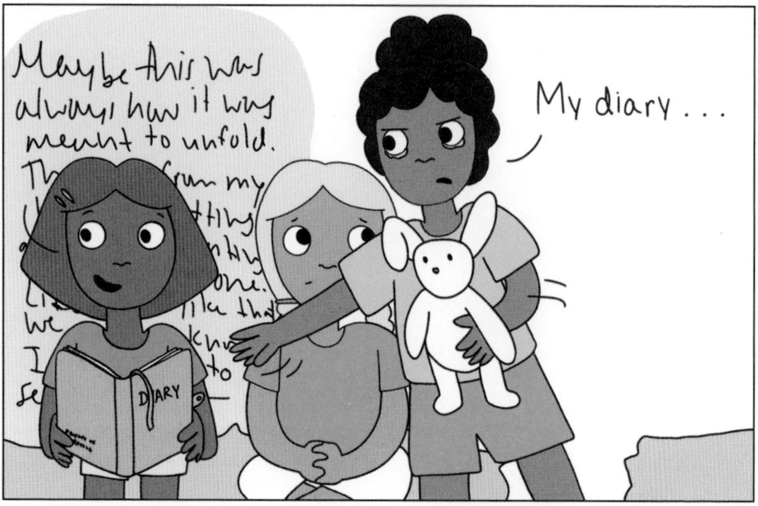

Maybe this was always how it was meant to unfold.
DIARY
My diary . . .

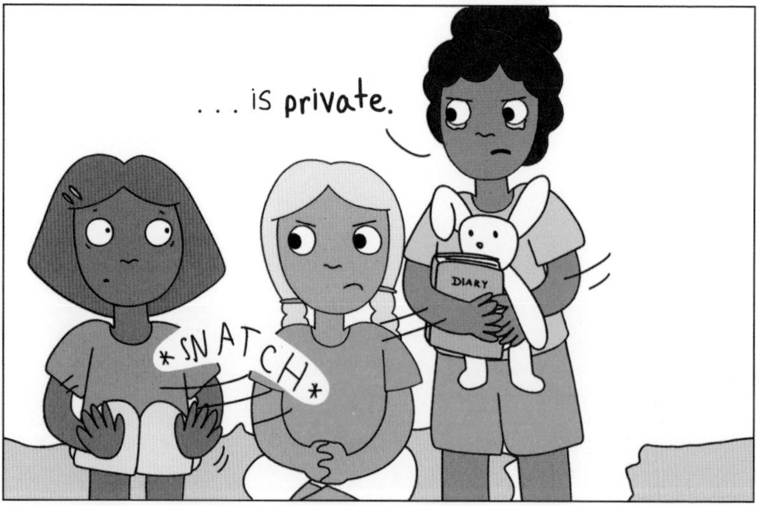

. . . is **private.**
SNATCH
DIARY

Bea, I'm—

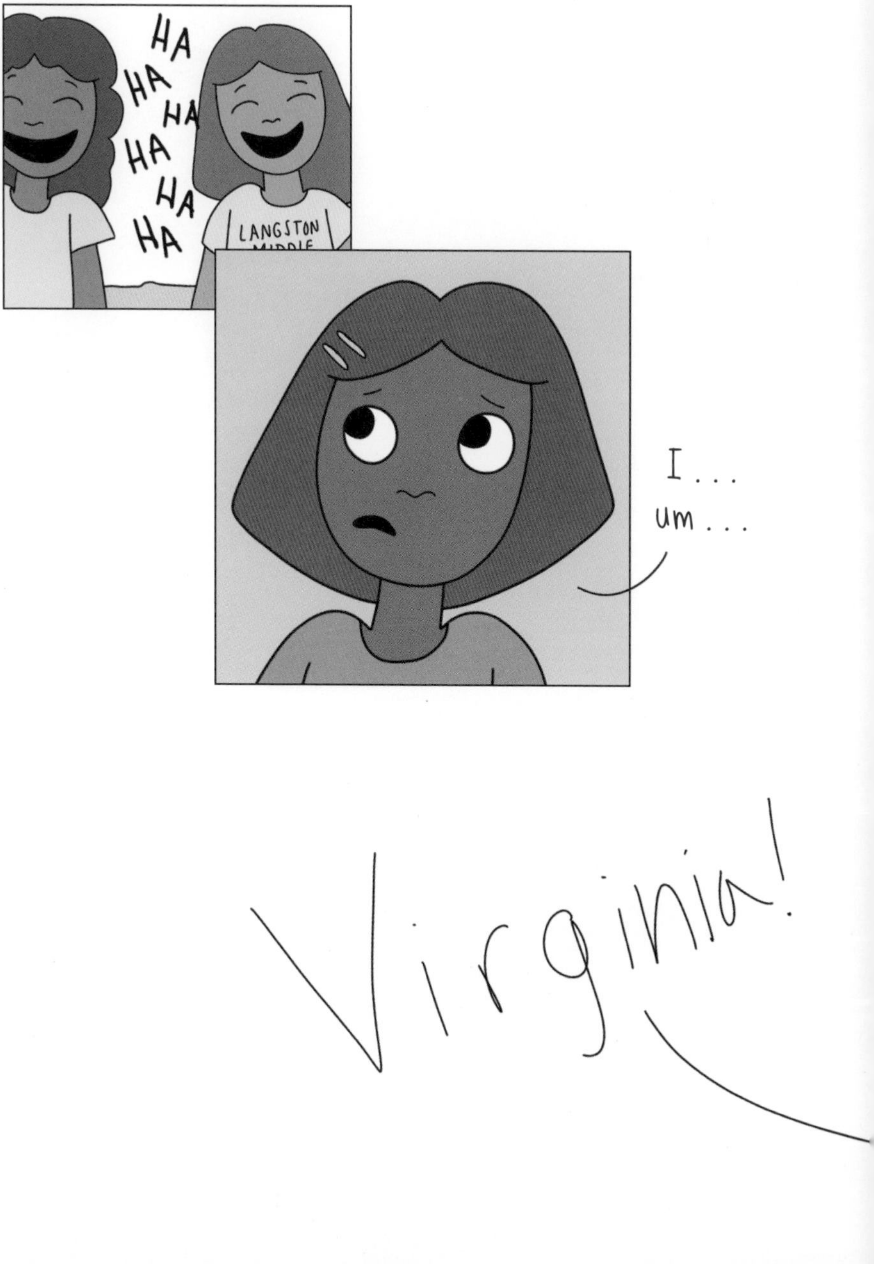
HA
HA
HA
HA
HA
HA
LANGSTON
I . . .
um . . .
Virginia!

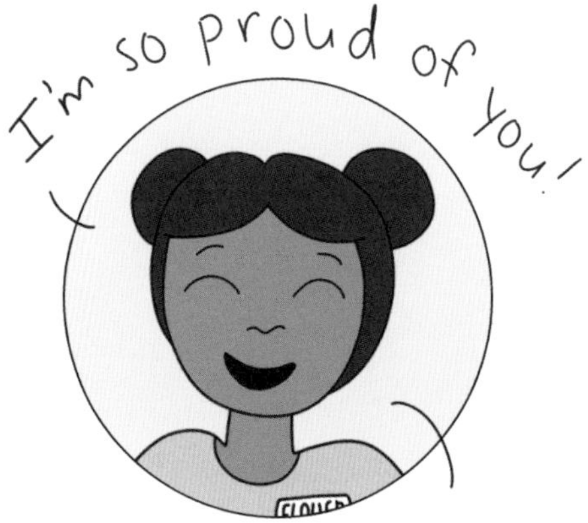
I'm so proud of you!
It takes a lot of bravery to share such vulnerable feelings. Now **that's** the campfire spirit!

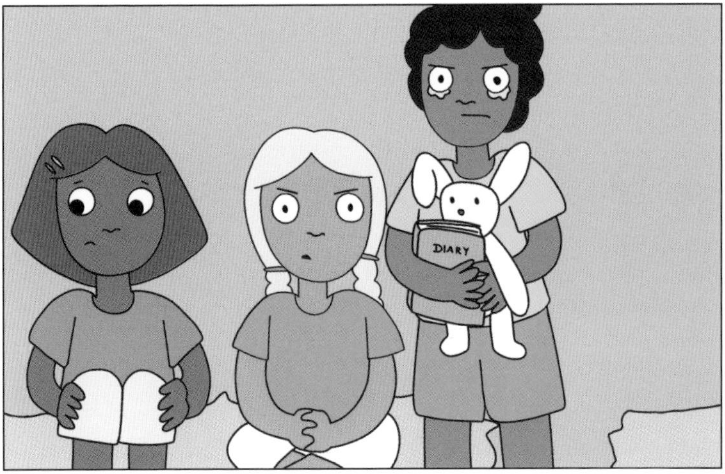
DIARY

CHAPTER 5

BEATRICE'S RUINED LIFE

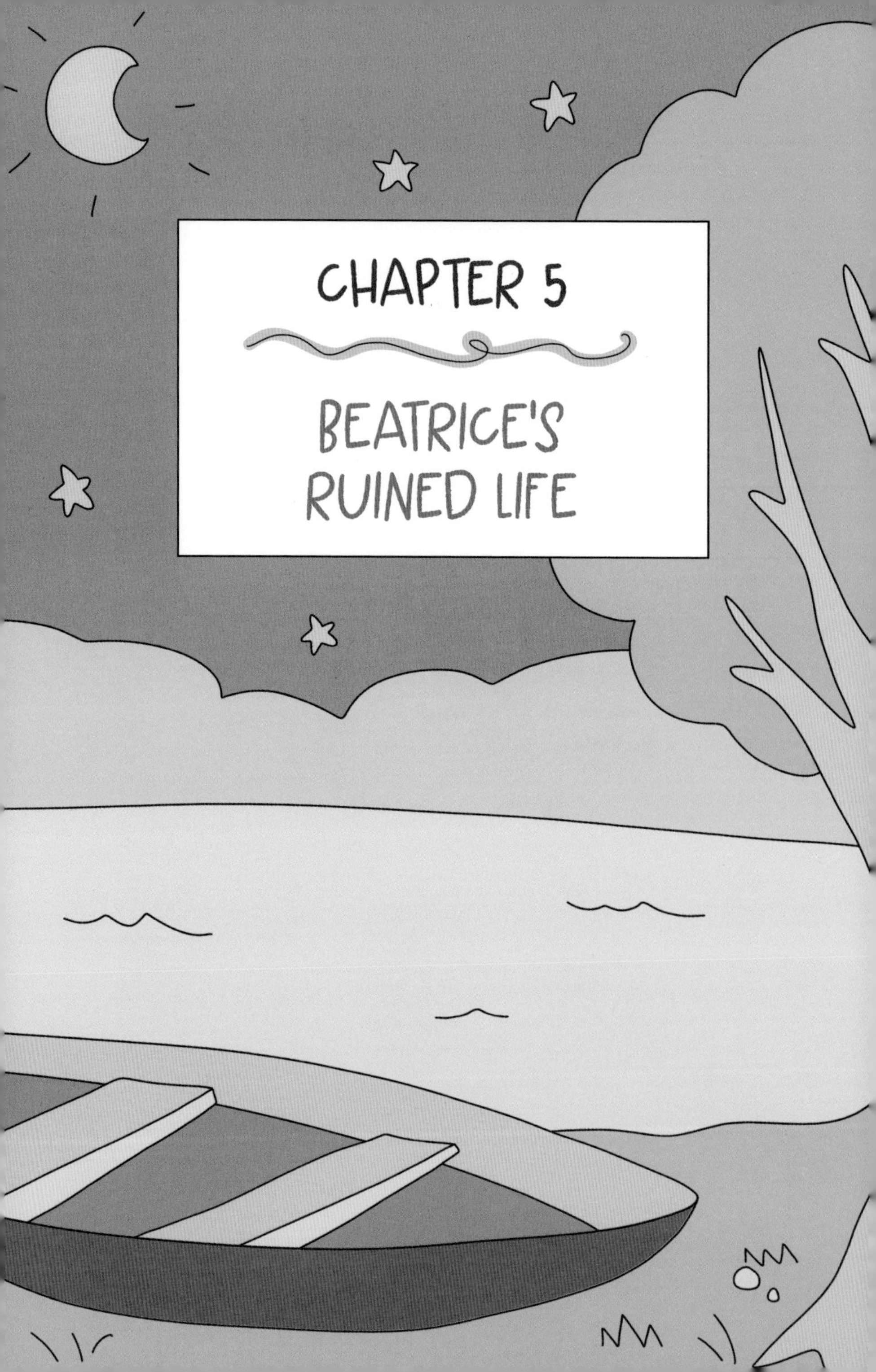

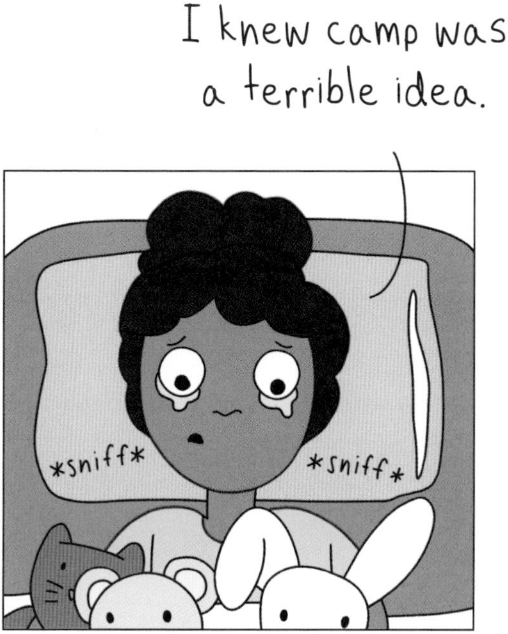
I knew camp was a terrible idea.
sniff
sniff

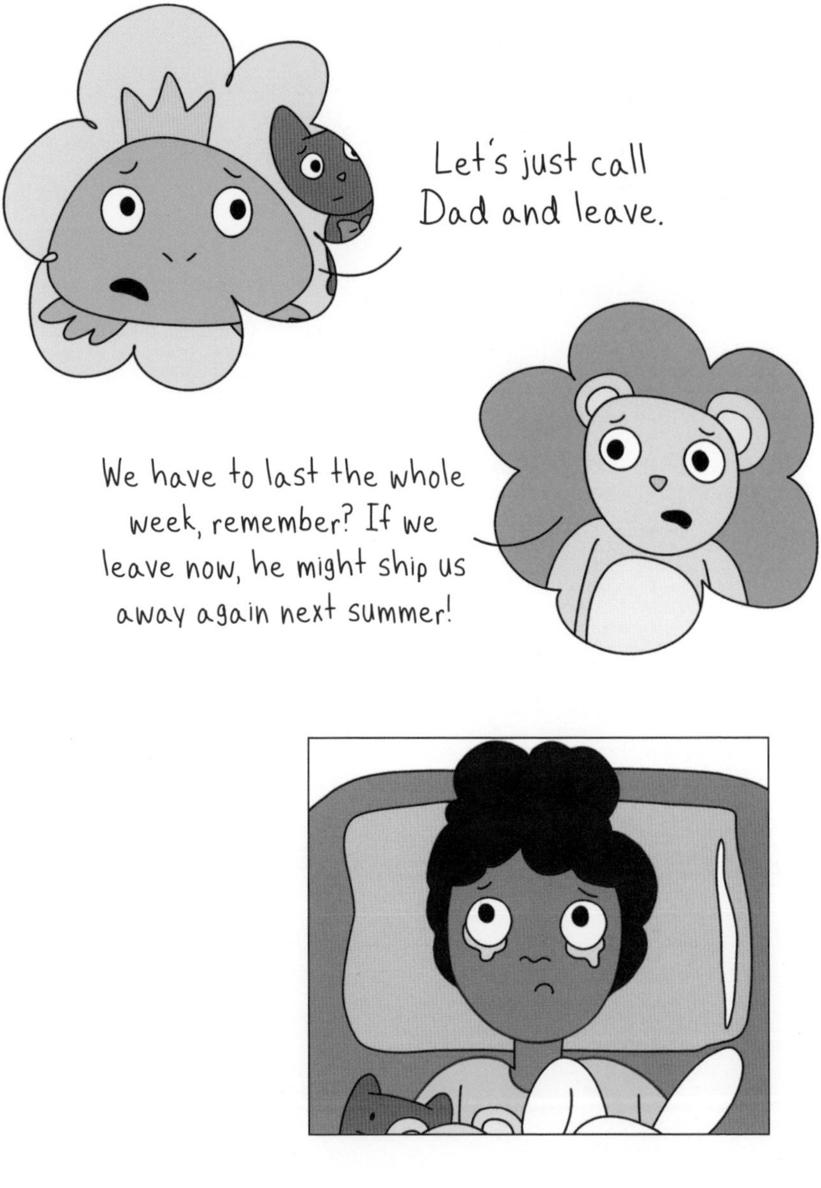
Let's just call
Dad and leave.
We have to last the whole
week, remember? If we
leave now, he might ship us
away again next summer!

whisper

That was so messed up, Virginia! You have to apologize.

You don't understand. I had **no** intention of reading her diary to everyone! It was an accident. *whisper*

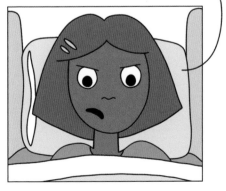

91

whisper

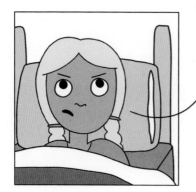

But you still did it! You've had it out for Bea this whole time. I know you were trying to fit in with those girls, but—

I was not!

Yes, you were!

There are girls like that on my team, I get it. But trust me, it's not worth it.

whisper

When did you become such an expert?
Just because you made your school team
doesn't mean you know everything.

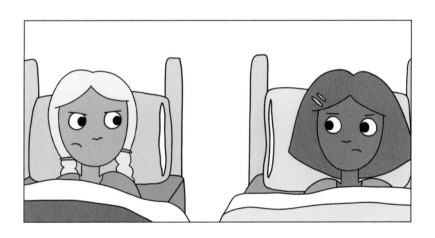

Soon you're going to have two nest mates not speaking to you instead of just one.

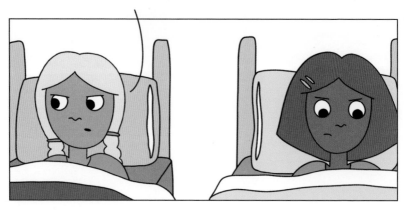

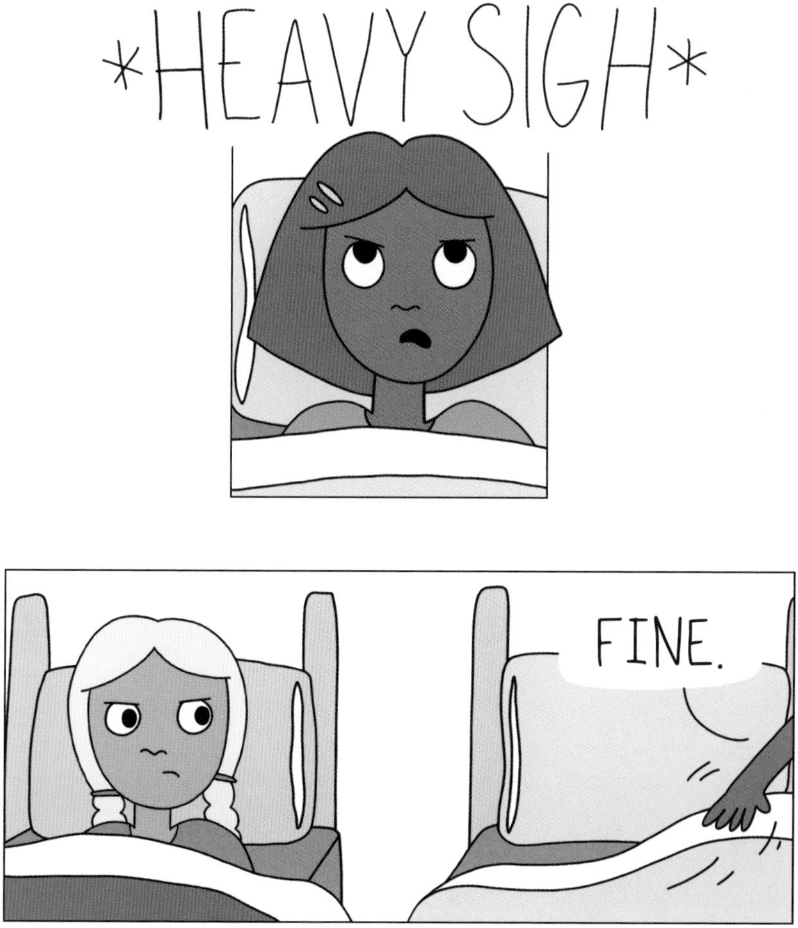
HEAVY SIGH
FINE.

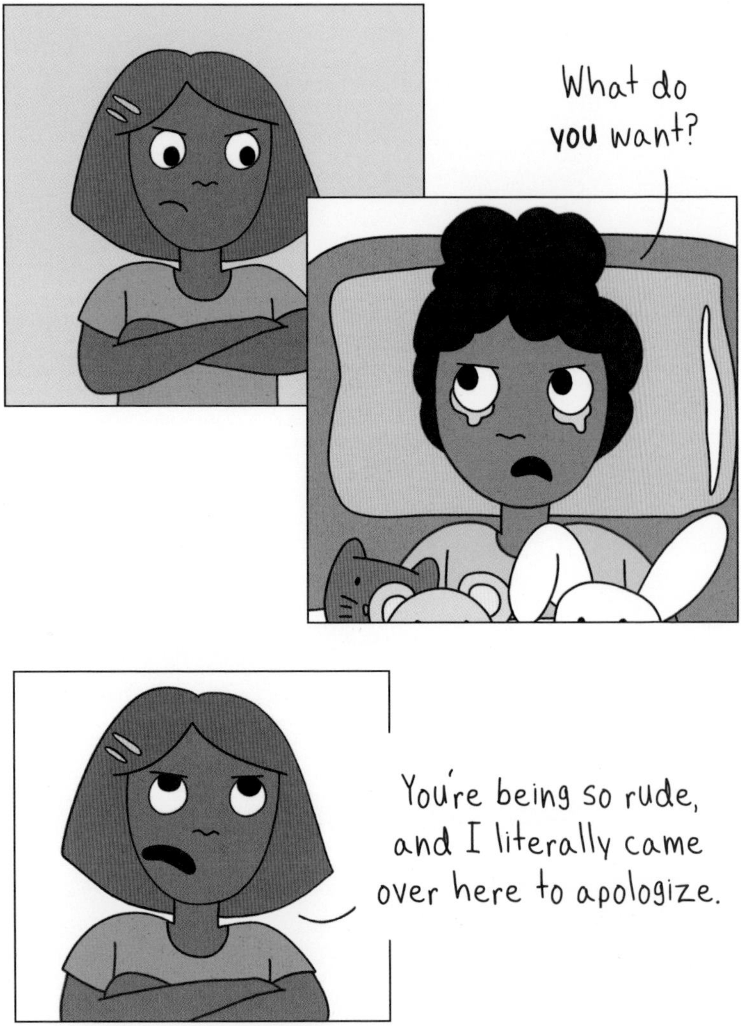
What do you want?
You're being so rude, and I literally came over here to apologize.

Apologize, then.

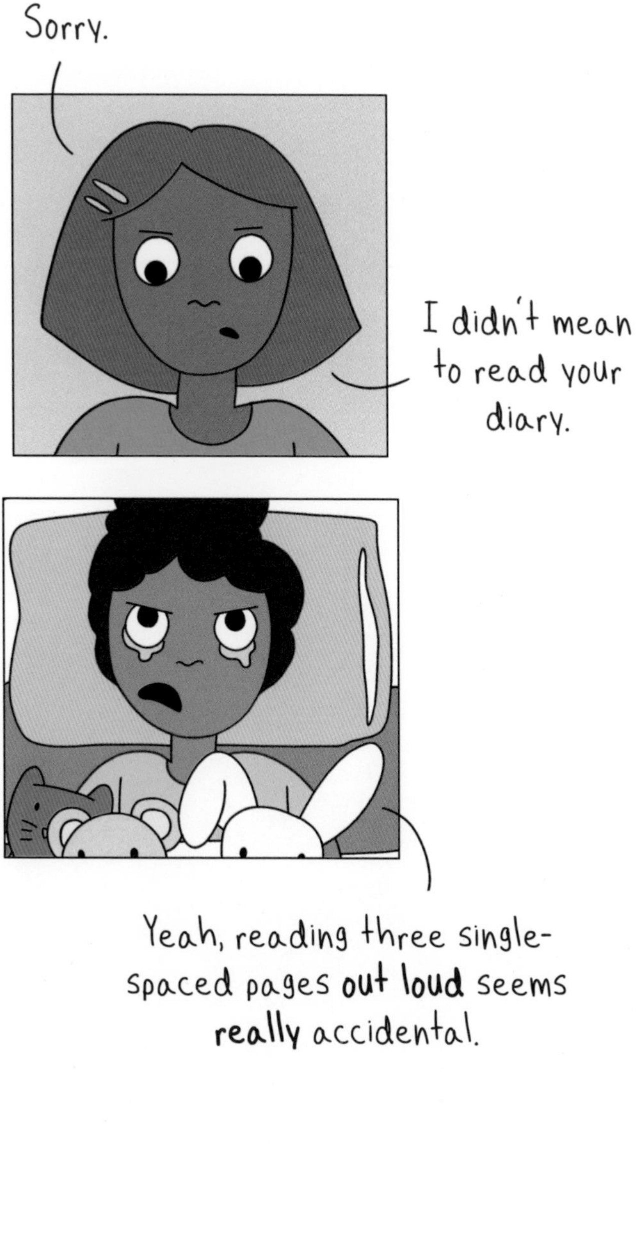
Sorry.
I didn't mean to read your diary.
Yeah, reading three single-spaced pages **out loud** seems **really** accidental.

I do not accept your apology.

Then why did you tell me to apologize?!

Because a better person might actually forgive you.

But I am not a better person, and I will **not** forgive you.

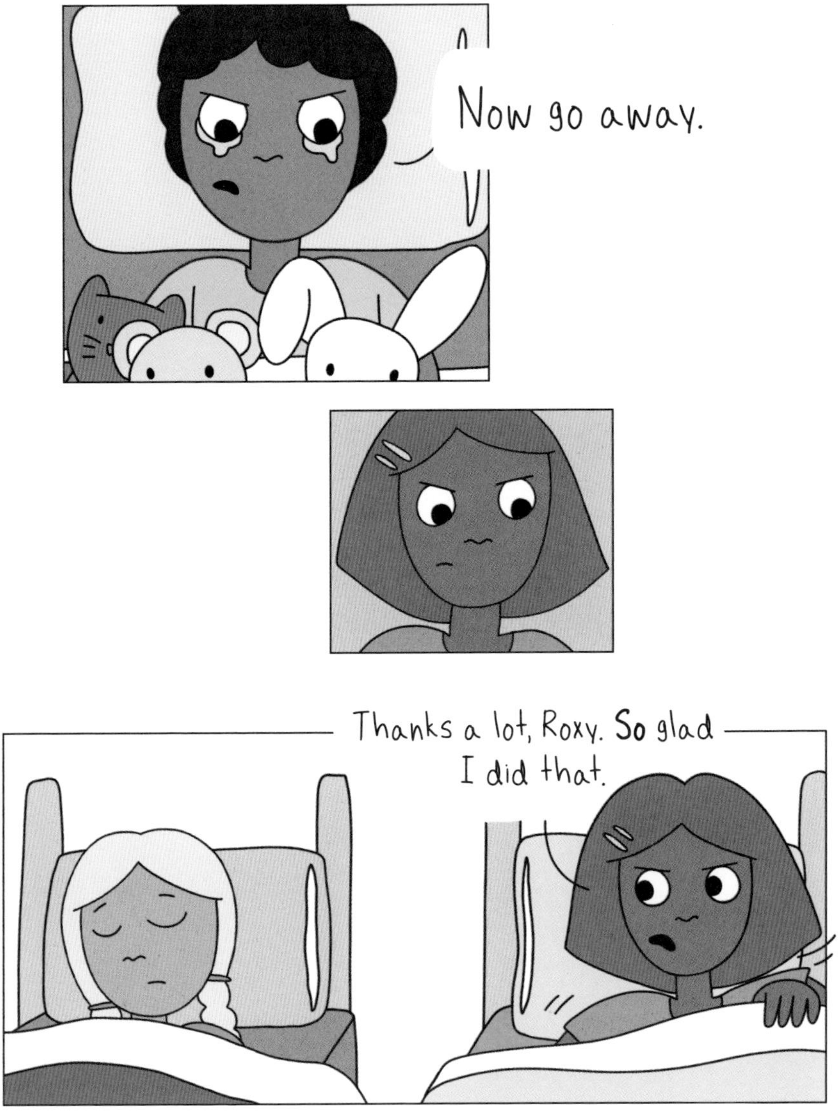
Now go away.
Thanks a lot, Roxy. So glad I did that.

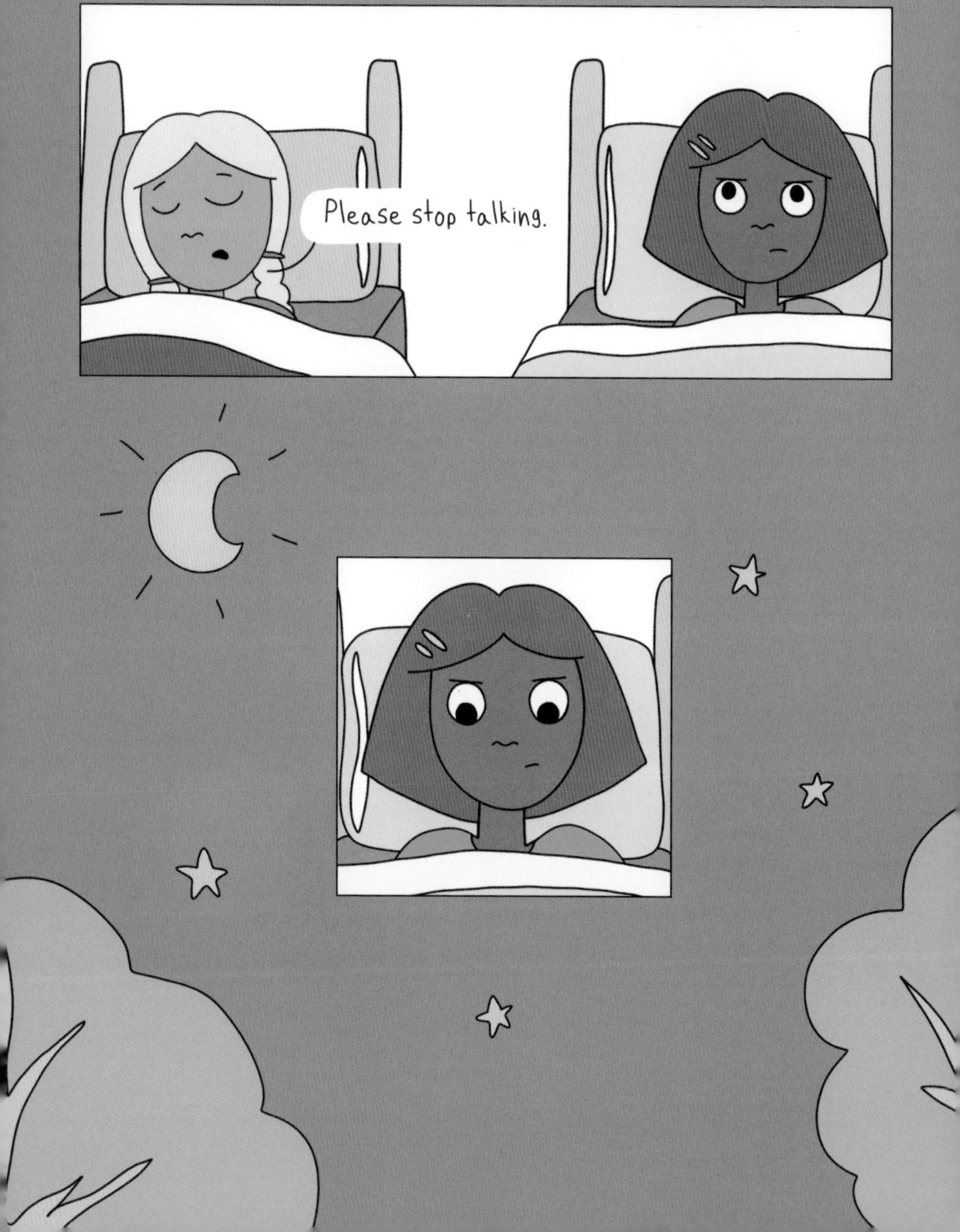
Please stop talking.

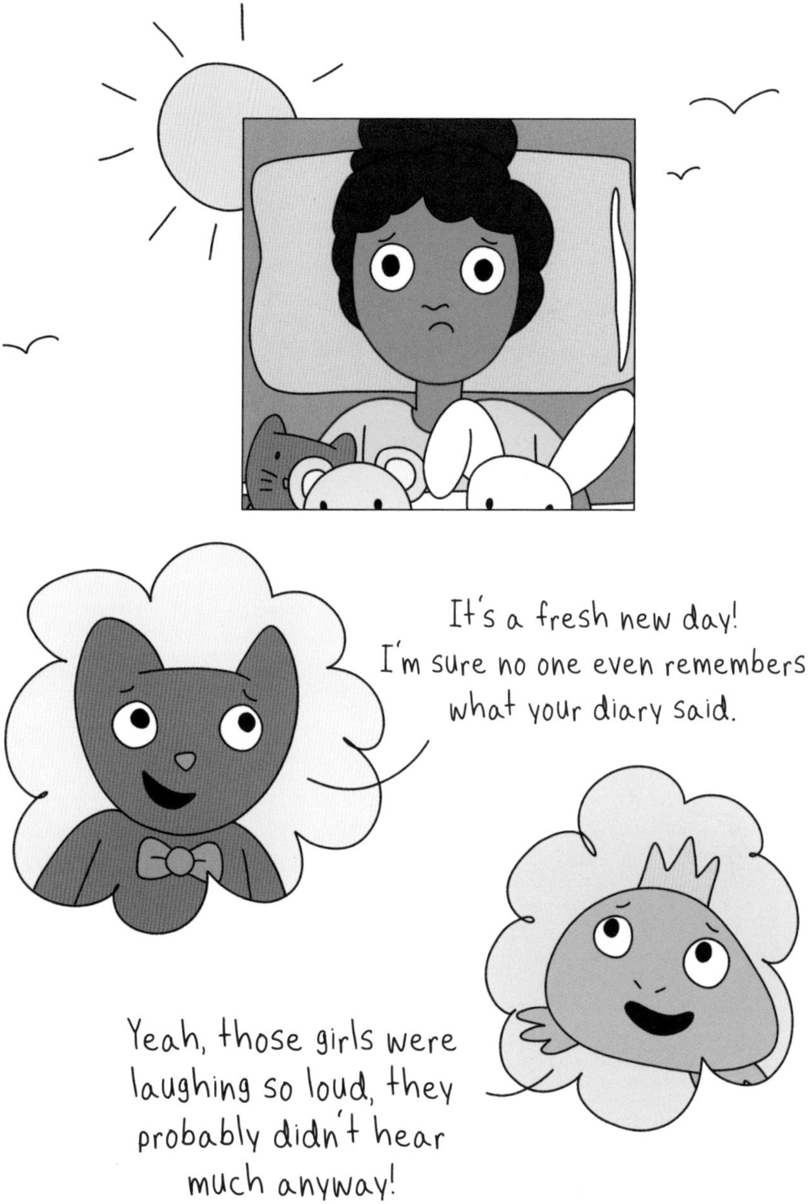
It's a fresh new day! I'm sure no one even remembers what your diary said.
Yeah, those girls were laughing so loud, they probably didn't hear much anyway!

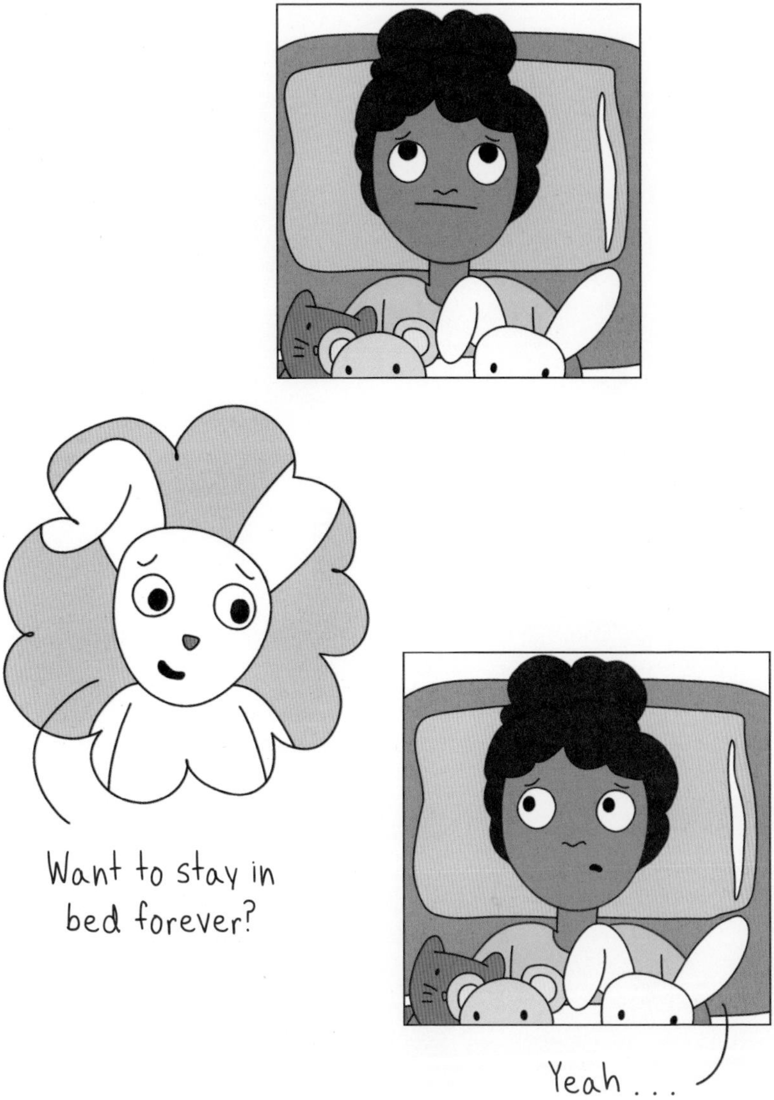
Want to stay in bed forever?
Yeah . . .

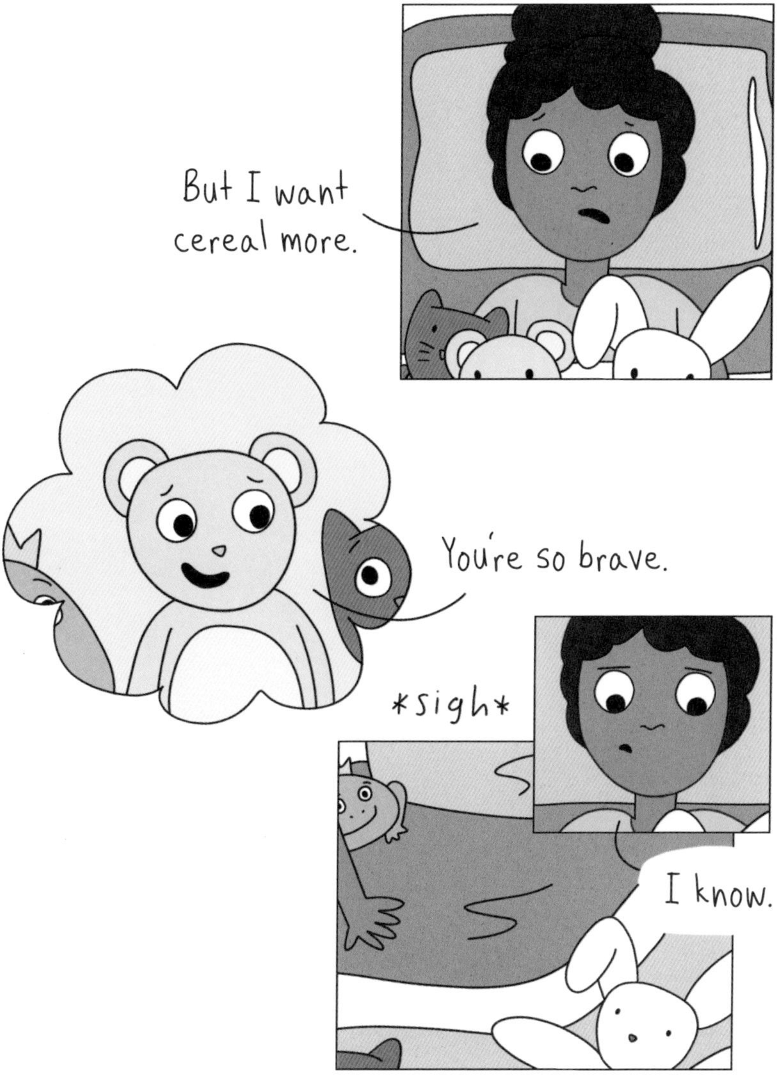
But I want cereal more.
You're so brave.
sigh
I know.

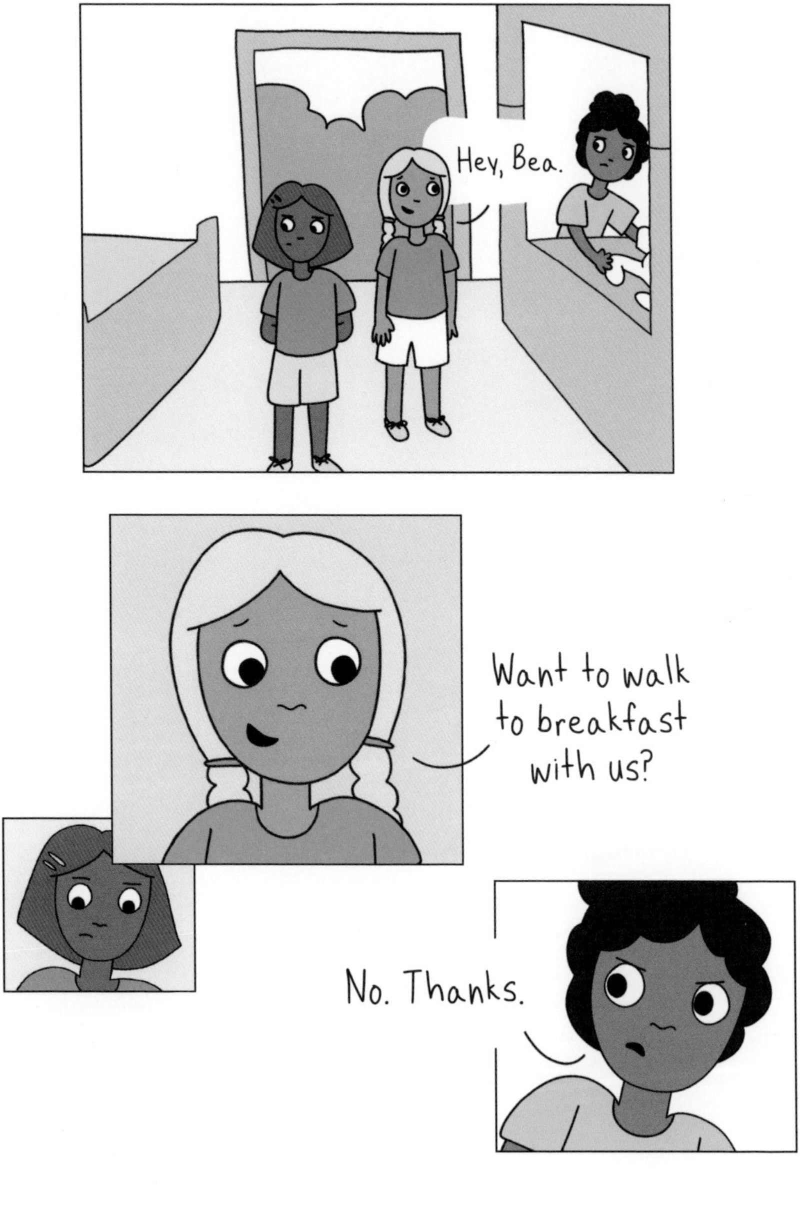
Hey, Bea.
Want to walk to breakfast with us?
No. Thanks.

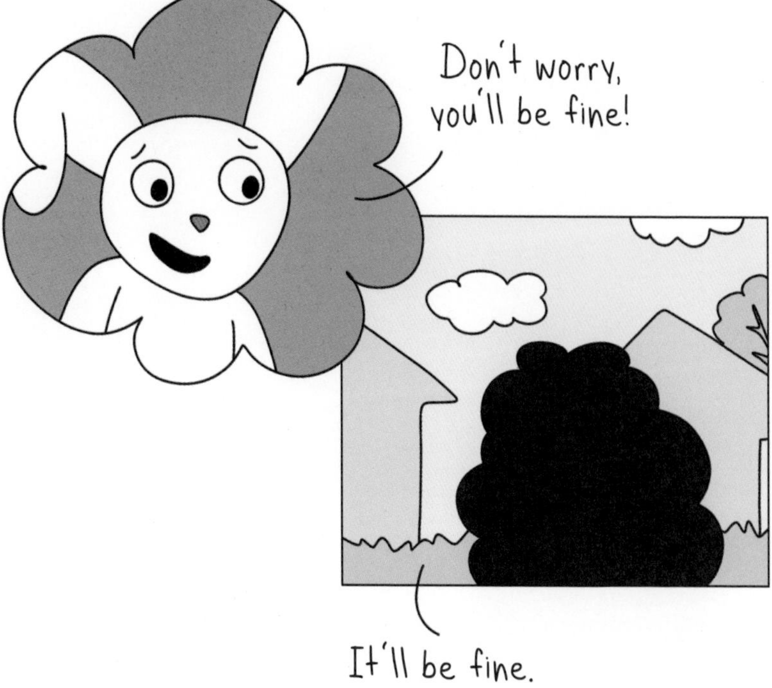
Don't worry,
you'll be fine!
It'll be fine.

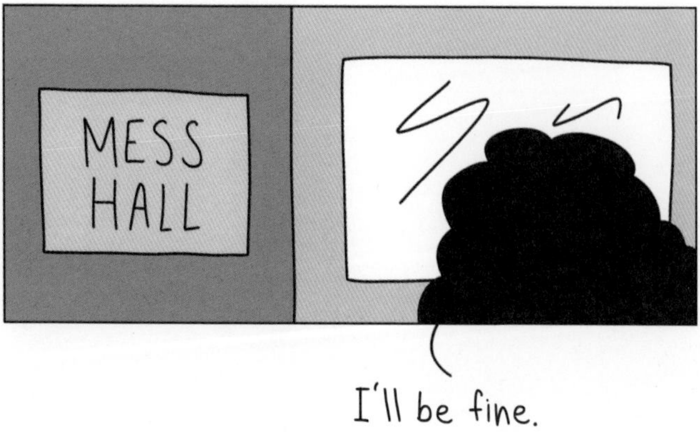
MESS
HALL
I'll be fine.

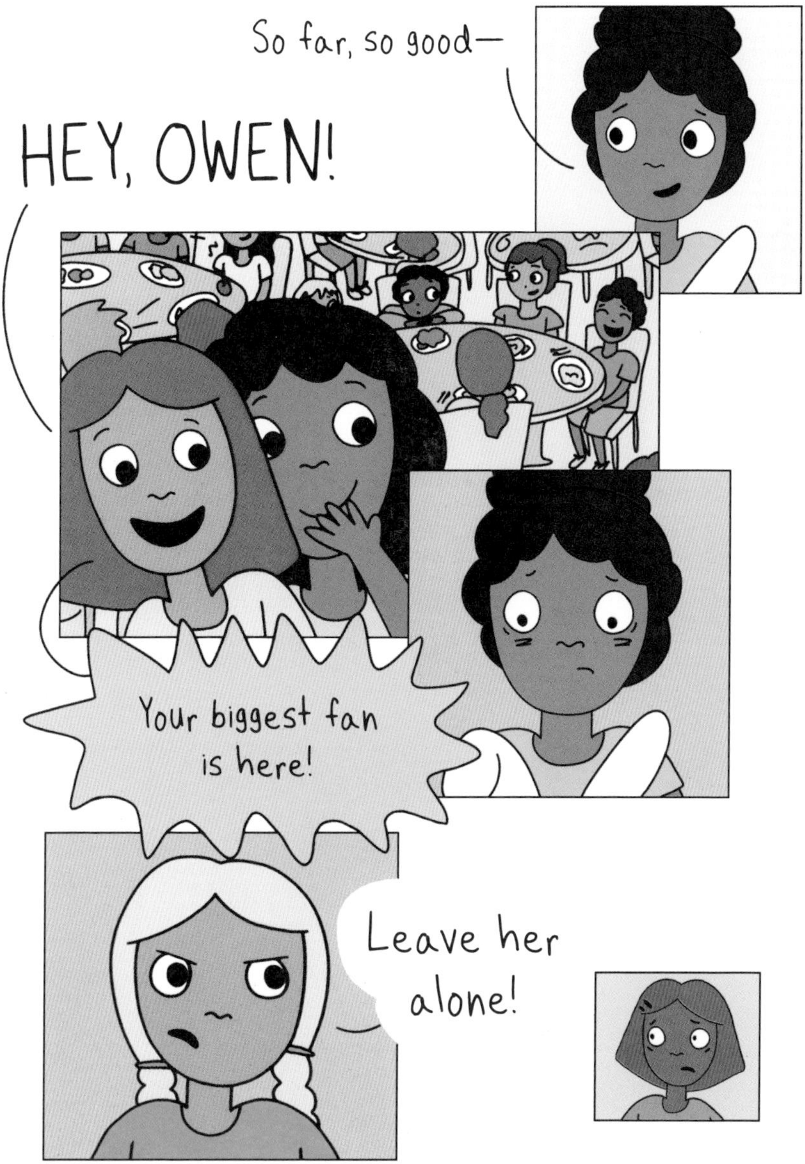
So far, so good—
HEY, OWEN!
Your biggest fan is here!
Leave her alone!

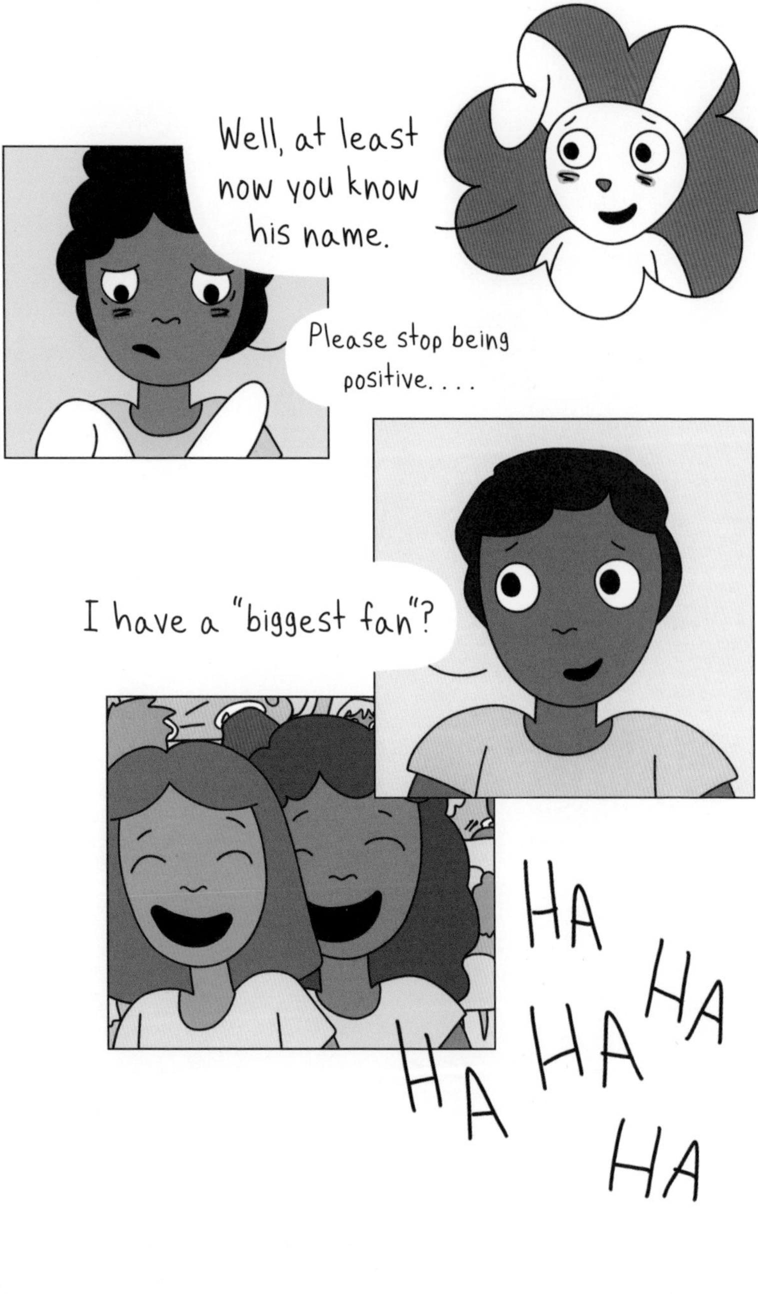
Well, at least now you know his name.
Please stop being positive. . . .
I have a "biggest fan"?
HA HA HA HA HA

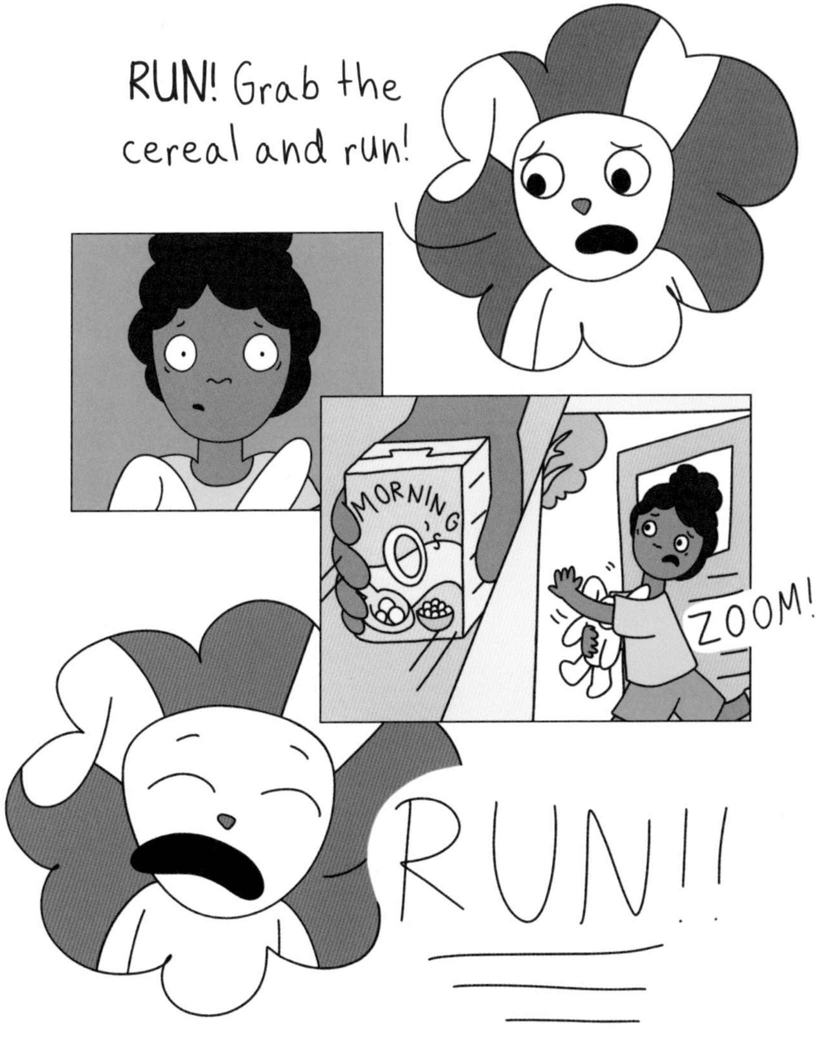
RUN! Grab the cereal and run!
MORNING O's
ZOOM!
RUN!!

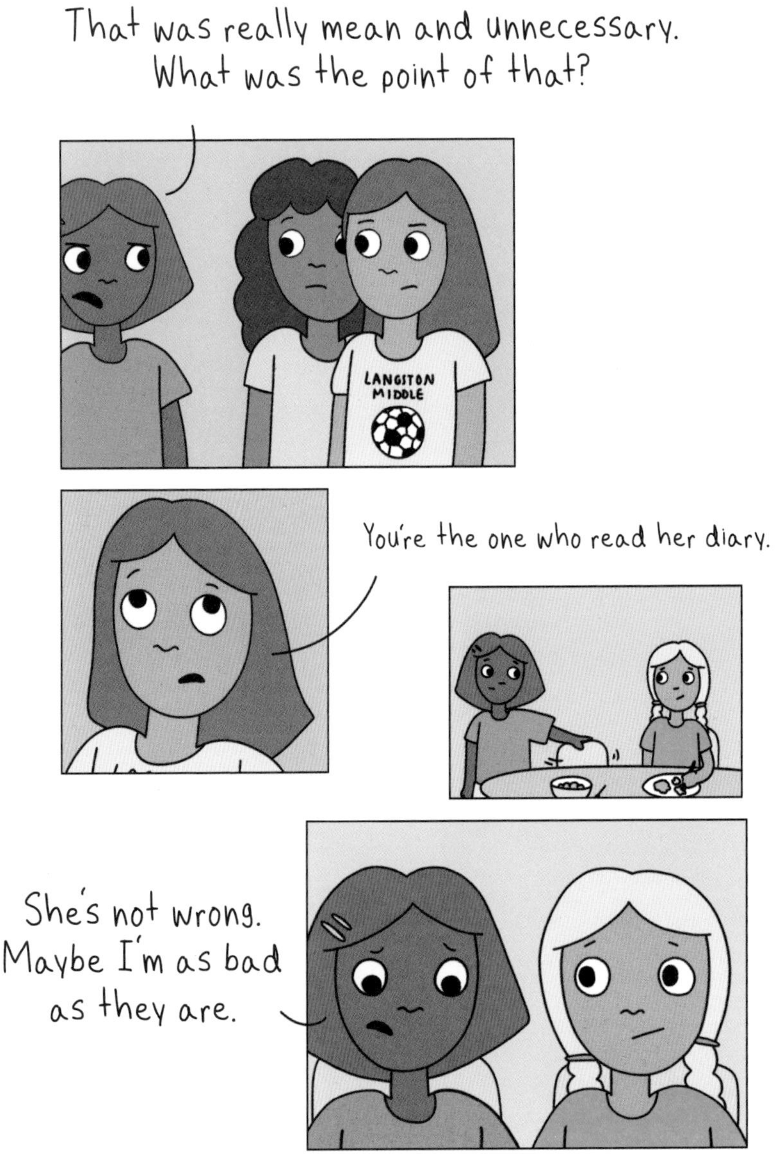
That was really mean and unnecessary. What was the point of that?
LANGSTON MIDDLE
You're the one who read her diary.
She's not wrong. Maybe I'm as bad as they are.

You're not like them.
You at least tried
to make it right.

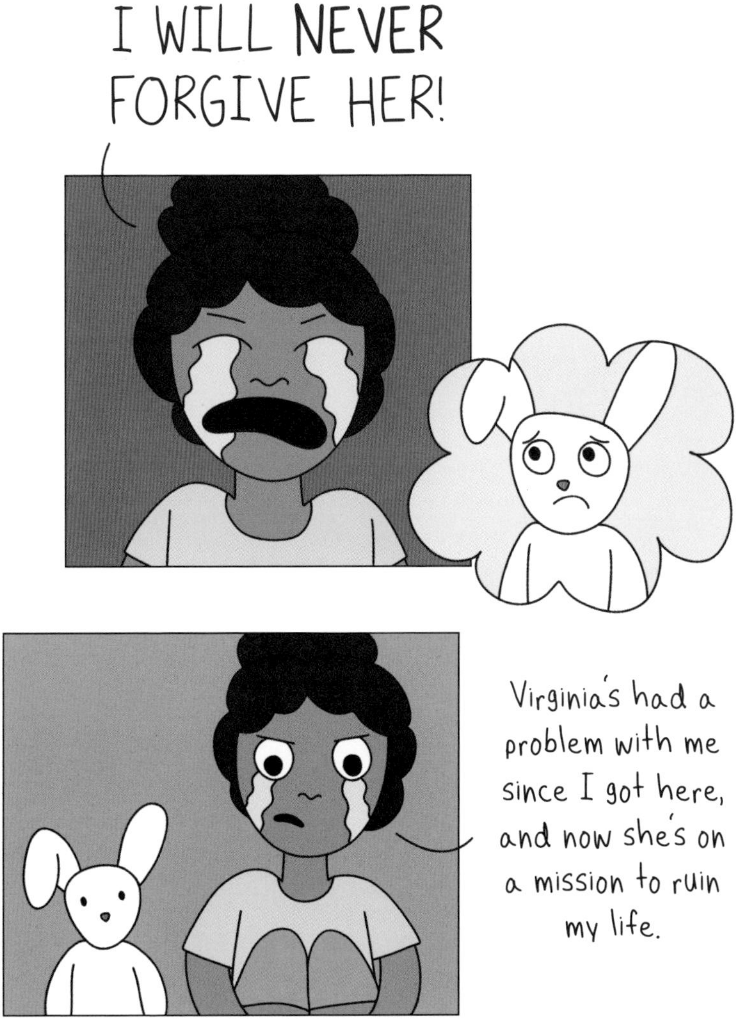
I WILL NEVER FORGIVE HER!
Virginia's had a problem with me since I got here, and now she's on a mission to ruin my life.

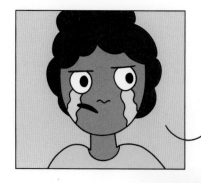

She's just a **bad** person.

sniff

sniff

A bad, mean, evil person.

sniff

She's a life-ruiner.

CHAPTER 6

TROUBLE AT SEA

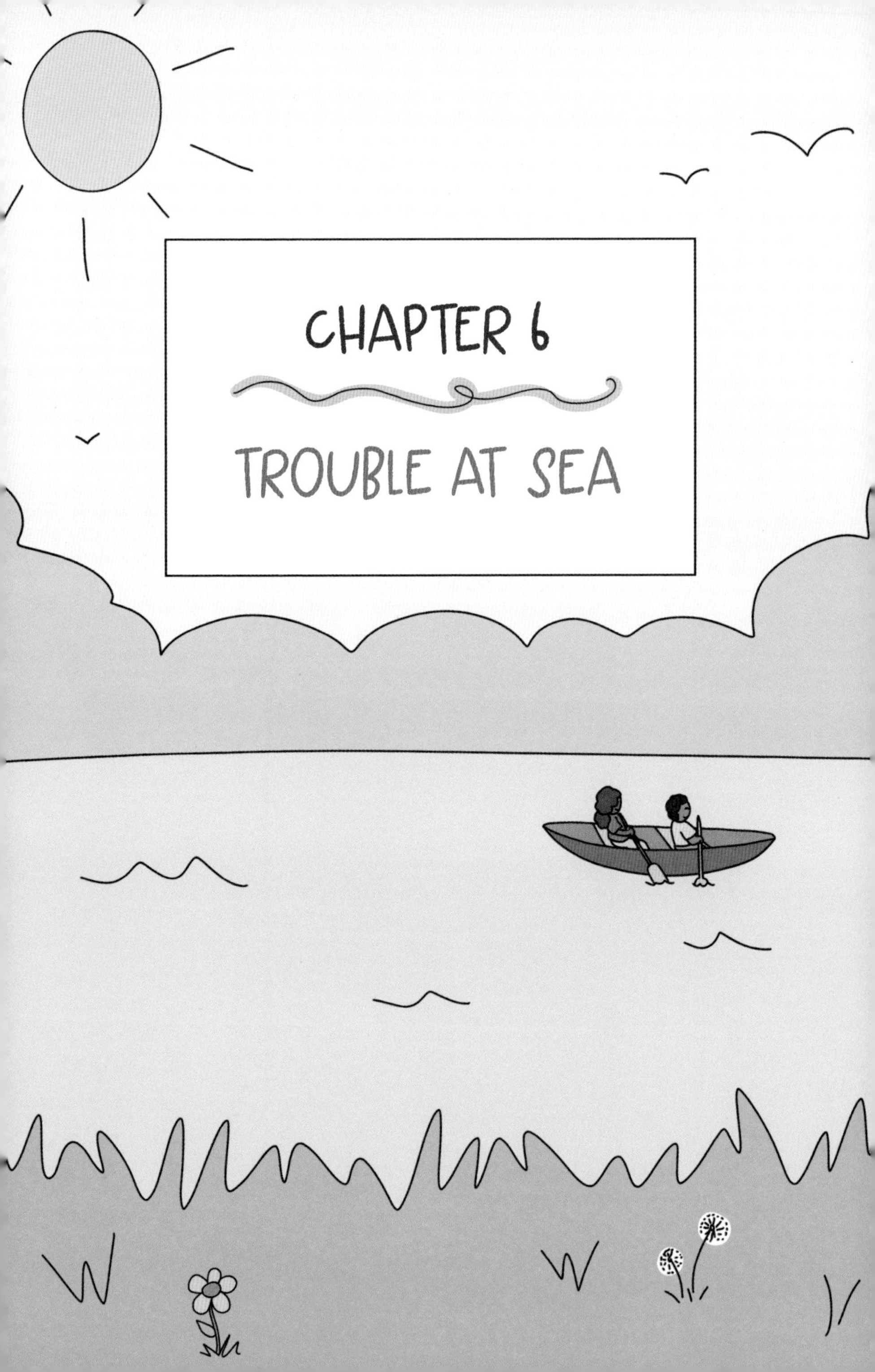

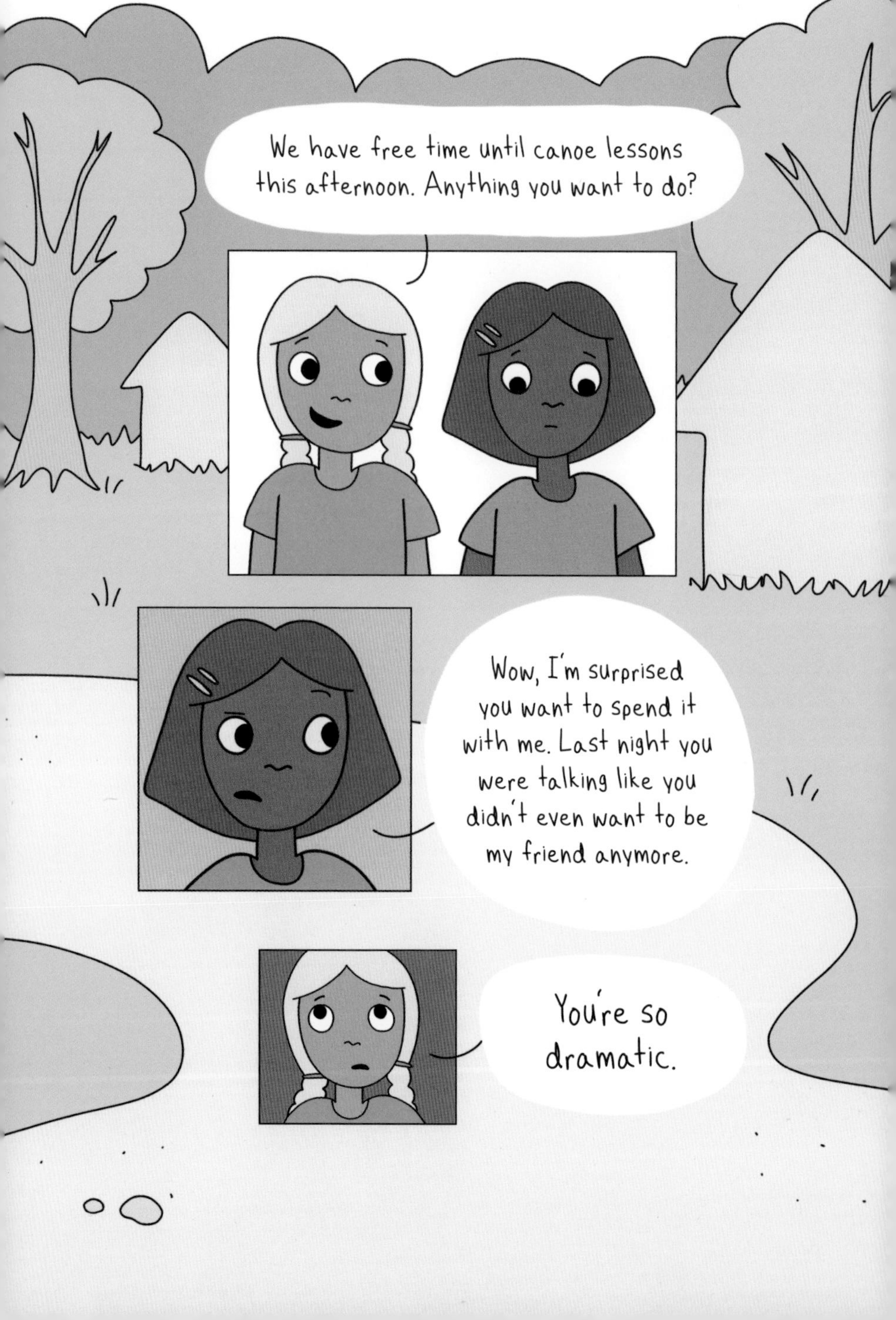
We have free time until canoe lessons this afternoon. Anything you want to do?
Wow, I'm surprised you want to spend it with me. Last night you were talking like you didn't even want to be my friend anymore.
You're so dramatic.

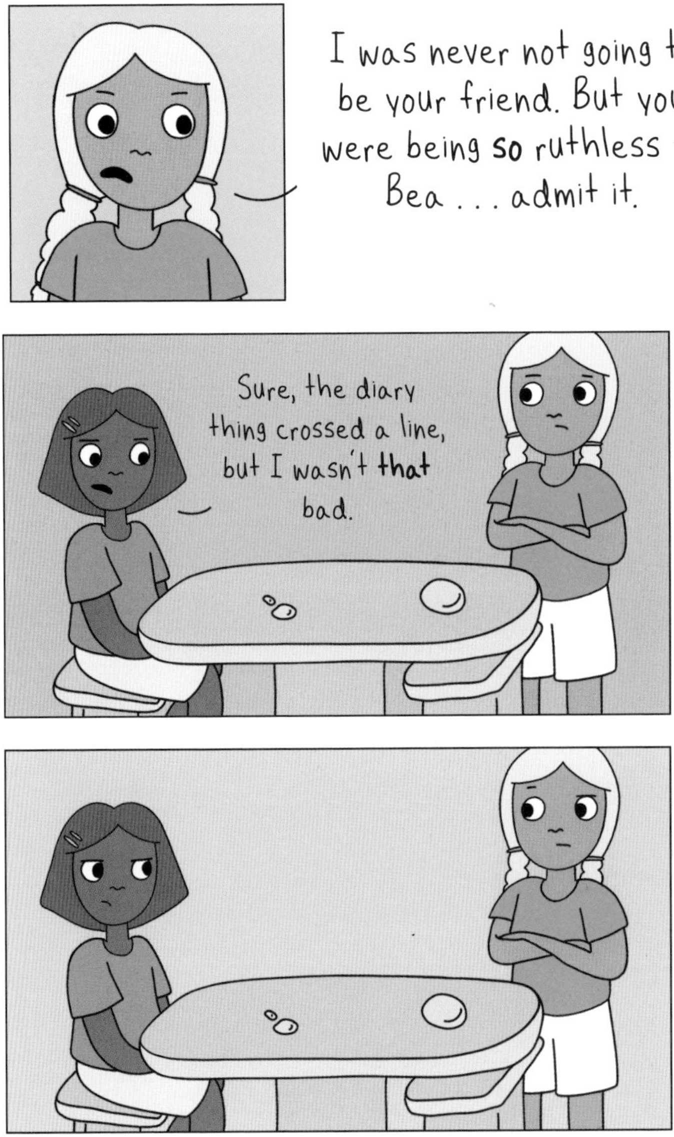
I was never not going to be your friend. But you were being **so** ruthless to Bea . . . admit it.
Sure, the diary thing crossed a line, but I wasn't **that** bad.

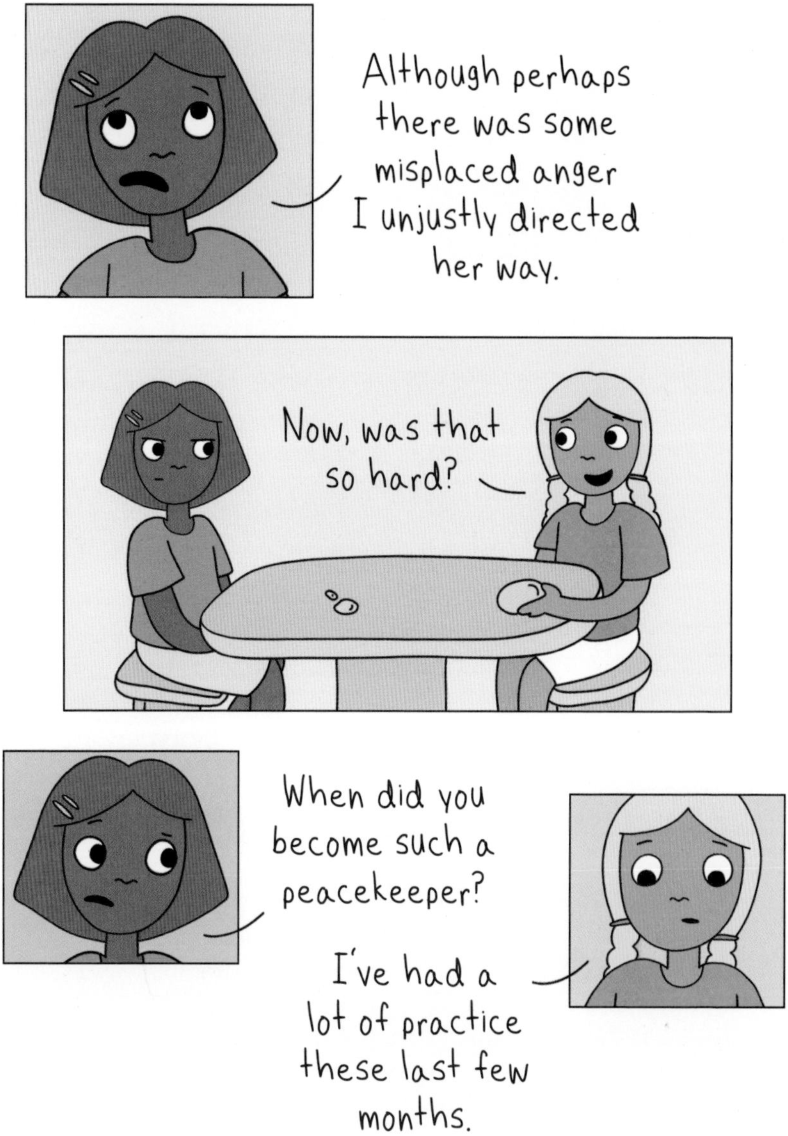
Although perhaps there was some misplaced anger I unjustly directed her way.
Now, was that so hard?
When did you become such a peacekeeper?
I've had a lot of practice these last few months.

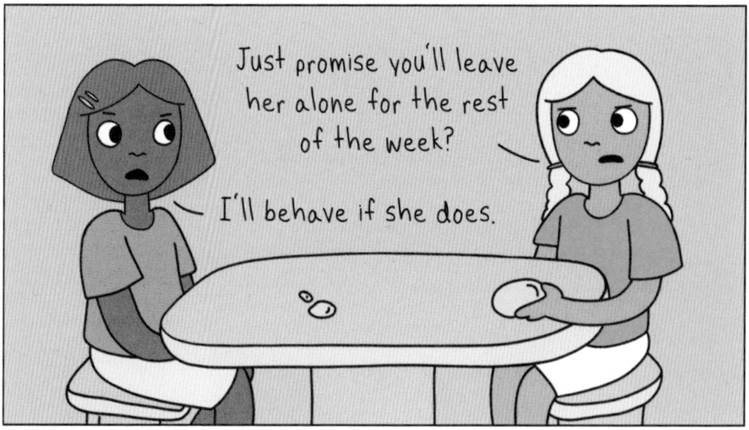
Just promise you'll leave her alone for the rest of the week?
I'll behave if she does.

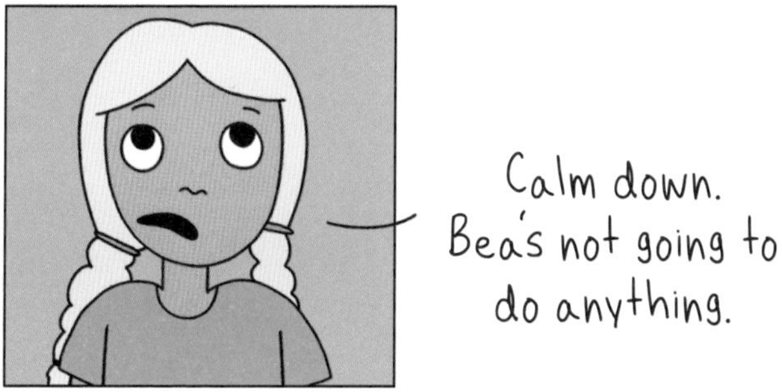
Calm down. Bea's not going to do anything.

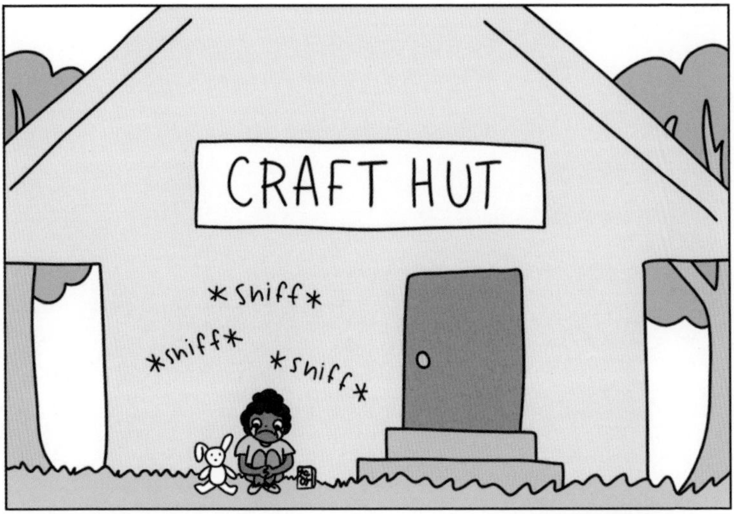
CRAFT HUT
sniff
sniff
sniff

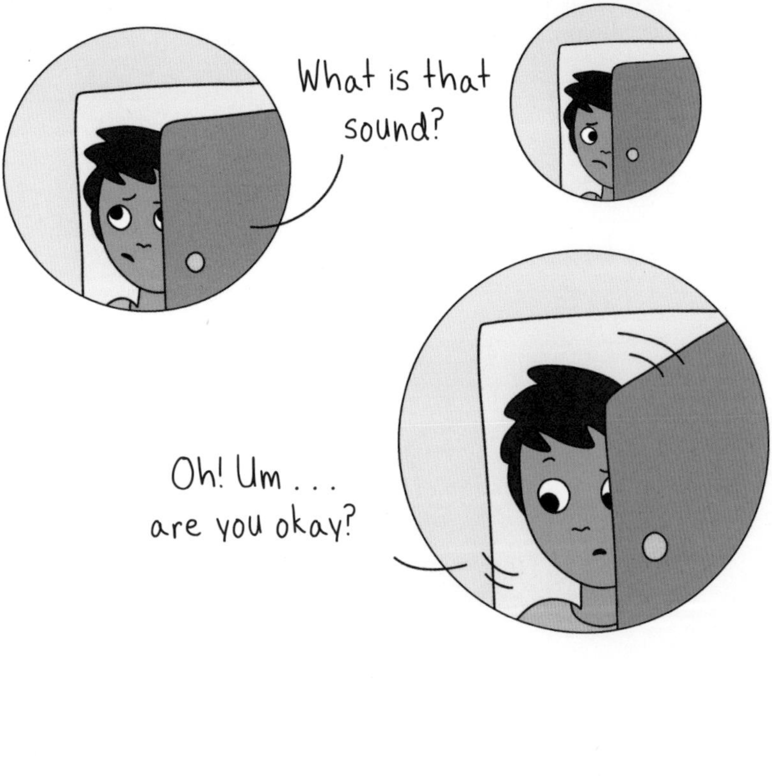
What is that sound?
Oh! Um . . . are you okay?

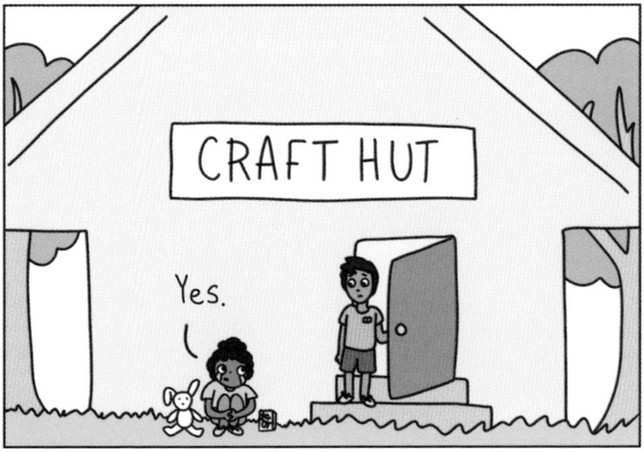
CRAFT HUT
Yes.

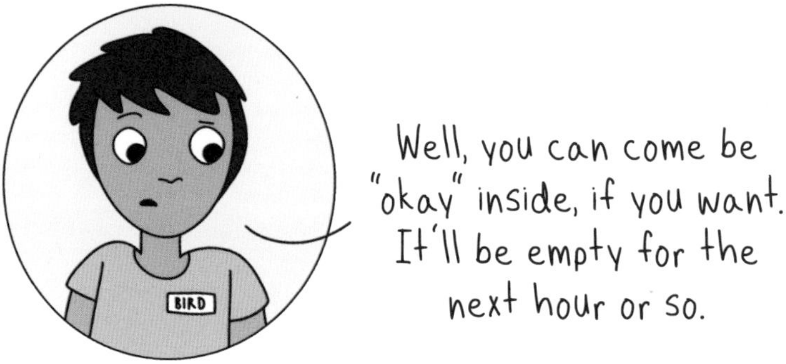
BIRD
Well, you can come be "okay" inside, if you want. It'll be empty for the next hour or so.

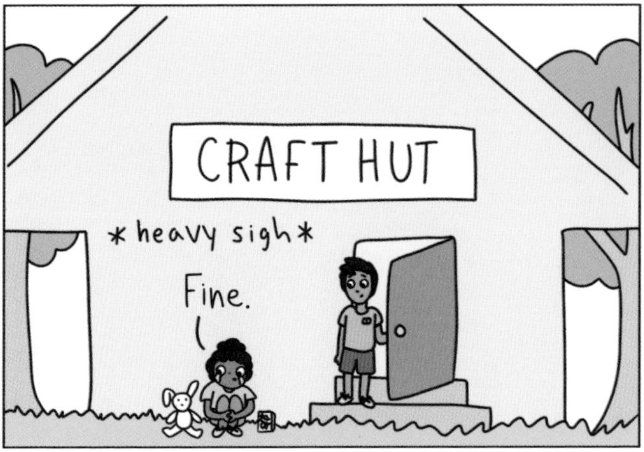
CRAFT HUT
heavy sigh
Fine.

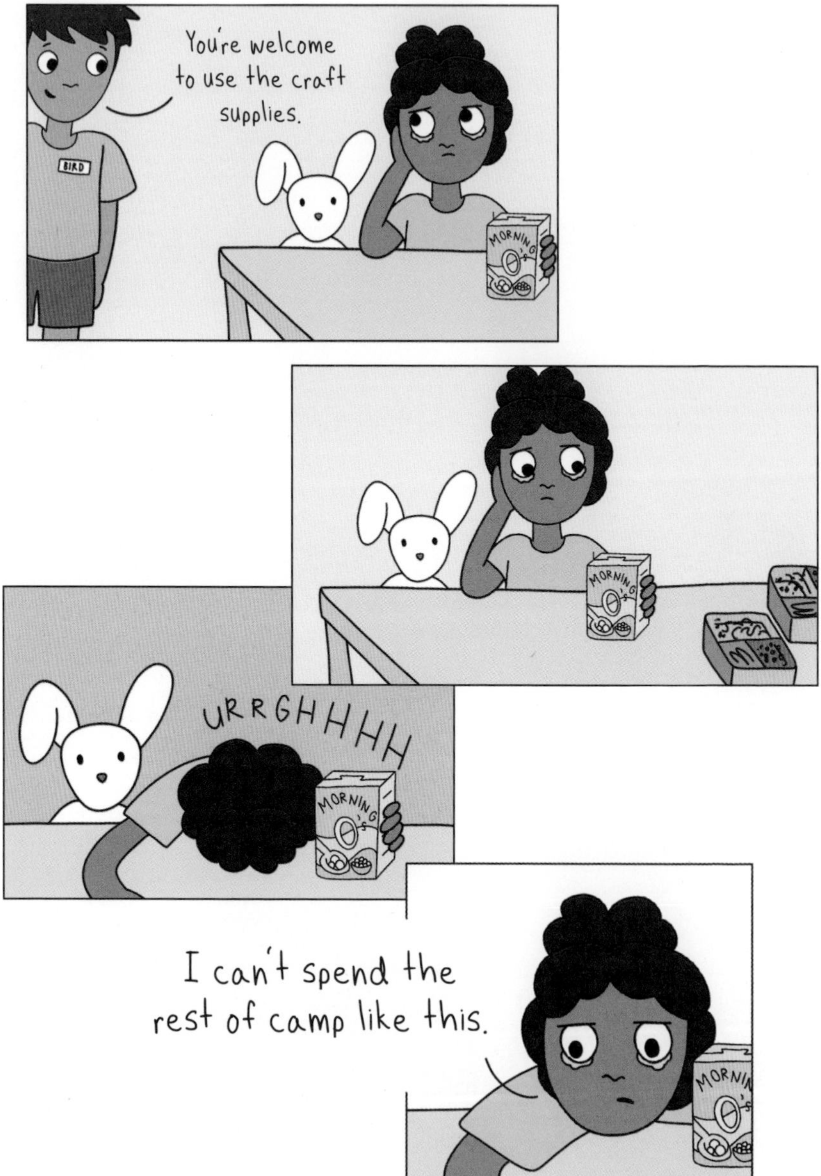
You're welcome to use the craft supplies.
BIRD
MORNING O's
URRGHHHH
I can't spend the rest of camp like this.

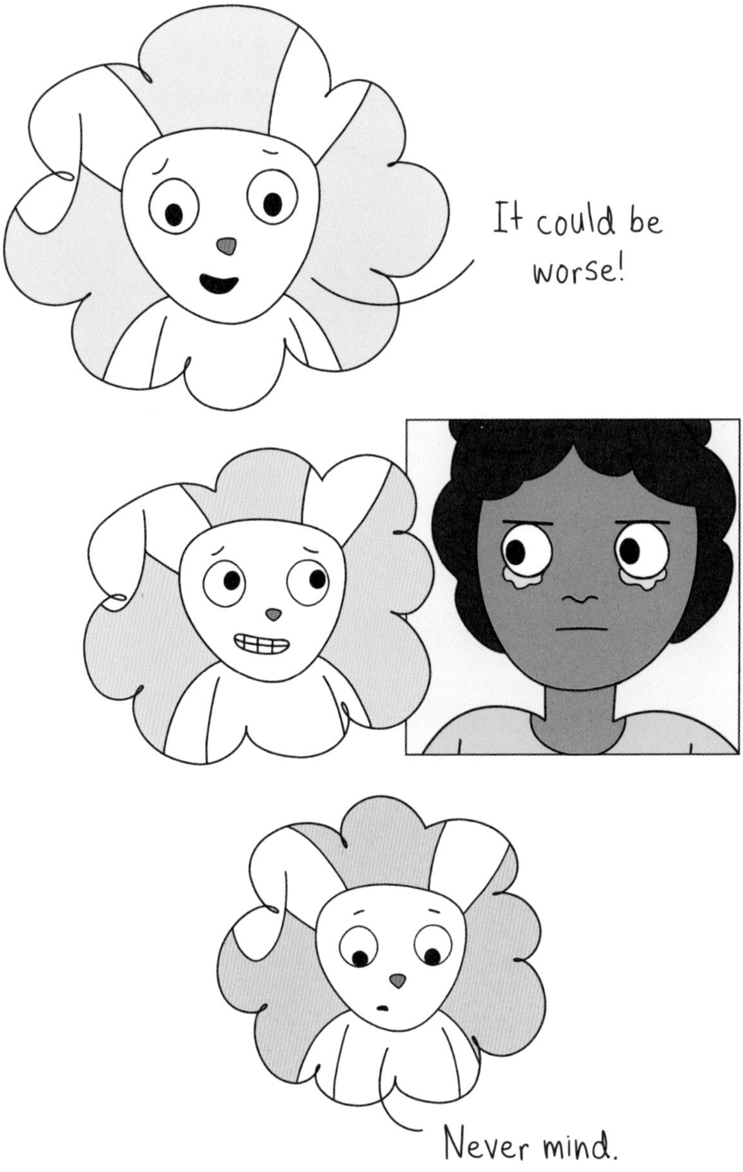
It could be worse!
Never mind.

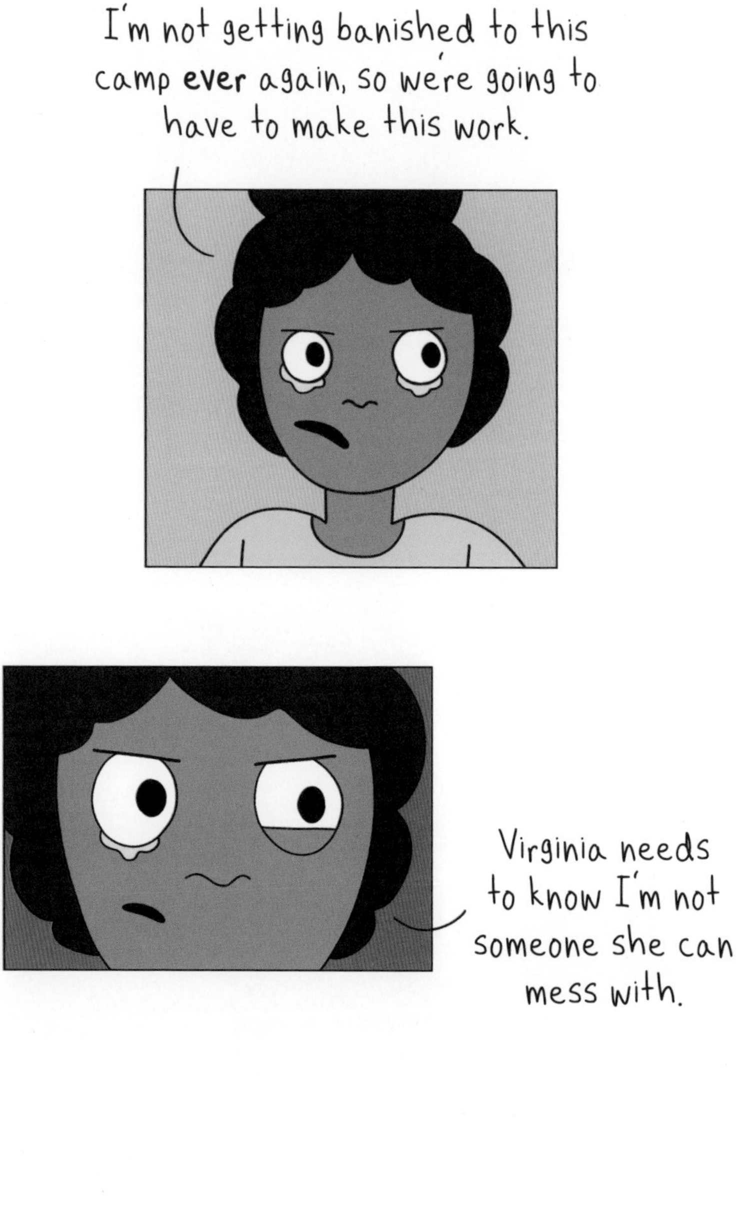
I'm not getting banished to this camp **ever** again, so we're going to have to make this work.
Virginia needs to know I'm not someone she can mess with.

She needs to
know I'm not an
easy target.

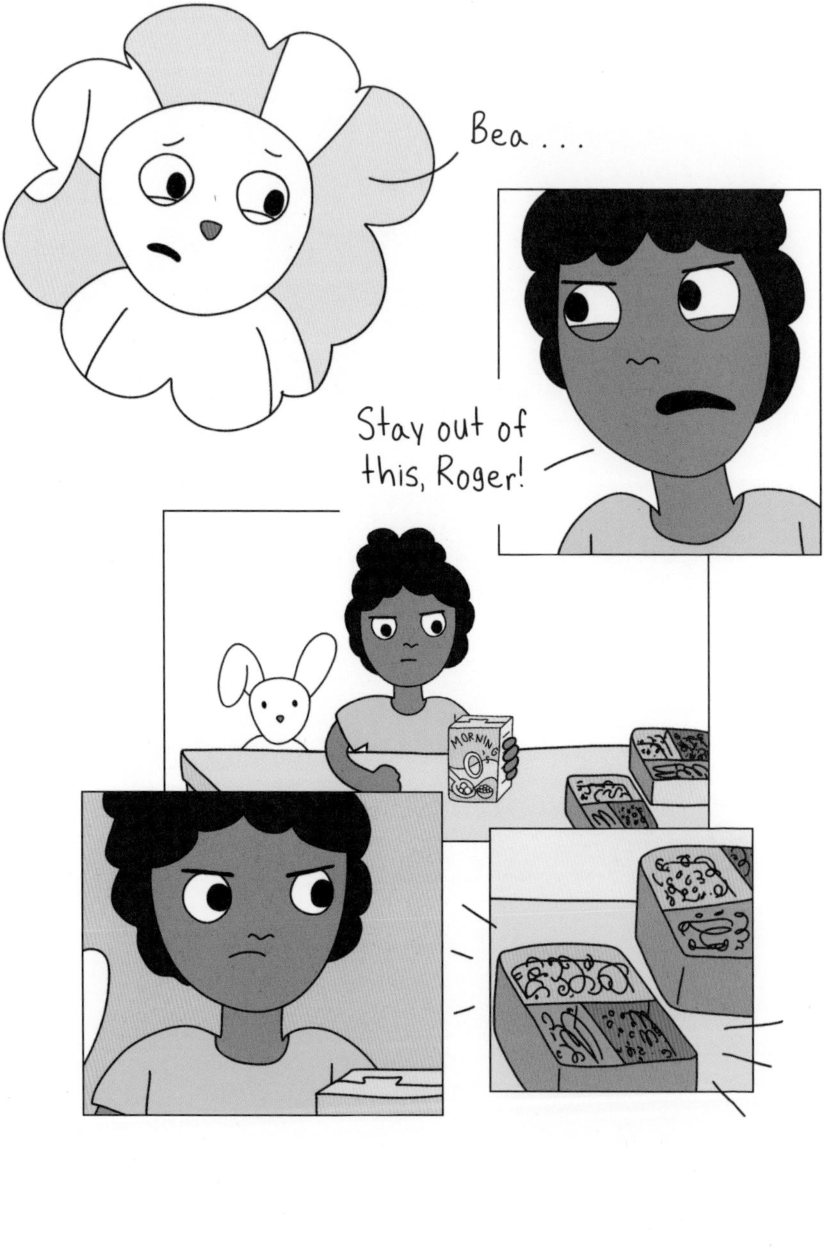
Bea . . .
Stay out of this, Roger!
MORNING O's

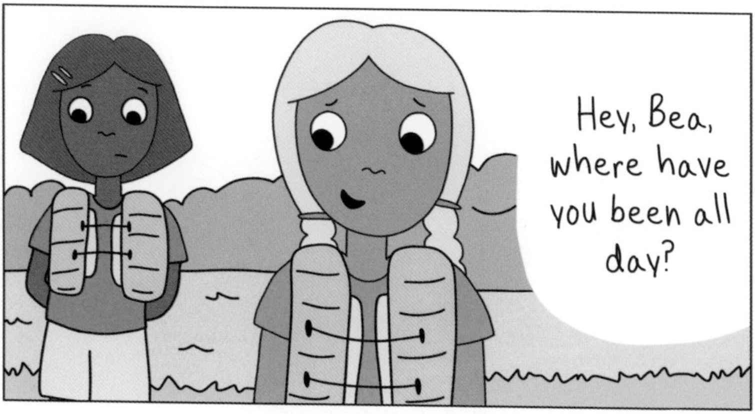
Hey, Bea, where have you been all day?

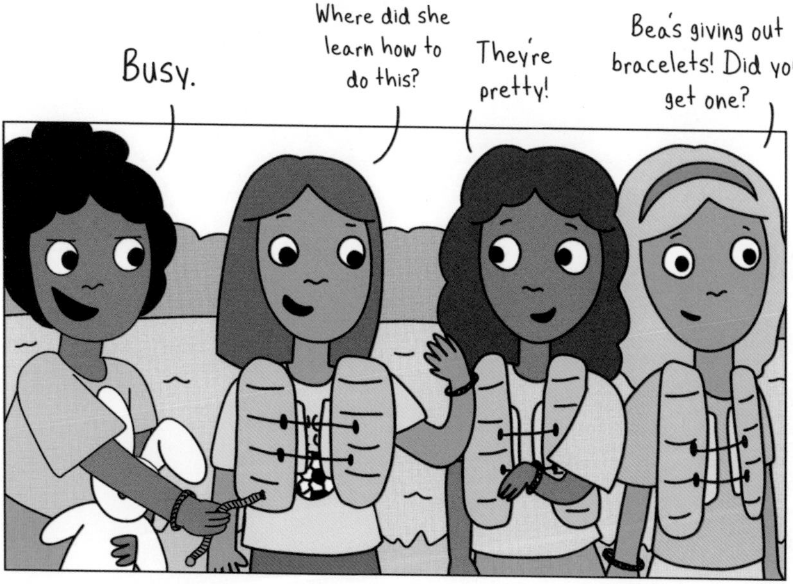
Busy.
Where did she learn how to do this?
They're pretty!
Bea's giving out bracelets! Did you get one?

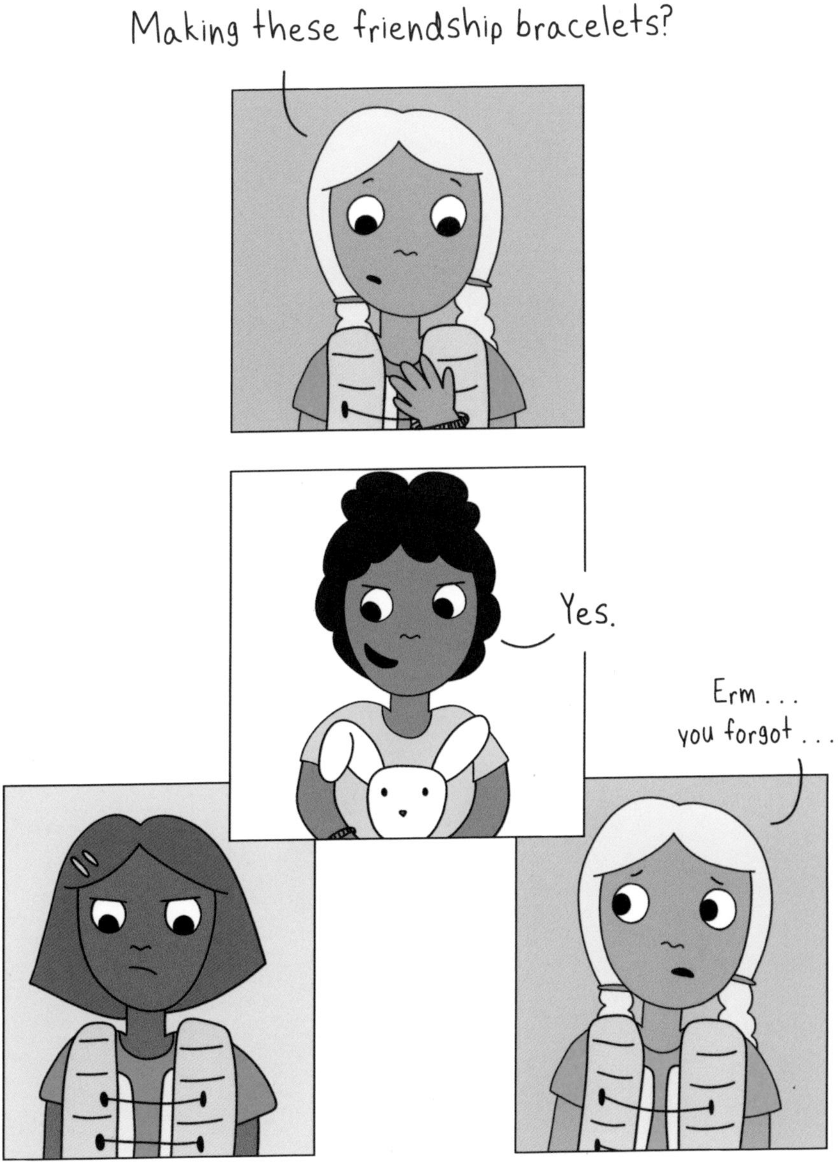
Making these friendship bracelets?
Yes.
Erm . . .
you forgot . . .

Oh no.

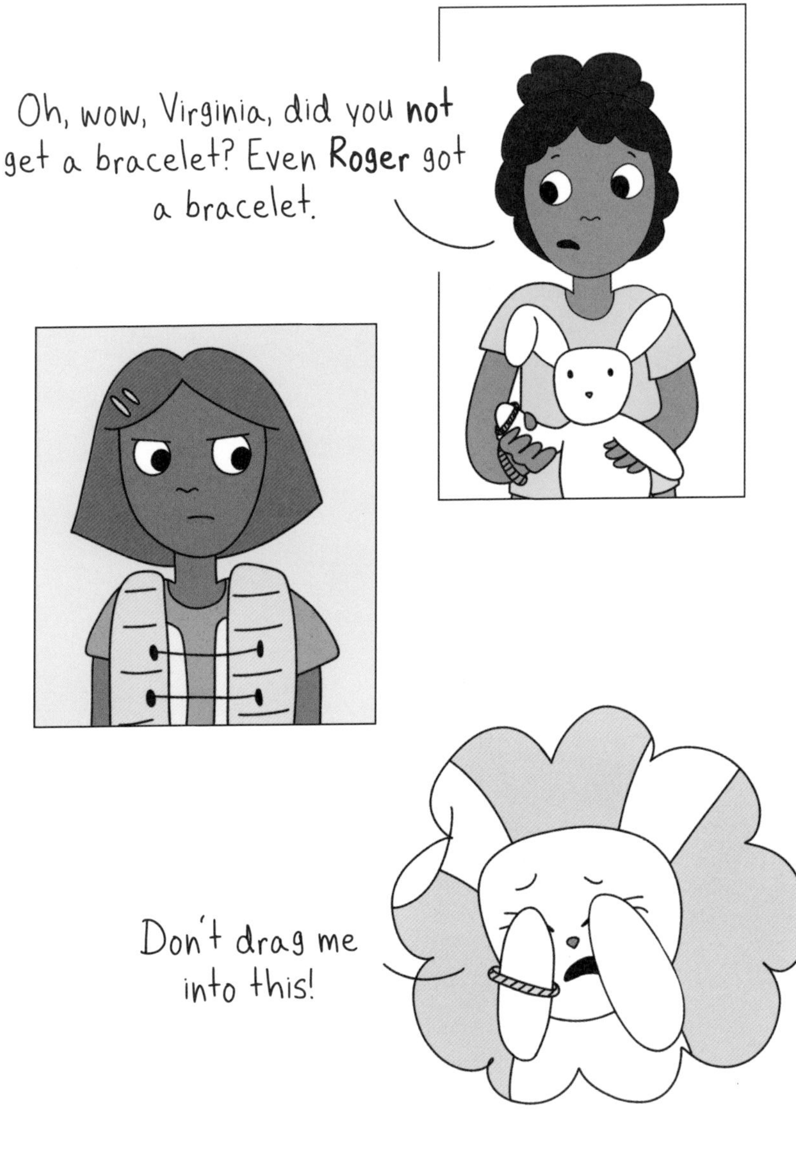
Oh, wow, Virginia, did you not get a bracelet? Even Roger got a bracelet.
Don't drag me into this!

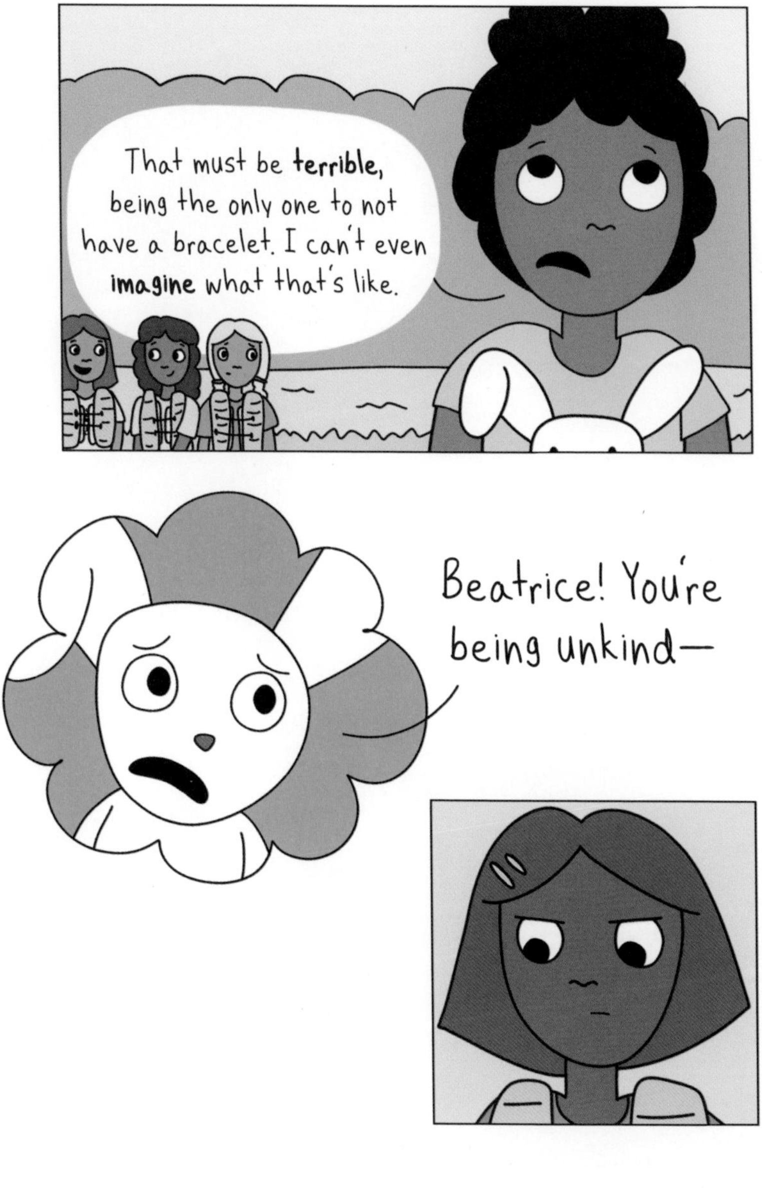
That must be **terrible,** being the only one to not have a bracelet. I can't even **imagine** what that's like.
Beatrice! You're being unkind—

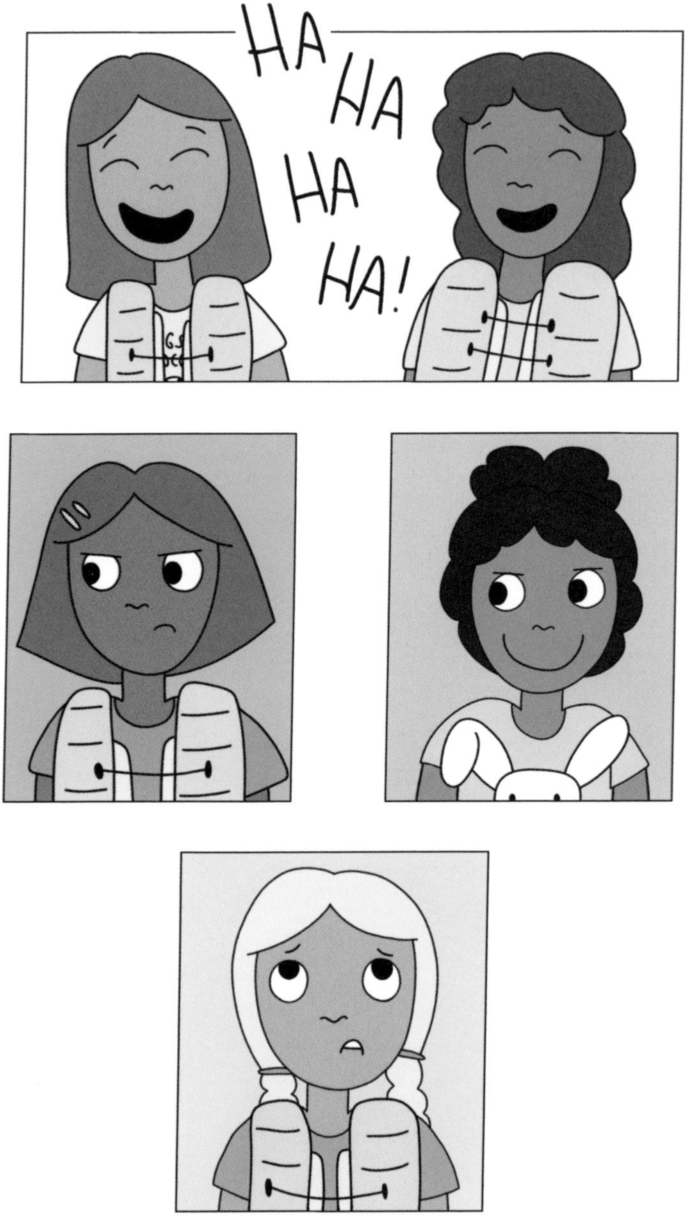
HA HA HA HA!

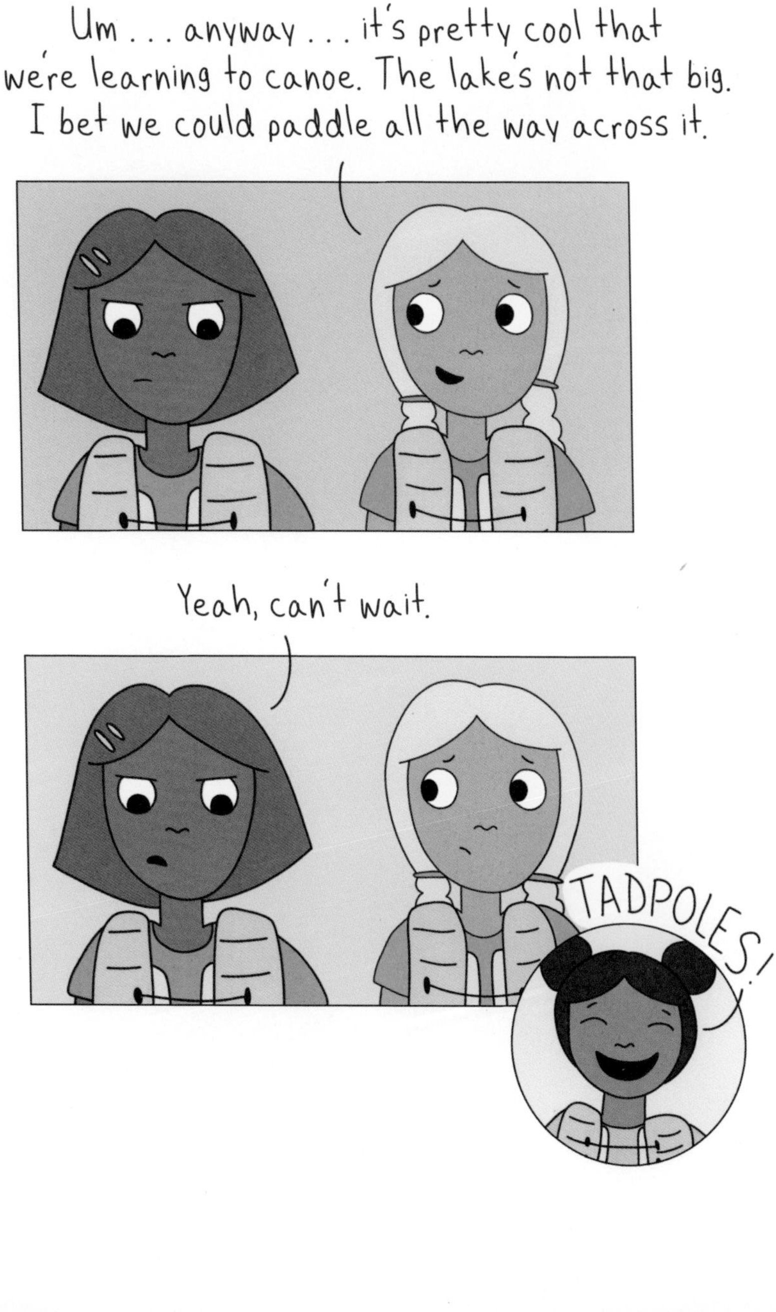
Um . . . anyway . . . it's pretty cool that we're learning to canoe. The lake's not that big. I bet we could paddle all the way across it.
Yeah, can't wait.
TADPOLES!

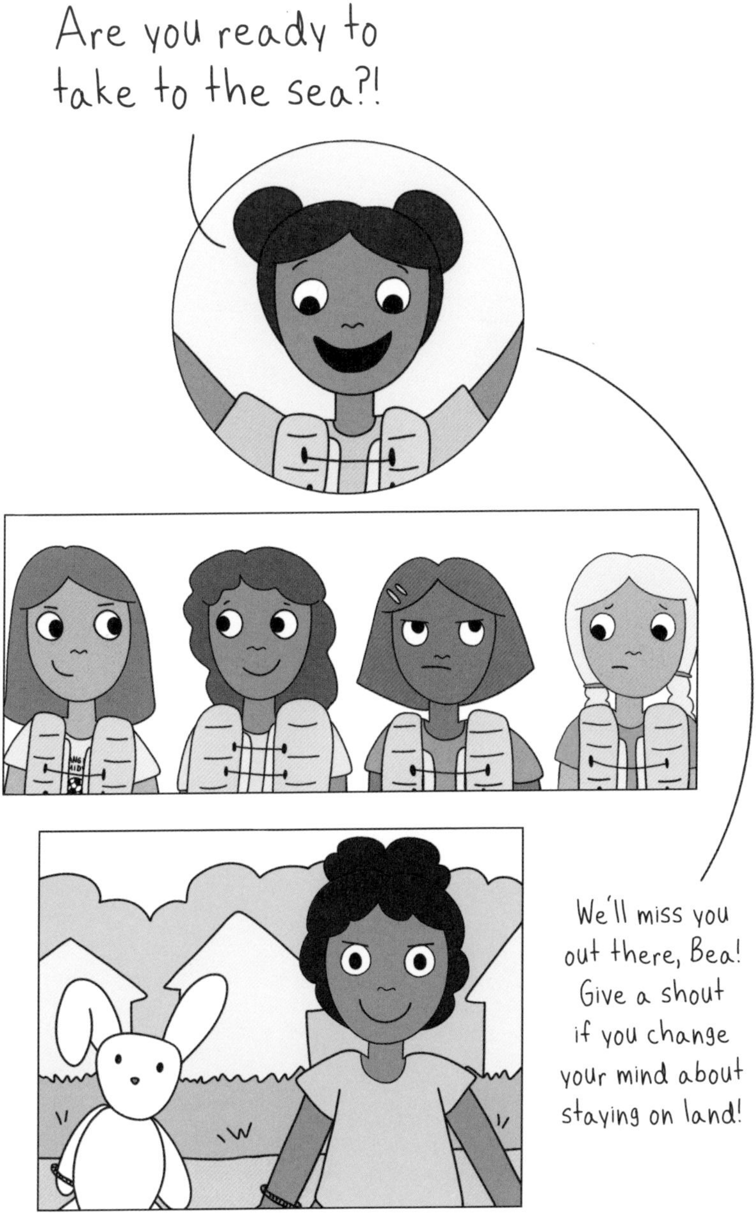
Are you ready to take to the sea?!
We'll miss you out there, Bea! Give a shout if you change your mind about staying on land!

What a lovely
afternoon by
the lake.

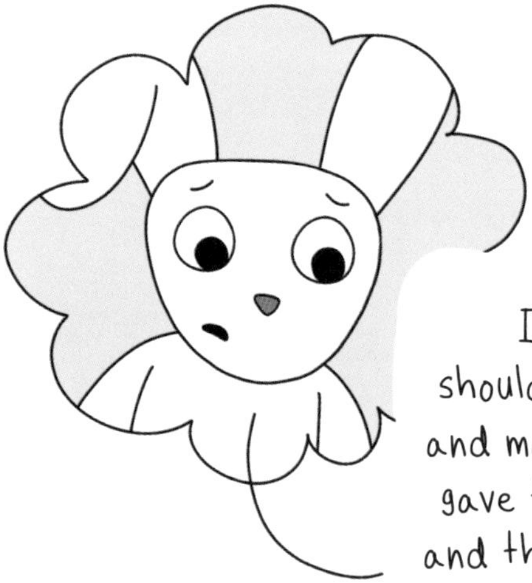
It is, but . . . maybe we should go back to the craft hut and make Virginia a bracelet. You gave them to those soccer girls, and they're the ones who teased you in the mess hall.

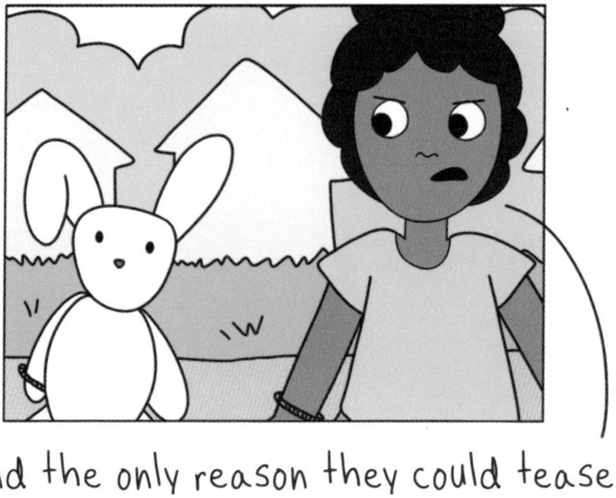
And the only reason they could tease me is because **Virginia** viciously violated my privacy—unprovoked, I might add.

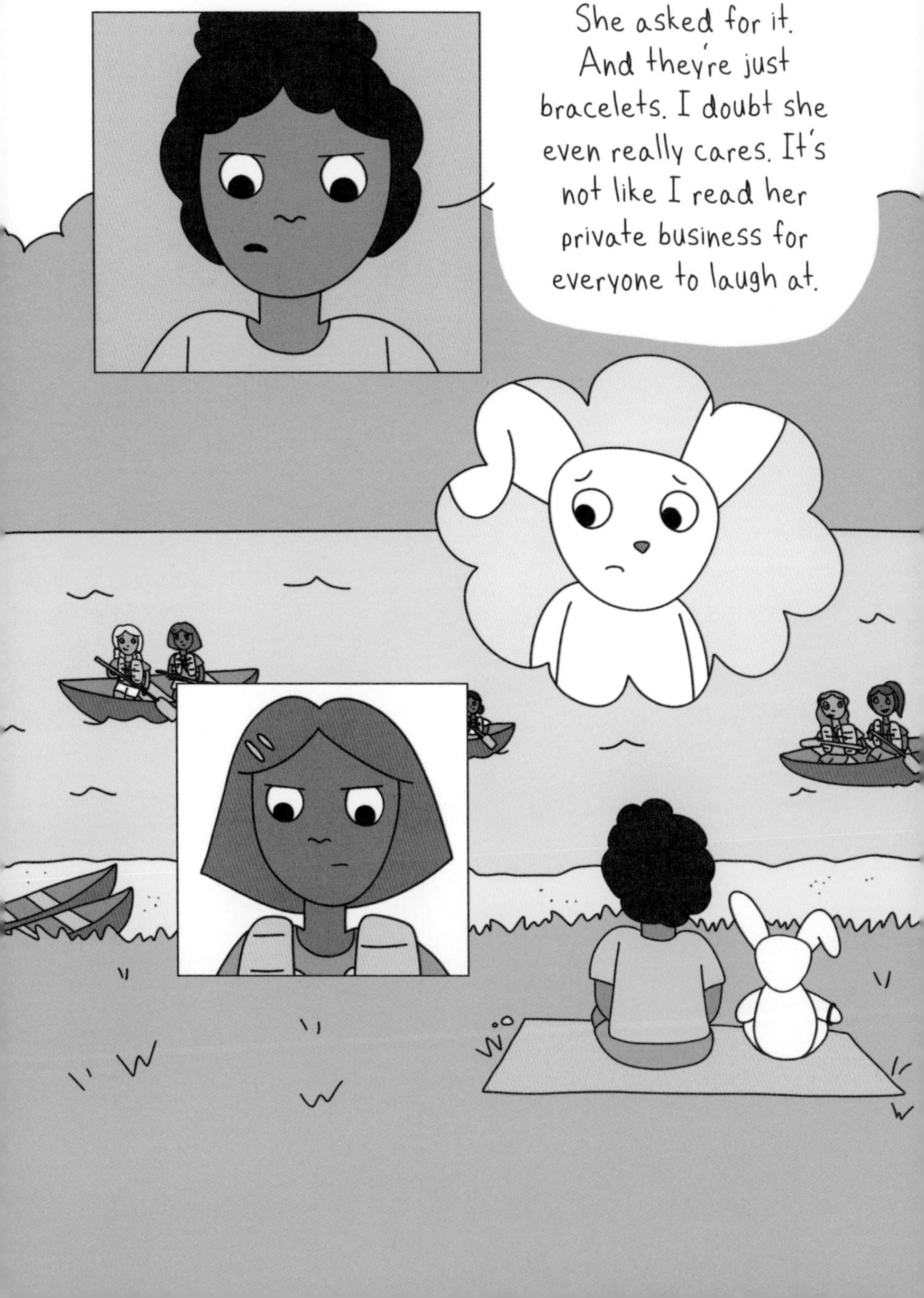
She asked for it. And they're just bracelets. I doubt she even really cares. It's not like I read her private business for everyone to laugh at.

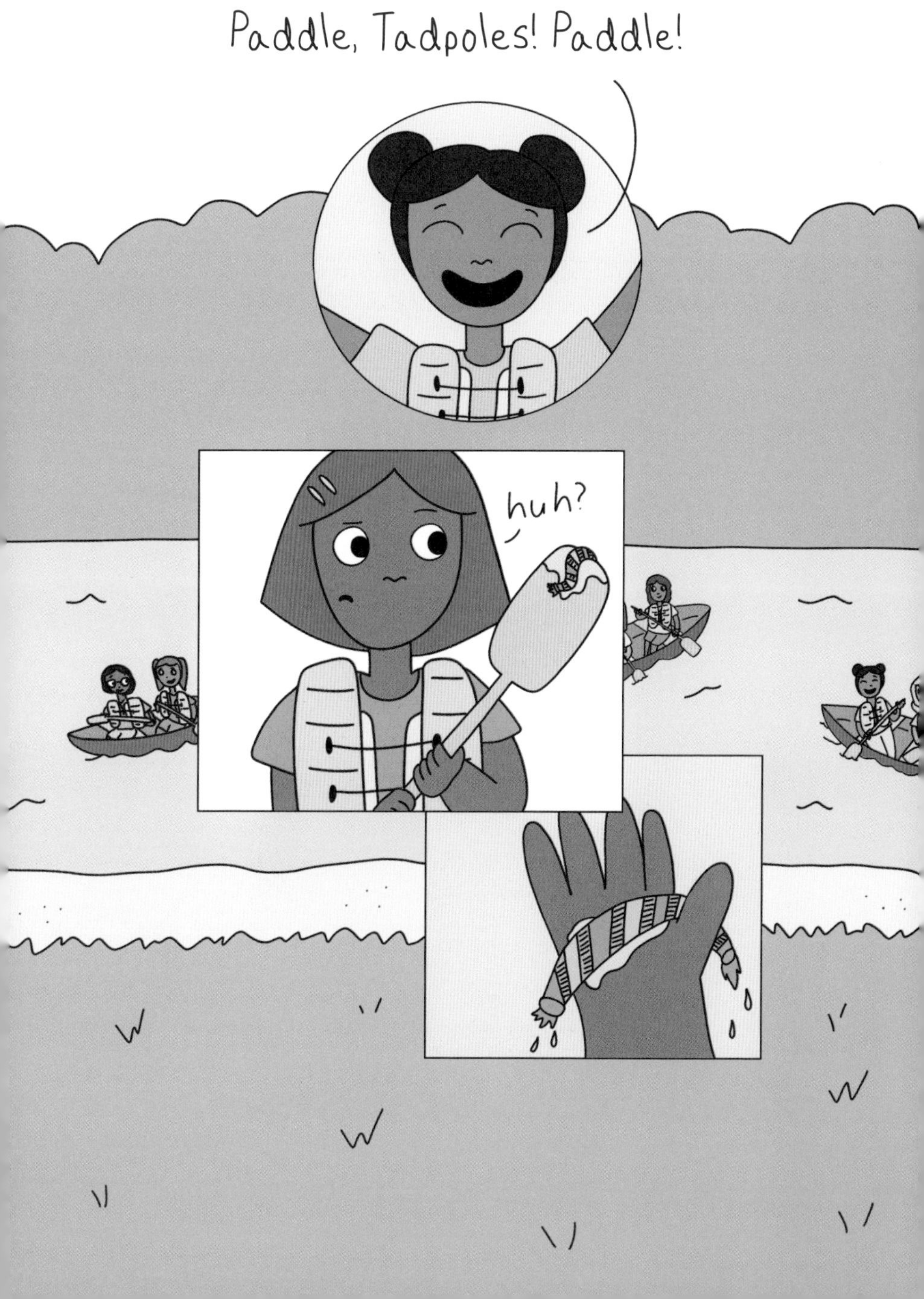
Paddle, Tadpoles! Paddle!
huh?

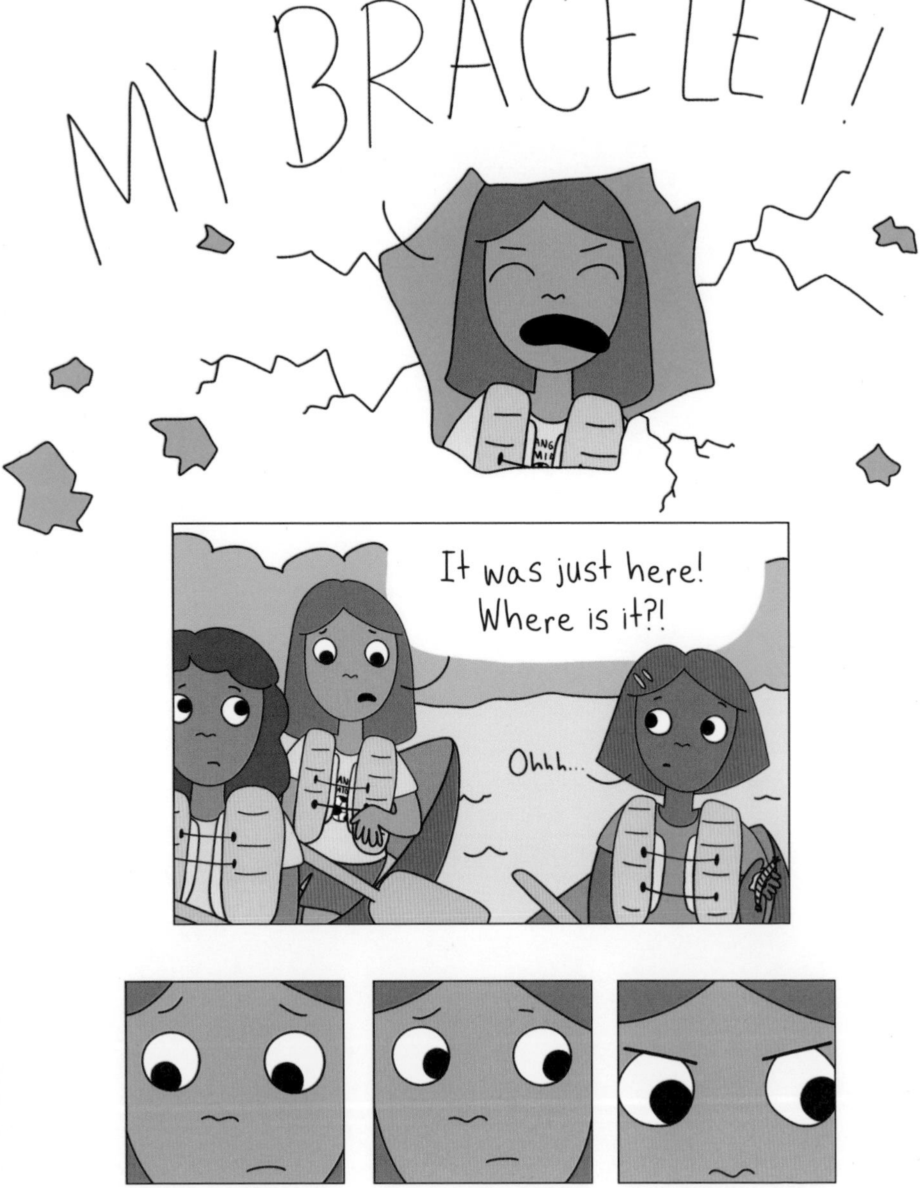
MY BRACELET!
It was just here!
Where is it?!
Ohhh...

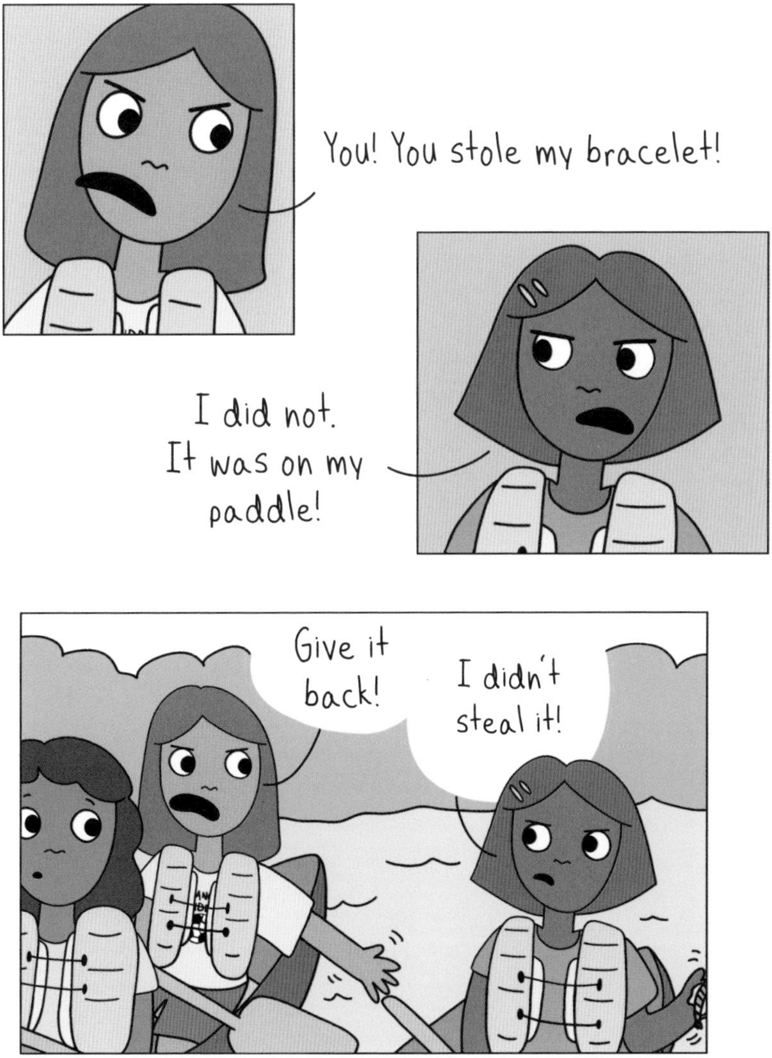
You! You stole my bracelet!
I did not. It was on my paddle!
Give it back!
I didn't steal it!

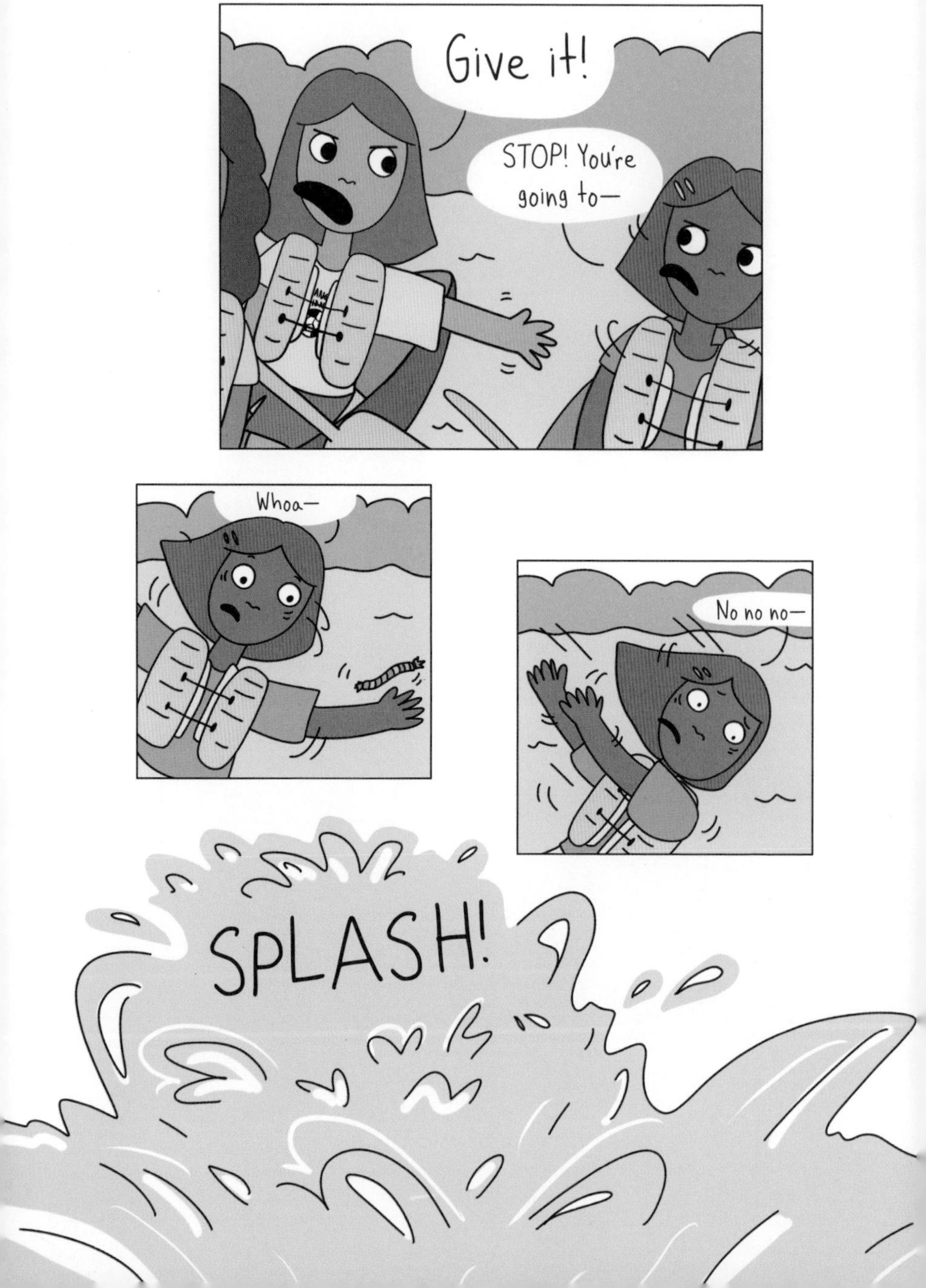
Give it!
STOP! You're going to—
Whoa—
No no no—
SPLASH!

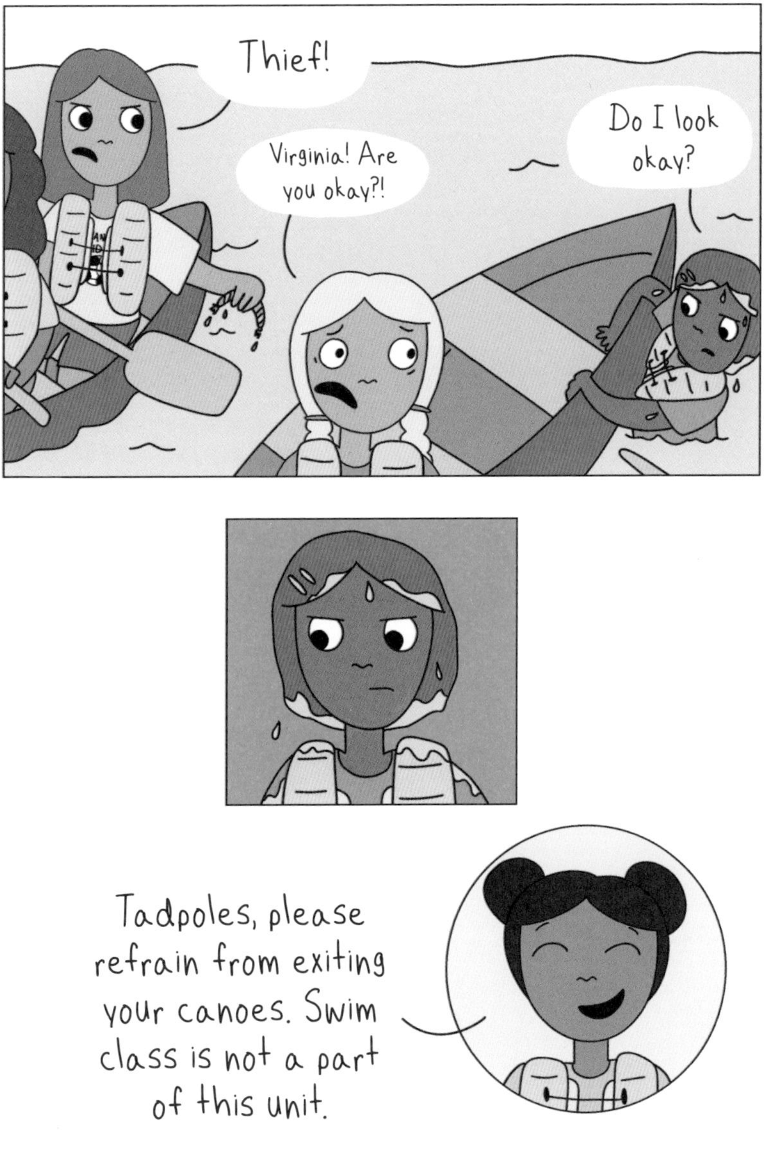
Thief!
Virginia! Are you okay?!
Do I look okay?
Tadpoles, please refrain from exiting your canoes. Swim class is not a part of this unit.

Virginia sure is having a tough day....

She had it coming.

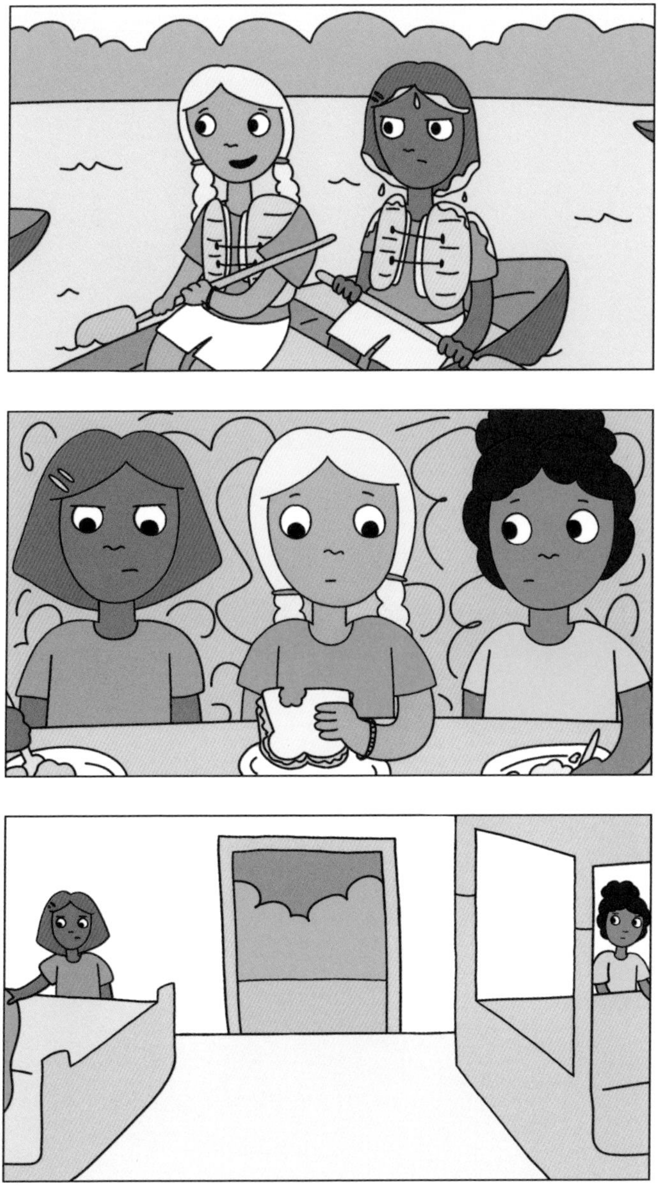

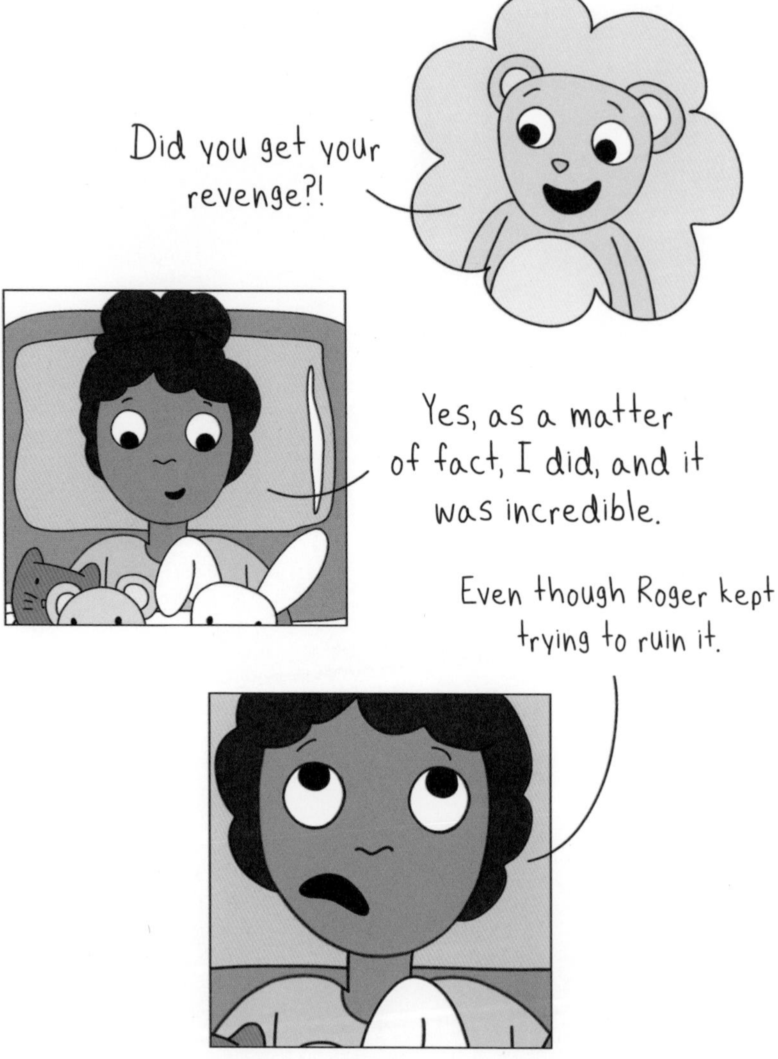
Did you get your revenge?!
Yes, as a matter of fact, I did, and it was incredible.
Even though Roger kept trying to ruin it.

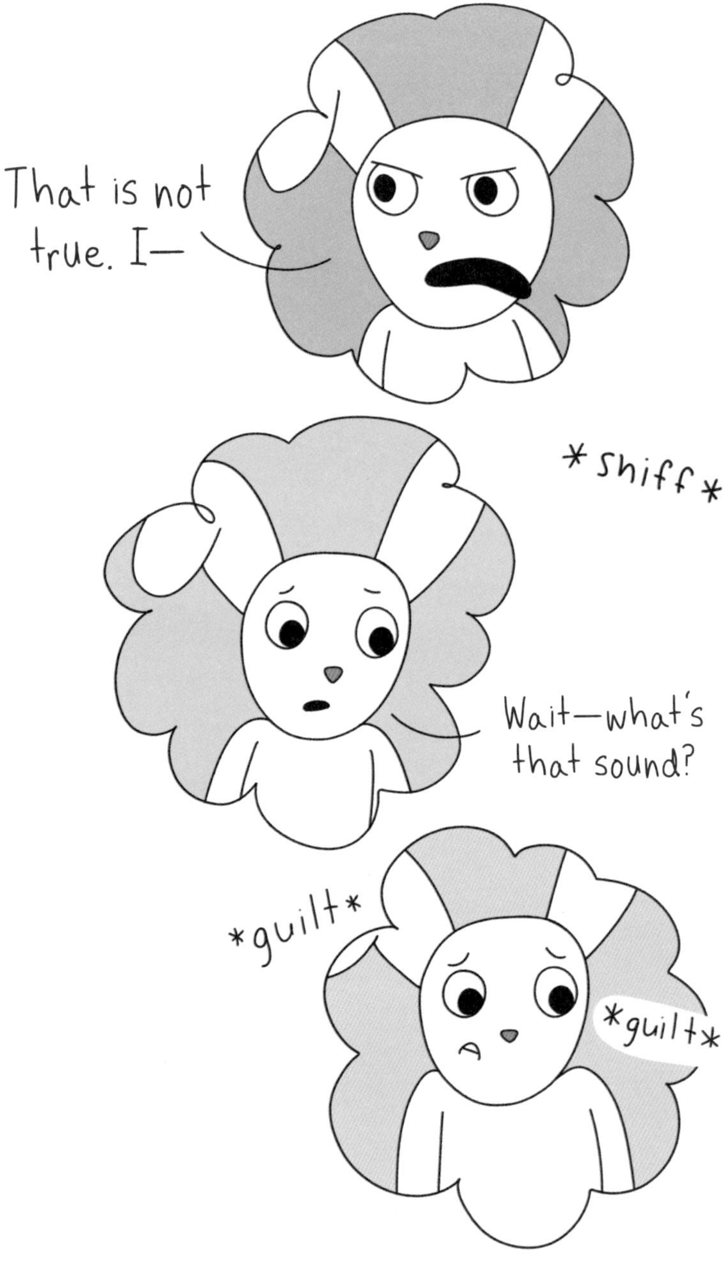
That is not true. I—
shiff
Wait—what's that sound?
guilt
guilt

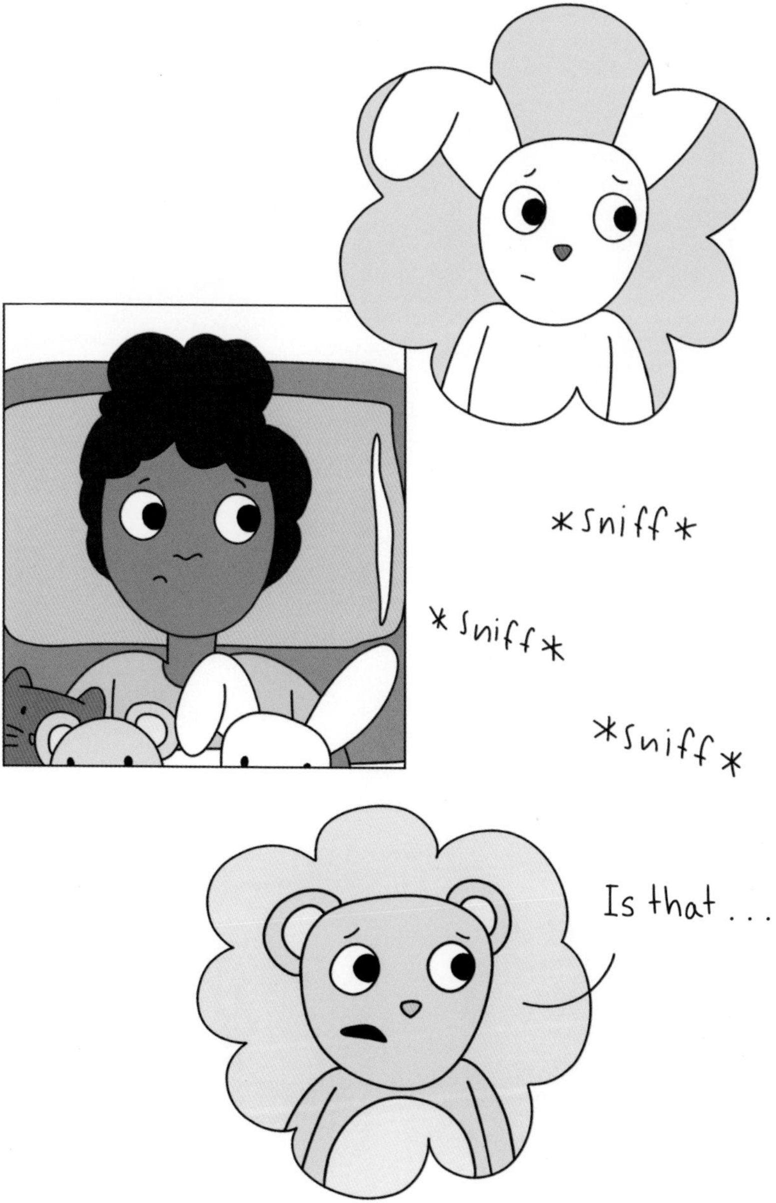
sniff
sniff
sniff
Is that . . .

sniff

sniff

sniff

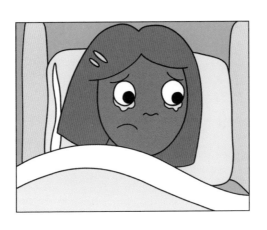

guilt

guilt

Why is someone crying every night?!

It must be a camp thing.

CHAPTER 7

ROXY'S LIMIT

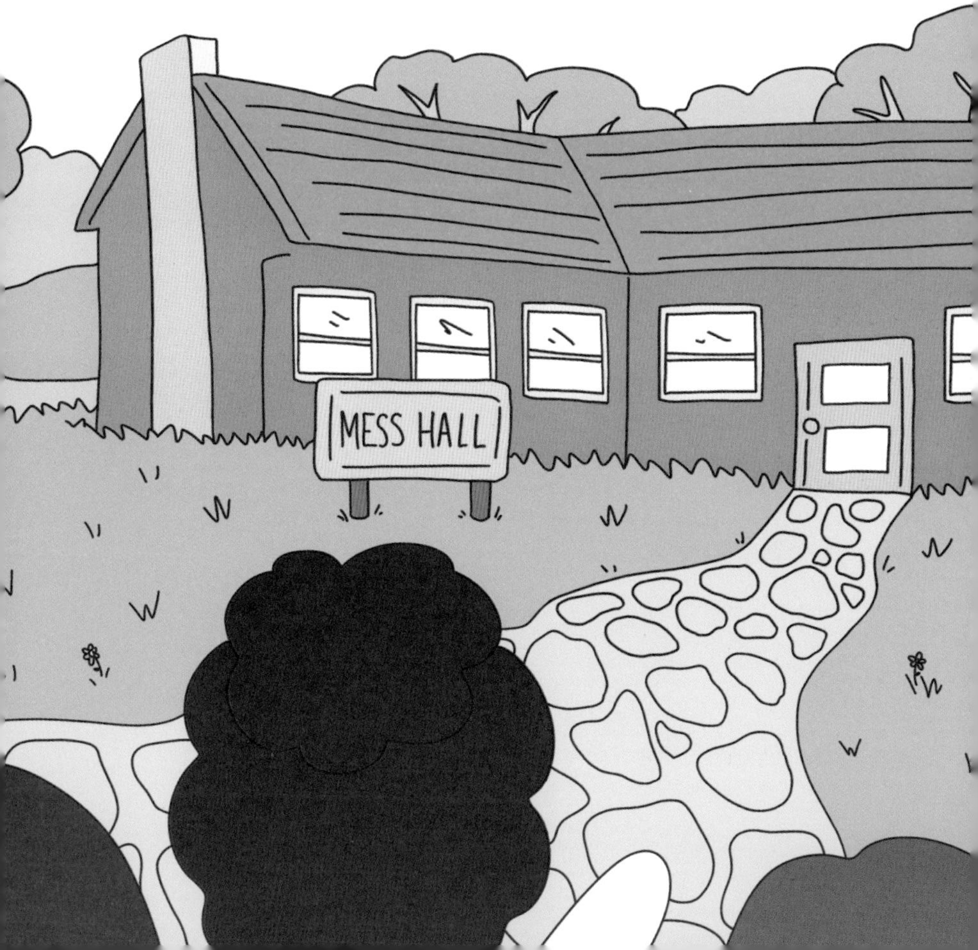
MESS HALL

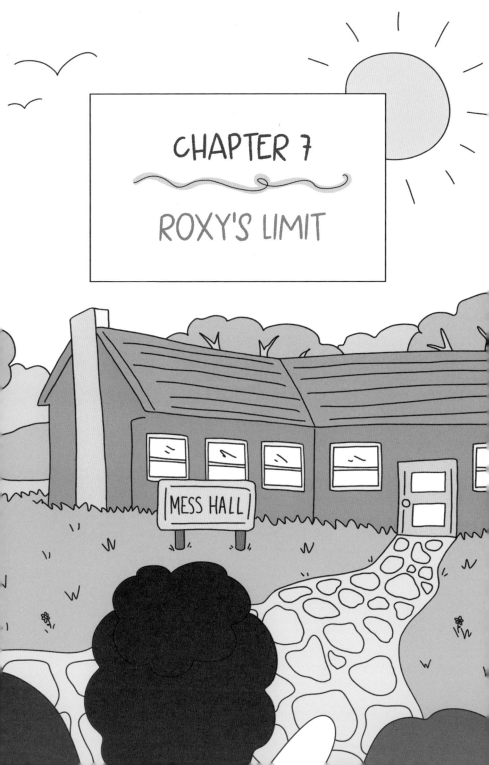

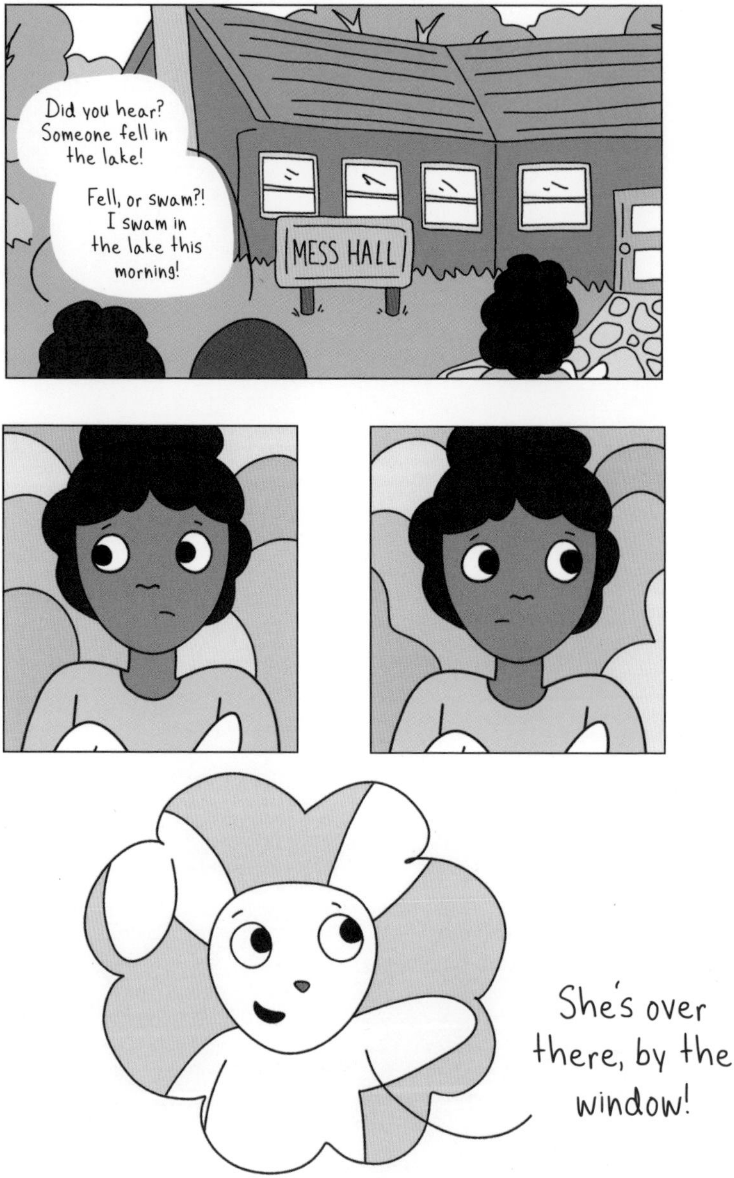
Did you hear? Someone fell in the lake!
Fell, or swam?! I swam in the lake this morning!
MESS HALL
She's over there, by the window!

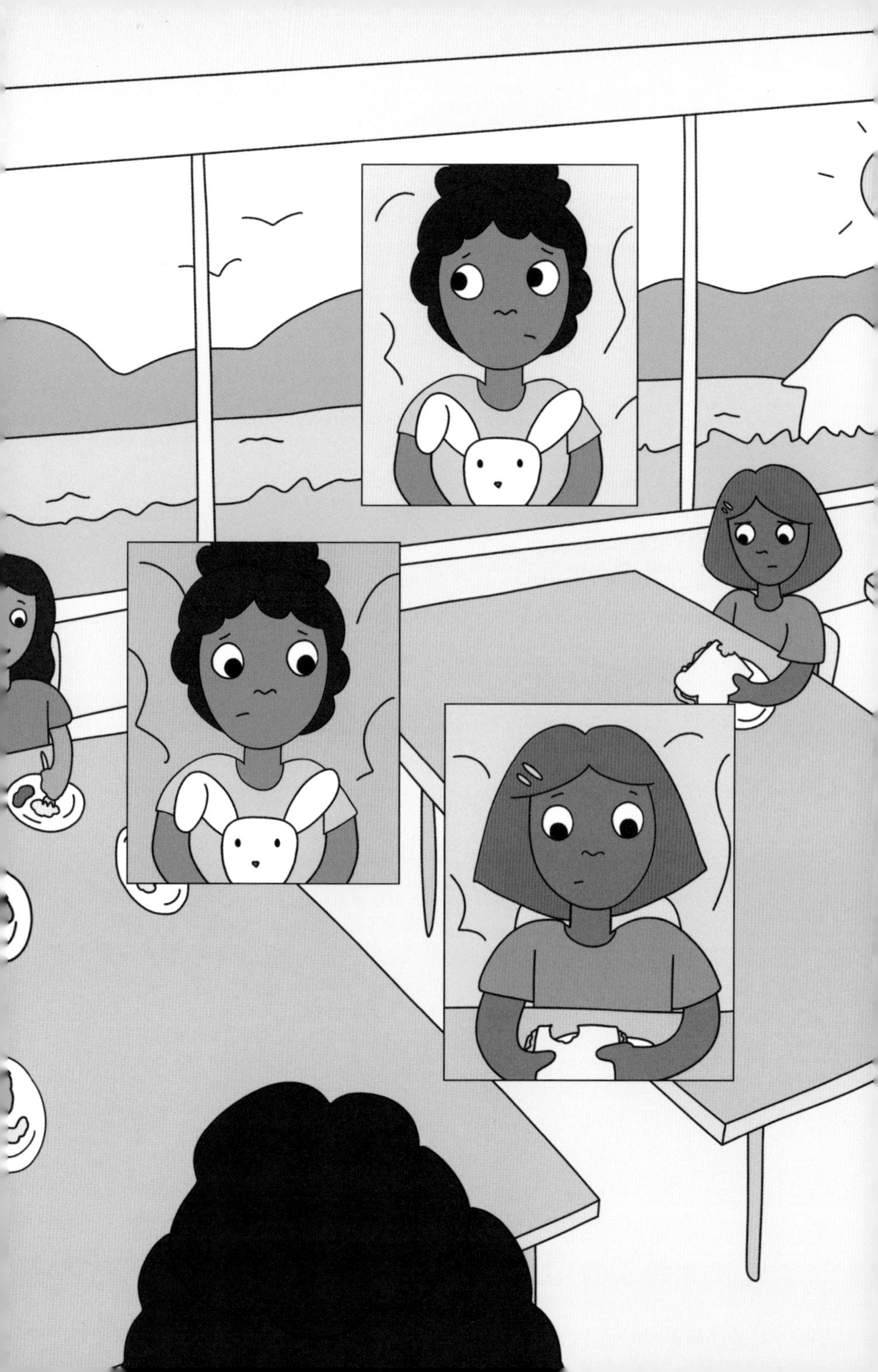

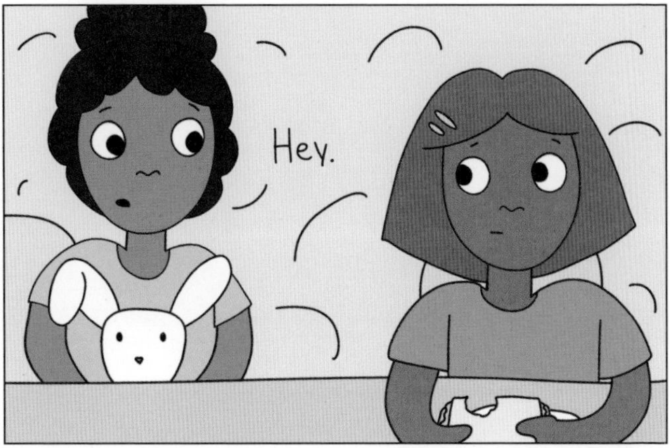
Hey.

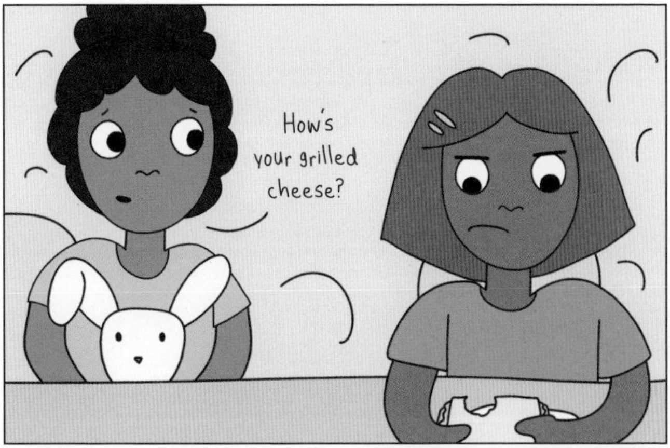
How's your grilled cheese?

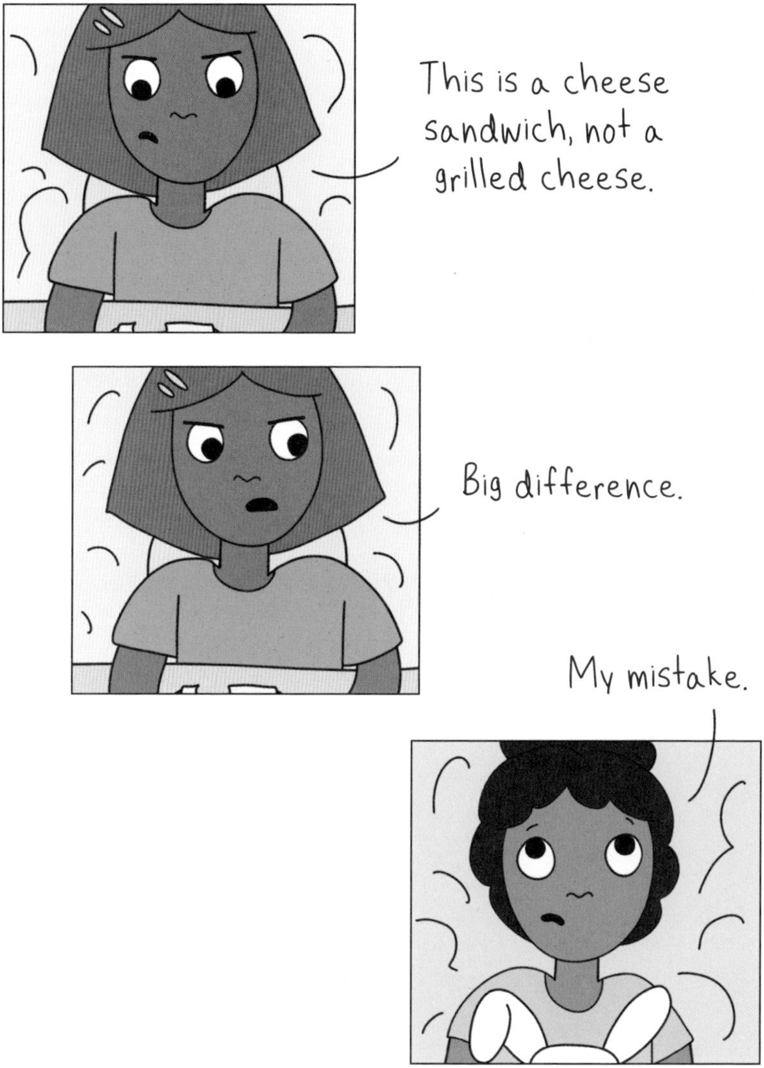
This is a cheese sandwich, not a grilled cheese.
Big difference.
My mistake.

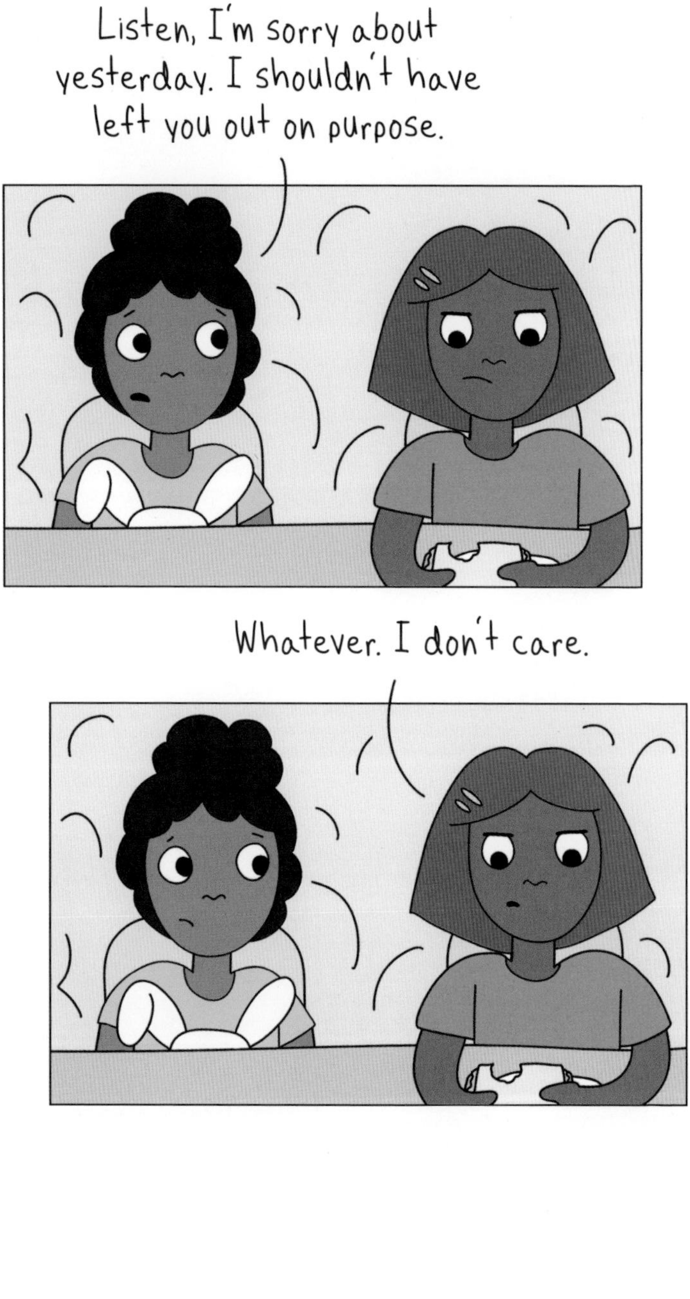
Listen, I'm sorry about yesterday. I shouldn't have left you out on purpose.
Whatever. I don't care.

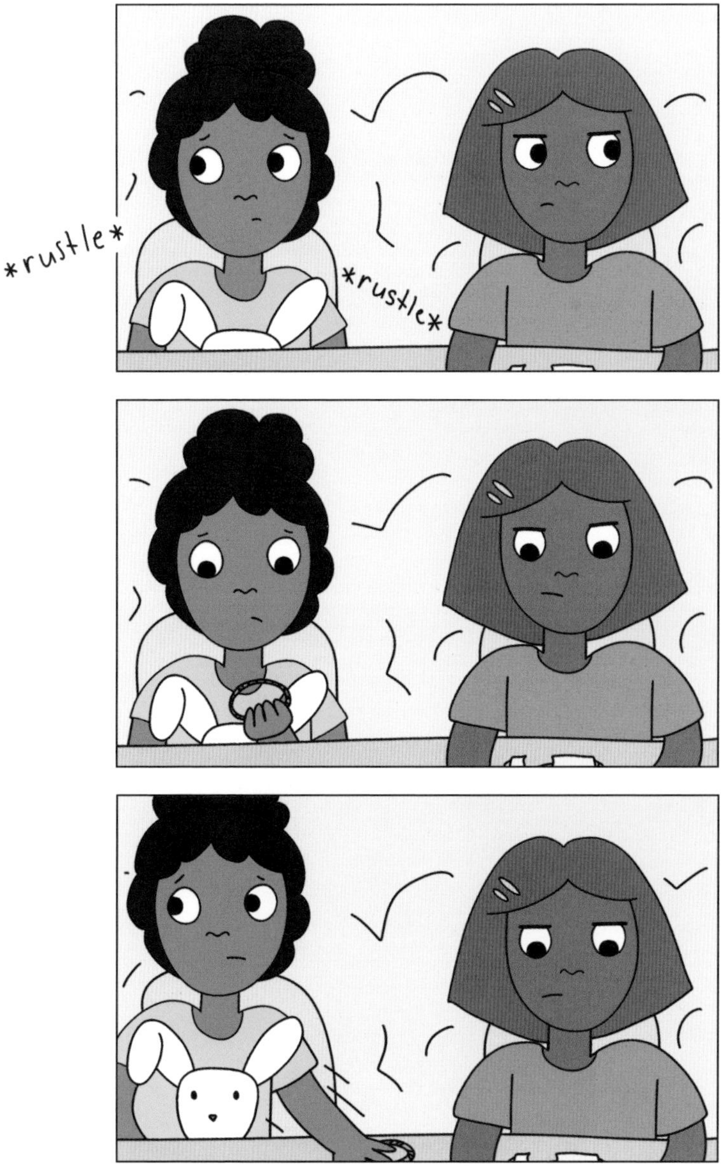
rustle
rustle

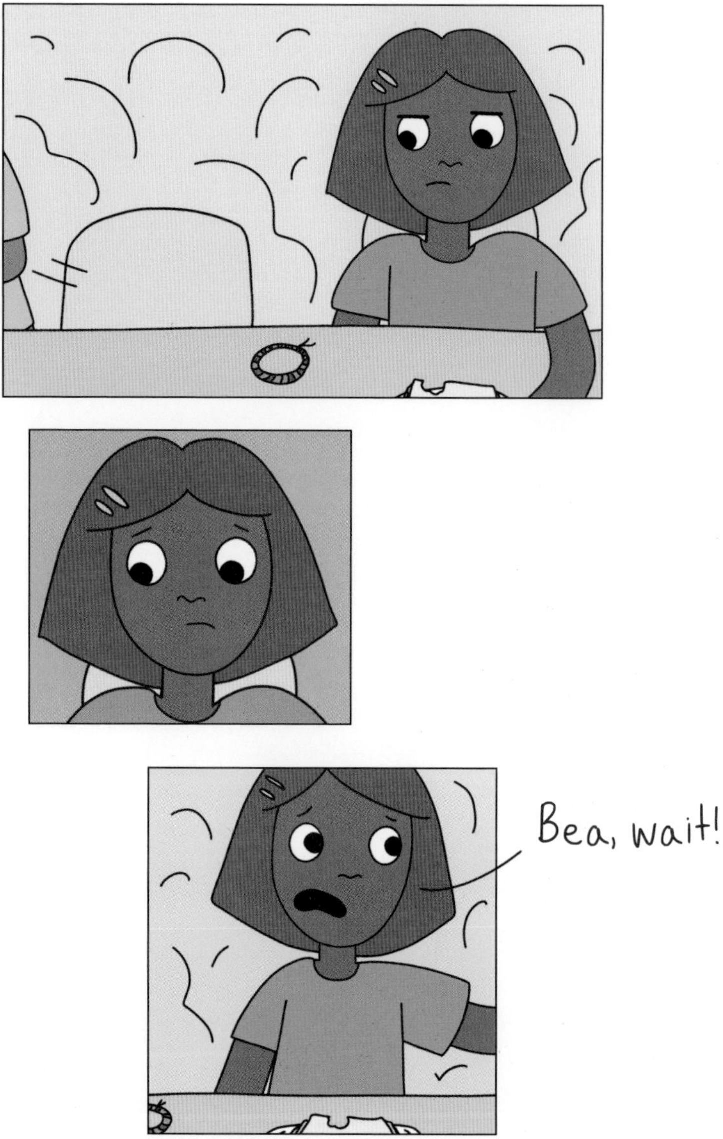
Bea, wait!

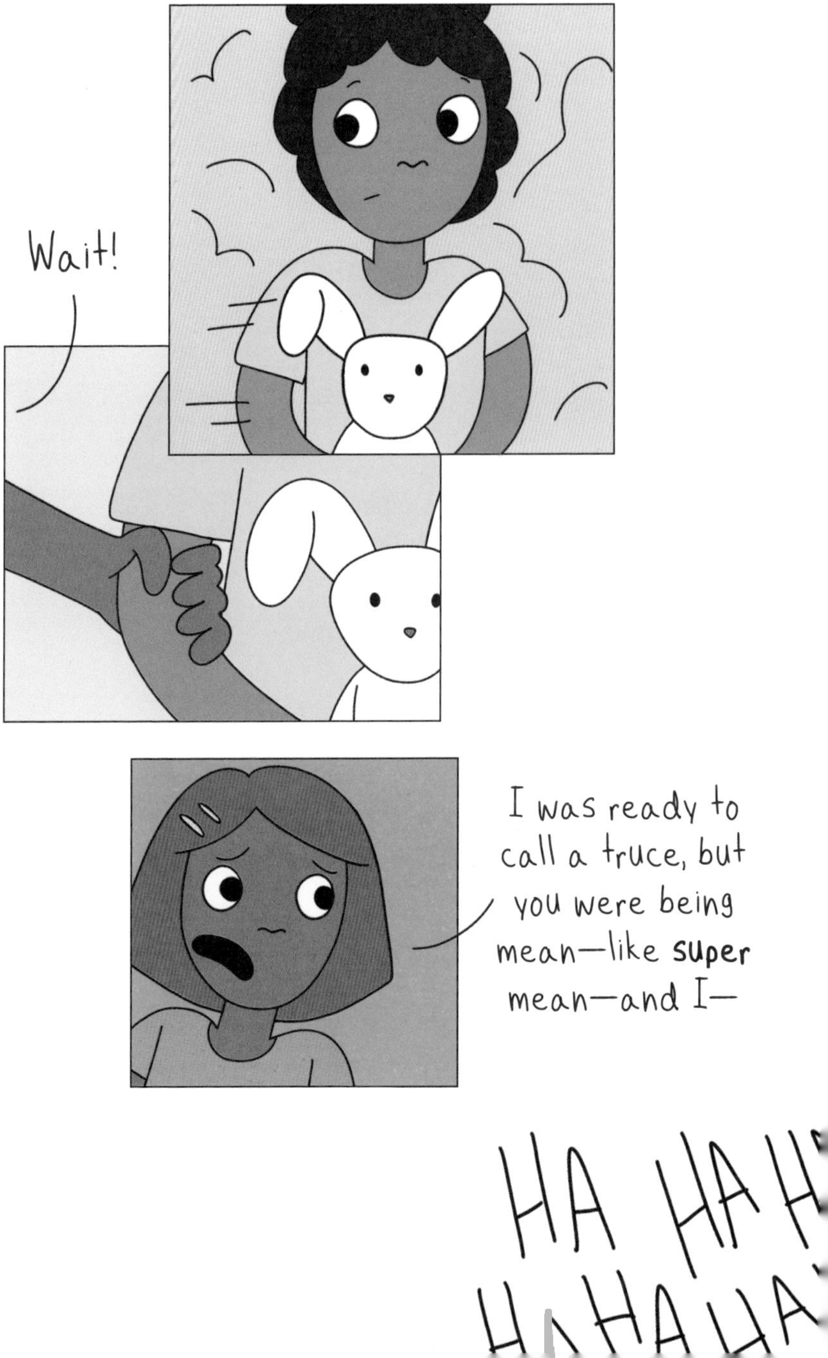
Wait!
I was ready to call a truce, but you were being mean—like **super** mean—and I—
HA HA

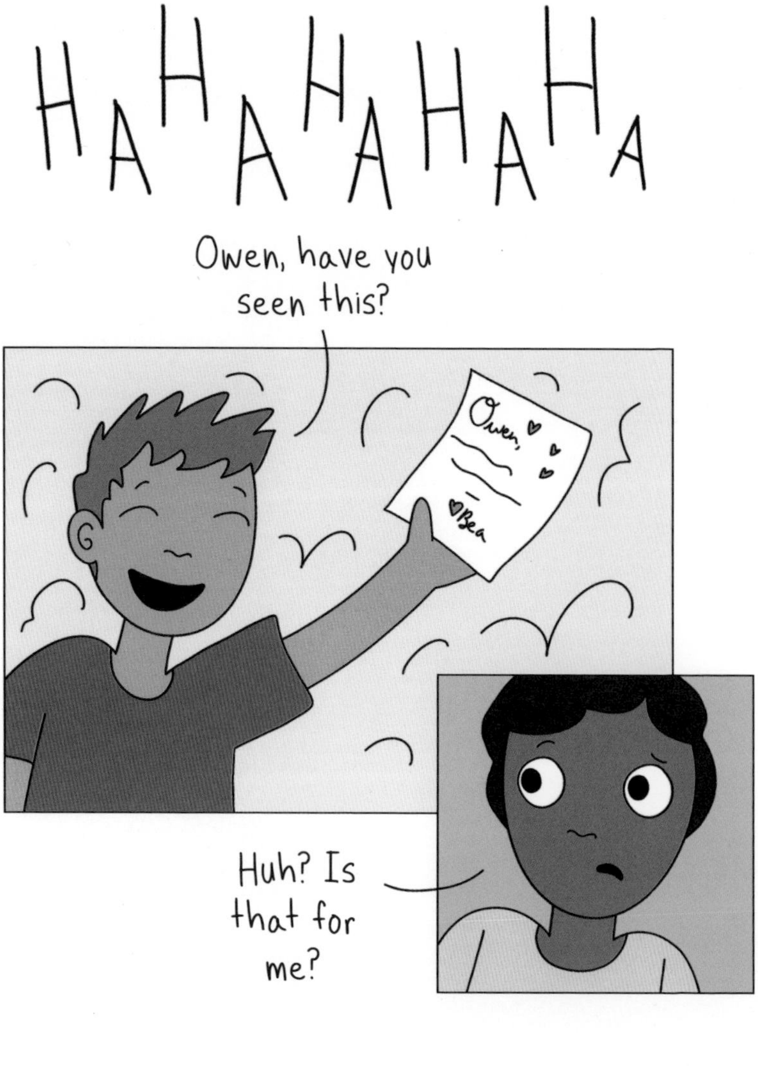
HAHAHAHAHAHAHAHA
Owen, have you seen this?
Owen,
Bea
Huh? Is that for me?

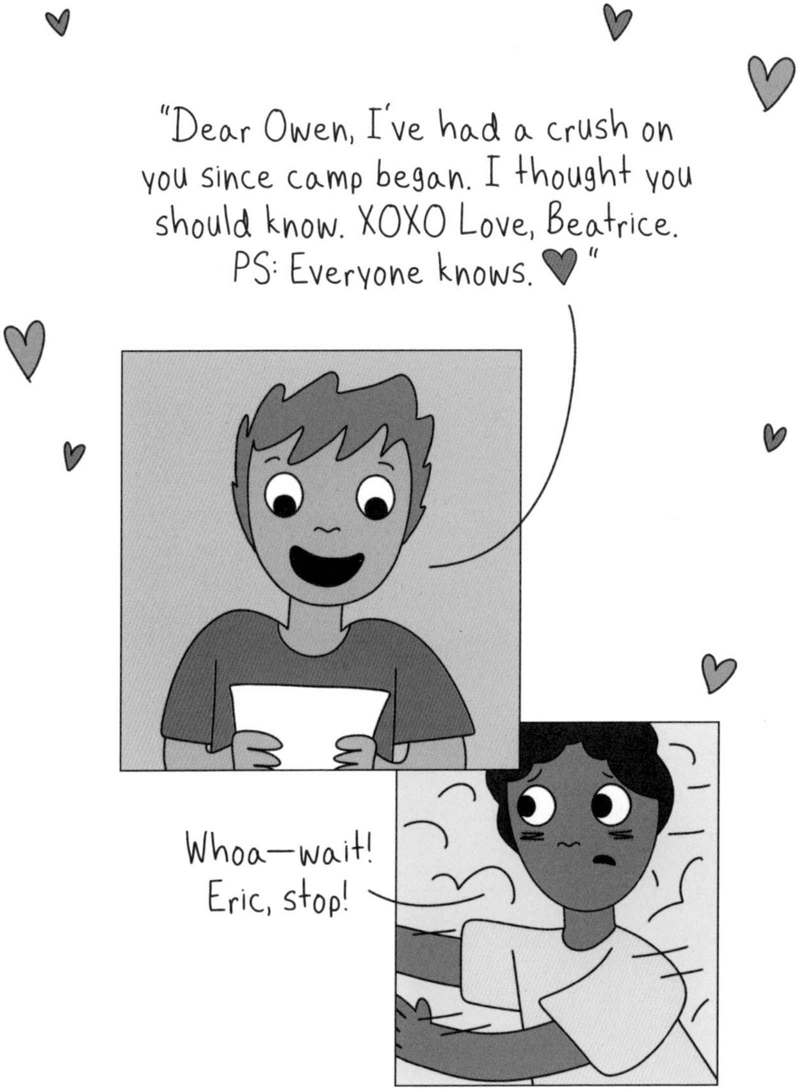
"Dear Owen, I've had a crush on you since camp began. I thought you should know. XOXO Love, Beatrice. PS: Everyone knows. ♥"
Whoa—wait! Eric, stop!

HA HA HA!

SNATCH

But I—
I didn't—

I'm sorry! I was mad—
I wasn't thinking—

GASP
YOU.
You wrote that note.

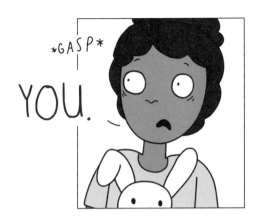

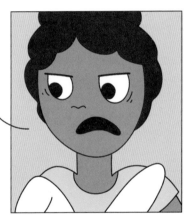

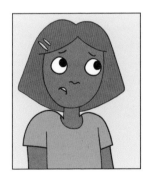

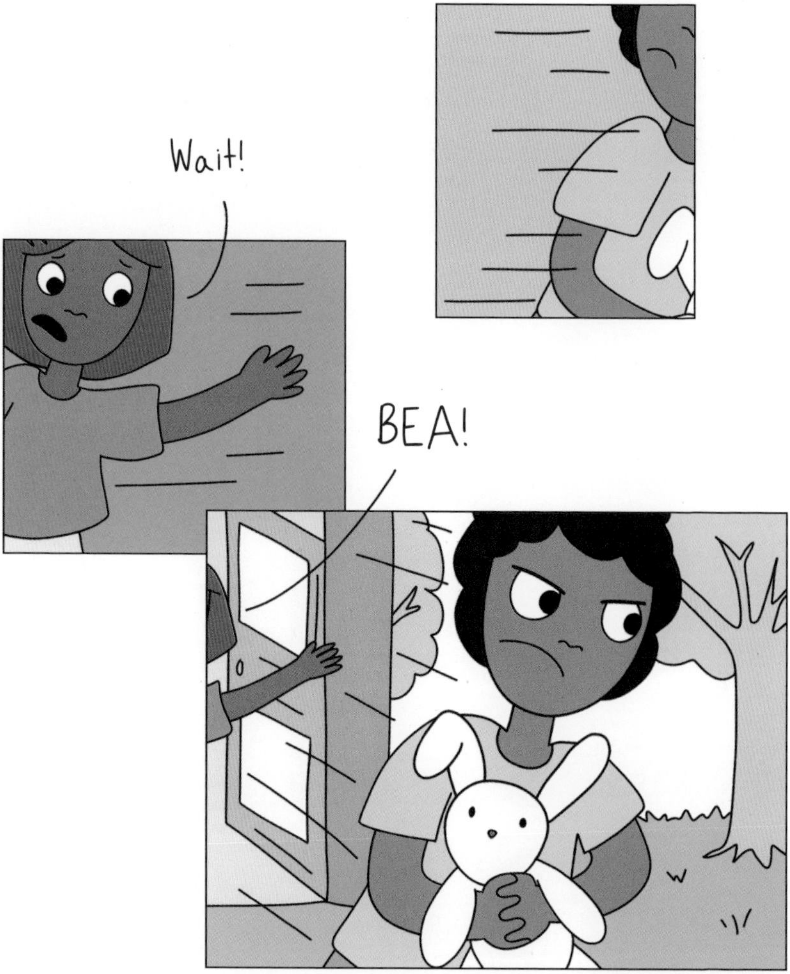
Wait!
BEA!

I had no desire **whatsoever** to go to camp. This wasn't something I chose! All I had to do was suffer through this week and I'd never have to come back!

My dad forced me to come here so I could learn how to "make friends" and "connect" with people, and you know what? This is exactly why I prefer spending time with Roger—people are **terrible.**

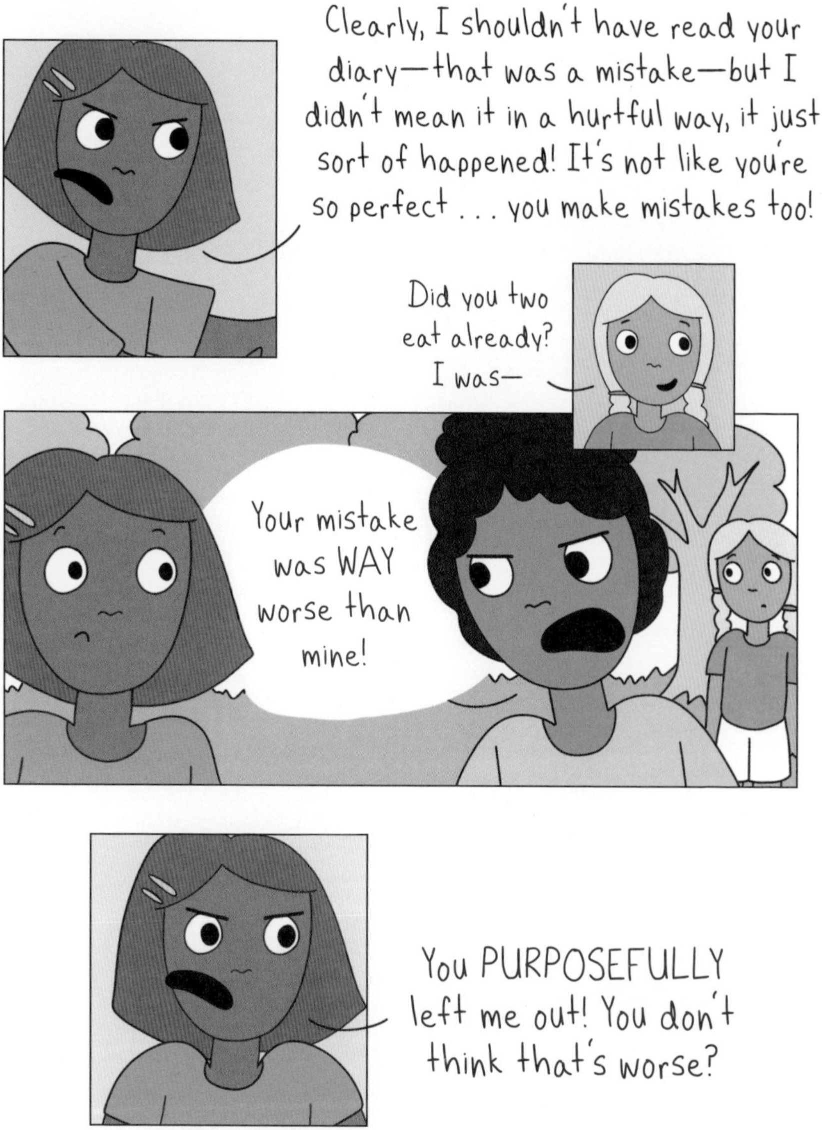
Clearly, I shouldn't have read your diary—that was a mistake—but I didn't mean it in a hurtful way, it just sort of happened! It's not like you're so perfect . . . you make mistakes too!
Did you two eat already? I was—
Your mistake was WAY worse than mine!
You PURPOSEFULLY left me out! You don't think that's worse?

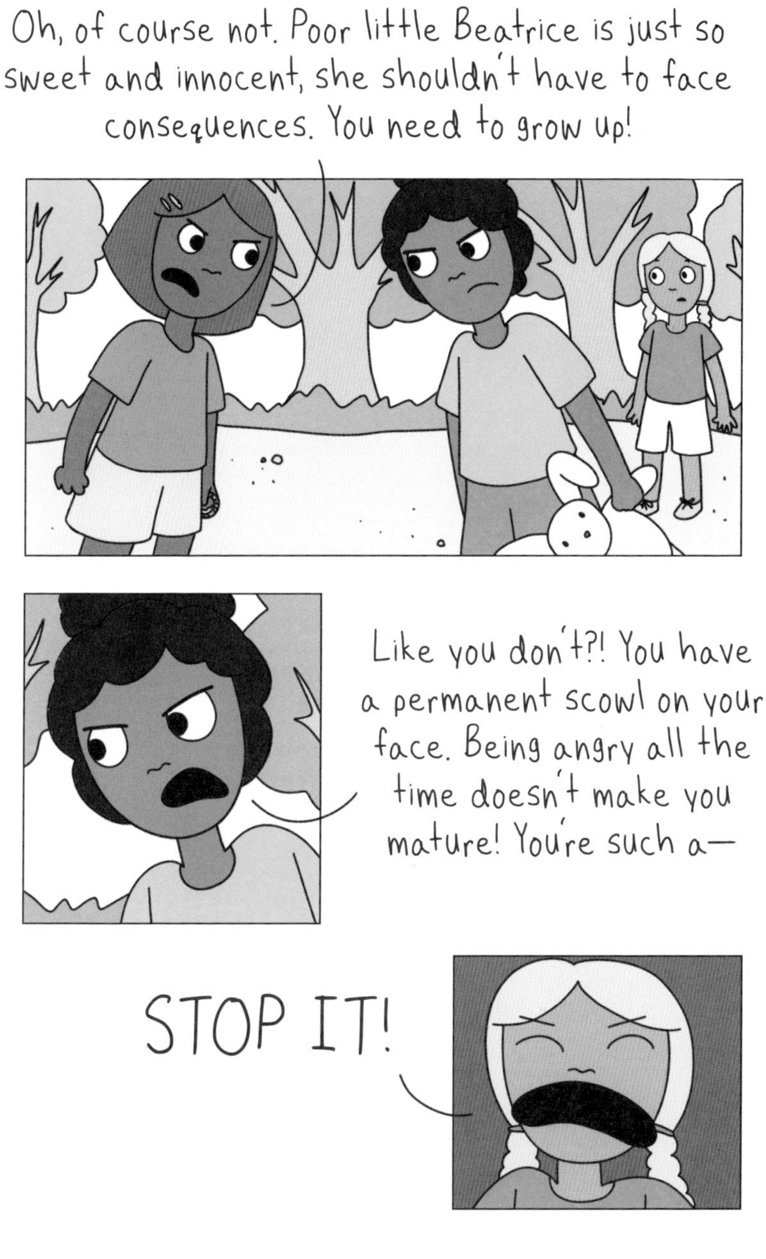
Oh, of course not. Poor little Beatrice is just so sweet and innocent, she shouldn't have to face consequences. You need to grow up!
Like you don't?! You have a permanent scowl on your face. Being angry all the time doesn't make you mature! You're such a—
STOP IT!

You two have done nothing but pick at each other, and I'm SICK OF IT!

If I wanted to be around a bunch of fighting, I would've stayed home!

heavy breathing

heavy breathing

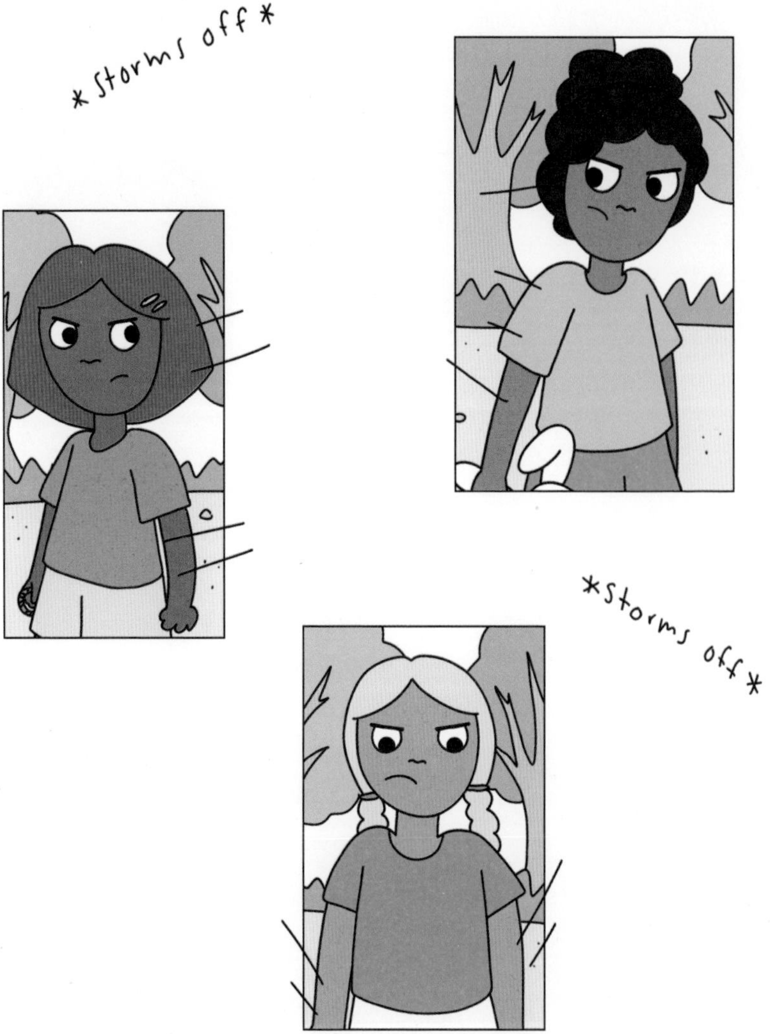
storms off
storms off

All anyone around me does is fight.

Here, at home, everywhere.

It's never going to end.

CHAPTER 8

A FEARFUL FLOWER

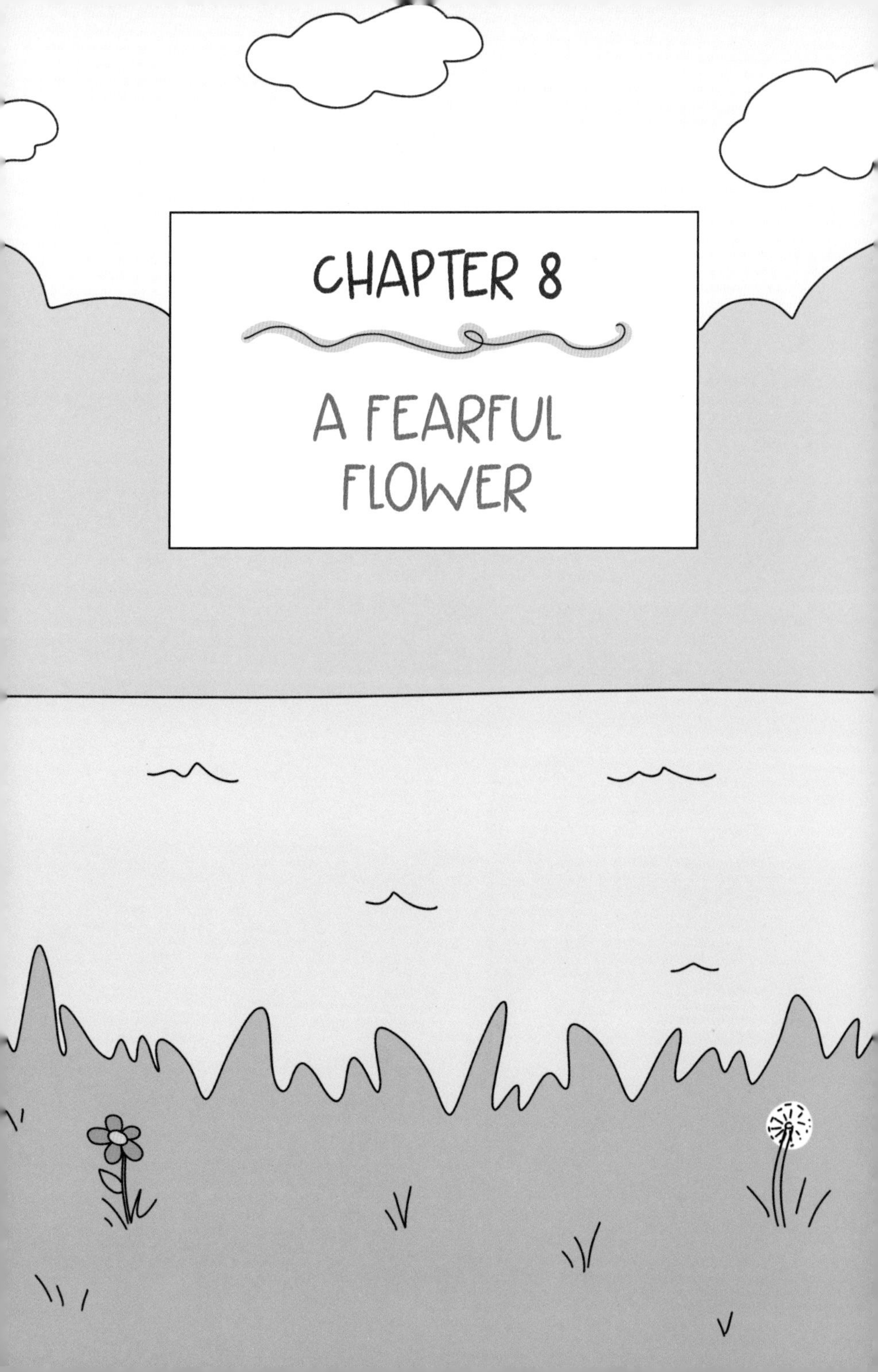

Ruin anyone else's life today?

No, you were the only one on my life-ruining schedule.

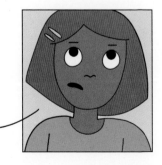

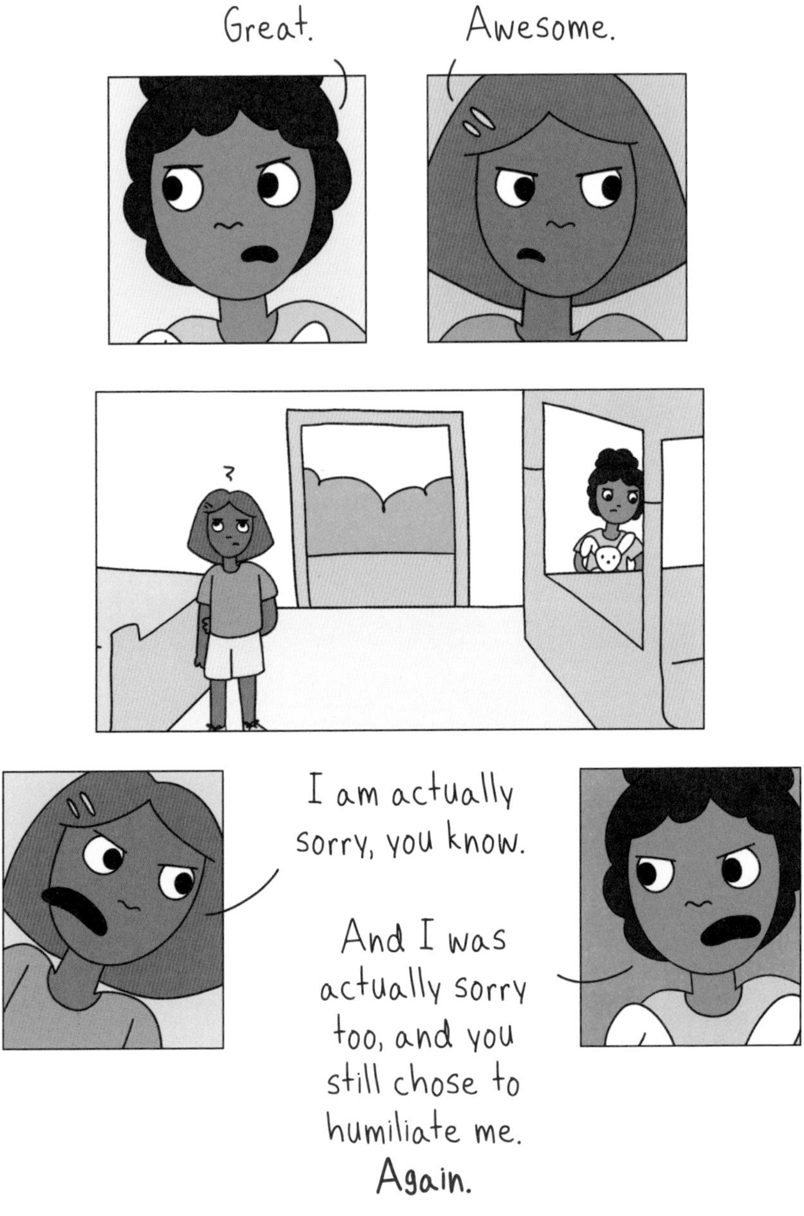
Great.
Awesome.
I am actually sorry, you know.
And I was actually sorry too, and you still chose to humiliate me. **Again.**

That was just bad timing!

Look, I'm not a bad person, and I know you're not a bad person either. When you're not being annoying, it's actually kind of brave how ... **you,** you are.

Gee, thanks.

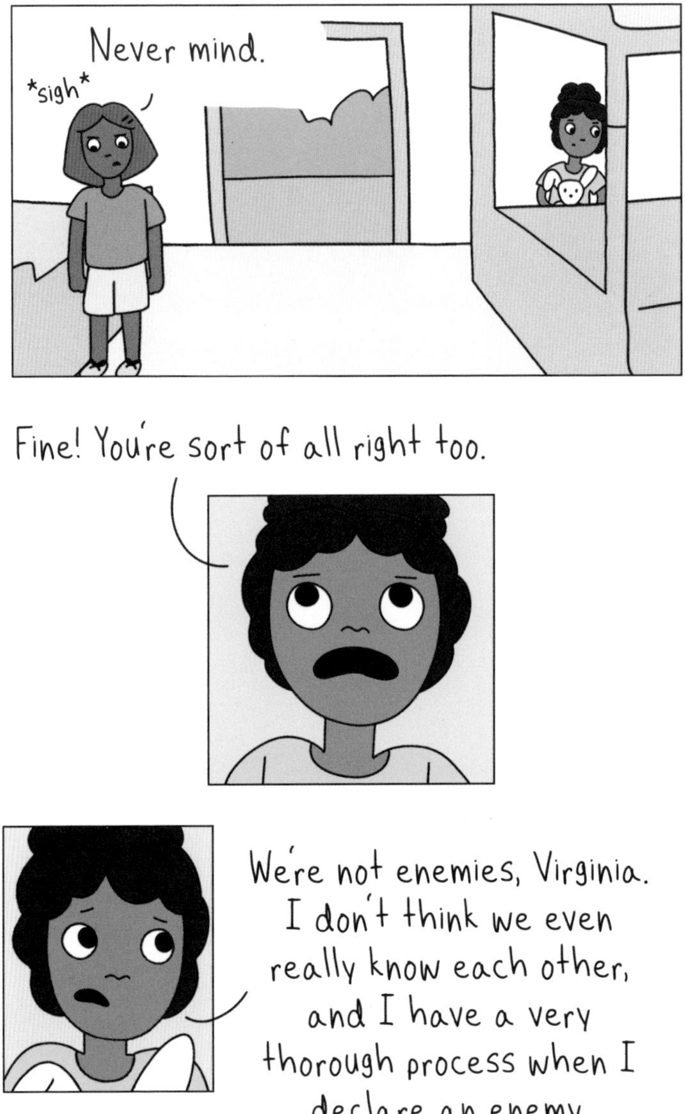
Never mind.
sigh
Fine! You're sort of all right too.
We're not enemies, Virginia. I don't think we even really know each other, and I have a very thorough process when I declare an enemy.

Well, do we want to really know each other?
huffing
puffing
Tadpoles!

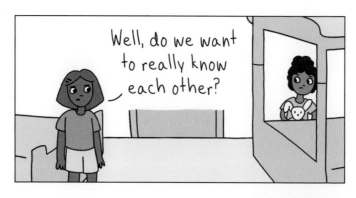

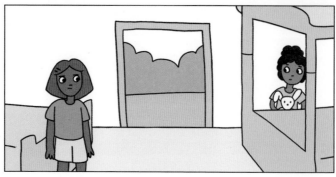

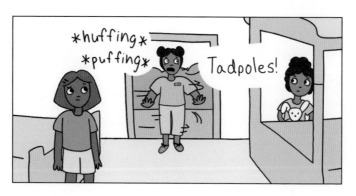

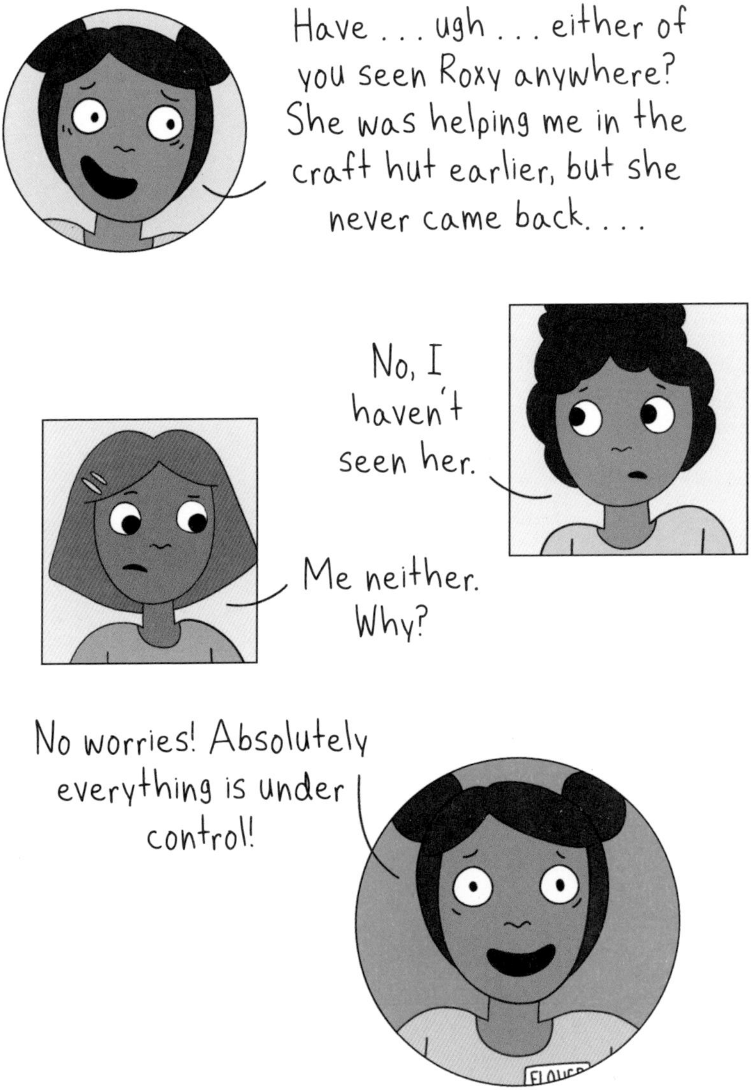

Have . . . ugh . . . either of you seen Roxy anywhere? She was helping me in the craft hut earlier, but she never came back. . . .
No, I haven't seen her.
Me neither. Why?
No worries! Absolutely everything is under control!

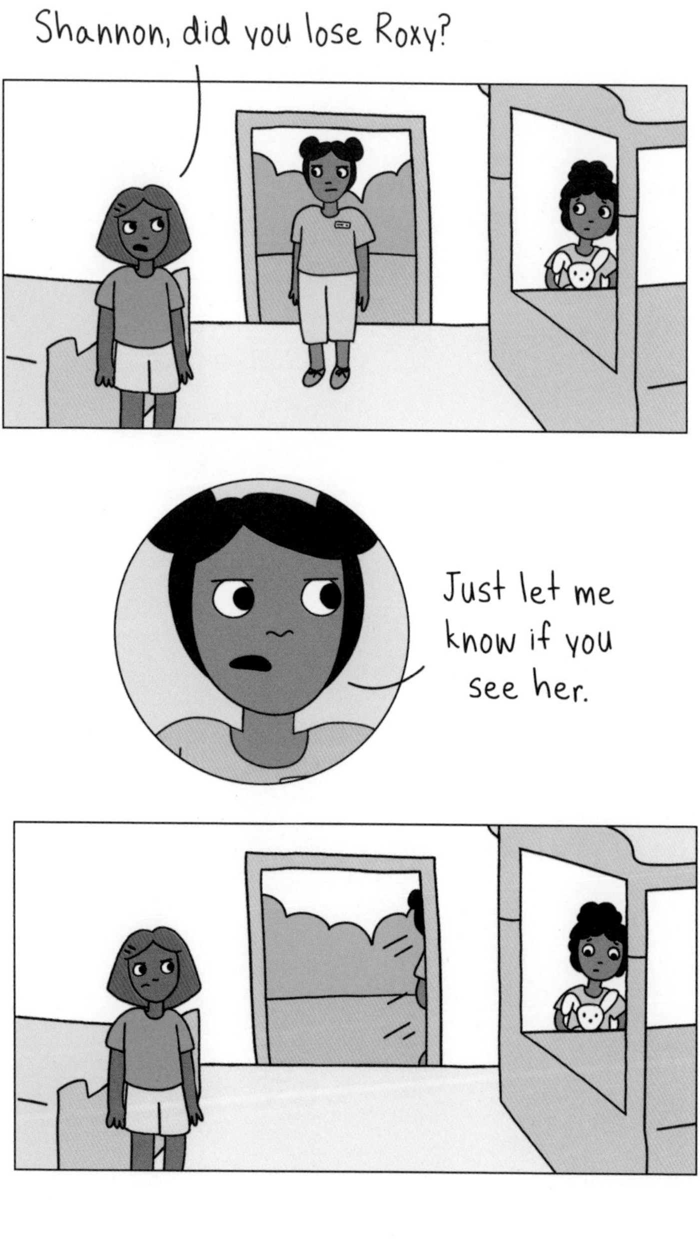
Shannon, did you lose Roxy?
Just let me know if you see her.

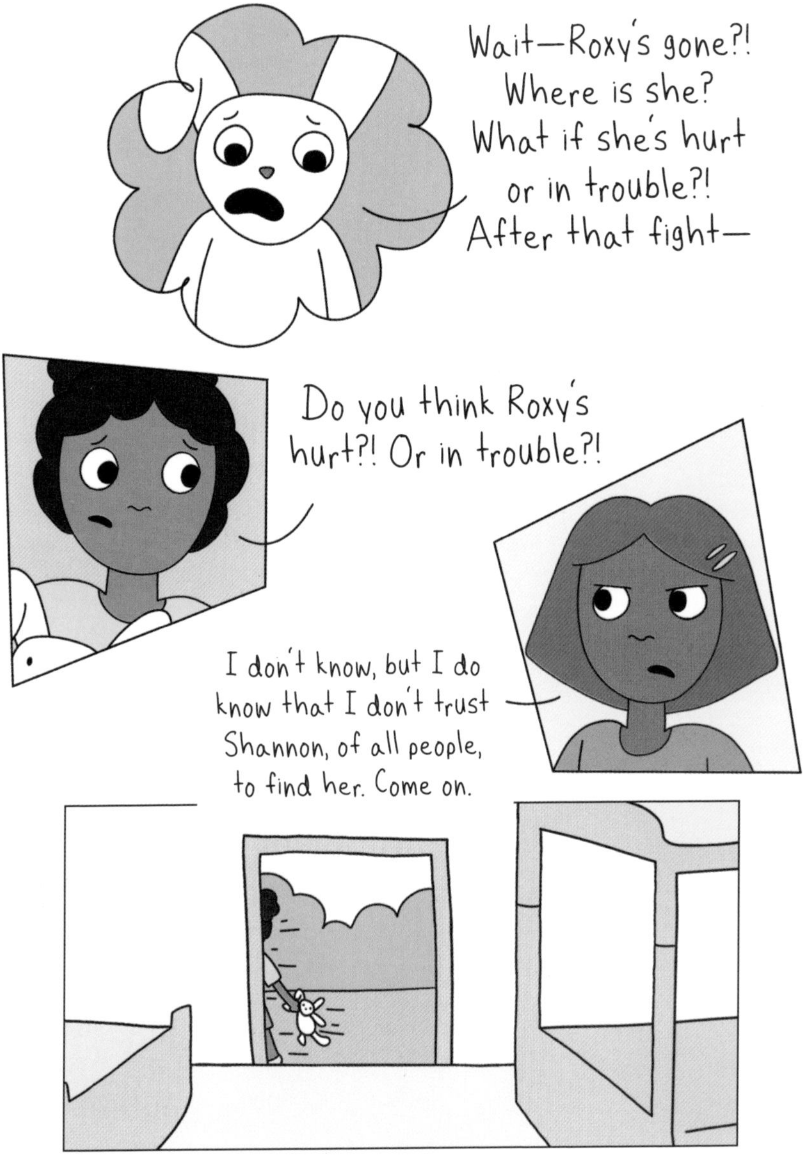
Wait—Roxy's gone?! Where is she? What if she's hurt or in trouble?! After that fight—
Do you think Roxy's hurt?! Or in trouble?!
I don't know, but I do know that I don't trust Shannon, of all people, to find her. Come on.

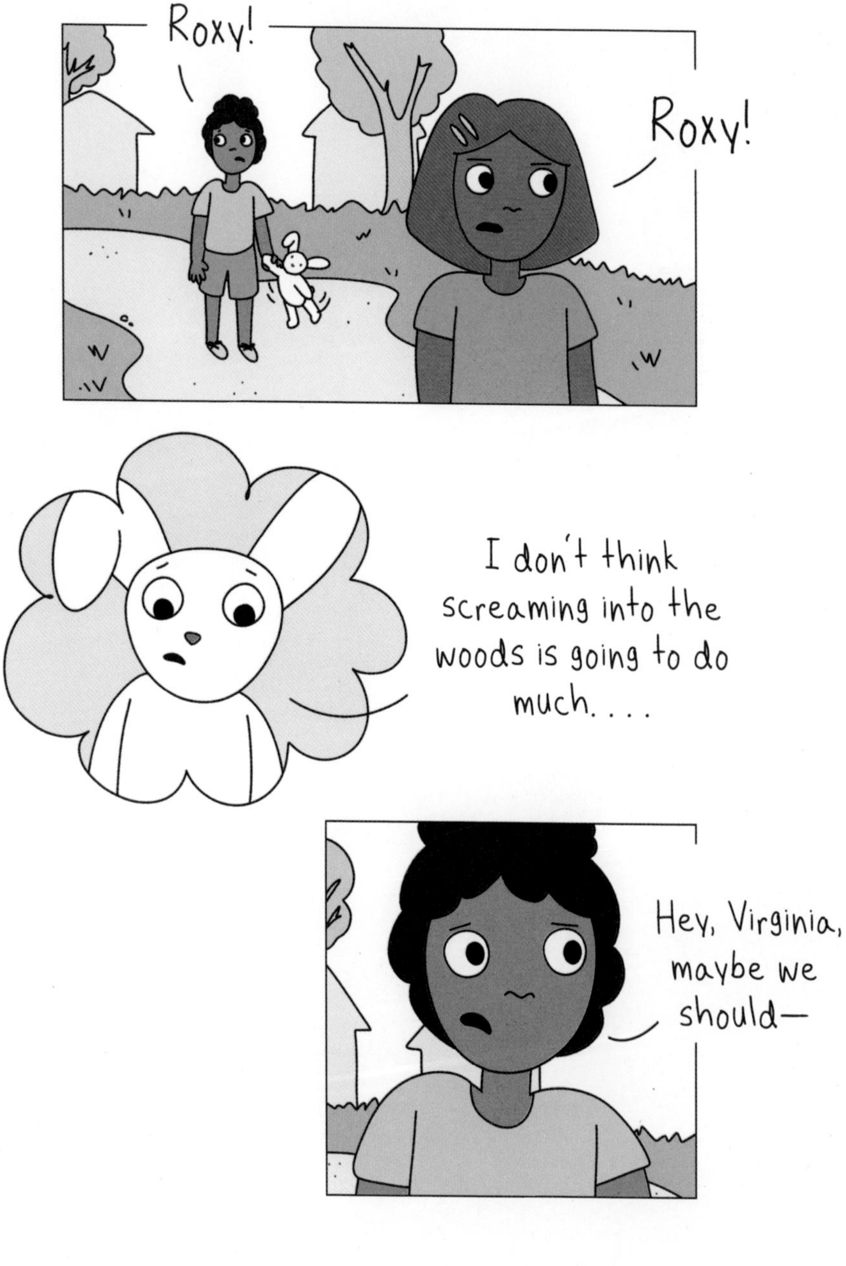
Roxy!
Roxy!
I don't think screaming into the woods is going to do much. . . .
Hey, Virginia, maybe we should—

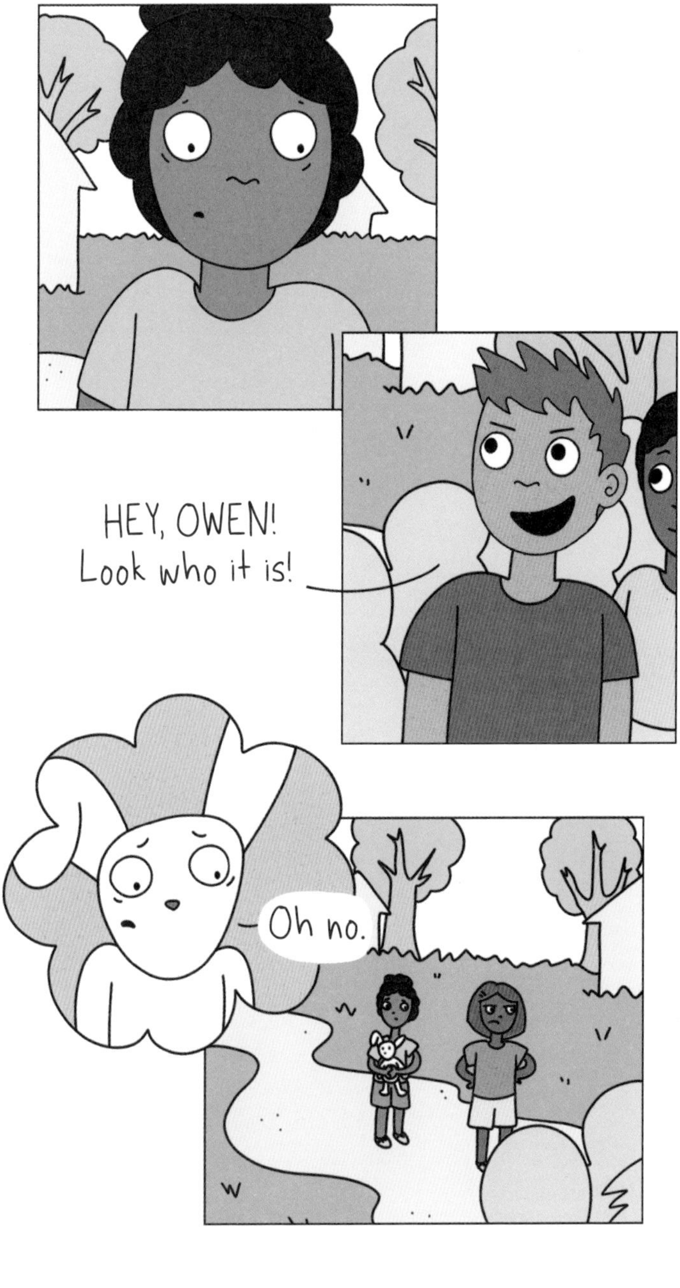
HEY, OWEN!
Look who it is!
Oh no.

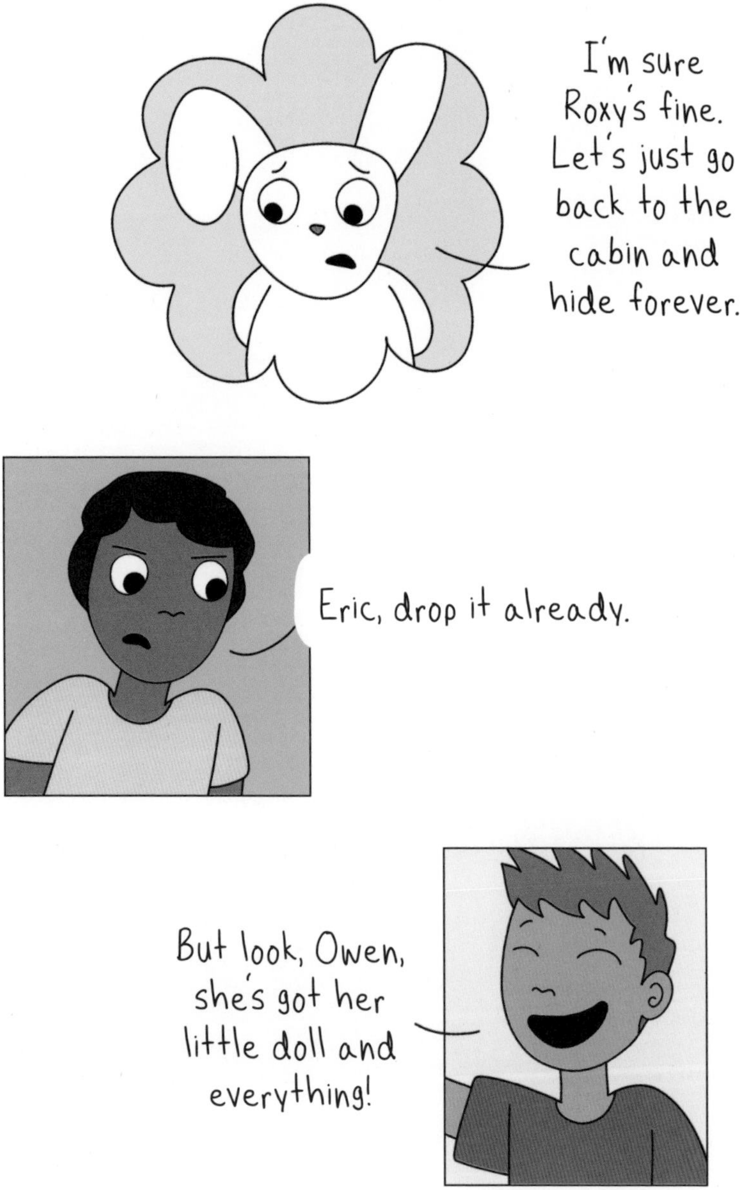
I'm sure Roxy's fine. Let's just go back to the cabin and hide forever.
Eric, drop it already.
But look, Owen, she's got her little doll and everything!

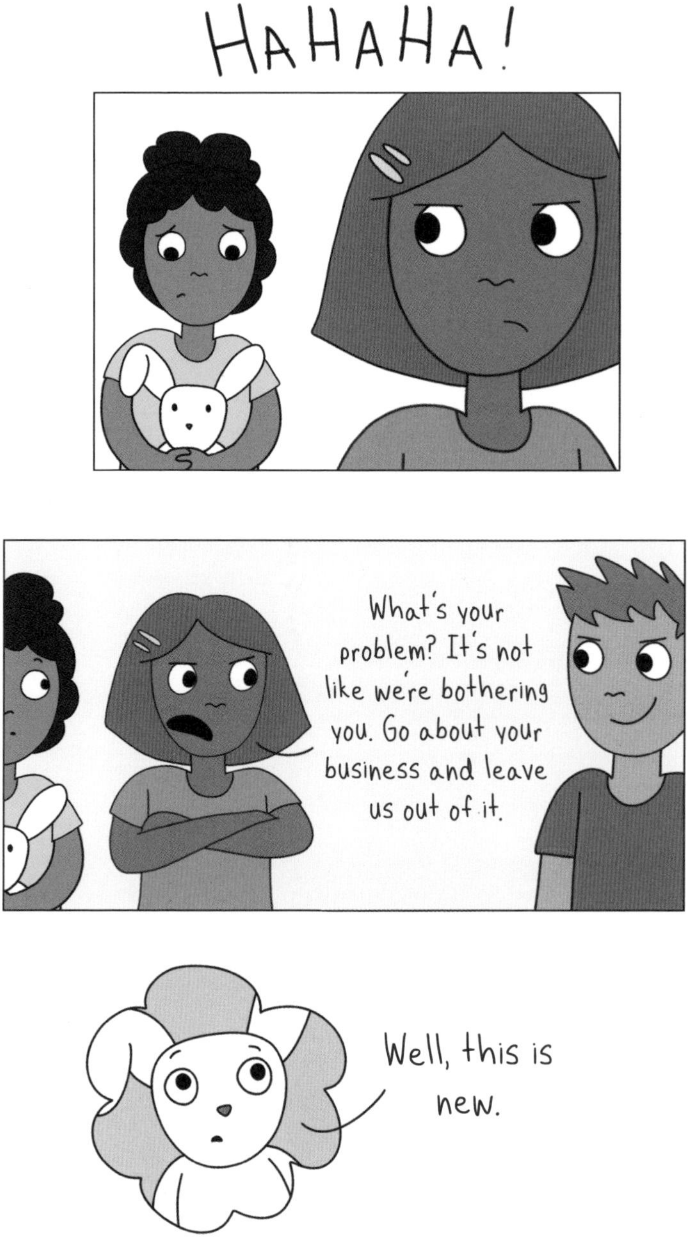
HAHAHA!
What's your problem? It's not like we're bothering you. Go about your business and leave us out of it.
Well, this is new.

HAHAHA!

Are you the bunny's bodyguard too?

Roger doesn't need a bodyguard because Bea's got more guts than all of you combined. And also, I made up all that stuff about her having a crush as a prank, so leave her alone and get on with your life.

Come on.

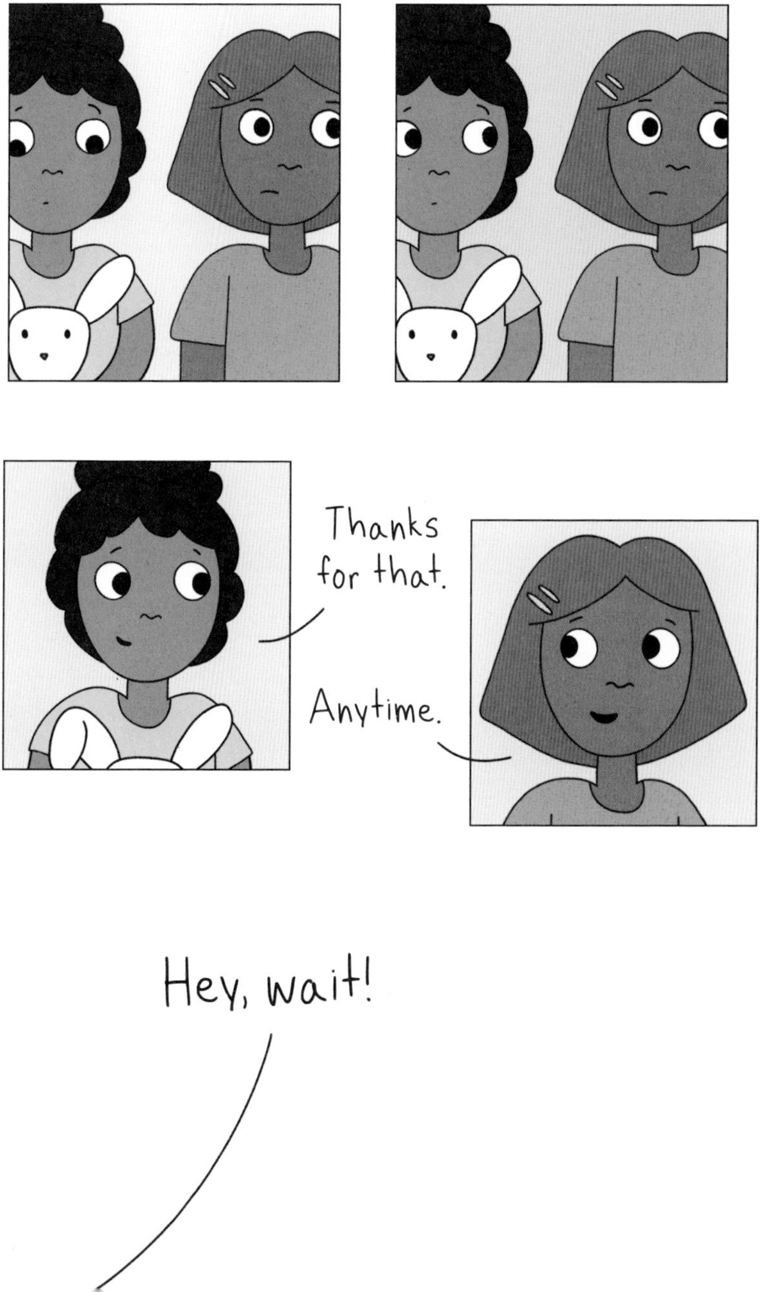
Thanks for that.
Anytime.
Hey, wait!

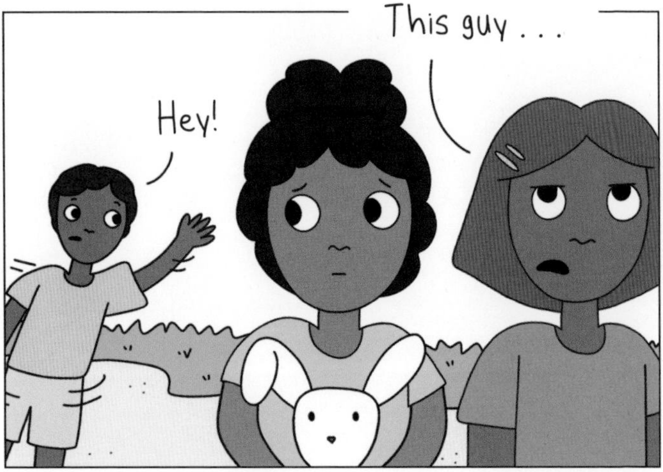
Hey!
This guy . . .

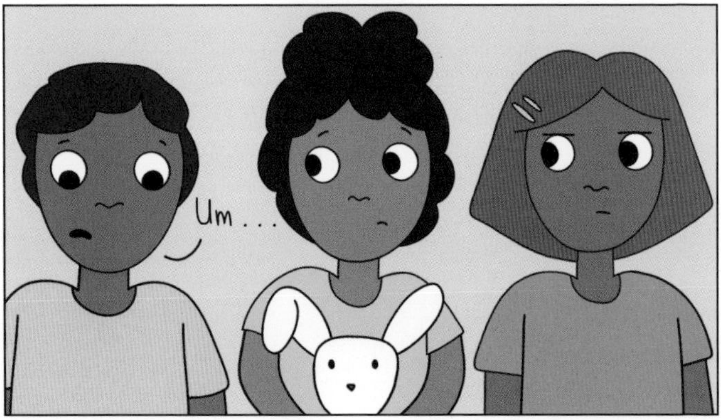
Um . . .

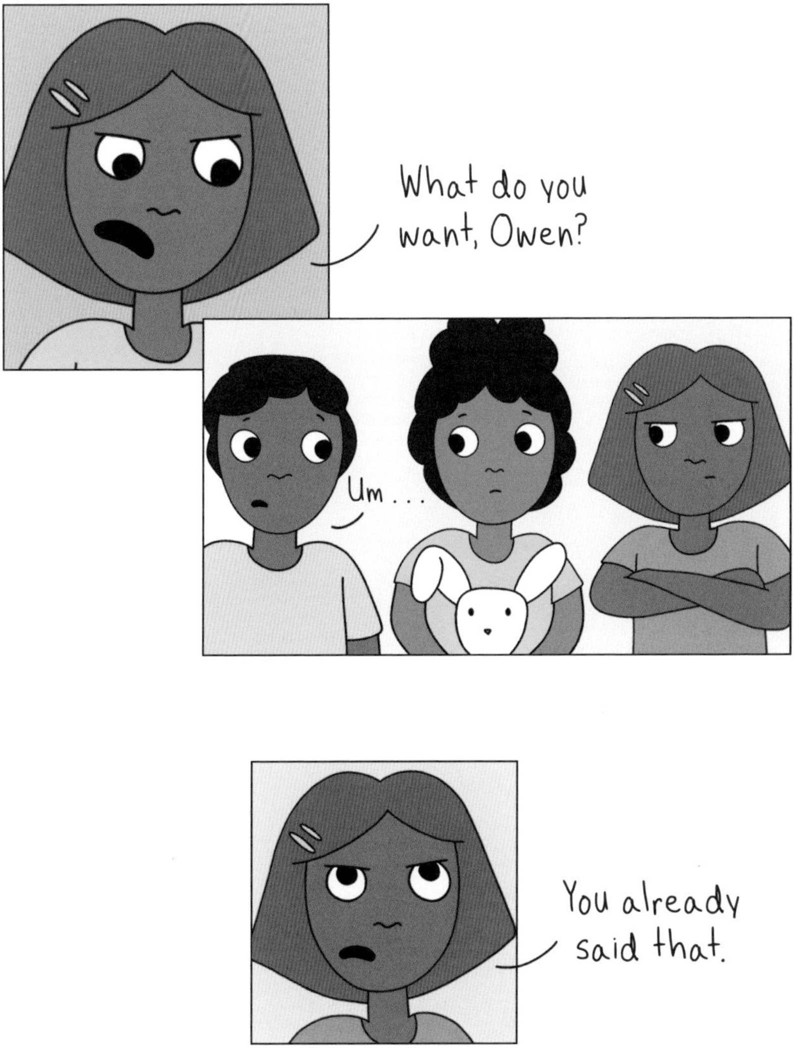
What do you want, Owen?
Um . . .
You already said that.

I mean . . . I, um, like your stuffed animal.

Thanks . . .

I have one just like it at home.

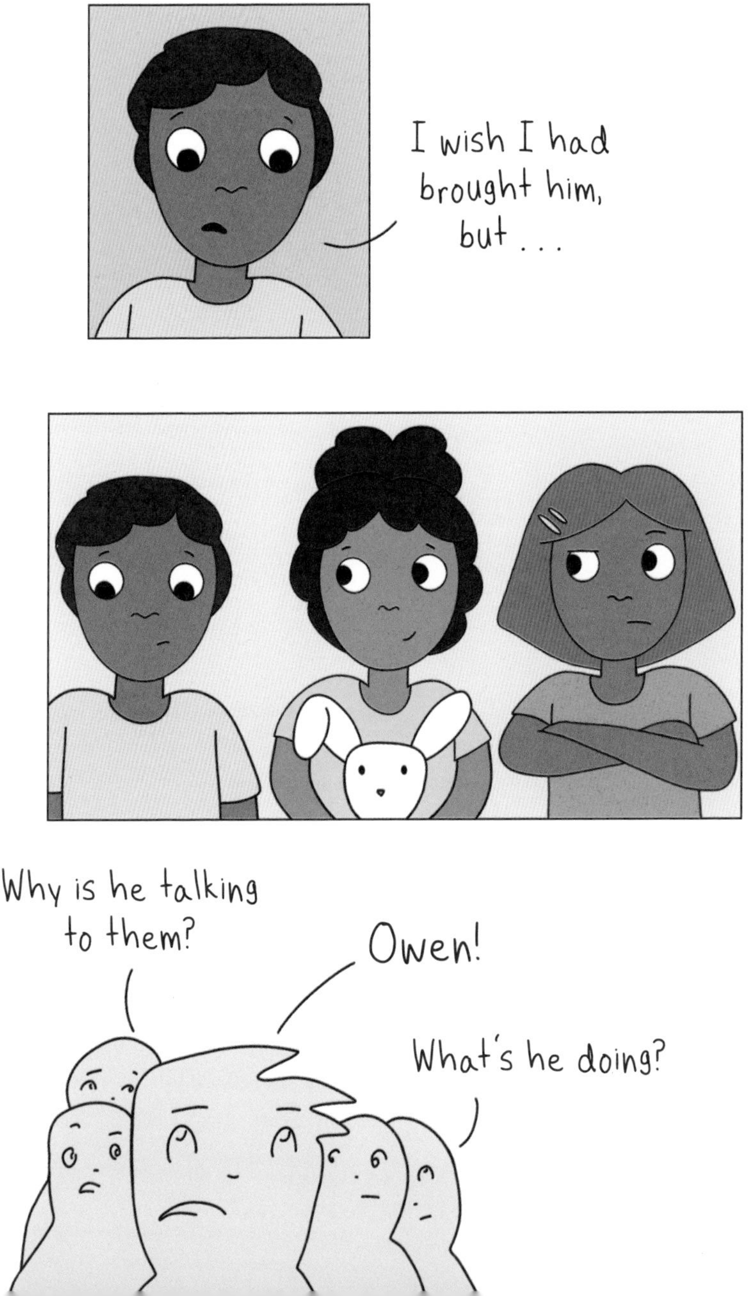
I wish I had brought him, but . . .
Why is he talking to them?
Owen!
What's he doing?

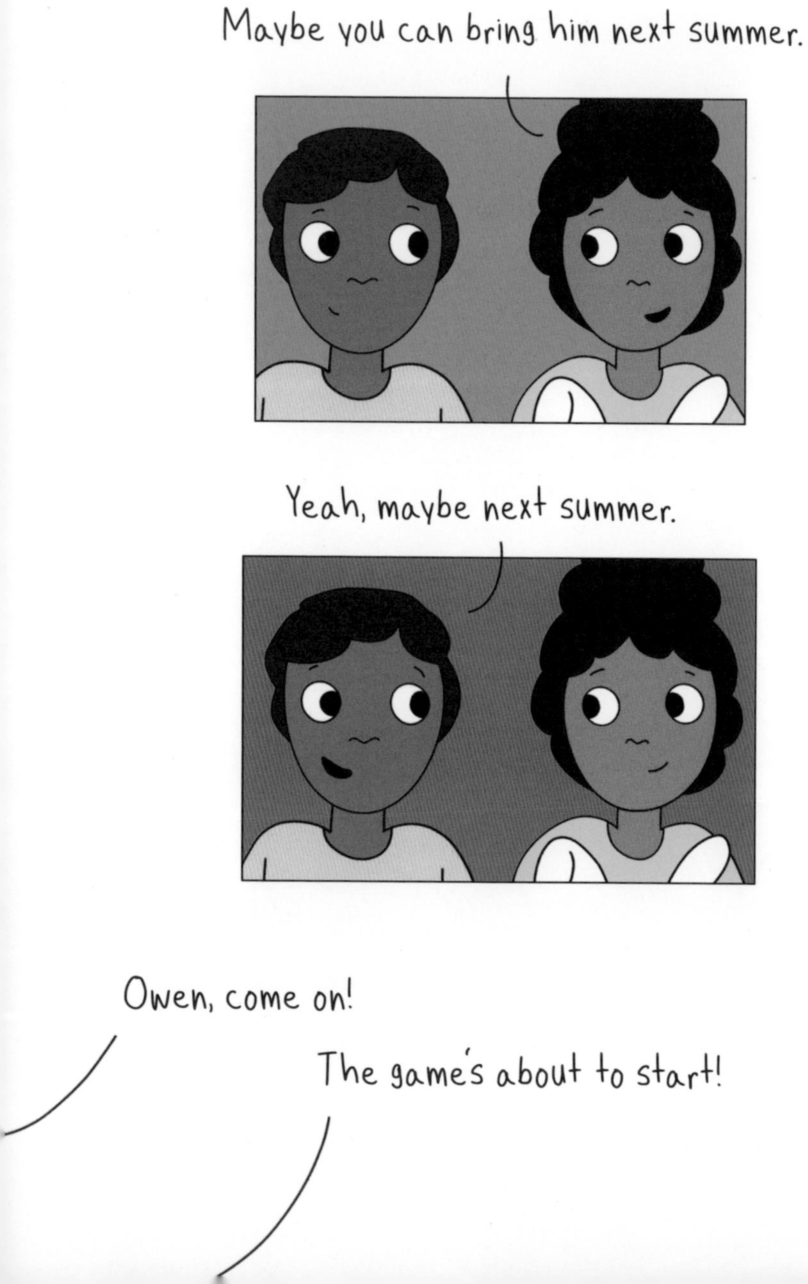
Maybe you can bring him next summer.
Yeah, maybe next summer.
Owen, come on!
The game's about to start!

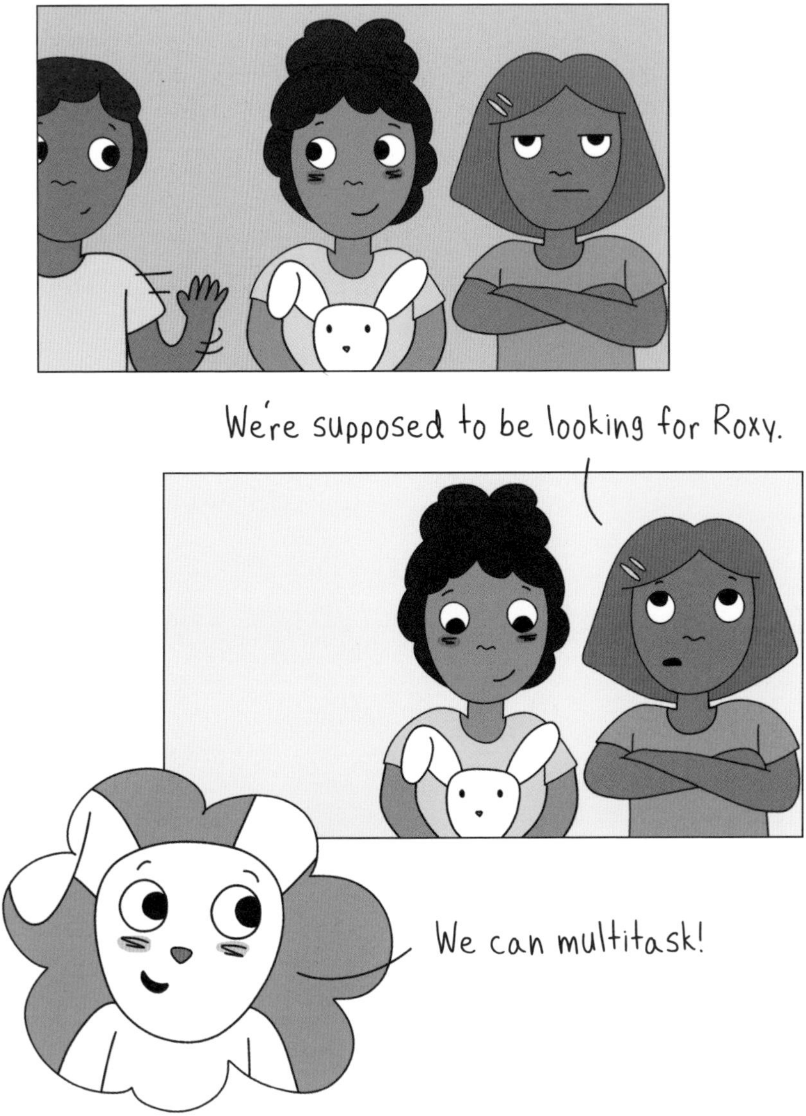
We're supposed to be looking for Roxy.
We can multitask!

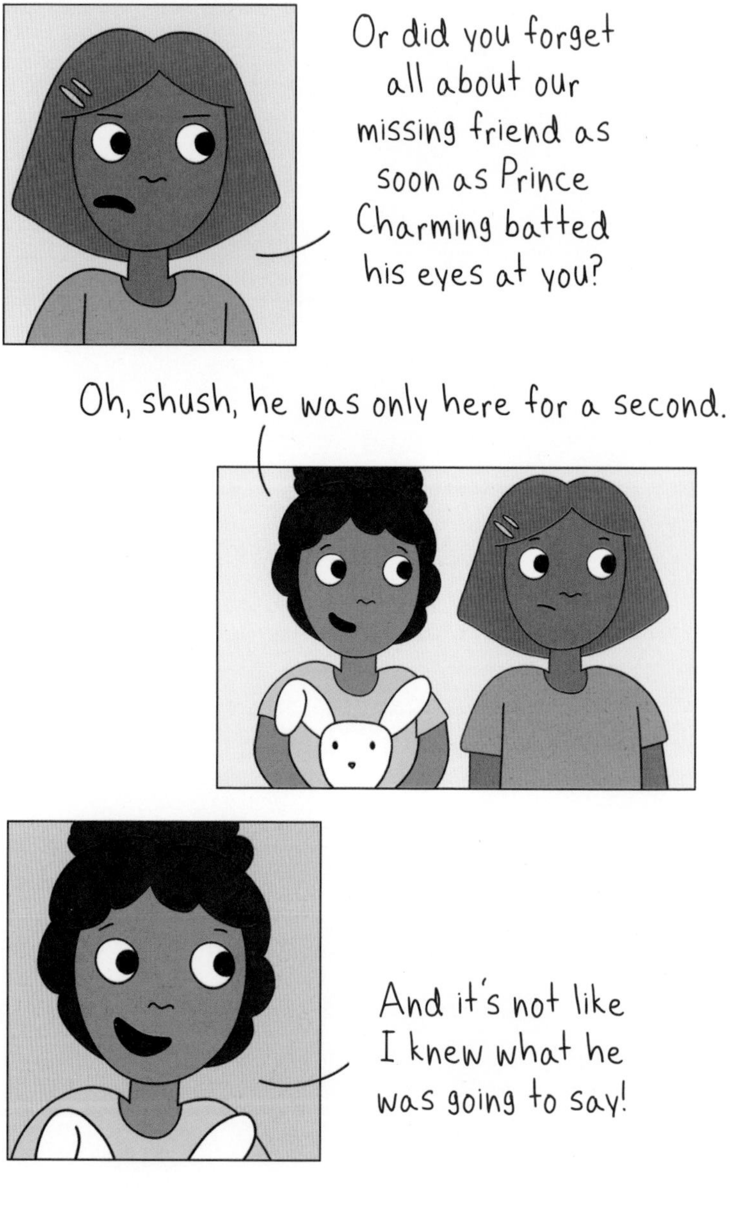
Or did you forget all about our missing friend as soon as Prince Charming batted his eyes at you?
Oh, shush, he was only here for a second.
And it's not like I knew what he was going to say!

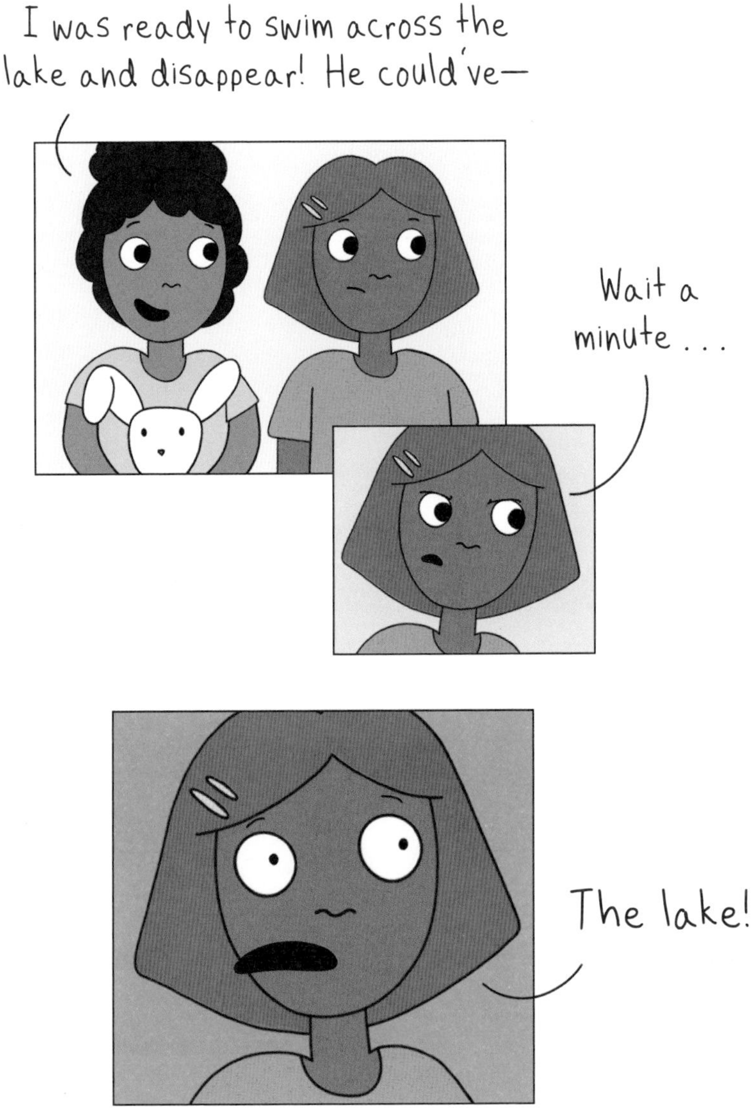
I was ready to swim across the lake and disappear! He could've—
Wait a minute . . .
The lake!

the other day at the lake

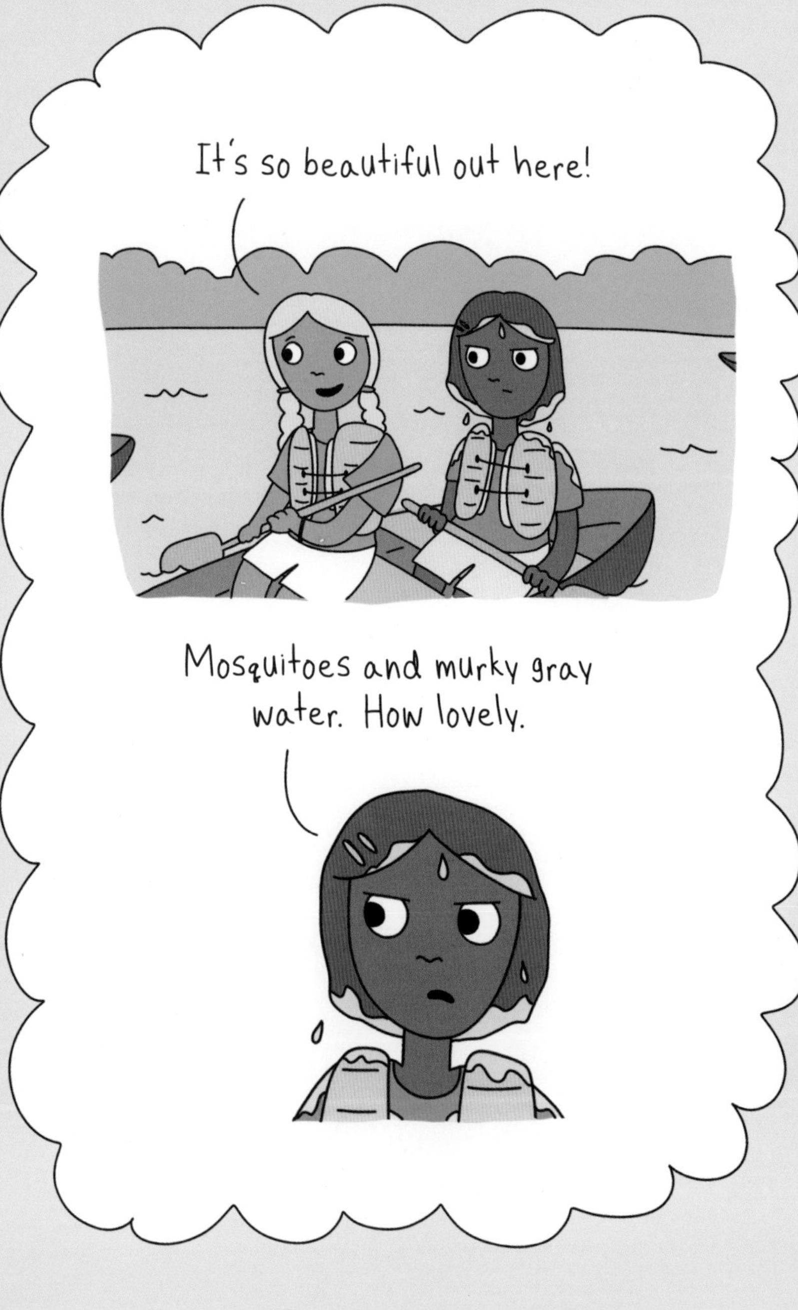

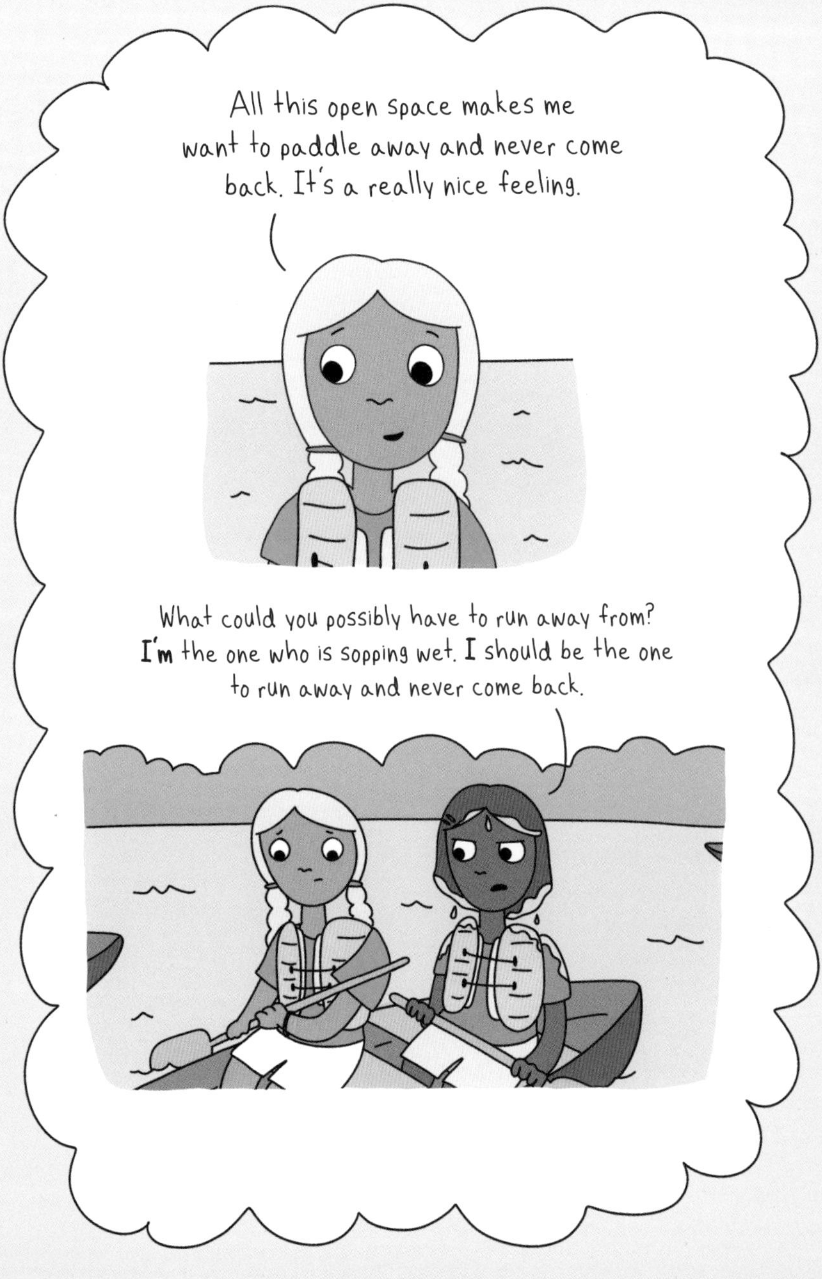
All this open space makes me want to paddle away and never come back. It's a really nice feeling.
What could you possibly have to run away from? **I'm** the one who is sopping wet. **I** should be the one to run away and never come back.

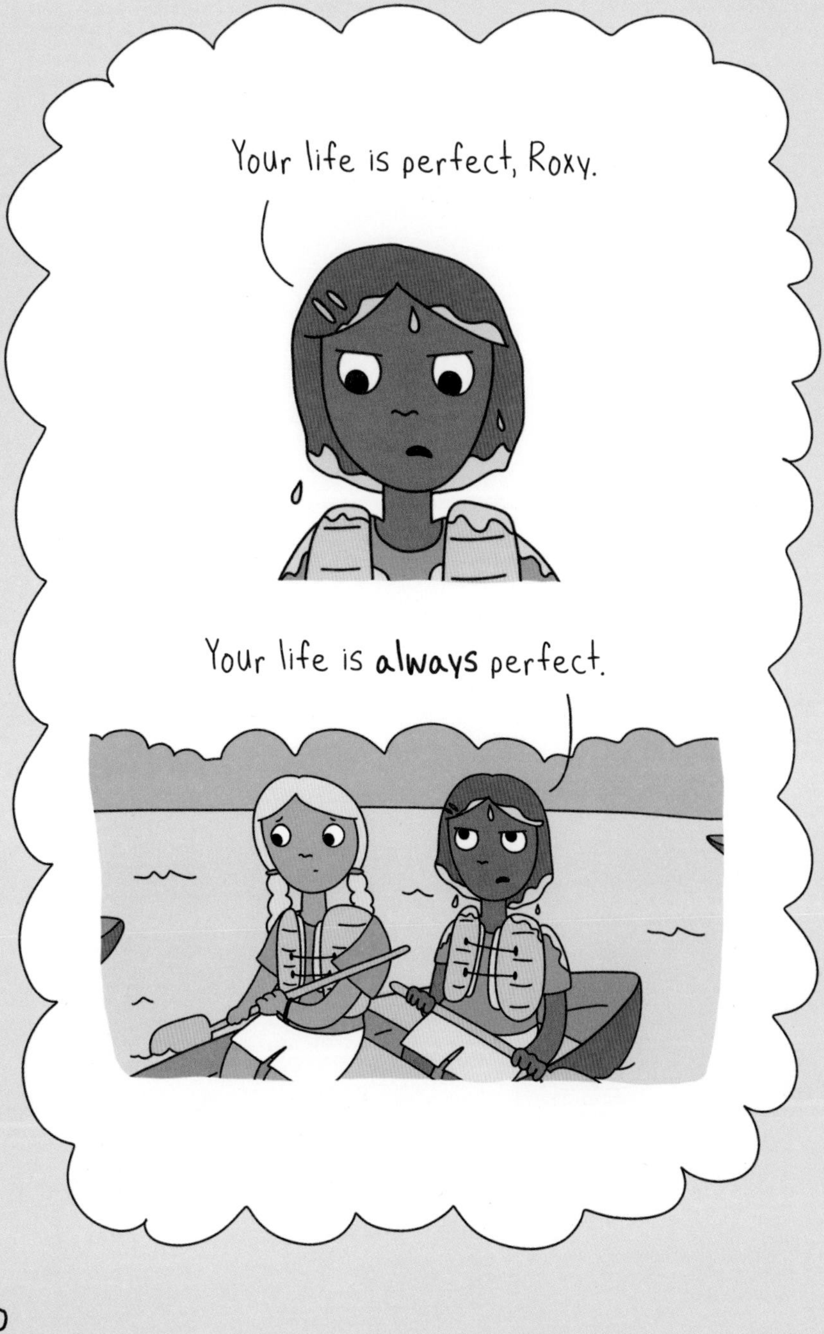
Your life is perfect, Roxy.
Your life is **always** perfect.

We have to check the lake!

CHAPTER 9

A LITTLE TO THE LEFT

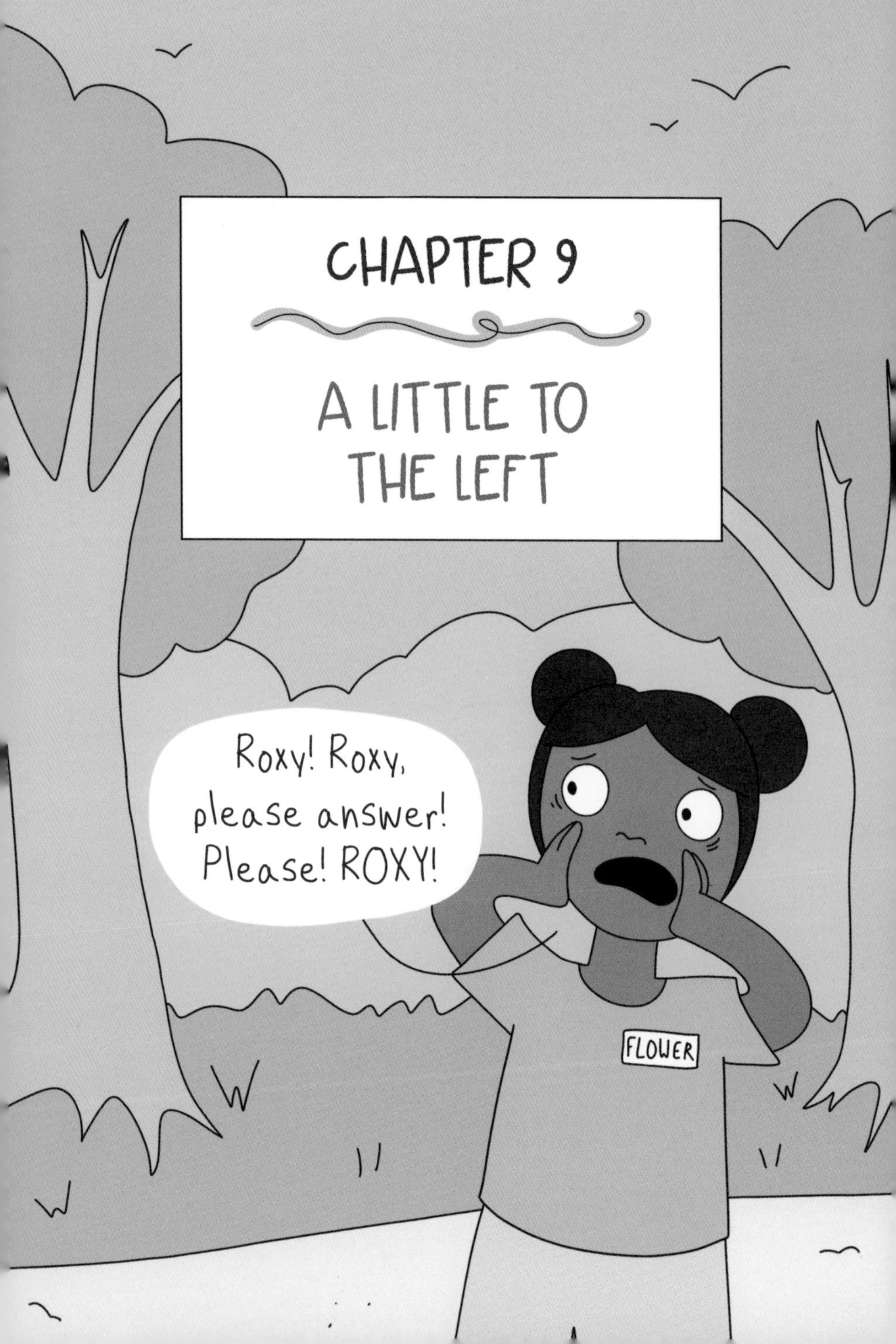
Roxy! Roxy, please answer! Please! ROXY!
FLOWER

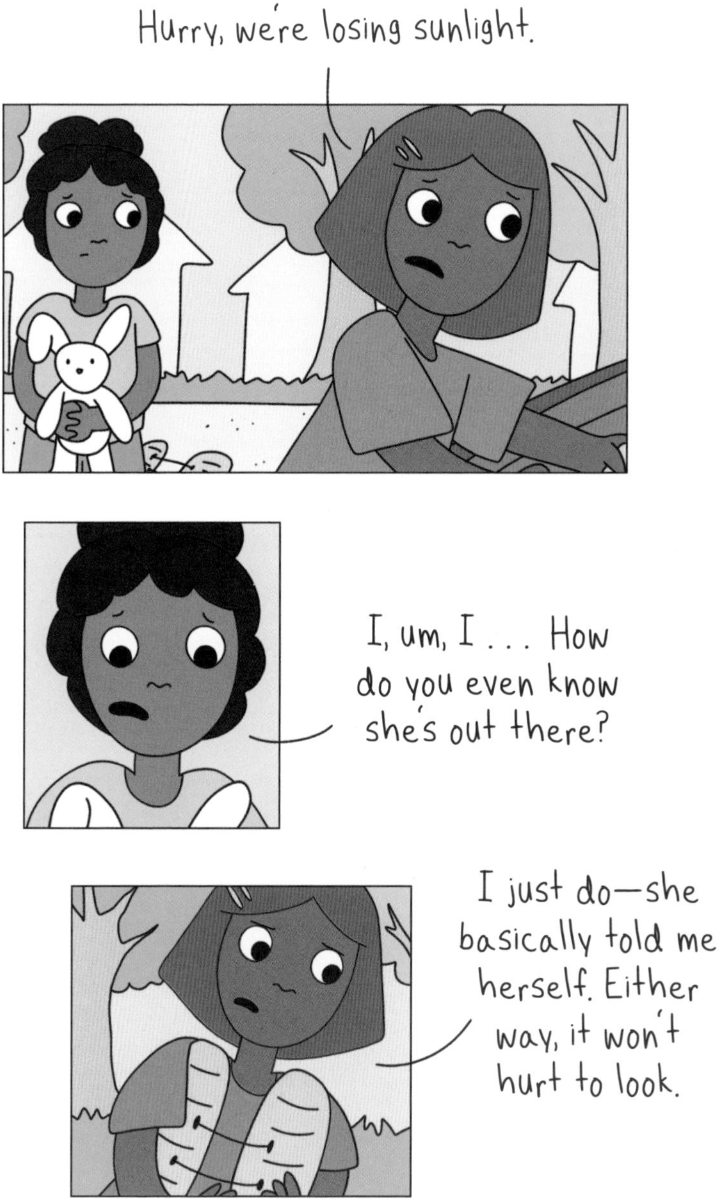
Hurry, we're losing sunlight.
I, um, I . . . How do you even know she's out there?
I just do—she basically told me herself. Either way, it won't hurt to look.

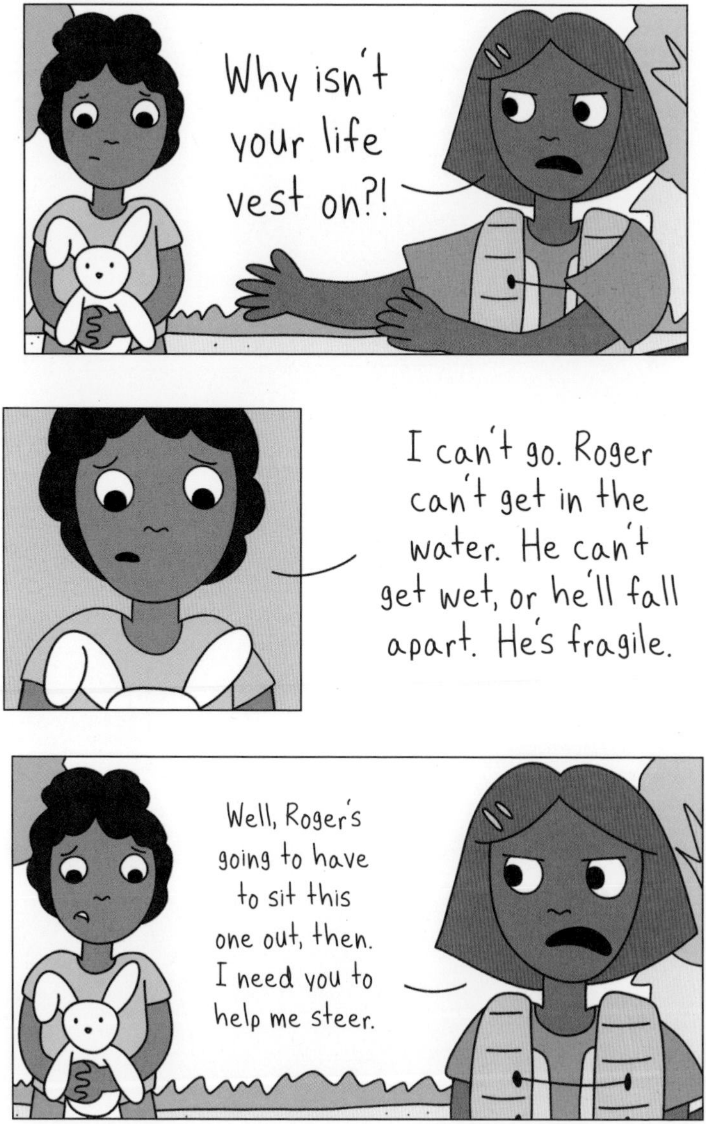
Why isn't your life vest on?!
I can't go. Roger can't get in the water. He can't get wet, or he'll fall apart. He's fragile.
Well, Roger's going to have to sit this one out, then. I need you to help me steer.

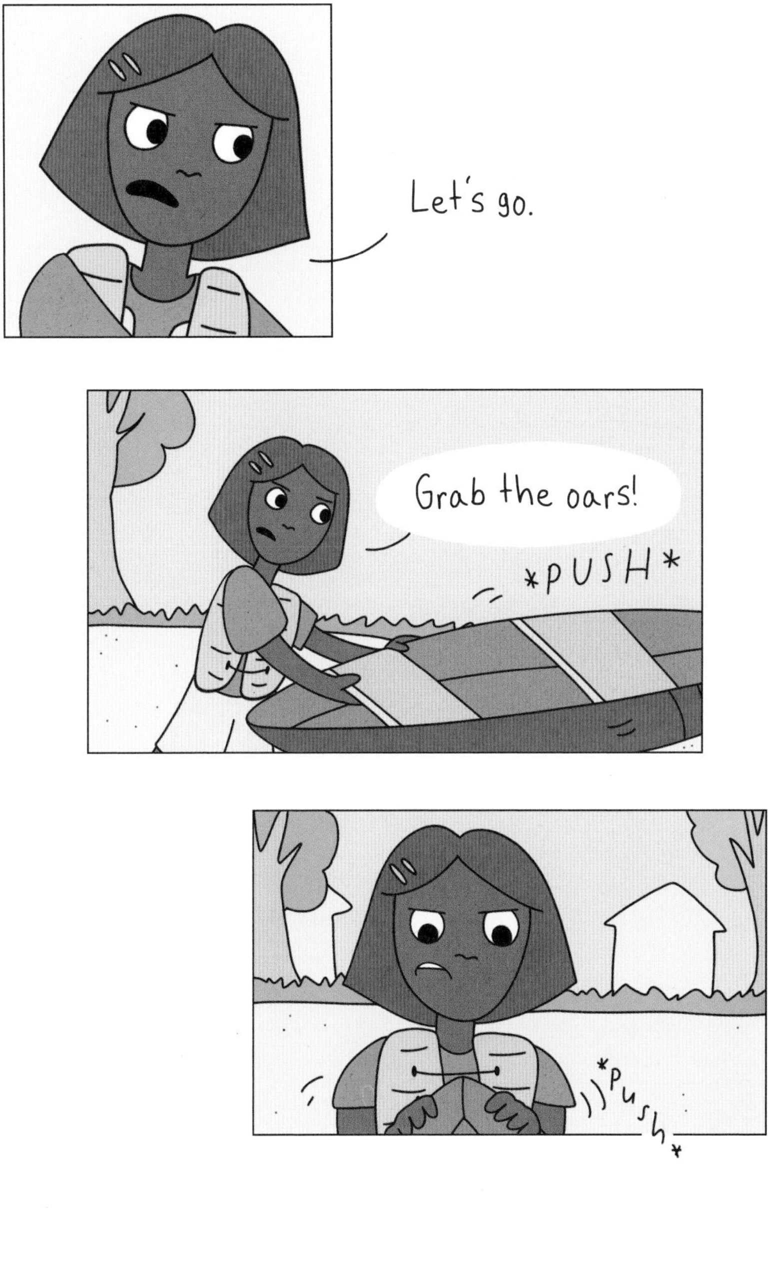
Let's go.
Grab the oars!
PUSH
Push

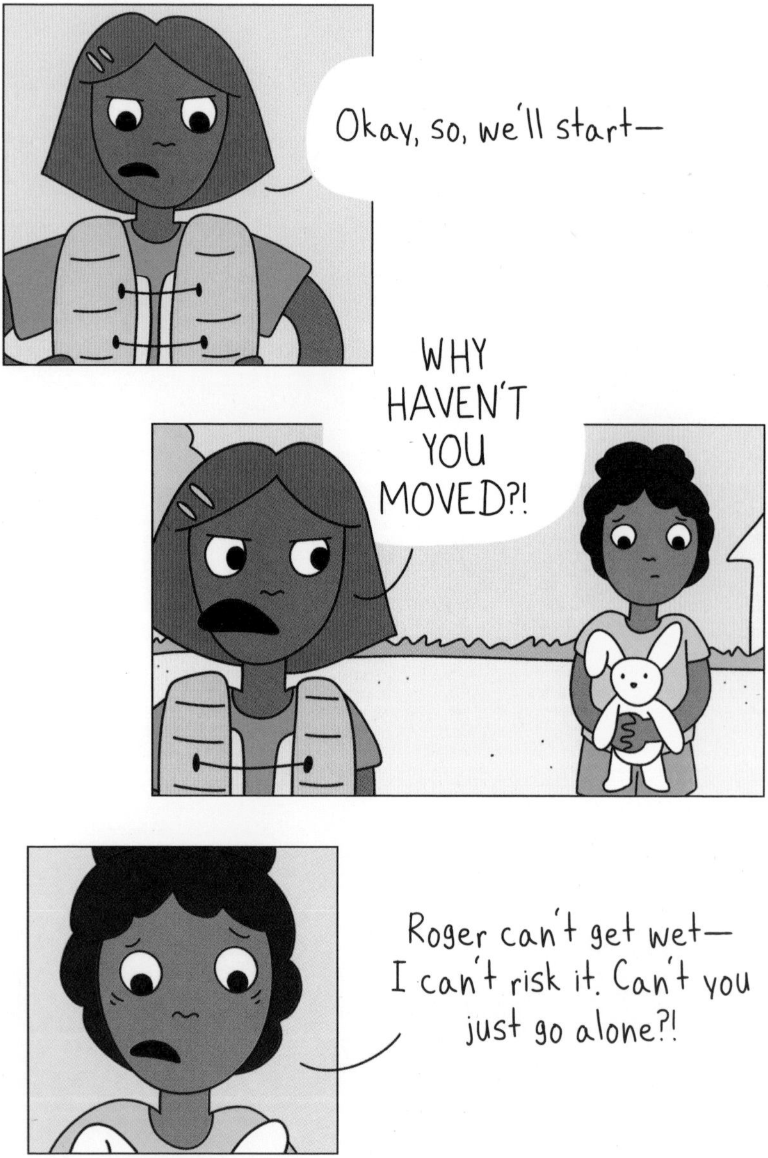
Okay, so, we'll start—
WHY HAVEN'T YOU MOVED?!
Roger can't get wet— I can't risk it. Can't you just go alone?!

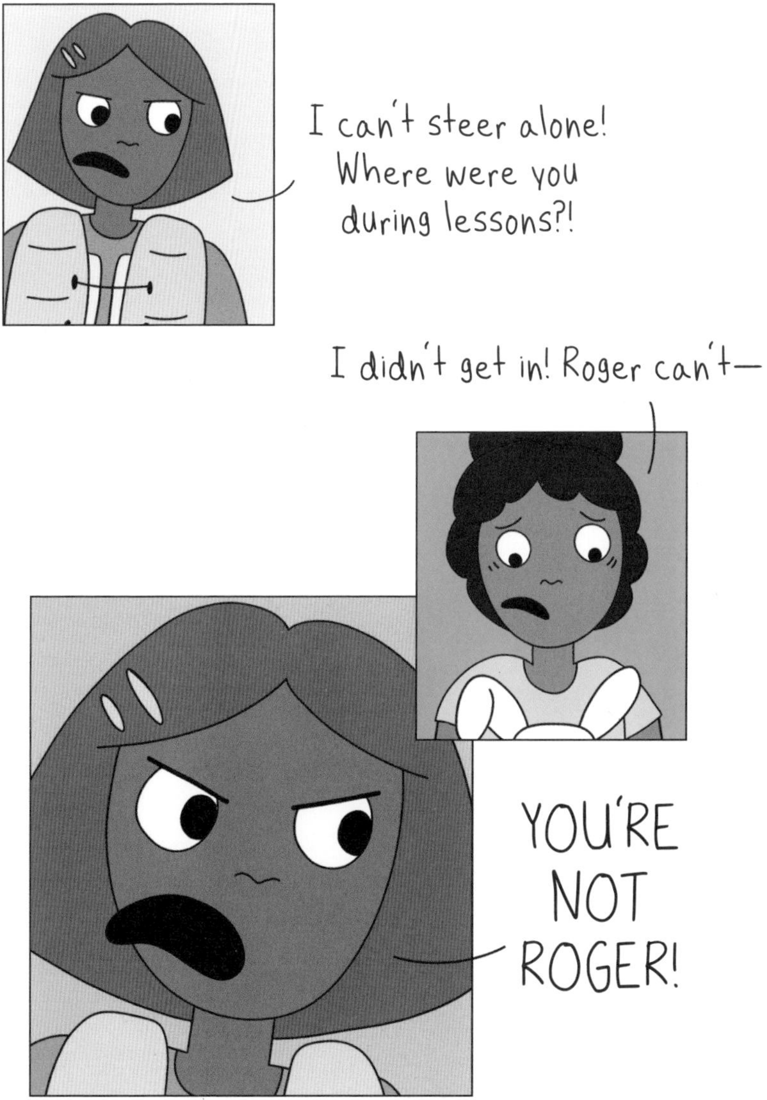
I can't steer alone! Where were you during lessons?!
I didn't get in! Roger can't—
YOU'RE NOT ROGER!

I KNOW THAT! But I can't just leave him here!

Yes, you can, because Roger is **a stuffed animal,** and Roxy, our living, breathing friend, could be in real trouble. I need you to help me steer.

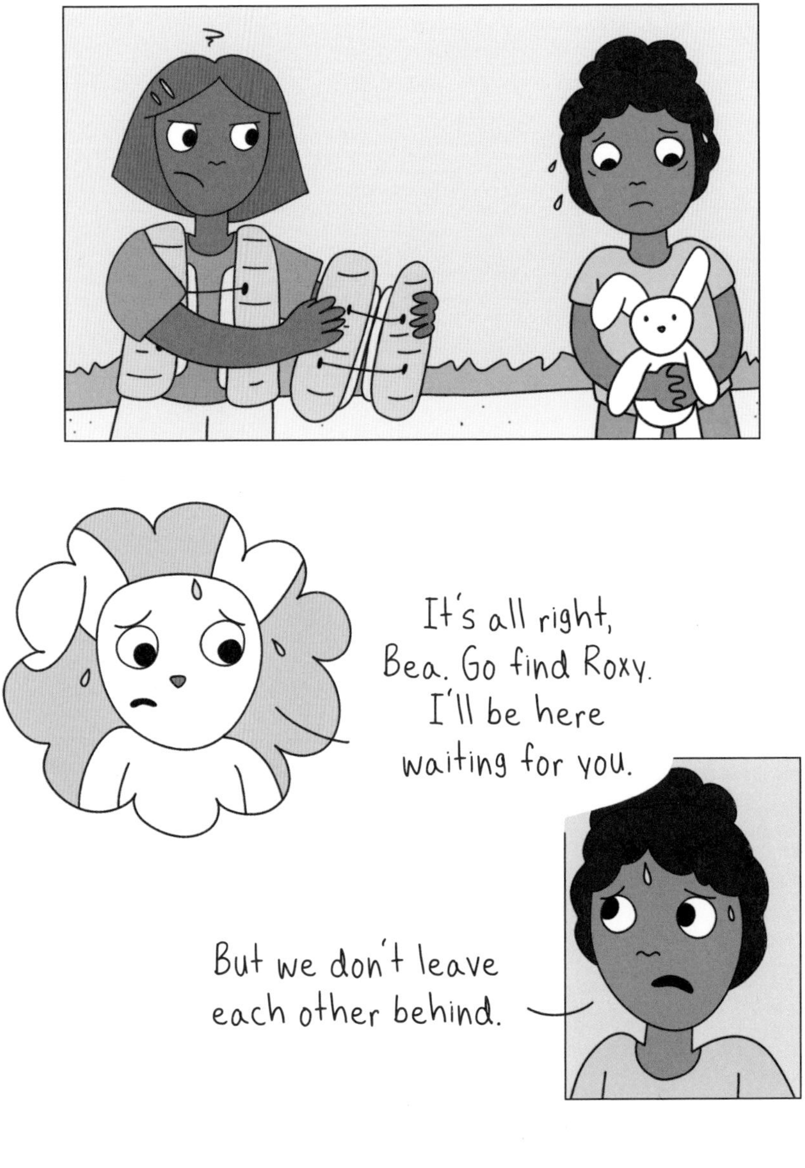
It's all right, Bea. Go find Roxy. I'll be here waiting for you.
But we don't leave each other behind.

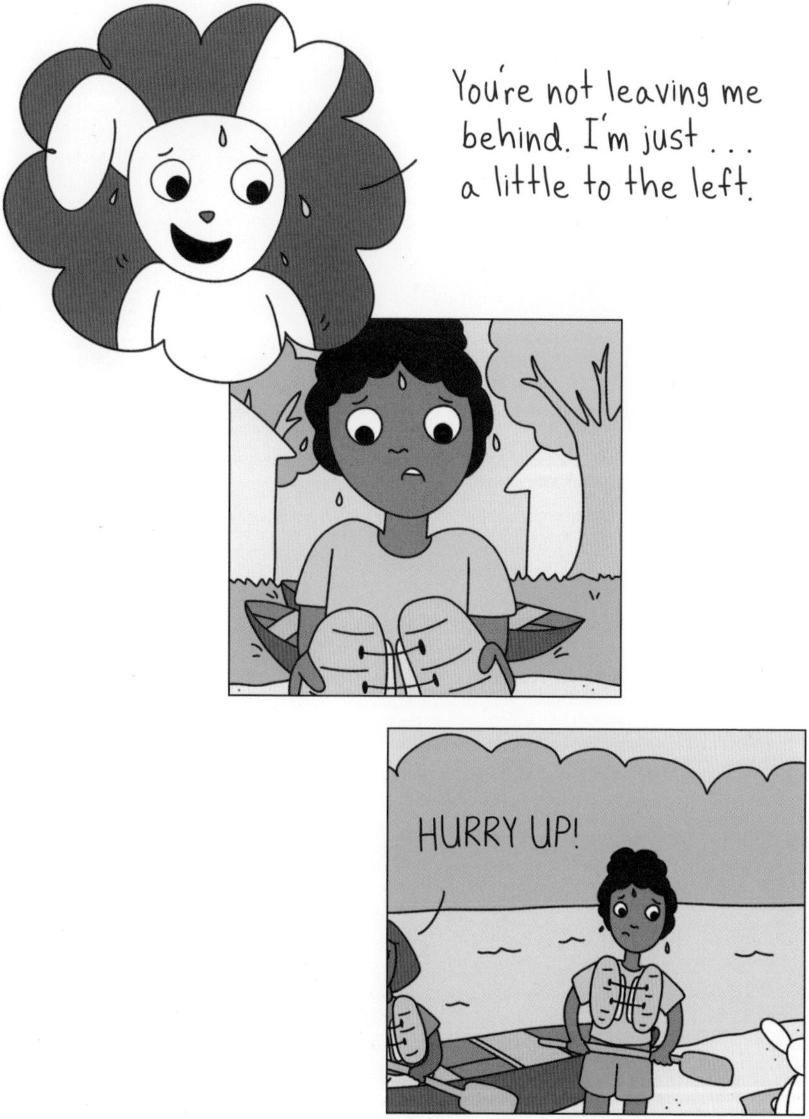
You're not leaving me behind. I'm just . . . a little to the left.
HURRY UP!

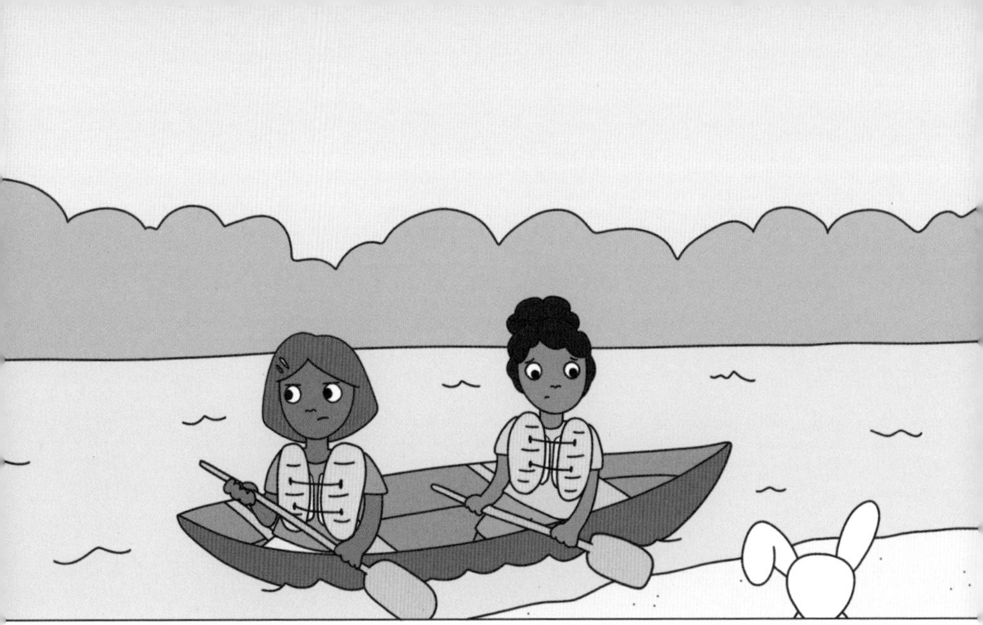

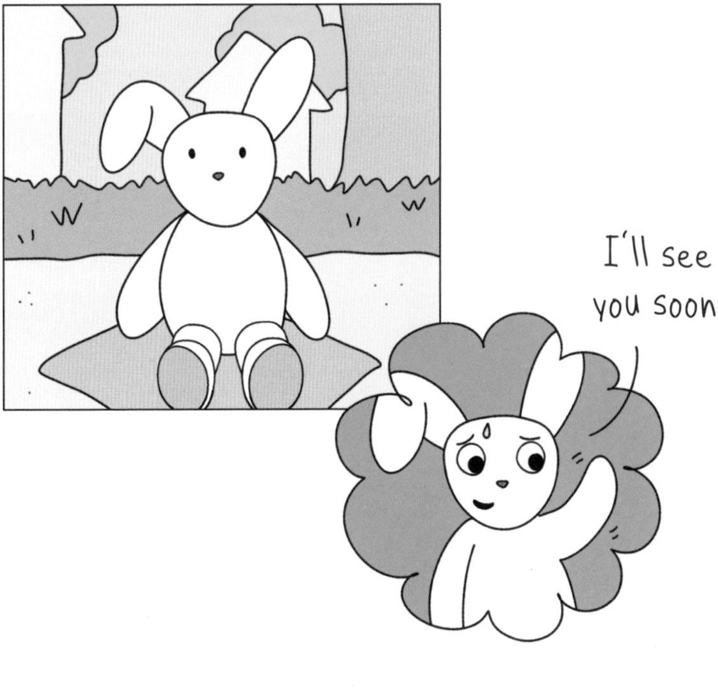
I'll see you soon.

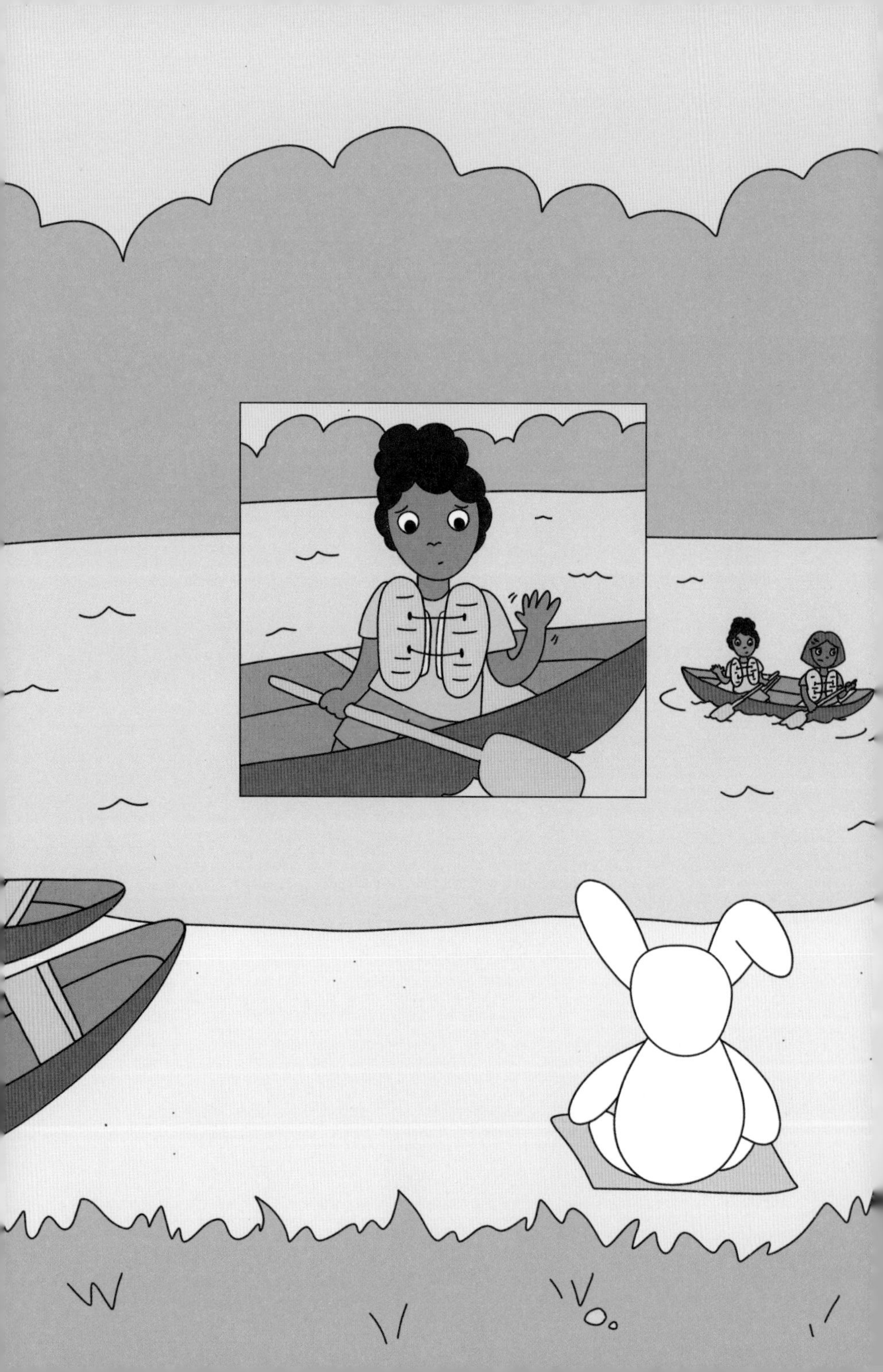

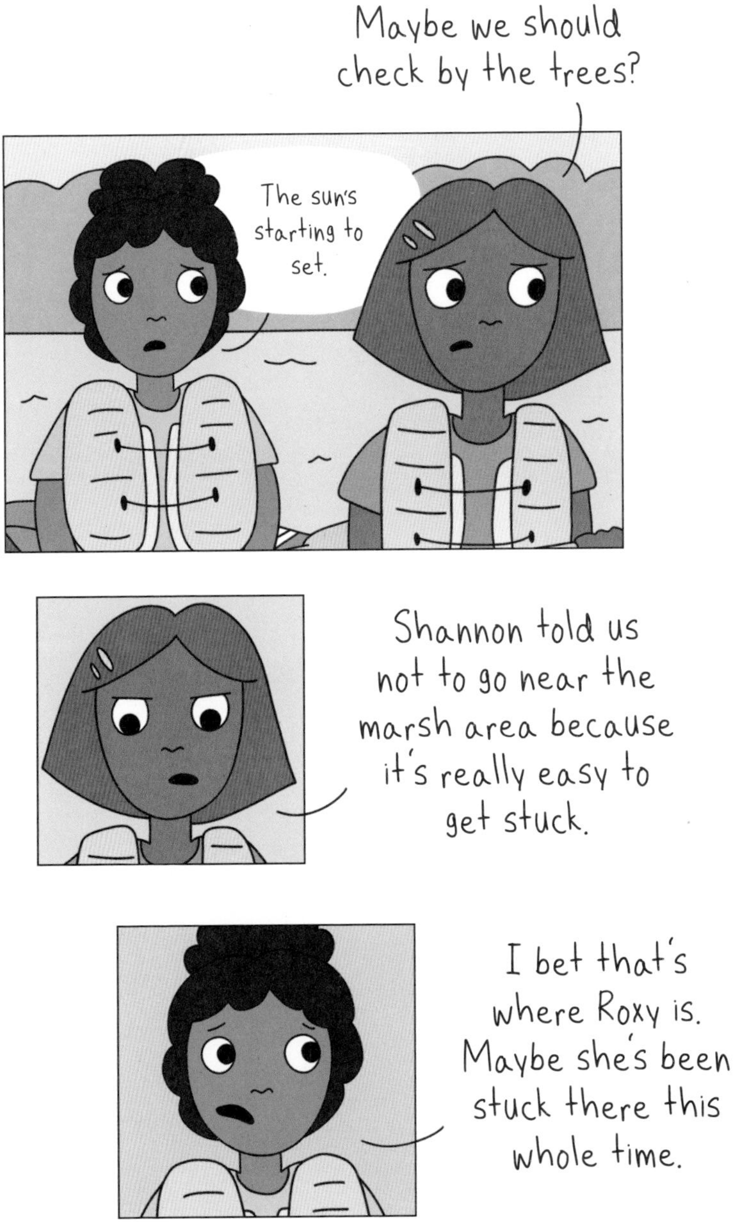
Maybe we should check by the trees?
The sun's starting to set.
Shannon told us not to go near the marsh area because it's really easy to get stuck.
I bet that's where Roxy is. Maybe she's been stuck there this whole time.

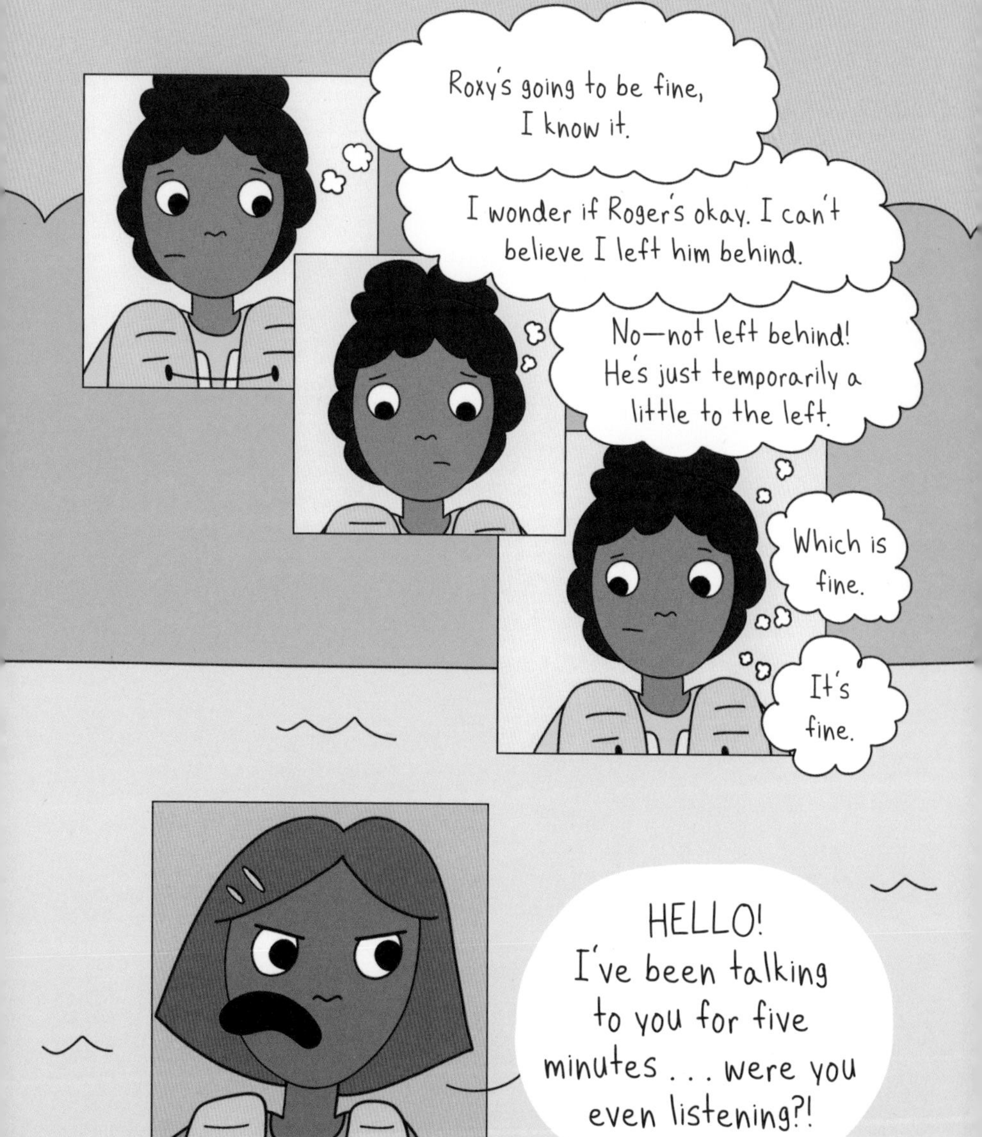
Roxy's going to be fine, I know it.
I wonder if Roger's okay. I can't believe I left him behind.
No—not left behind! He's just temporarily a little to the left.
Which is fine.
It's fine.
HELLO! I've been talking to you for five minutes . . . were you even listening?!

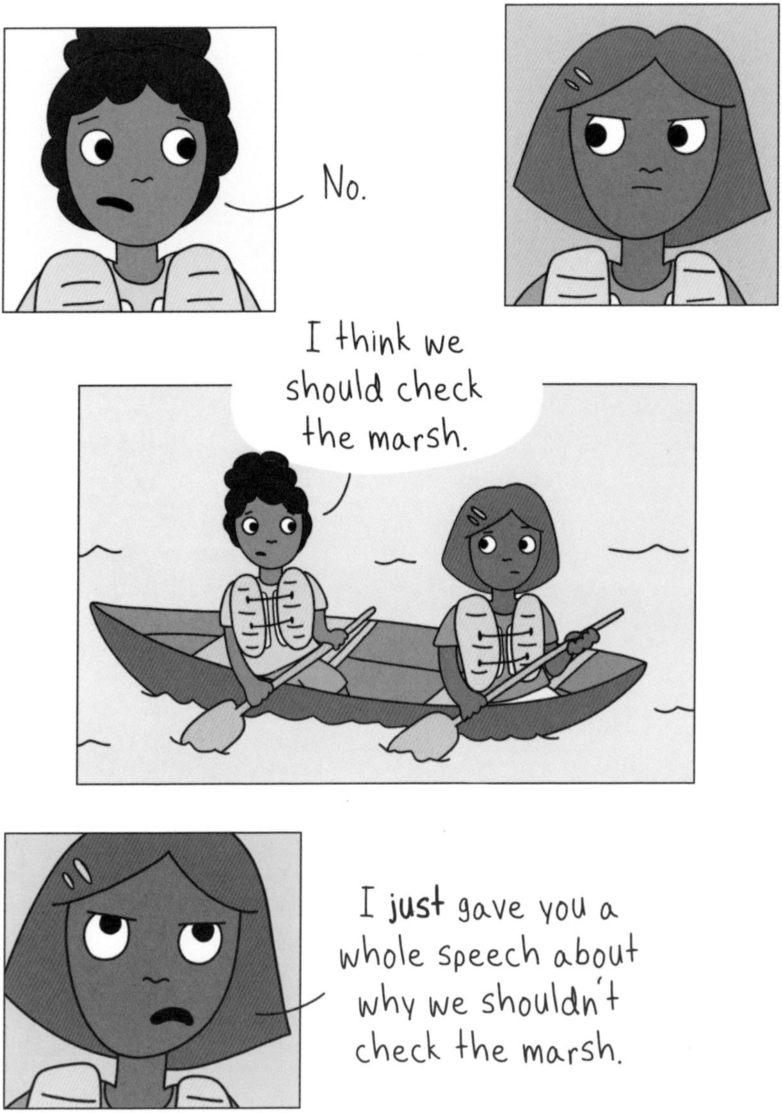
No.
I think we should check the marsh.
I **just** gave you a whole speech about why we shouldn't check the marsh.

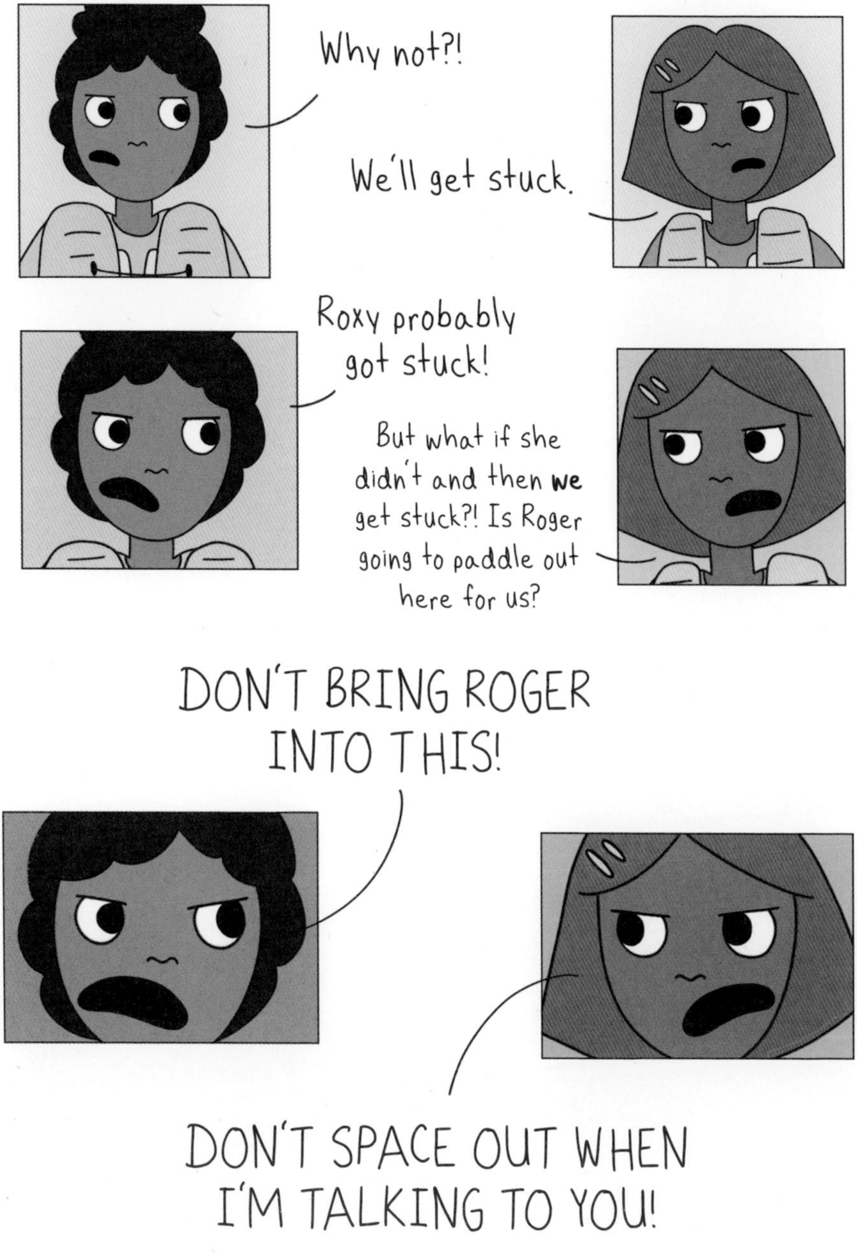
Why not?!
We'll get stuck.
Roxy probably got stuck!
But what if she didn't and then **we** get stuck?! Is Roger going to paddle out here for us?
DON'T BRING ROGER INTO THIS!
DON'T SPACE OUT WHEN I'M TALKING TO YOU!

Can you just trust me?

Please?

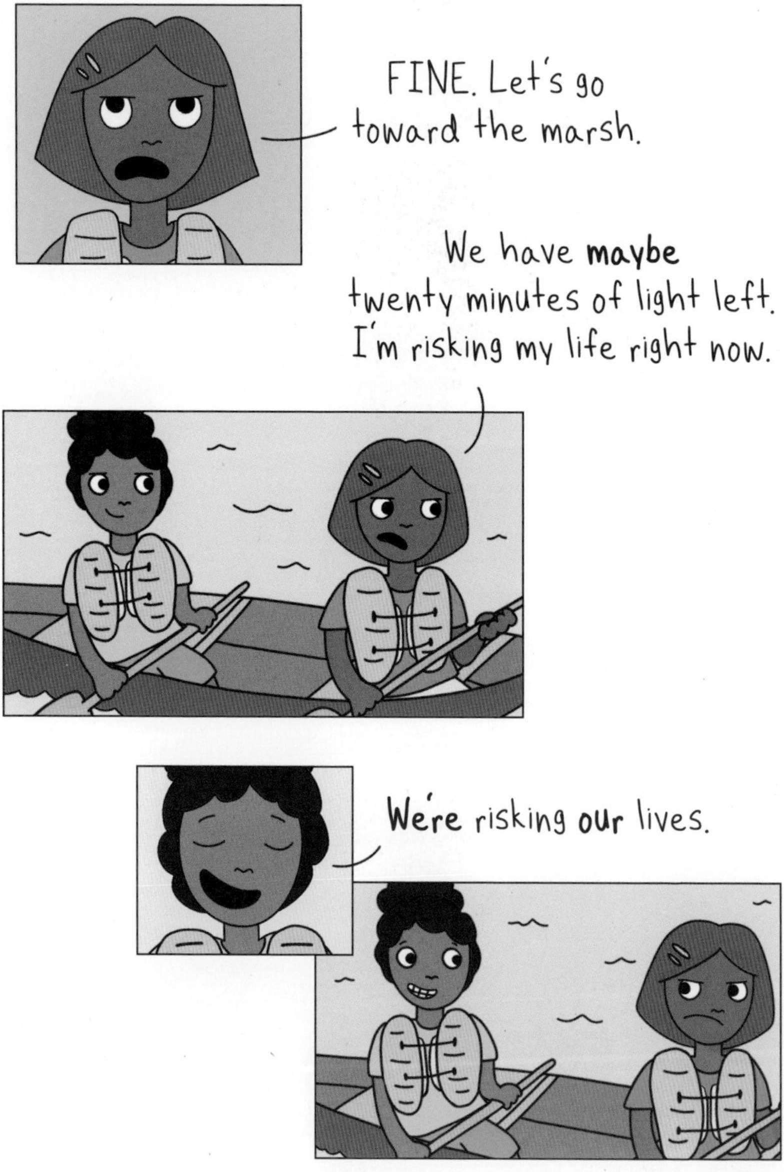
FINE. Let's go toward the marsh.
We have **maybe** twenty minutes of light left. I'm risking my life right now.
We're risking **our** lives.

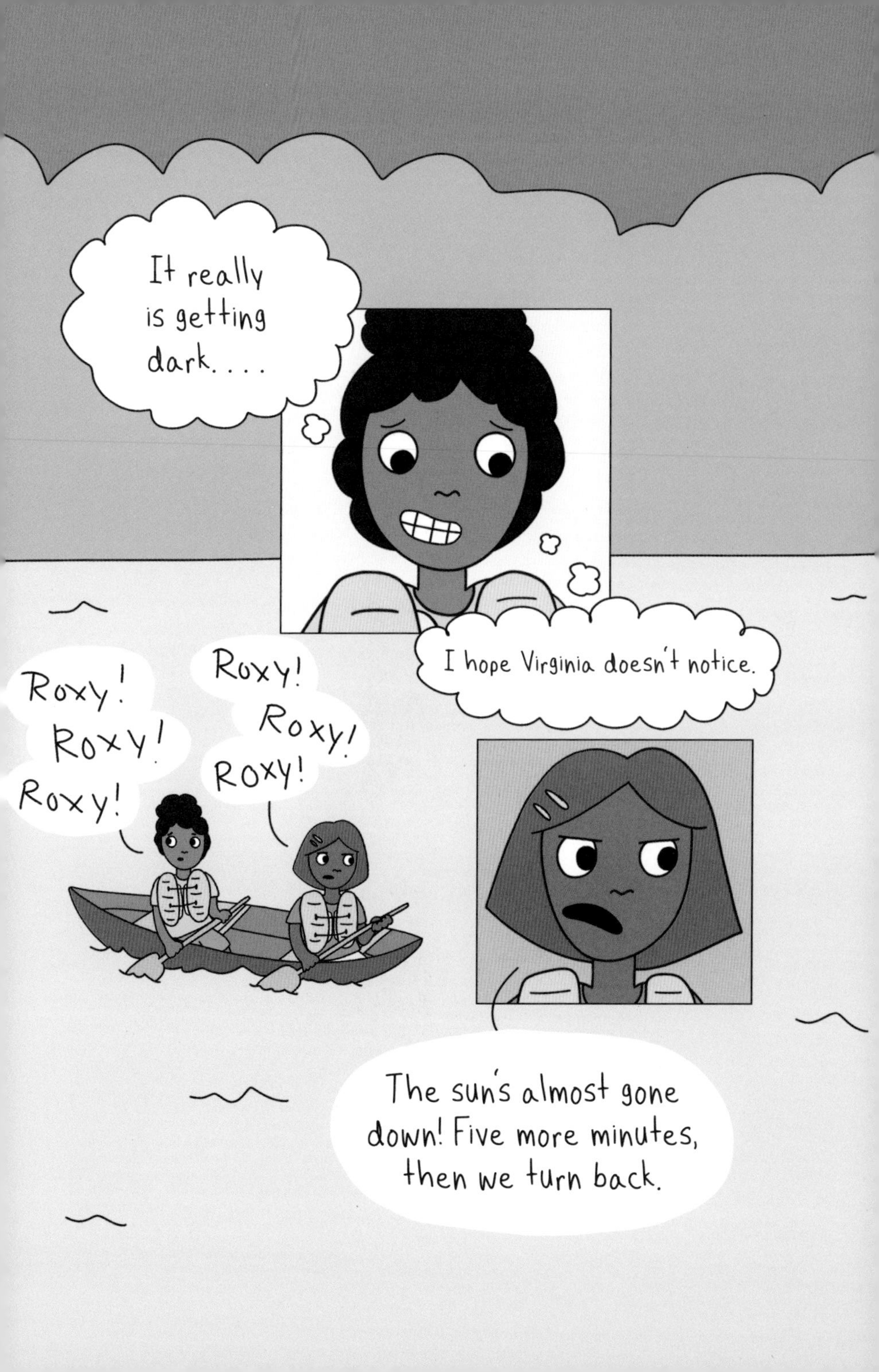
It really is getting dark. . . .
I hope Virginia doesn't notice.
Roxy! Roxy! Roxy!
Roxy! Roxy! ROXY!
The sun's almost gone down! Five more minutes, then we turn back.

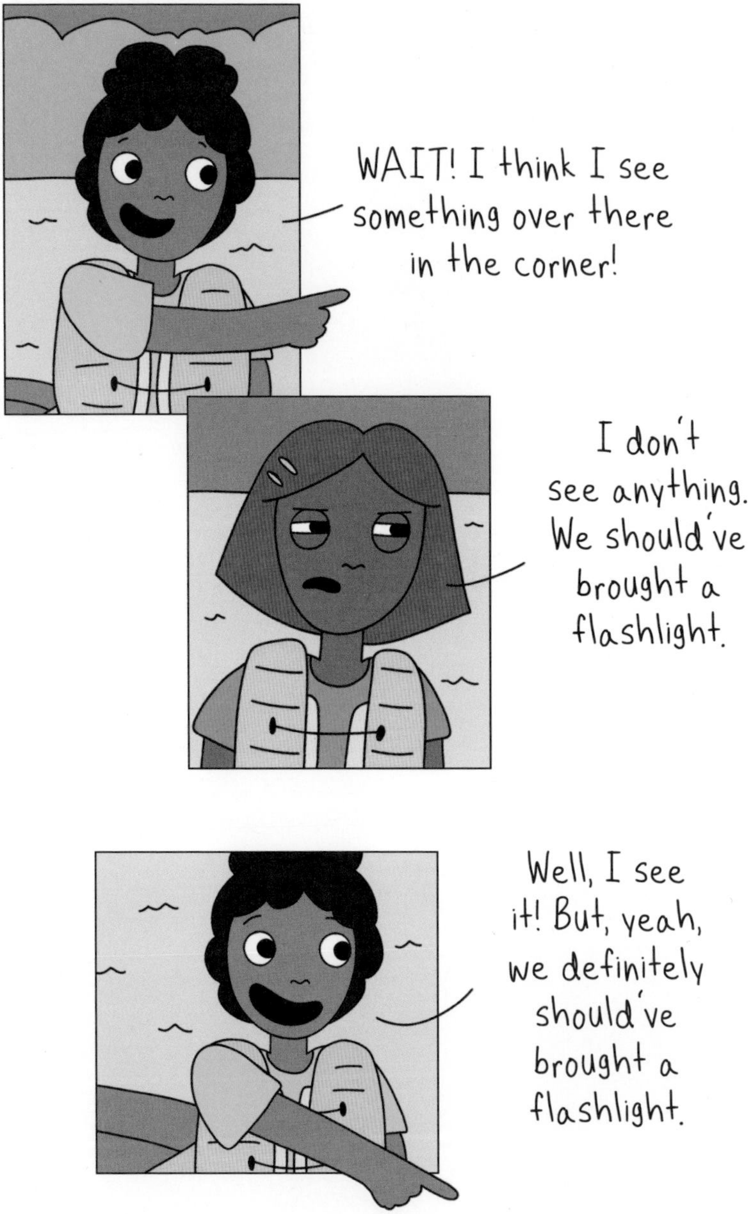
WAIT! I think I see something over there in the corner!
I don't see anything. We should've brought a flashlight.
Well, I see it! But, yeah, we definitely should've brought a flashlight.

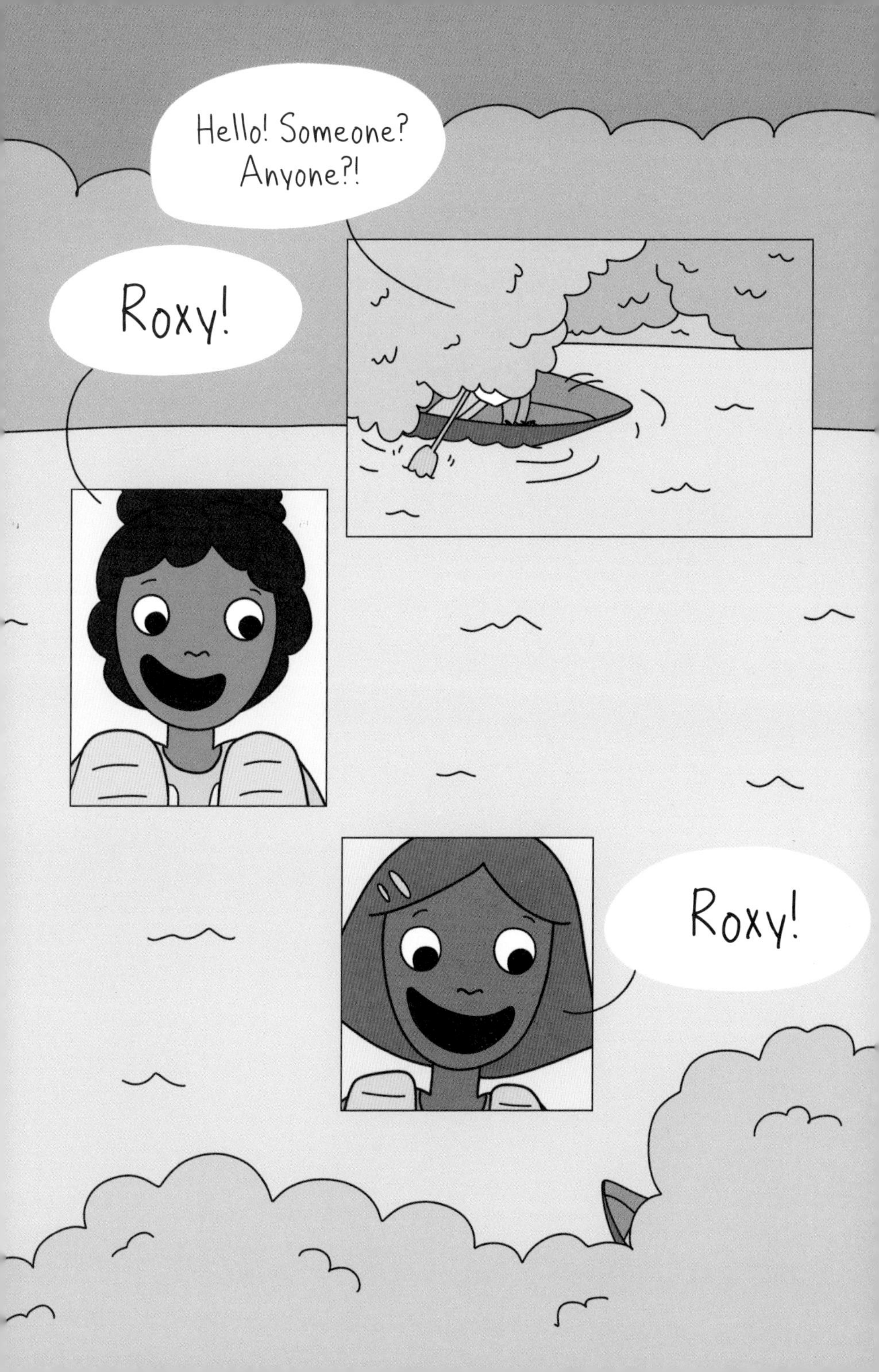
Hello! Someone? Anyone?!
Roxy!
Roxy!

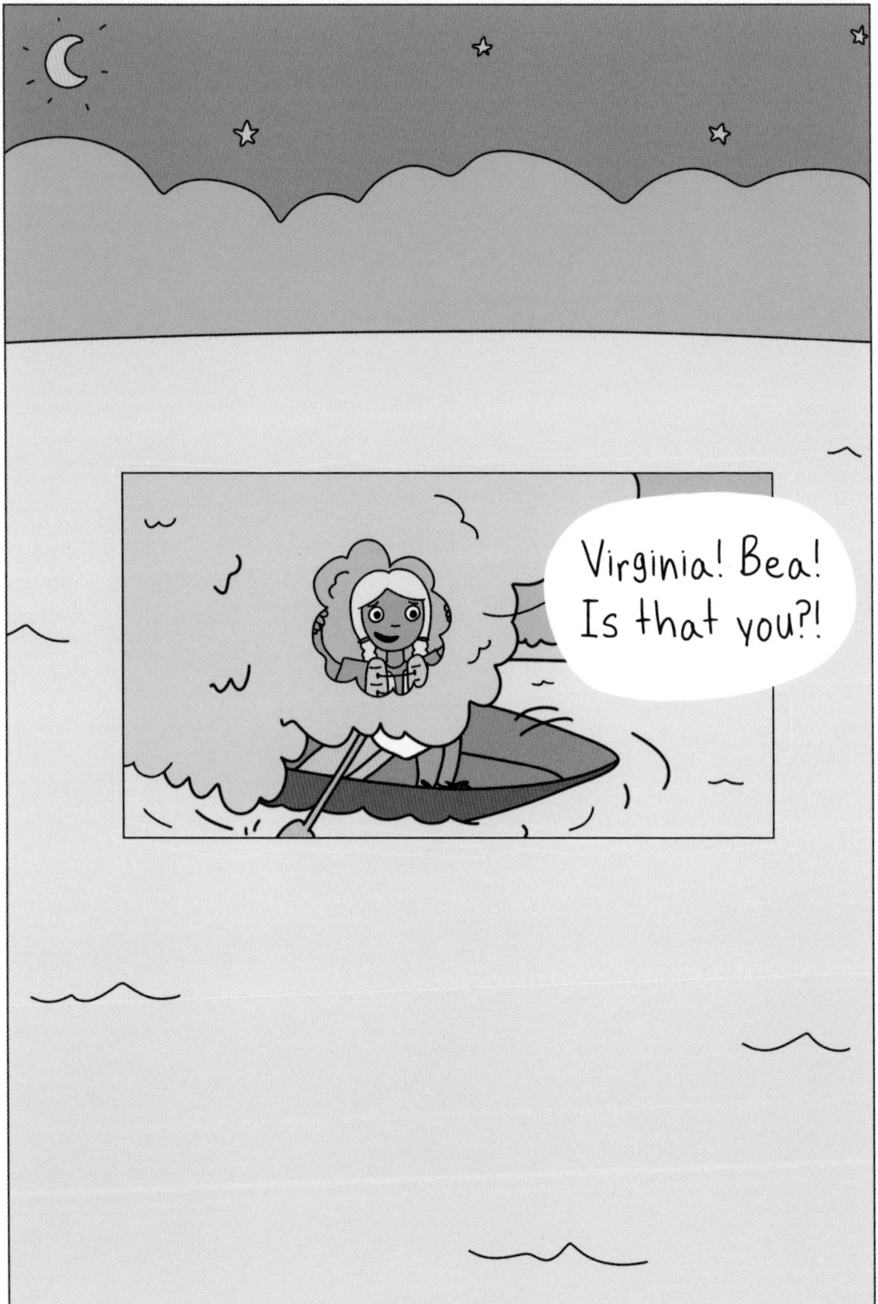
Virginia! Bea! Is that you?!

CHAPTER 10

PLEASE DON'T HATE ME

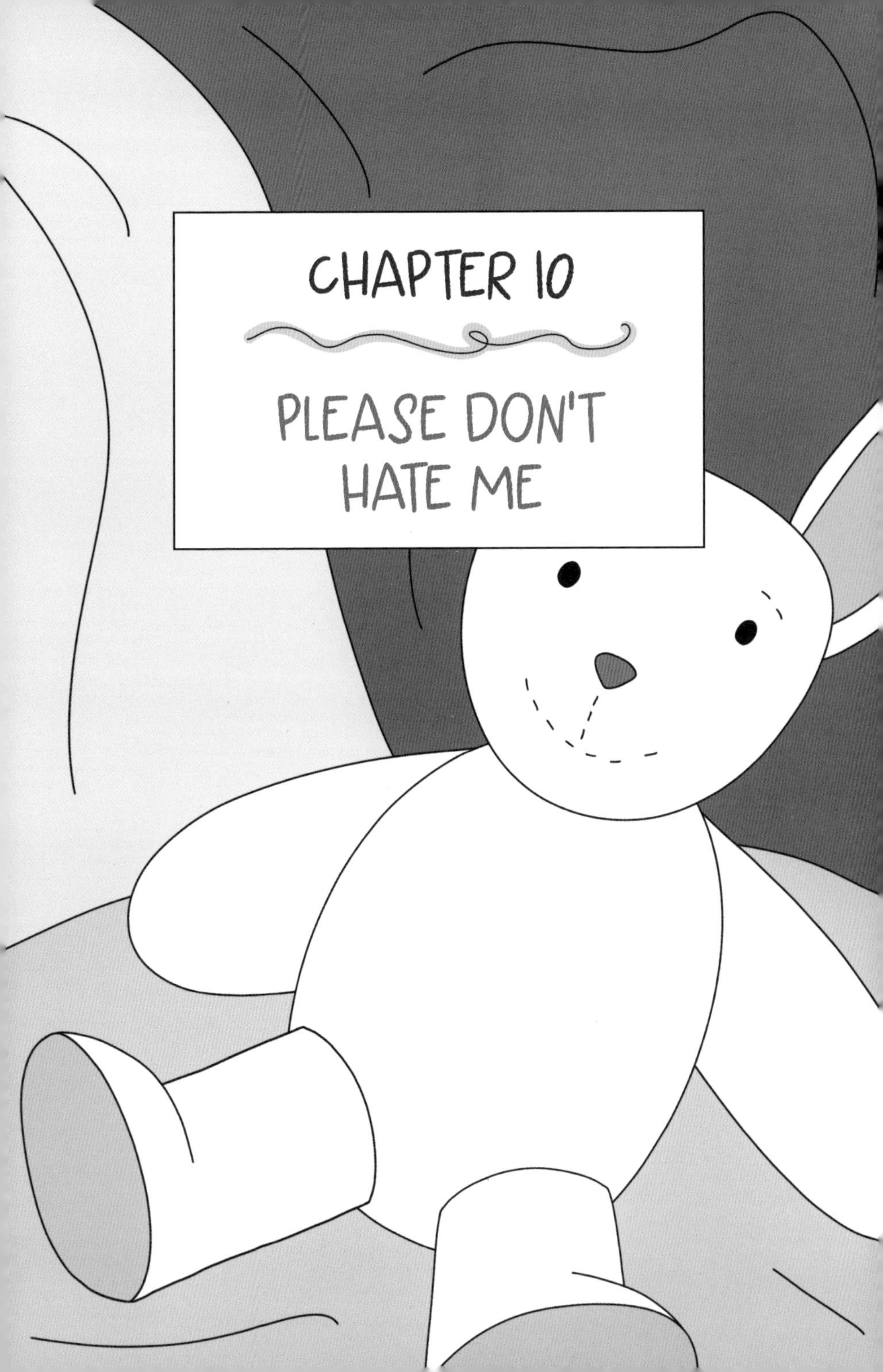

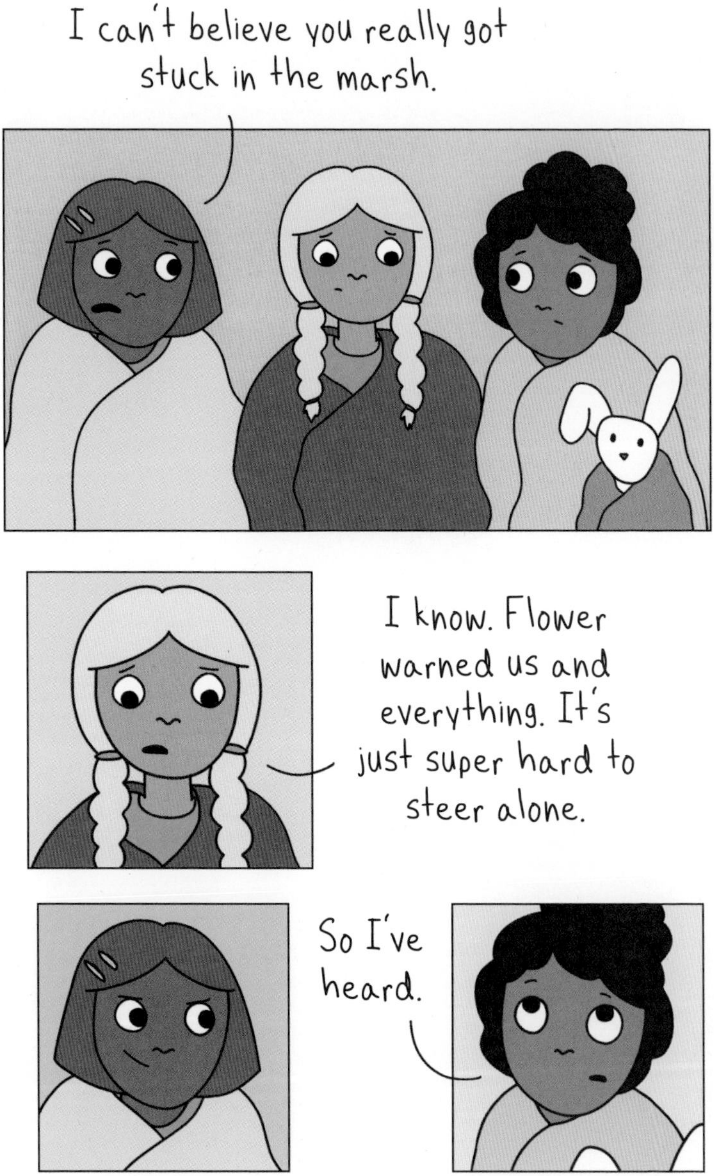
I can't believe you really got stuck in the marsh.
I know. Flower warned us and everything. It's just super hard to steer alone.
So I've heard.

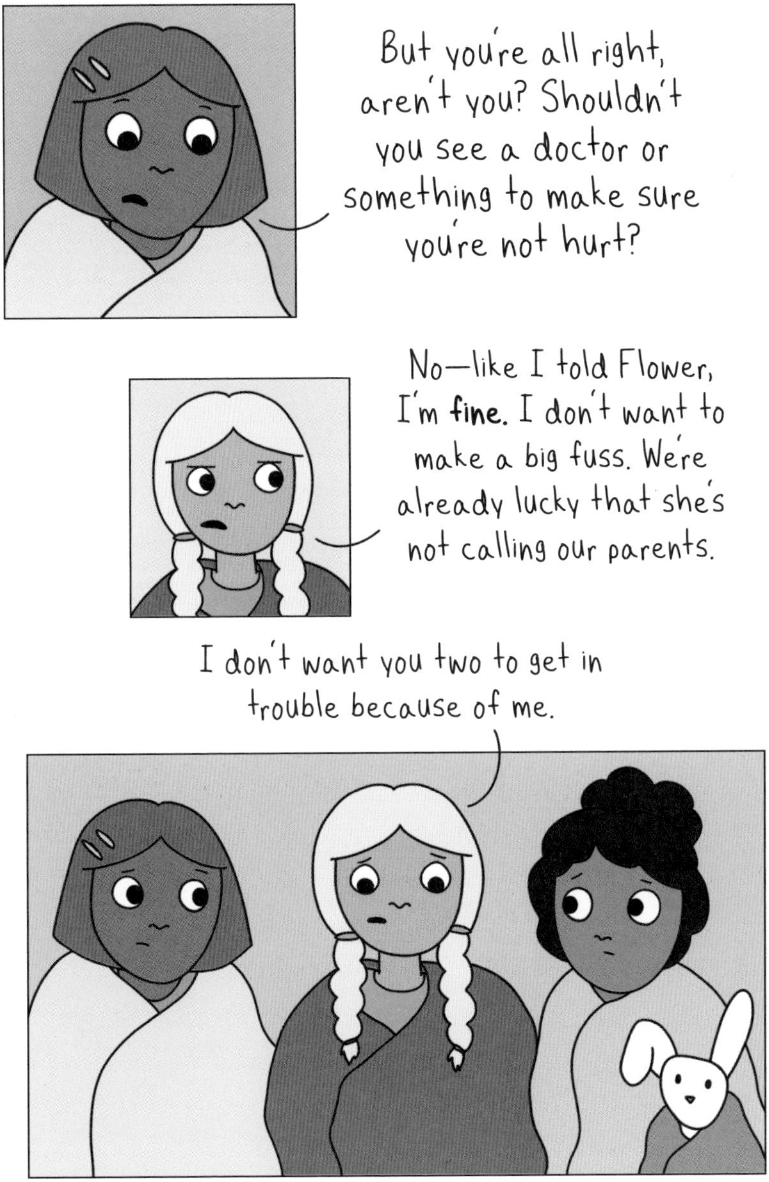
But you're all right, aren't you? Shouldn't you see a doctor or something to make sure you're not hurt?
No—like I told Flower, I'm **fine.** I don't want to make a big fuss. We're already lucky that she's not calling our parents.
I don't want you two to get in trouble because of me.

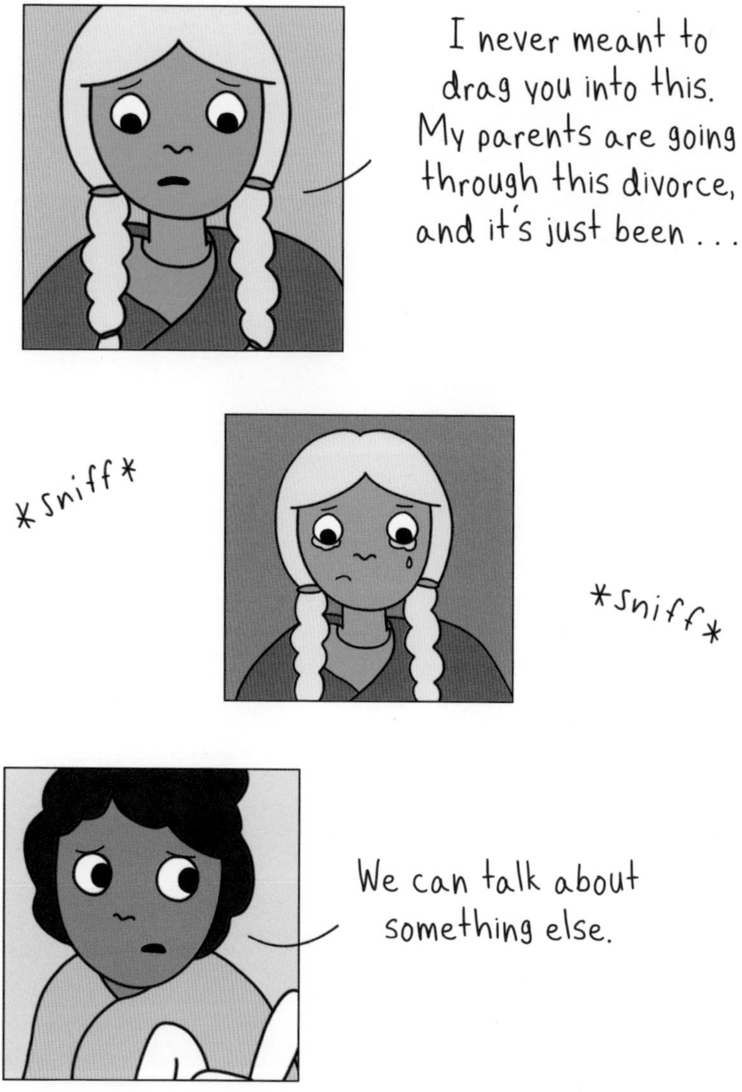
I never meant to drag you into this. My parents are going through this divorce, and it's just been . . .
sniff
sniff
We can talk about something else.

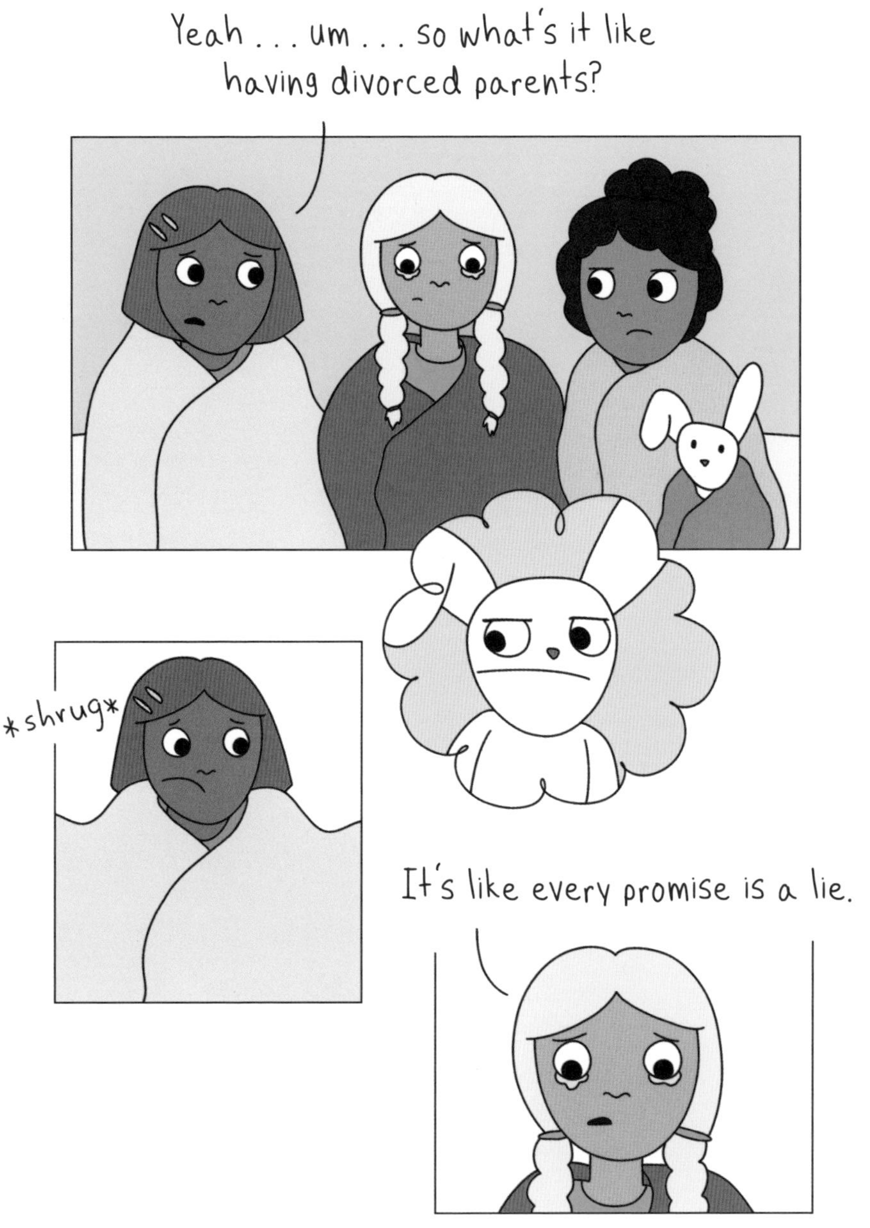
Yeah . . . um . . . so what's it like having divorced parents?
shrug
It's like every promise is a lie.

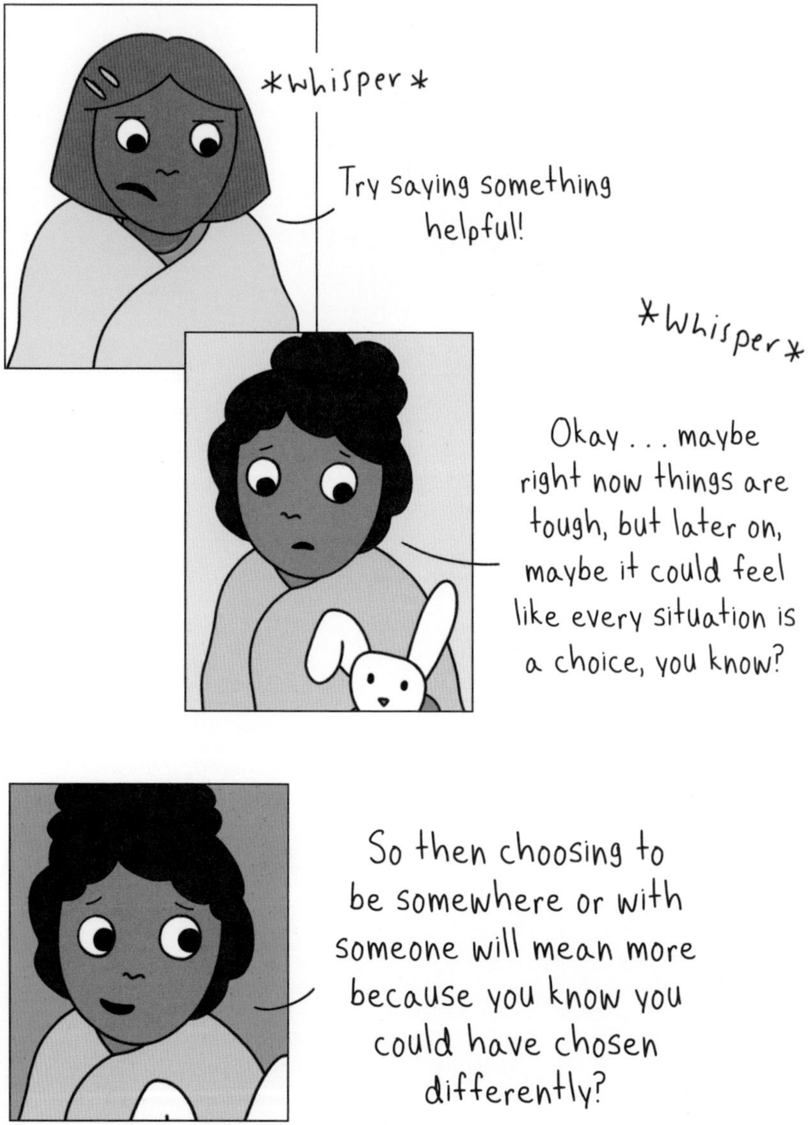
whisper
Try saying something helpful!
Whisper
Okay . . . maybe right now things are tough, but later on, maybe it could feel like every situation is a choice, you know?
So then choosing to be somewhere or with someone will mean more because you know you could have chosen differently?

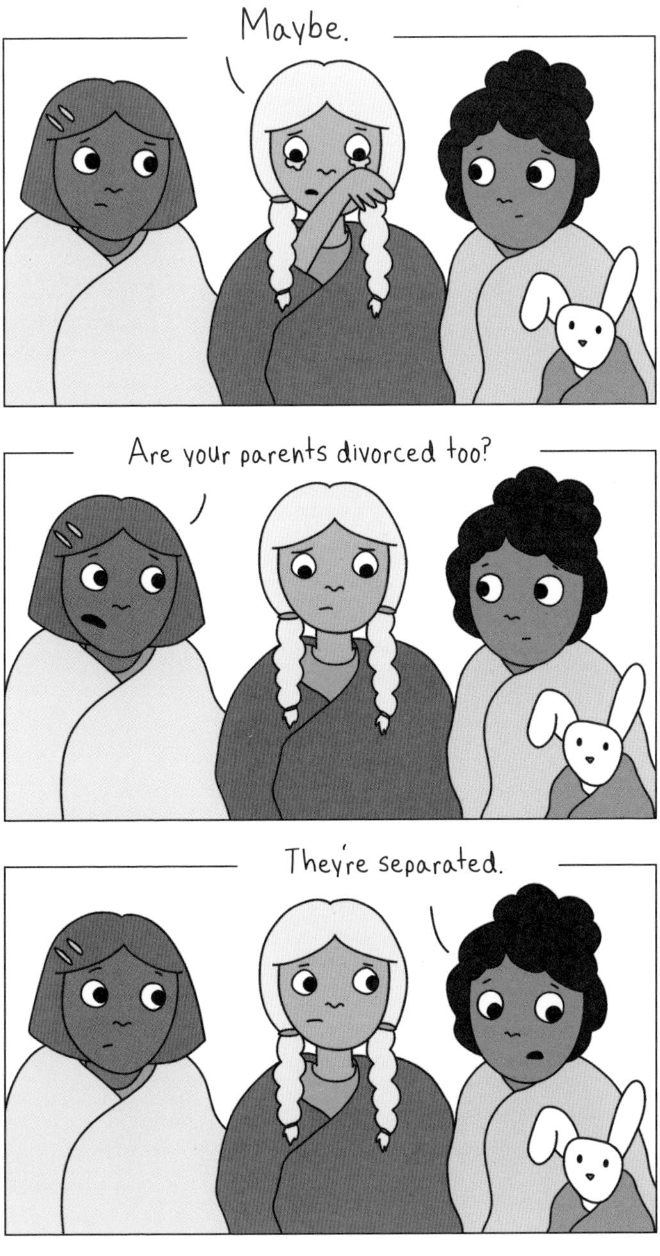
Maybe.
Are your parents divorced too?
They're separated.

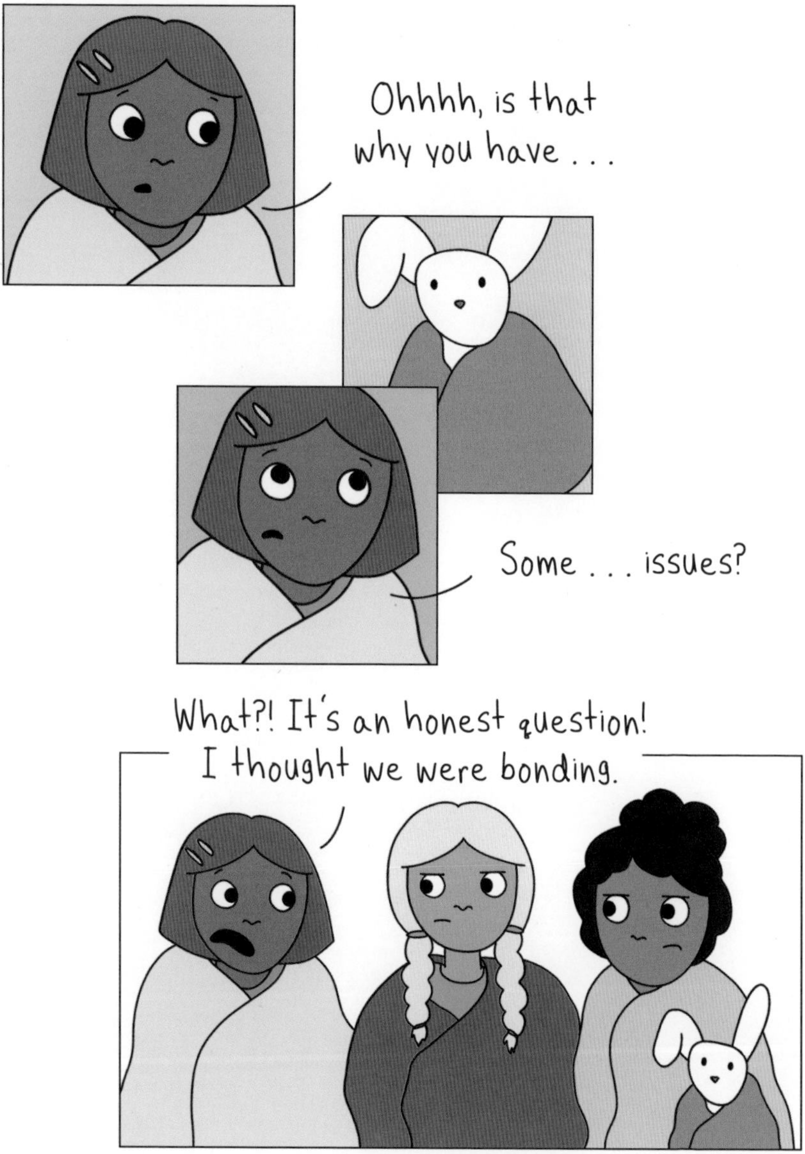
Ohhhh, is that why you have . . .
Some . . . issues?
What?! It's an honest question! I thought we were bonding.

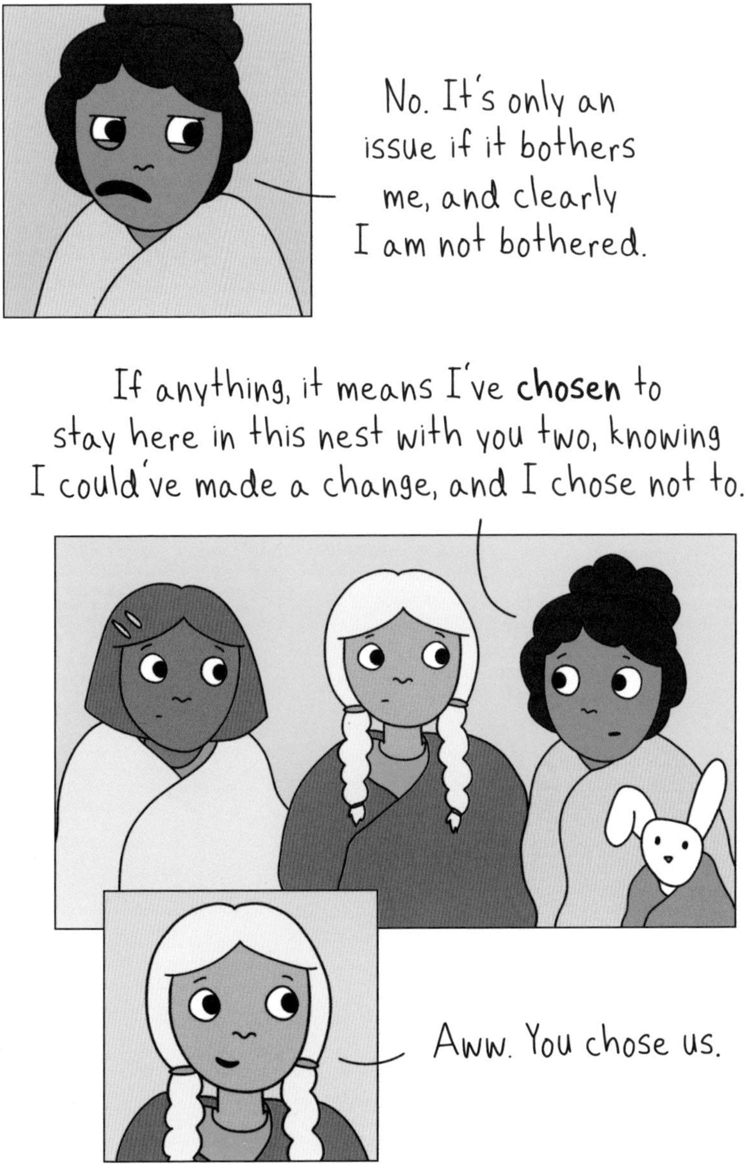
No. It's only an issue if it bothers me, and clearly I am not bothered.
If anything, it means I've **chosen** to stay here in this nest with you two, knowing I could've made a change, and I chose not to.
Aww. You chose us.

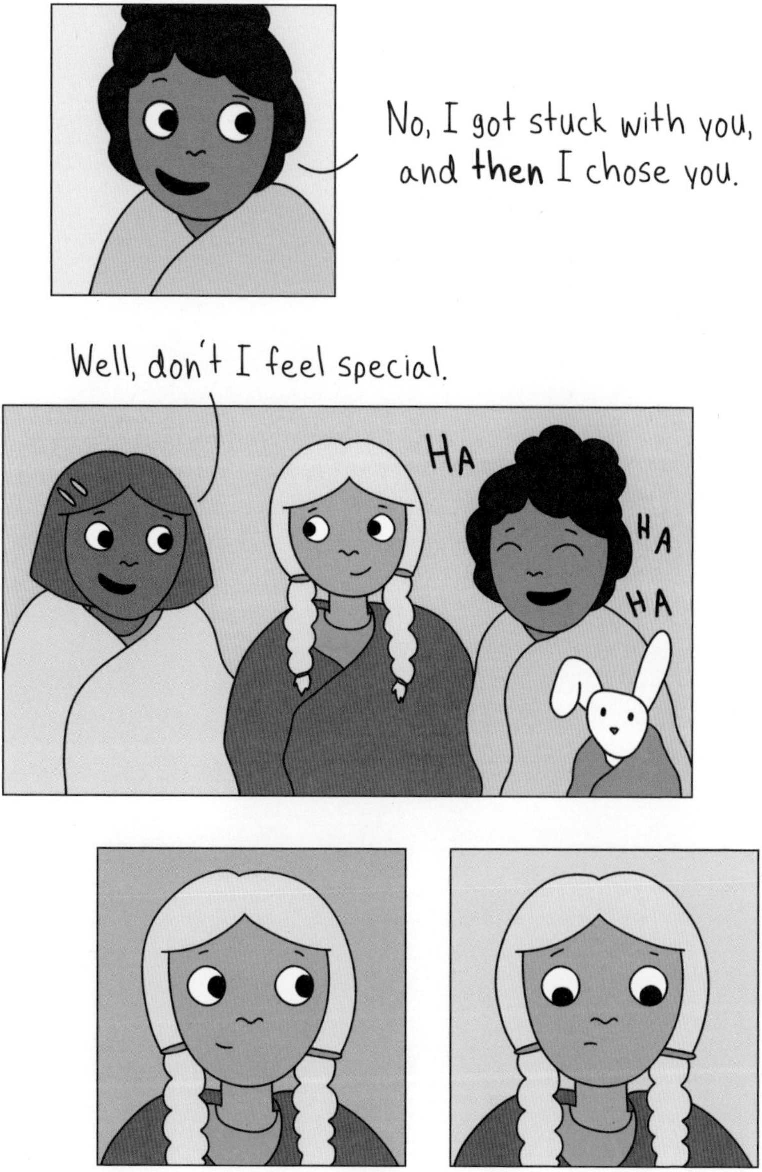
No, I got stuck with you, and **then** I chose you.
Well, don't I feel special.
HA
HA
HA

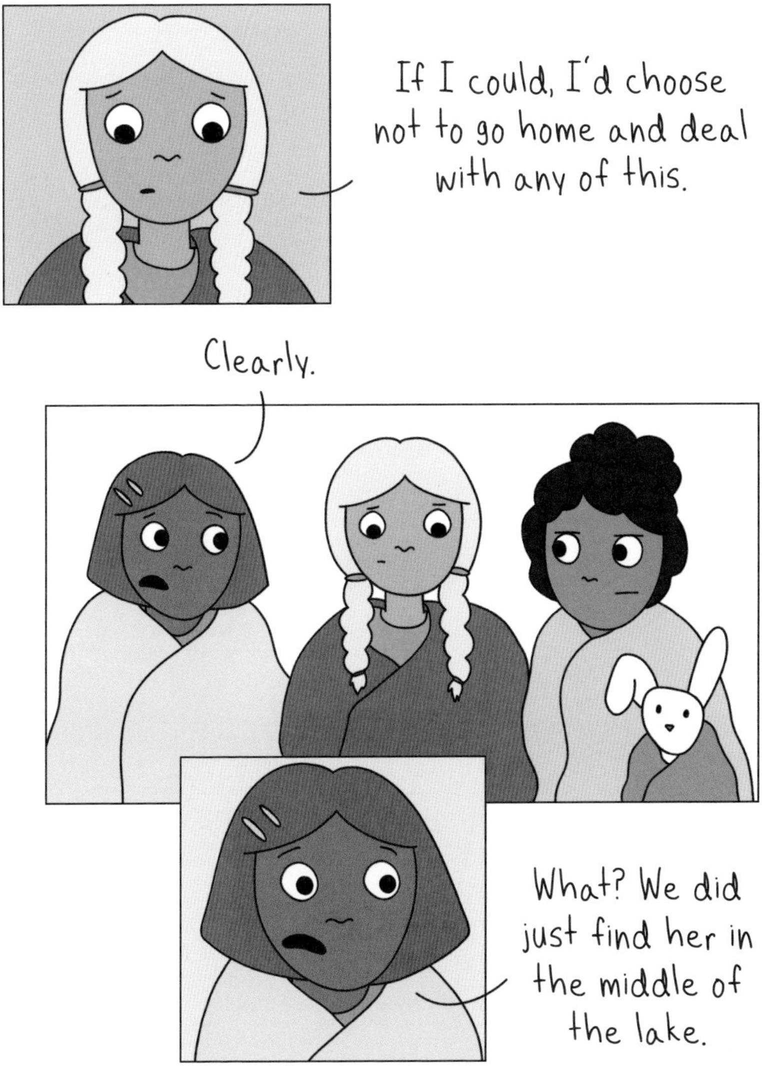
If I could, I'd choose not to go home and deal with any of this.
Clearly.
What? We did just find her in the middle of the lake.

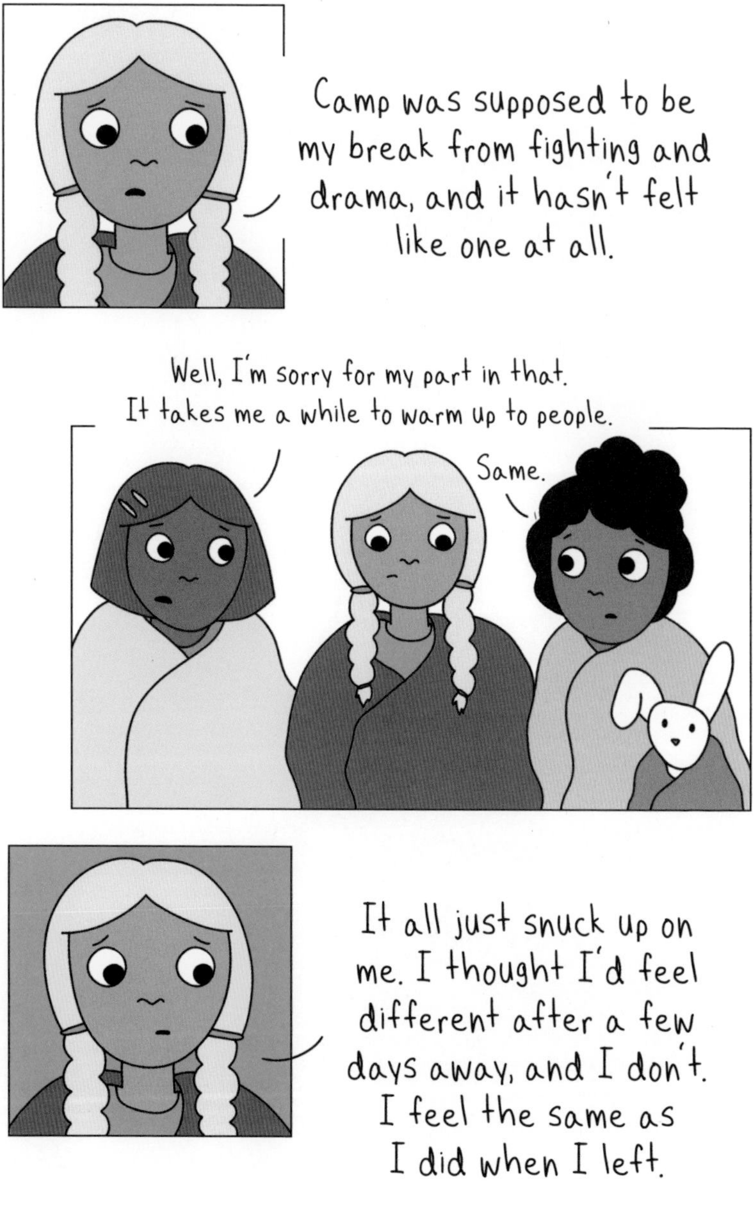
Camp was supposed to be my break from fighting and drama, and it hasn't felt like one at all.
Well, I'm sorry for my part in that. It takes me a while to warm up to people.
Same.
It all just snuck up on me. I thought I'd feel different after a few days away, and I don't. I feel the same as I did when I left.

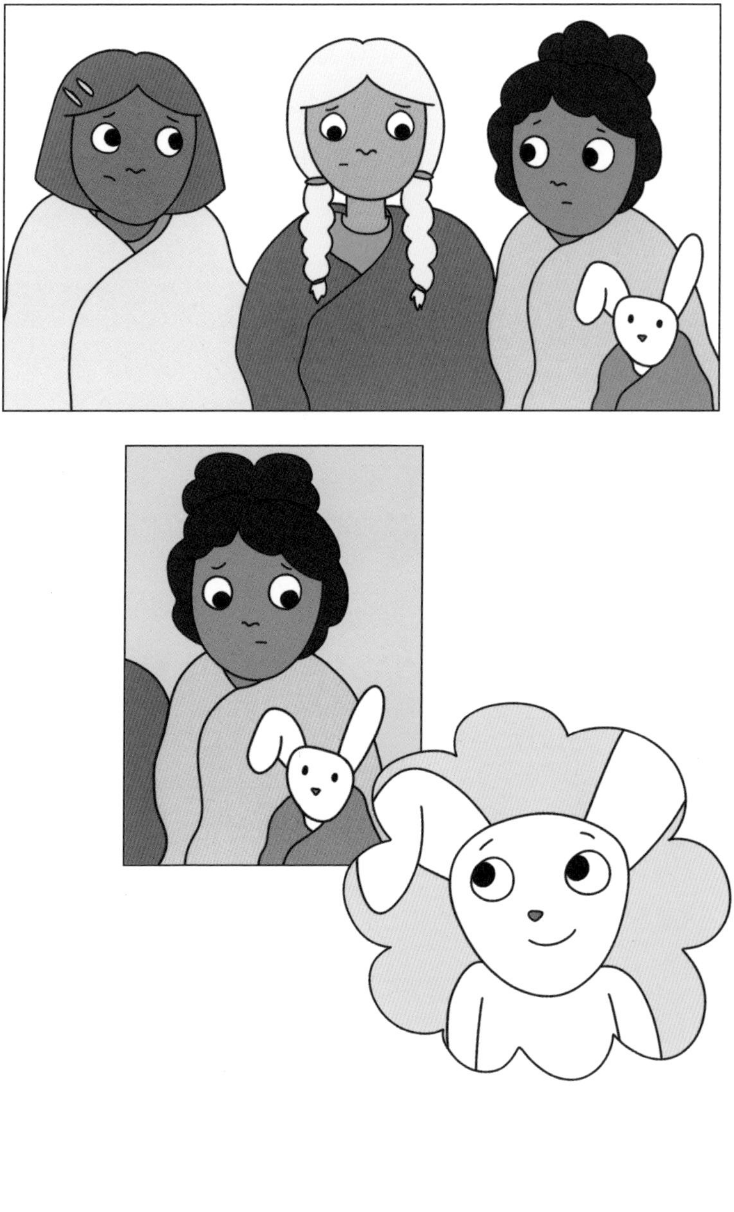

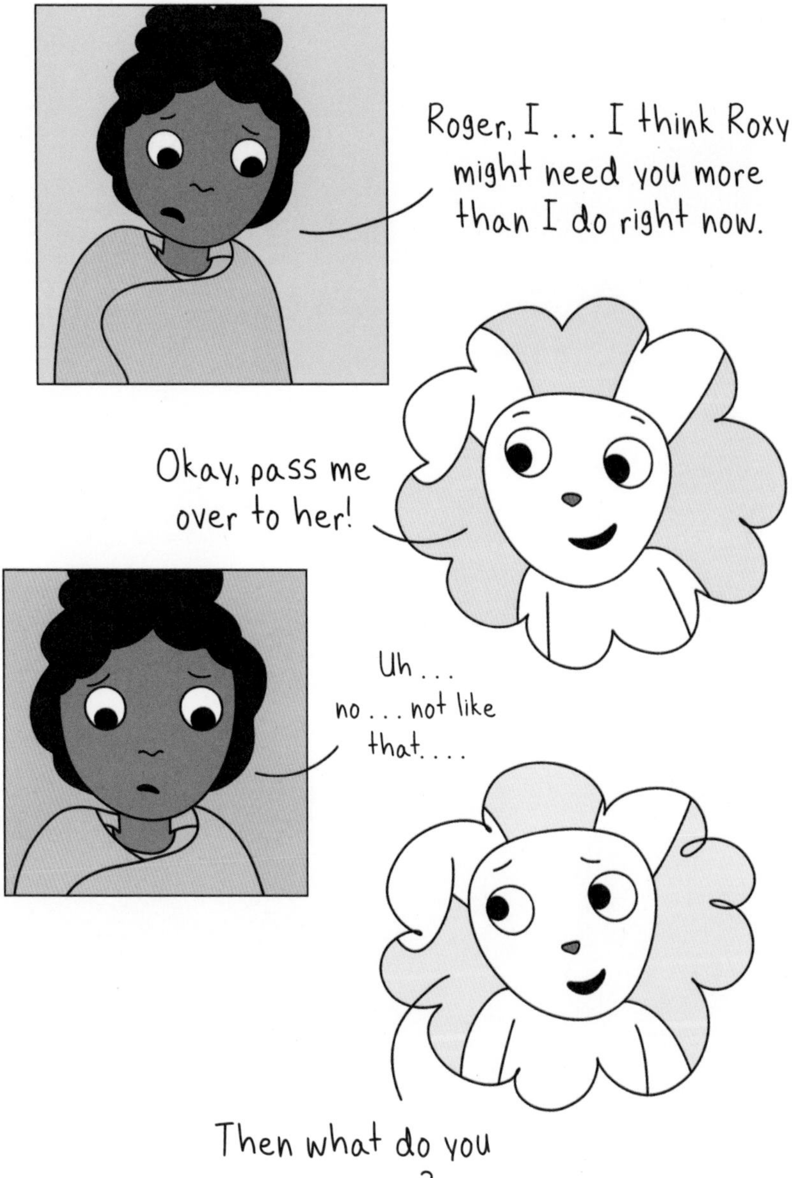
Roger, I . . . I think Roxy might need you more than I do right now.
Okay, pass me over to her!
Uh . . . no . . . not like that. . . .
Then what do you mean . . . ?

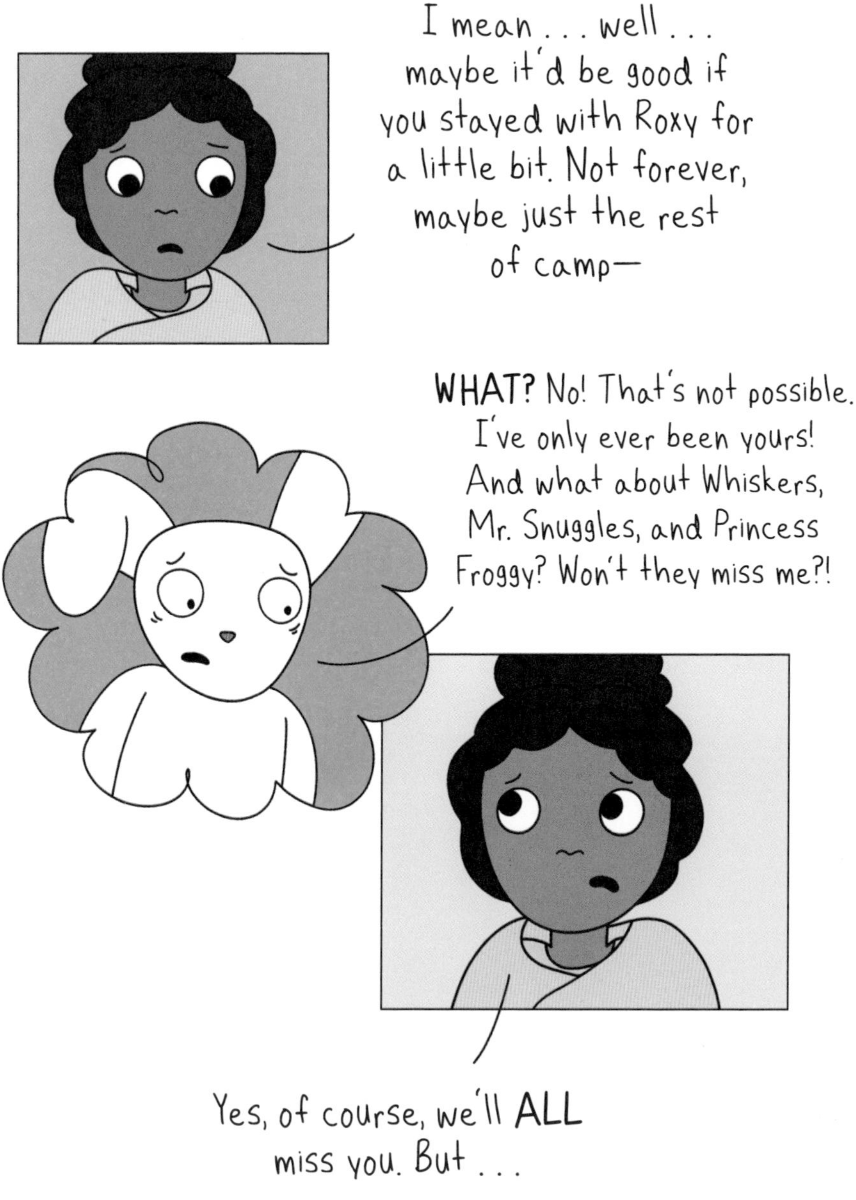
I mean . . . well . . . maybe it'd be good if you stayed with Roxy for a little bit. Not forever, maybe just the rest of camp—
WHAT? No! That's not possible. I've only ever been yours! And what about Whiskers, Mr. Snuggles, and Princess Froggy? Won't they miss me?!
Yes, of course, we'll **ALL** miss you. But . . .

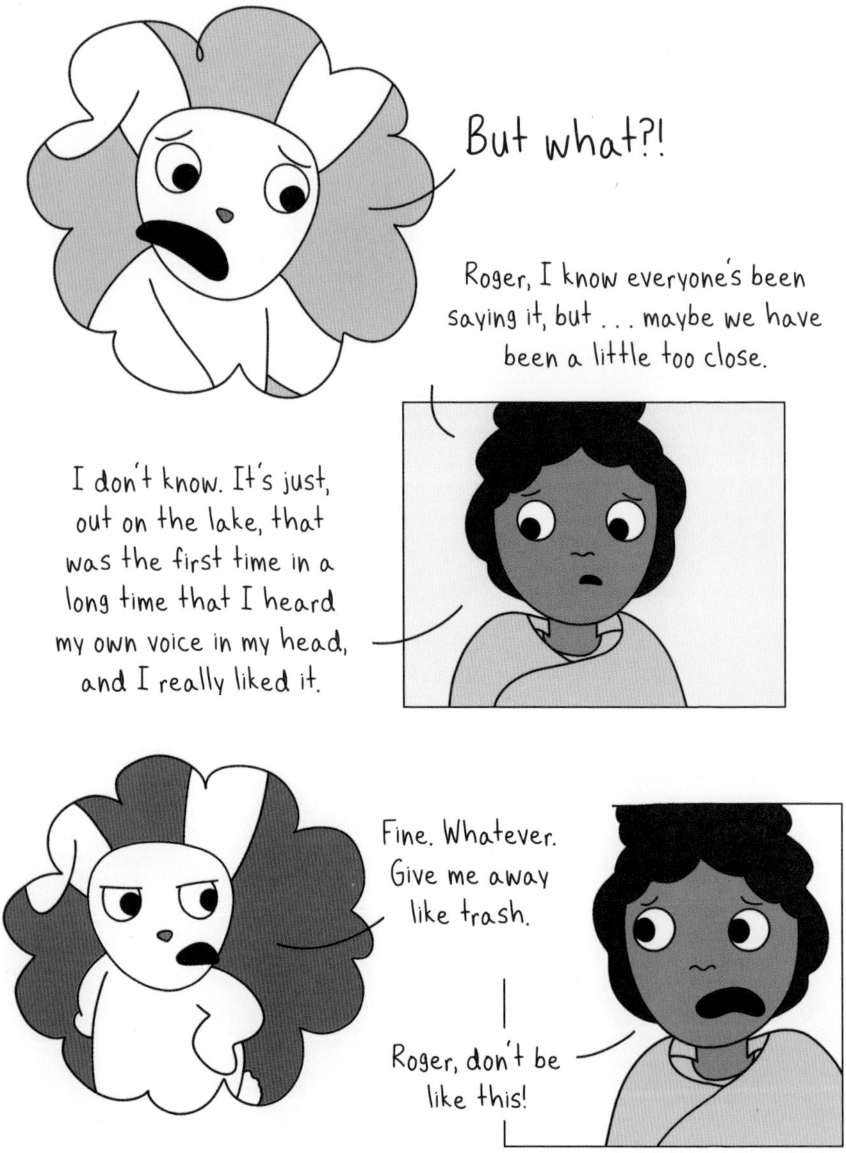
But what?!
Roger, I know everyone's been saying it, but . . . maybe we have been a little too close.
I don't know. It's just, out on the lake, that was the first time in a long time that I heard my own voice in my head, and I really liked it.
Fine. Whatever. Give me away like trash.
Roger, don't be like this!

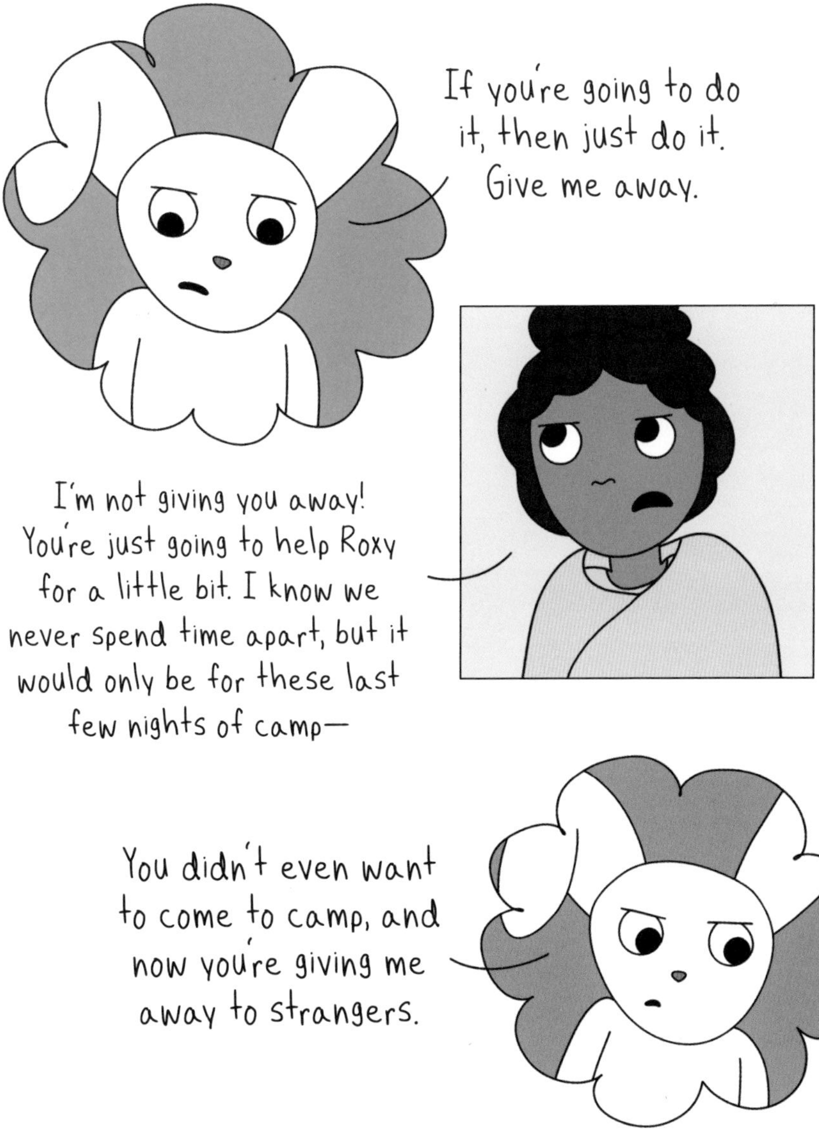
If you're going to do it, then just do it. Give me away.
I'm not giving you away! You're just going to help Roxy for a little bit. I know we never spend time apart, but it would only be for these last few nights of camp—
You didn't even want to come to camp, and now you're giving me away to strangers.

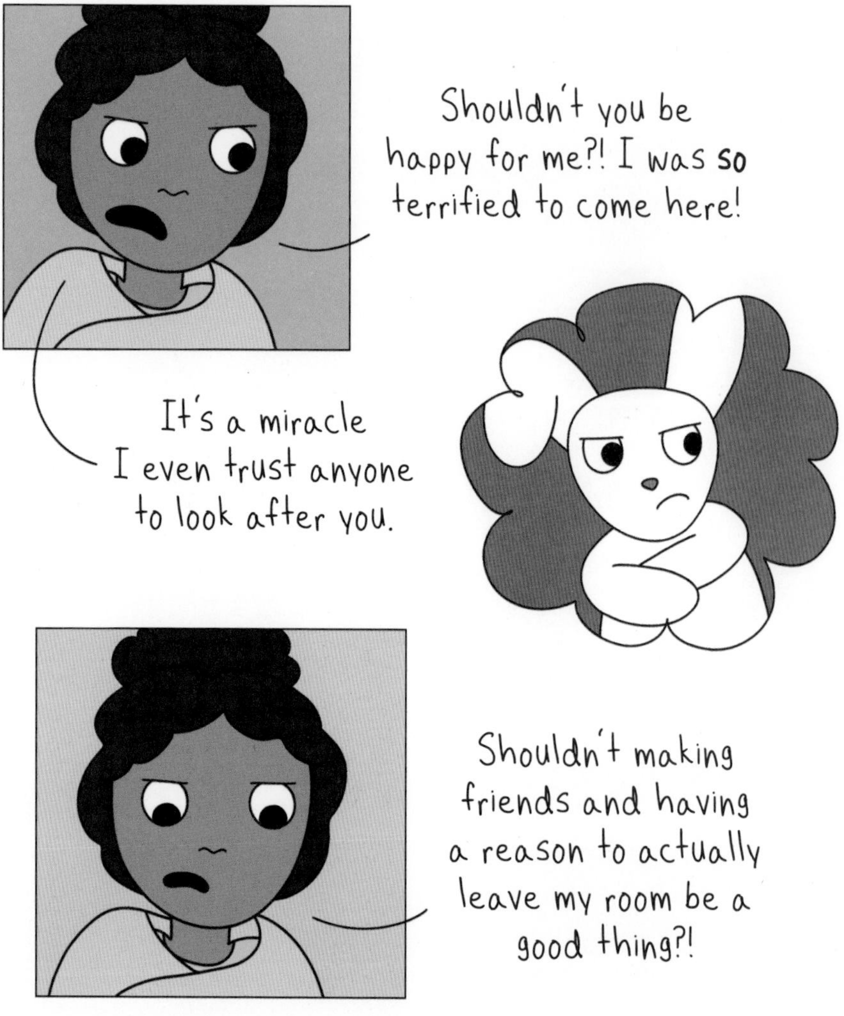
Shouldn't you be happy for me?! I was **SO** terrified to come here!
It's a miracle I even trust anyone to look after you.
Shouldn't making friends and having a reason to actually leave my room be a good thing?!

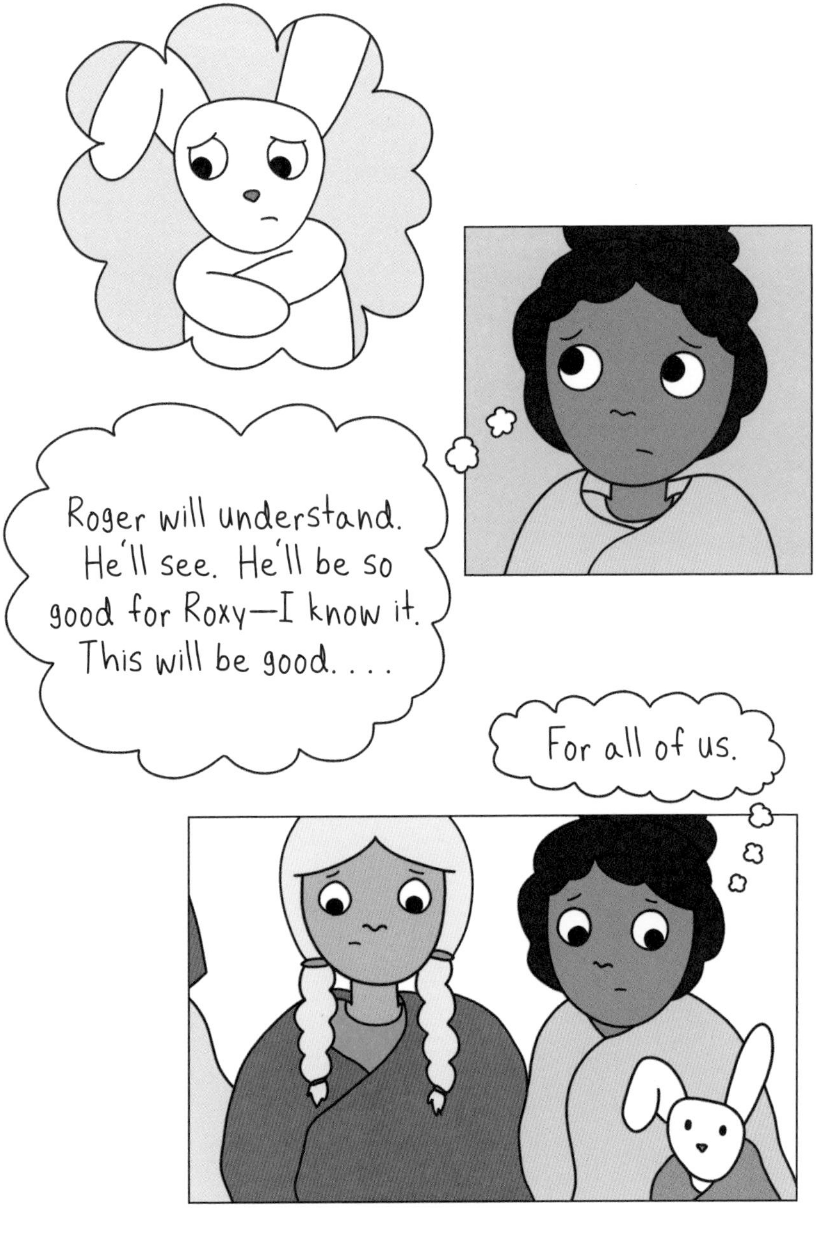
Roger will understand. He'll see. He'll be so good for Roxy—I know it. This will be good. . . .
For all of us.

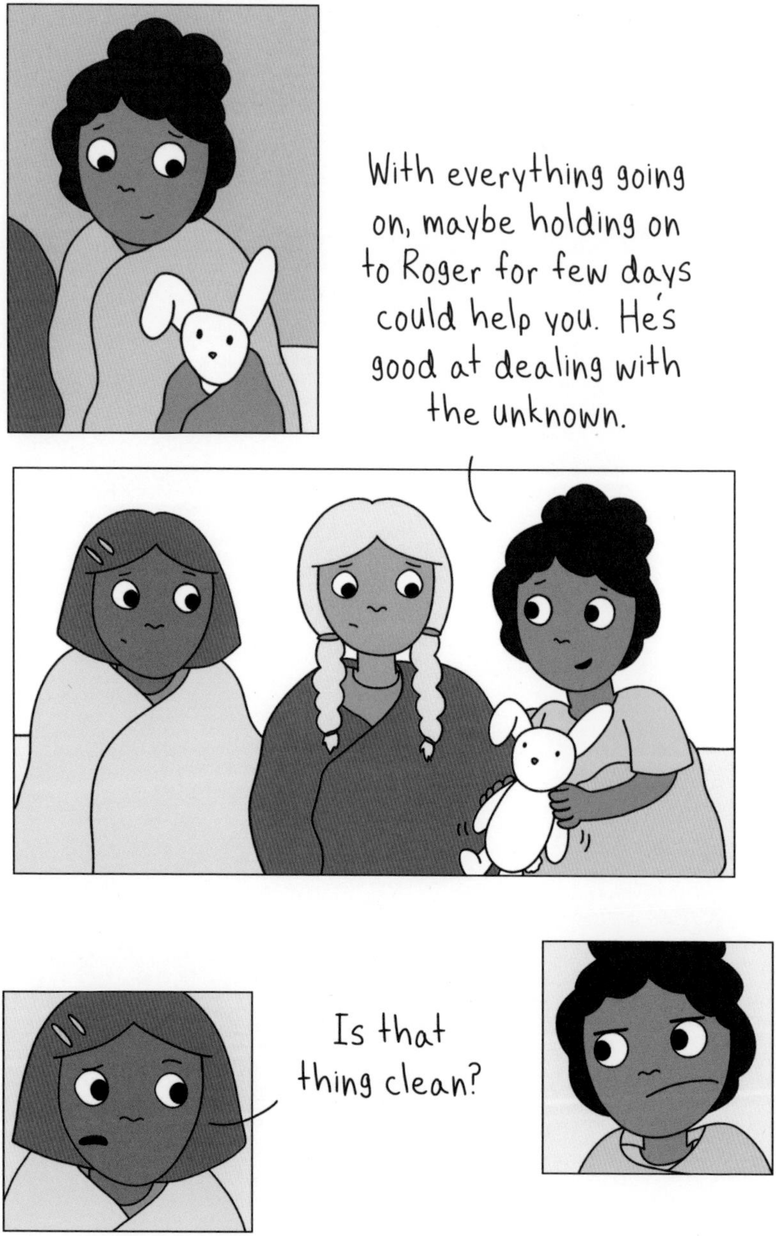
With everything going on, maybe holding on to Roger for few days could help you. He's good at dealing with the unknown.
Is that thing clean?

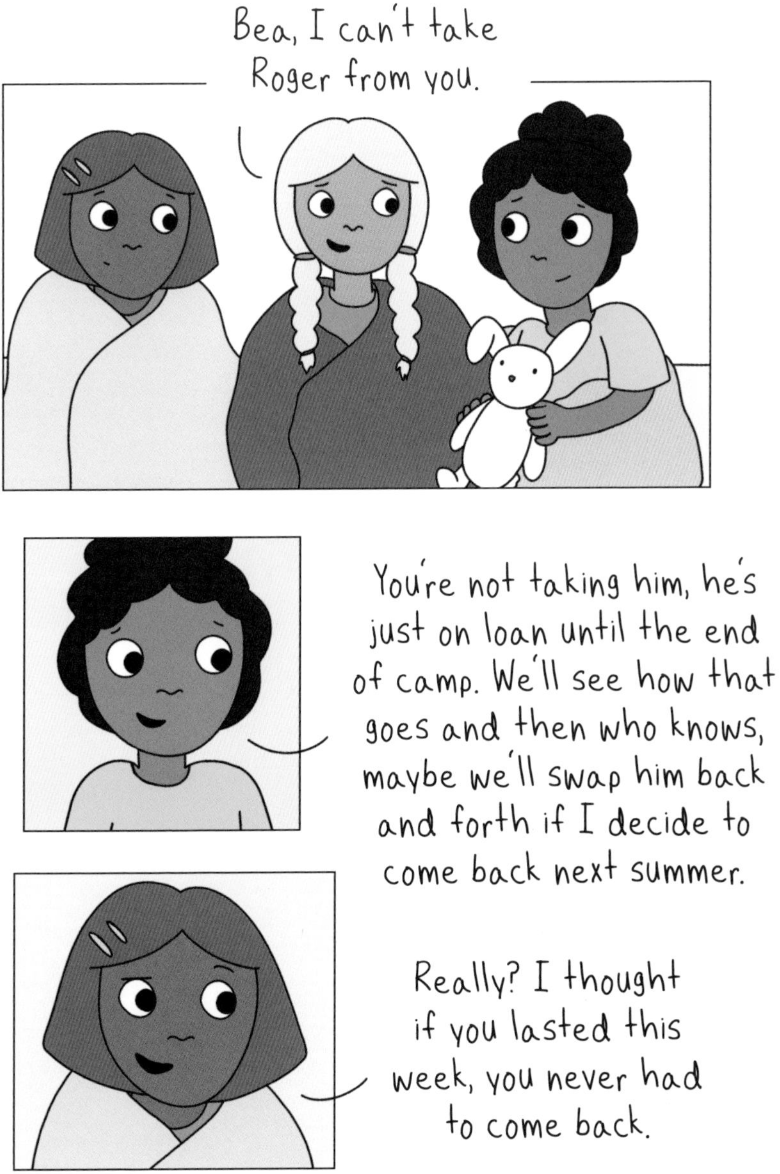
Bea, I can't take Roger from you.
You're not taking him, he's just on loan until the end of camp. We'll see how that goes and then who knows, maybe we'll swap him back and forth if I decide to come back next summer.
Really? I thought if you lasted this week, you never had to come back.

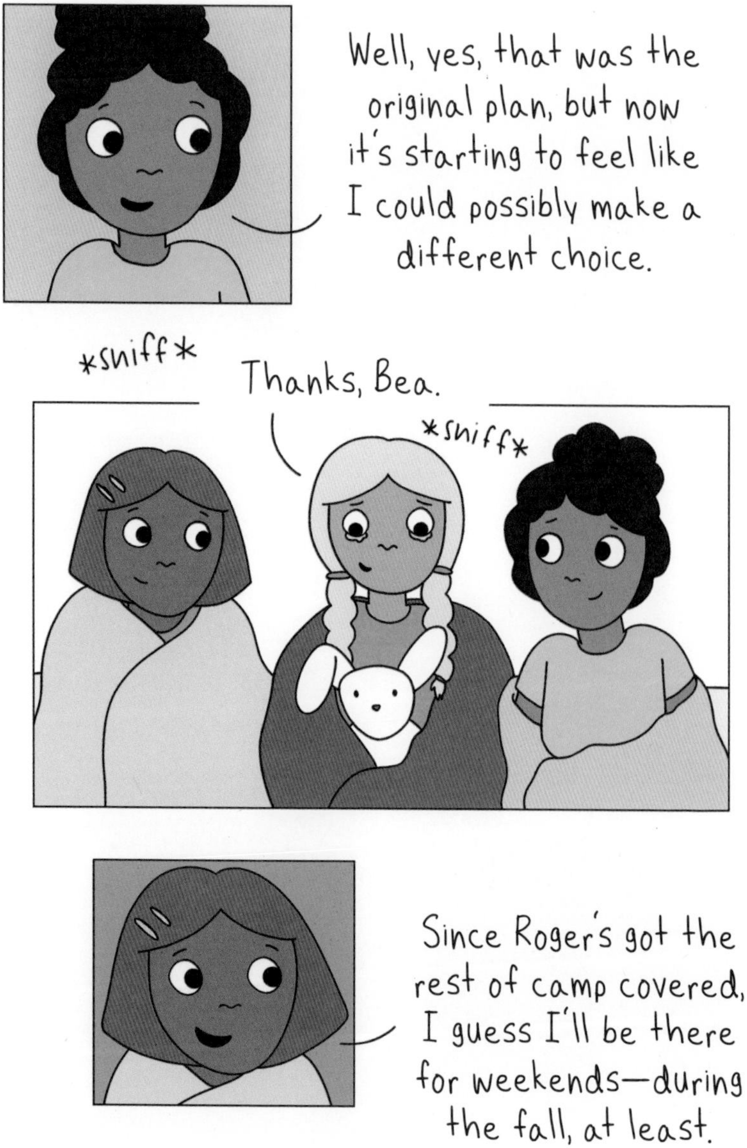
Well, yes, that was the original plan, but now it's starting to feel like I could possibly make a different choice.
sniff
Thanks, Bea.
sniff
Since Roger's got the rest of camp covered, I guess I'll be there for weekends—during the fall, at least.

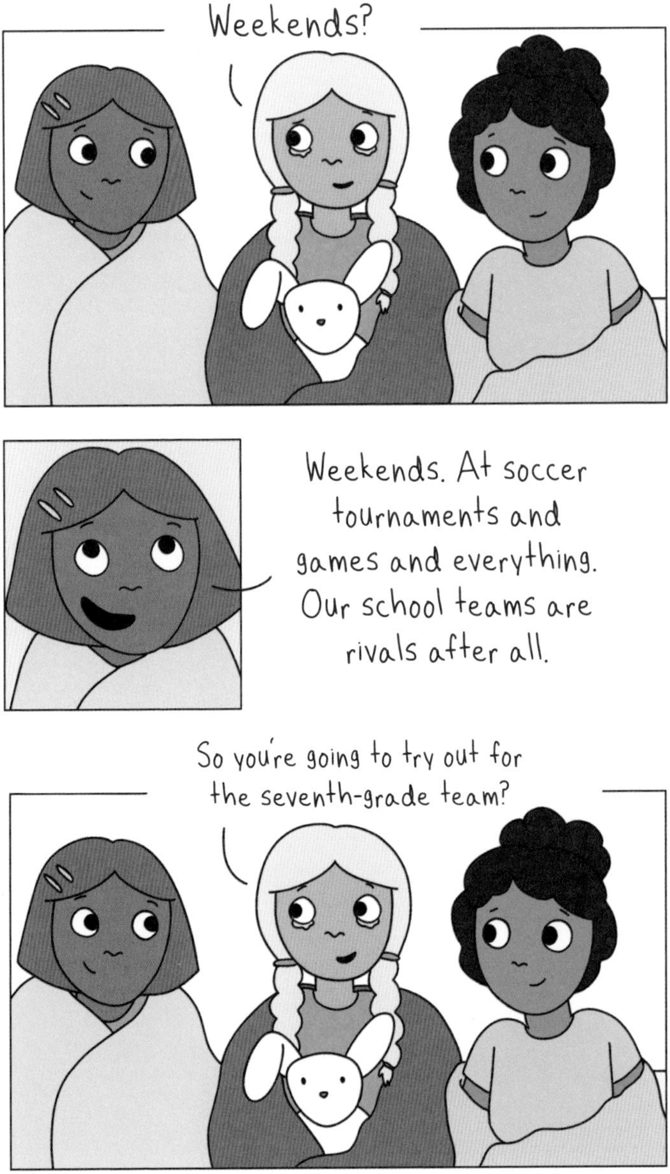
Weekends?
Weekends. At soccer tournaments and games and everything. Our school teams are rivals after all.
So you're going to try out for the seventh-grade team?

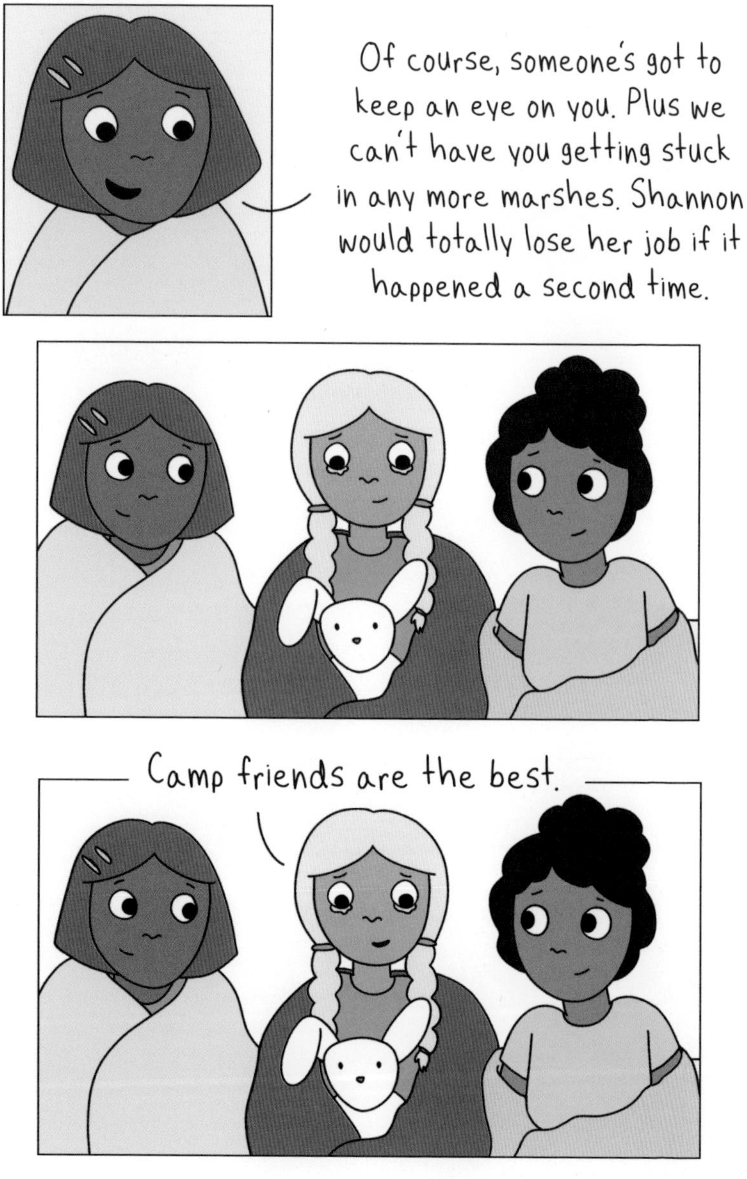
Of course, someone's got to keep an eye on you. Plus we can't have you getting stuck in any more marshes. Shannon would totally lose her job if it happened a second time.
Camp friends are the best.

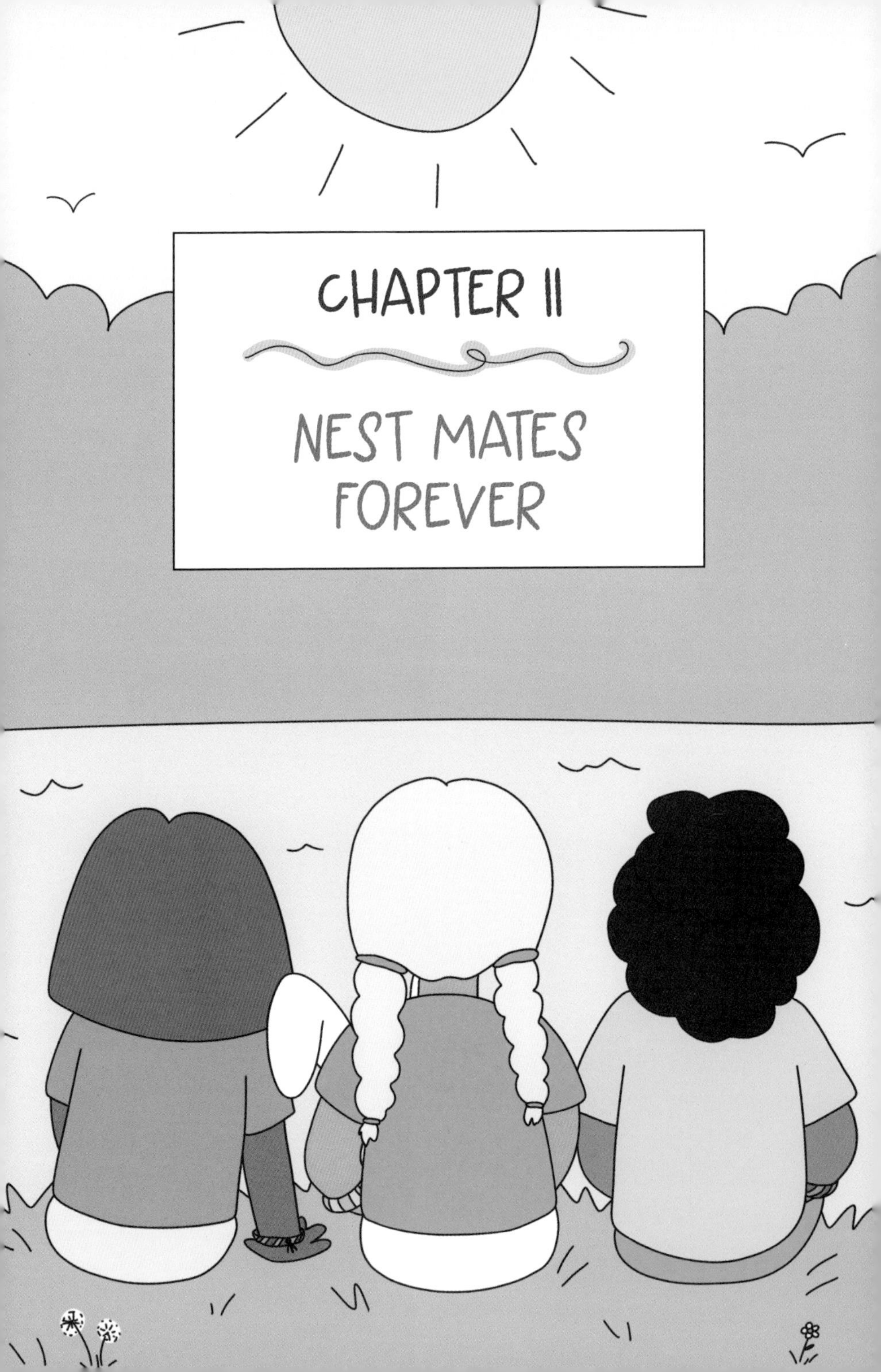
CHAPTER 11
NEST MATES FOREVER

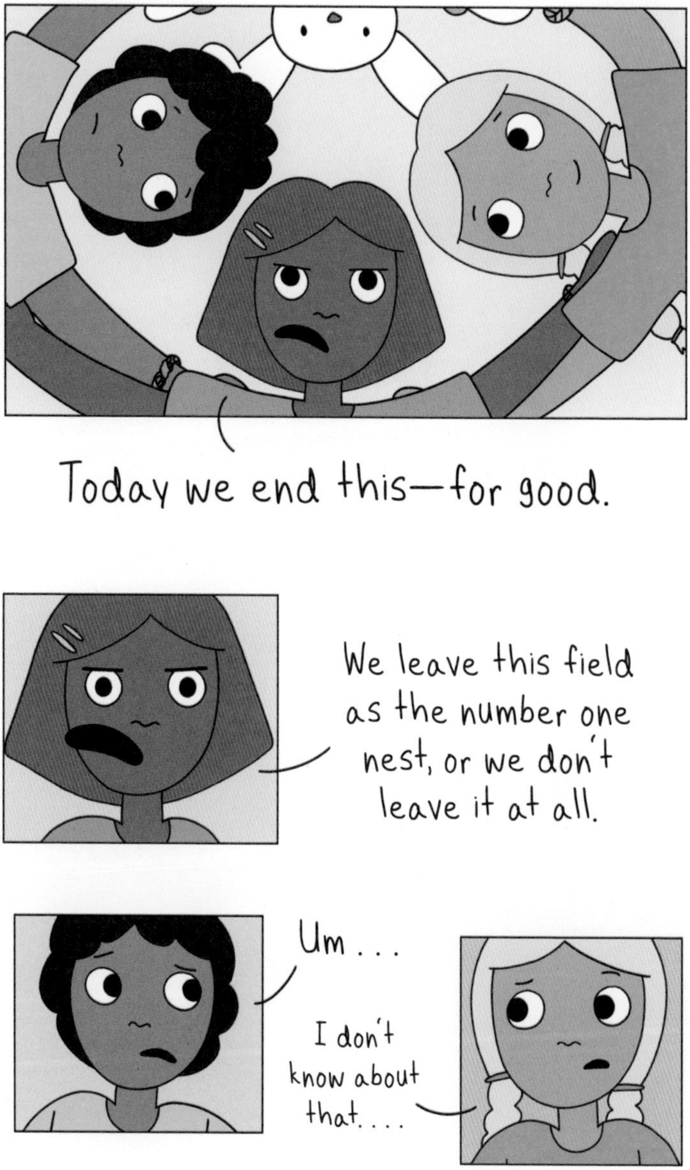
Today we end this—for good.
We leave this field as the number one nest, or we don't leave it at all.
Um . . .
I don't know about that. . . .

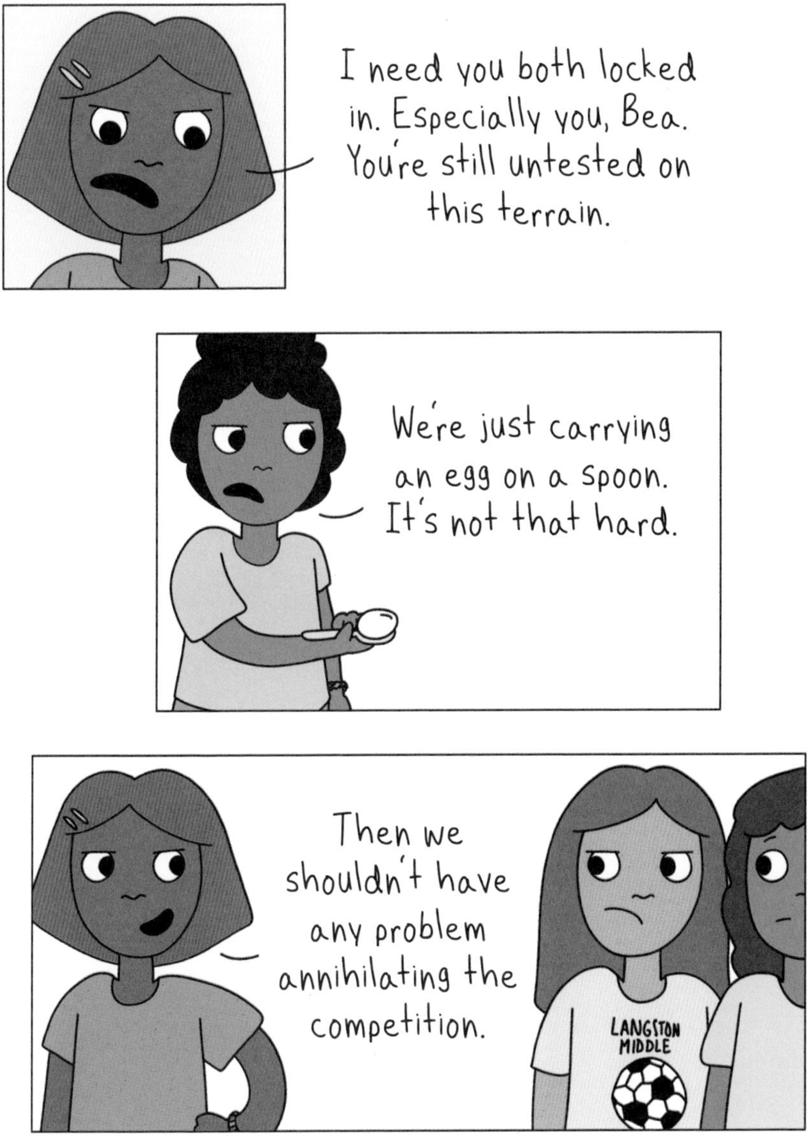
I need you both locked in. Especially you, Bea. You're still untested on this terrain.
We're just carrying an egg on a spoon. It's not that hard.
Then we shouldn't have any problem annihilating the competition.
LANGSTON MIDDLE

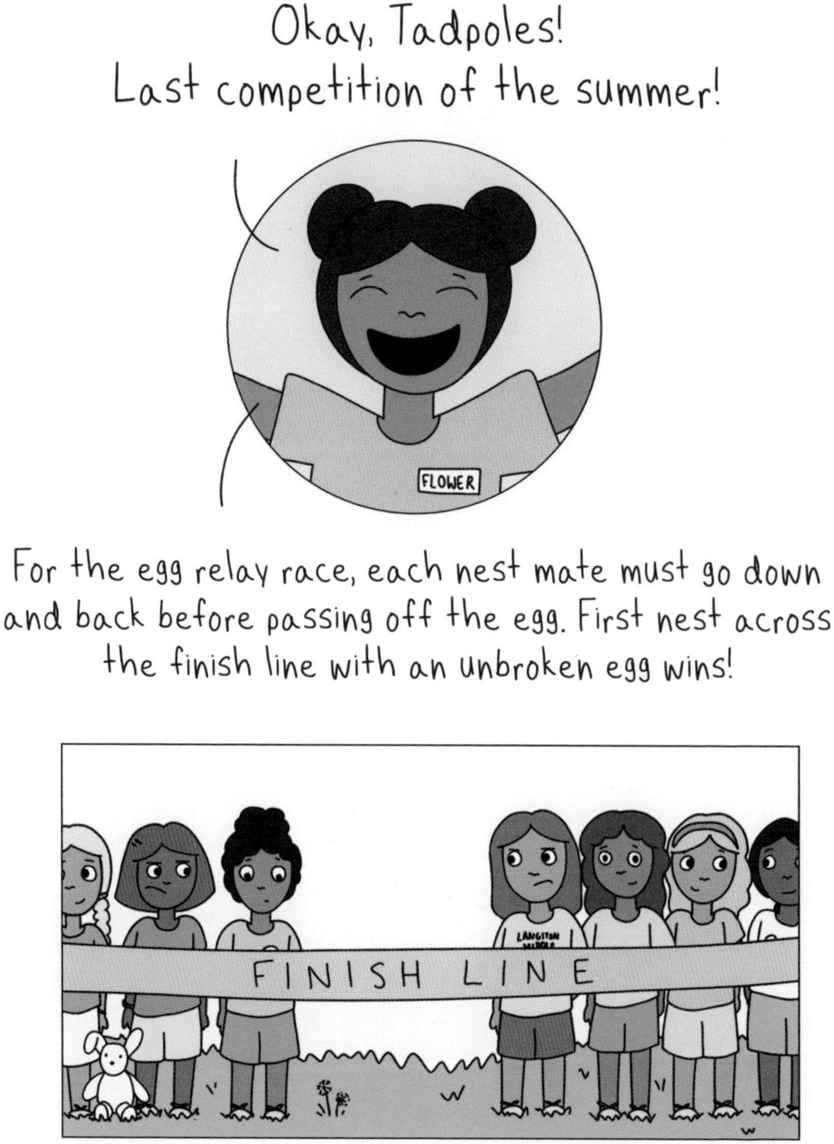
Okay, Tadpoles!
Last competition of the summer!
FLOWER
For the egg relay race, each nest mate must go down and back before passing off the egg. First nest across the finish line with an unbroken egg wins!
FINISH LINE

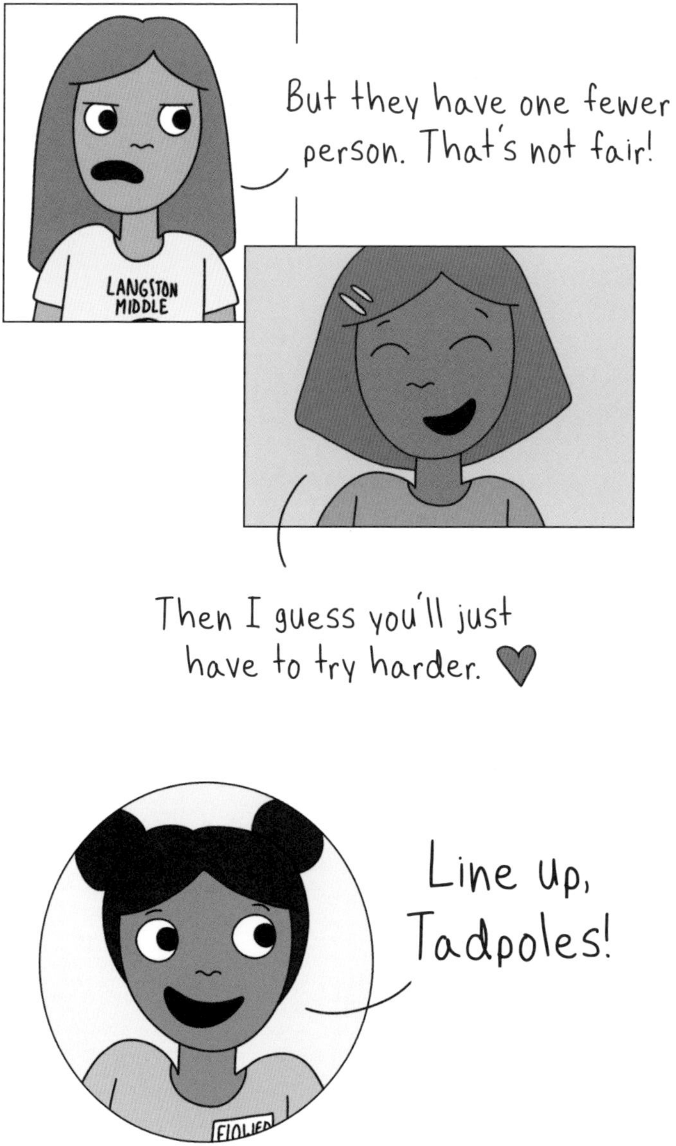
But they have one fewer person. That's not fair!
LANGSTON MIDDLE
Then I guess you'll just have to try harder. ♥
Line up, Tadpoles!

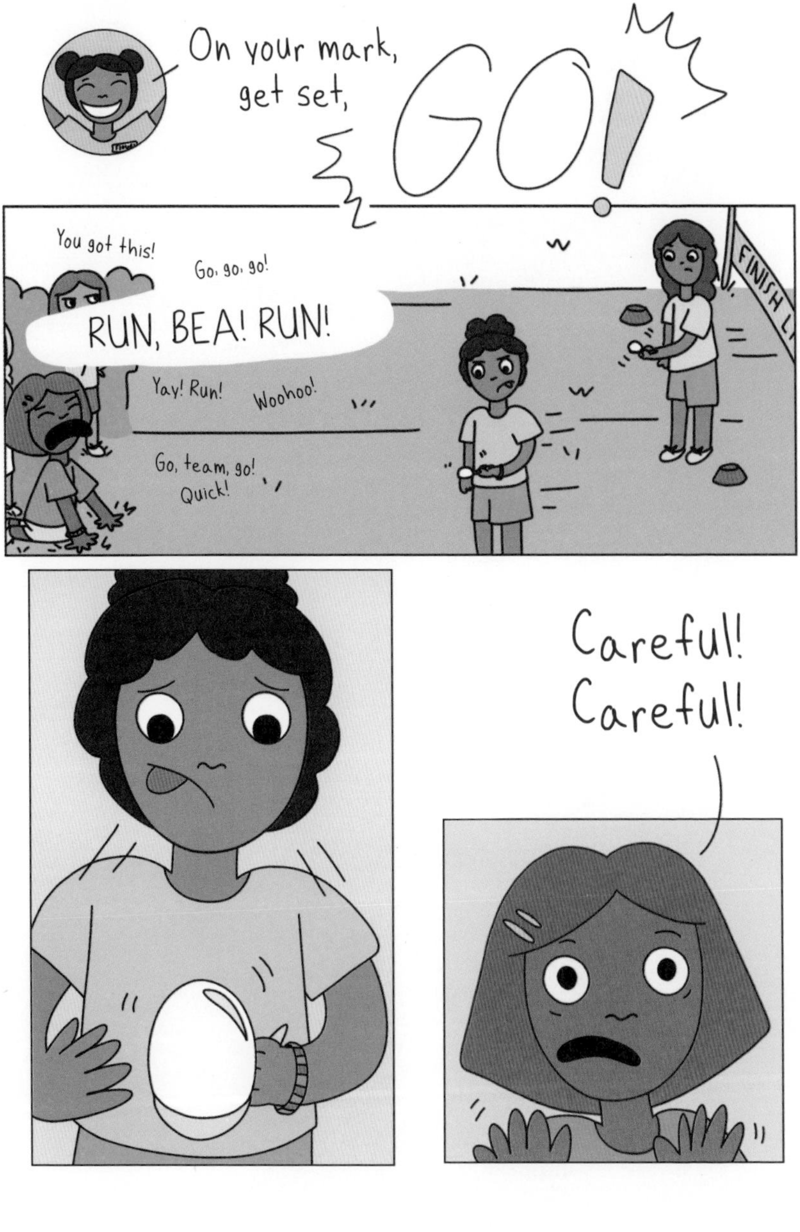
On your mark, get set,
GO!
You got this!
Go, go, go!
RUN, BEA! RUN!
Yay! Run!
Woohoo!
Go, team, go!
Quick!
FINISH L
Careful! Careful!

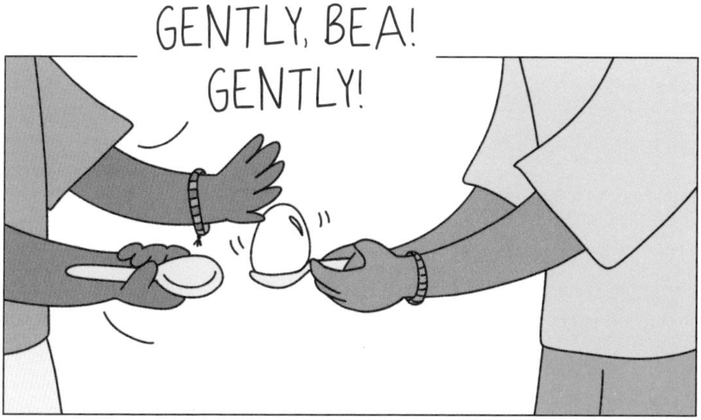
GENTLY, BEA! GENTLY!

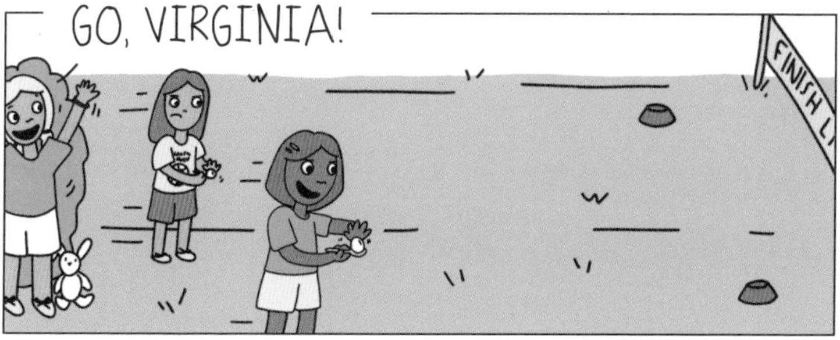
GO, VIRGINIA!
FINISH L

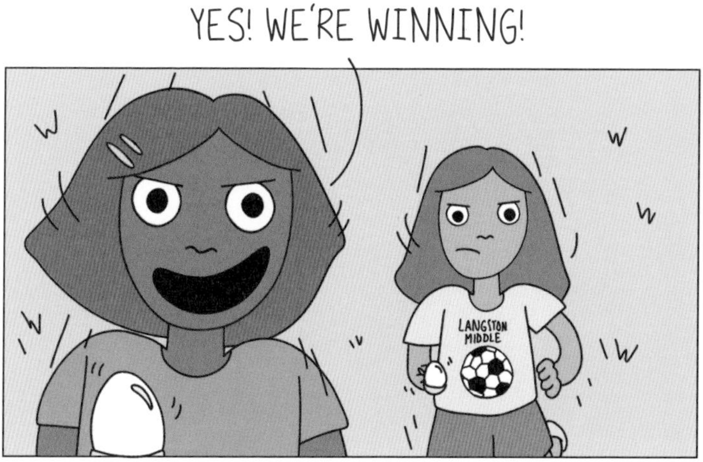
YES! WE'RE WINNING!
LANGSTON MIDDLE

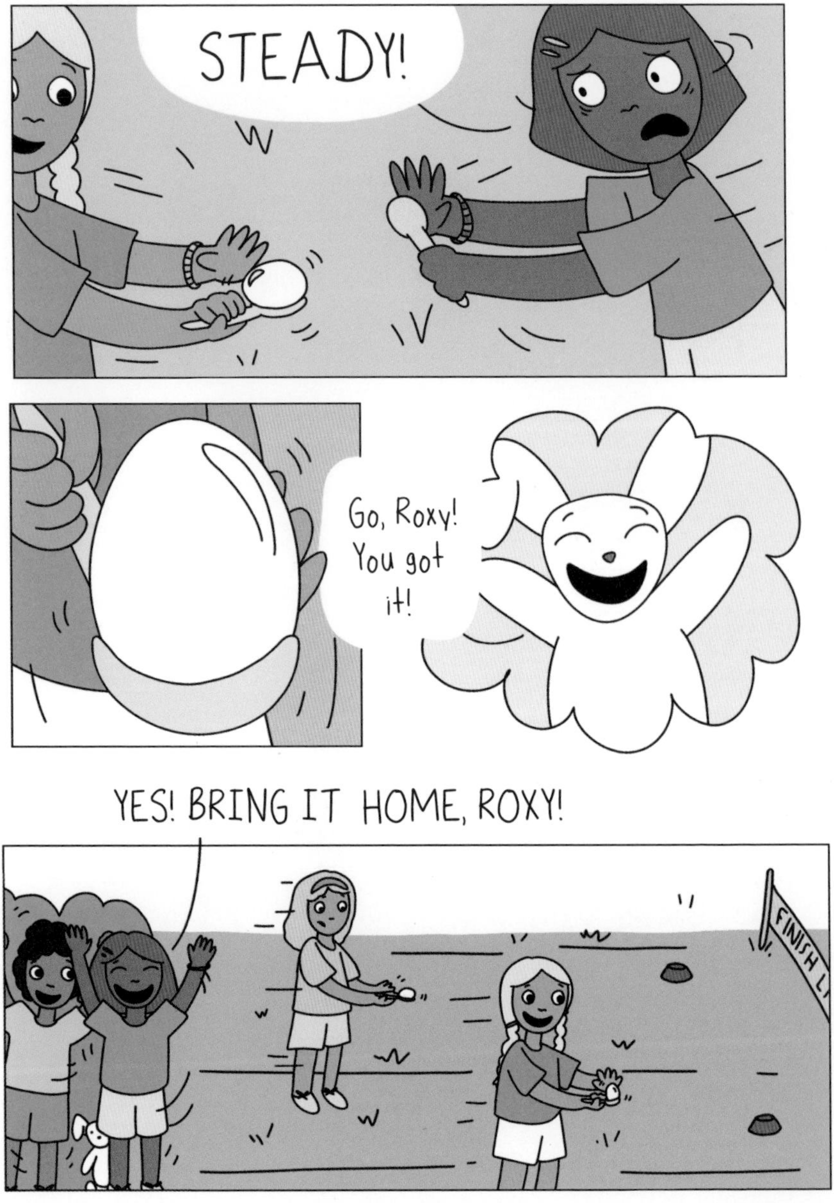
STEADY!
Go, Roxy! You got it!
YES! BRING IT HOME, ROXY!

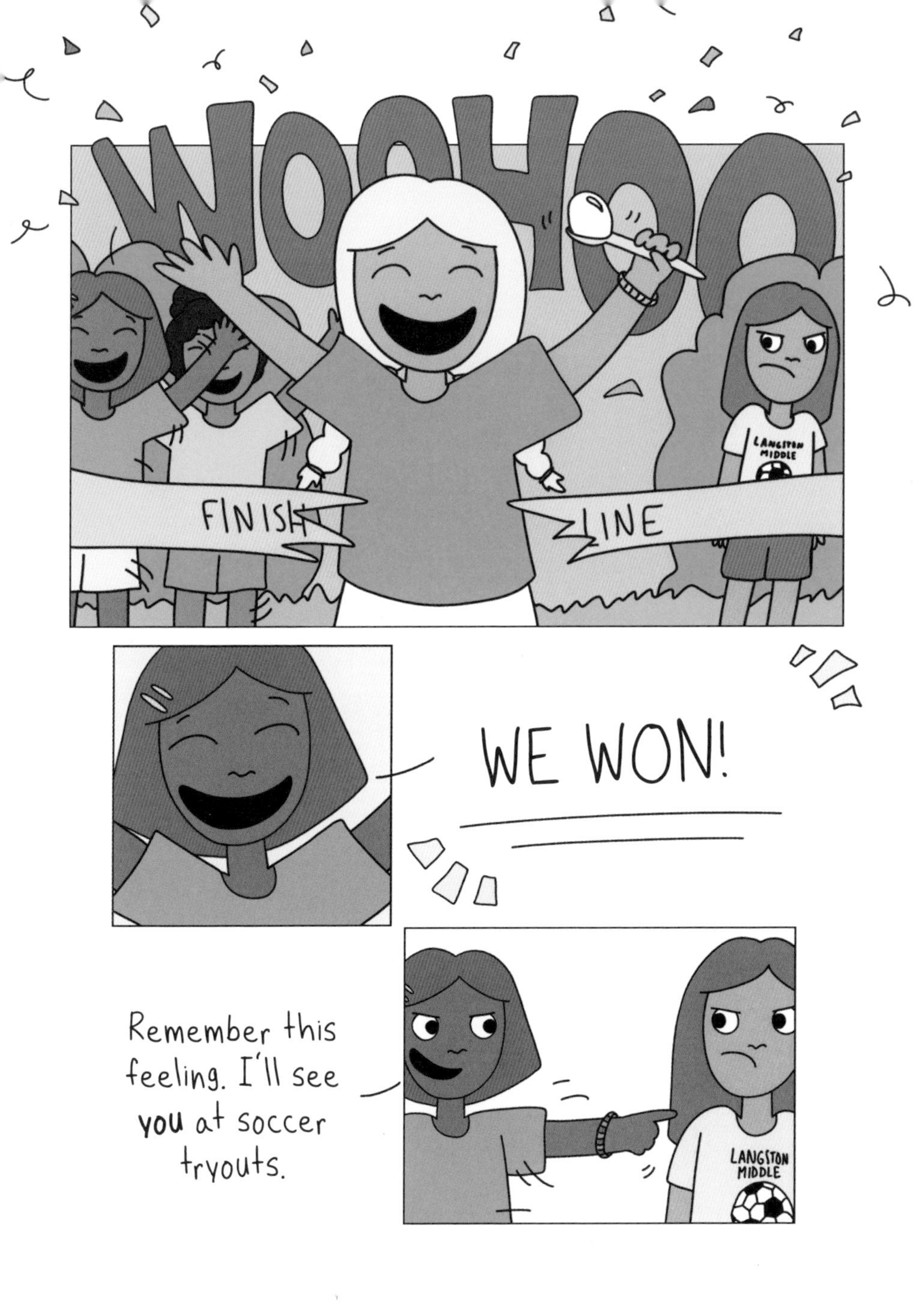
WOOHOO
FINISH LINE
LANGSTON MIDDLE
WE WON!
Remember this feeling. I'll see **you** at soccer tryouts.
LANGSTON MIDDLE

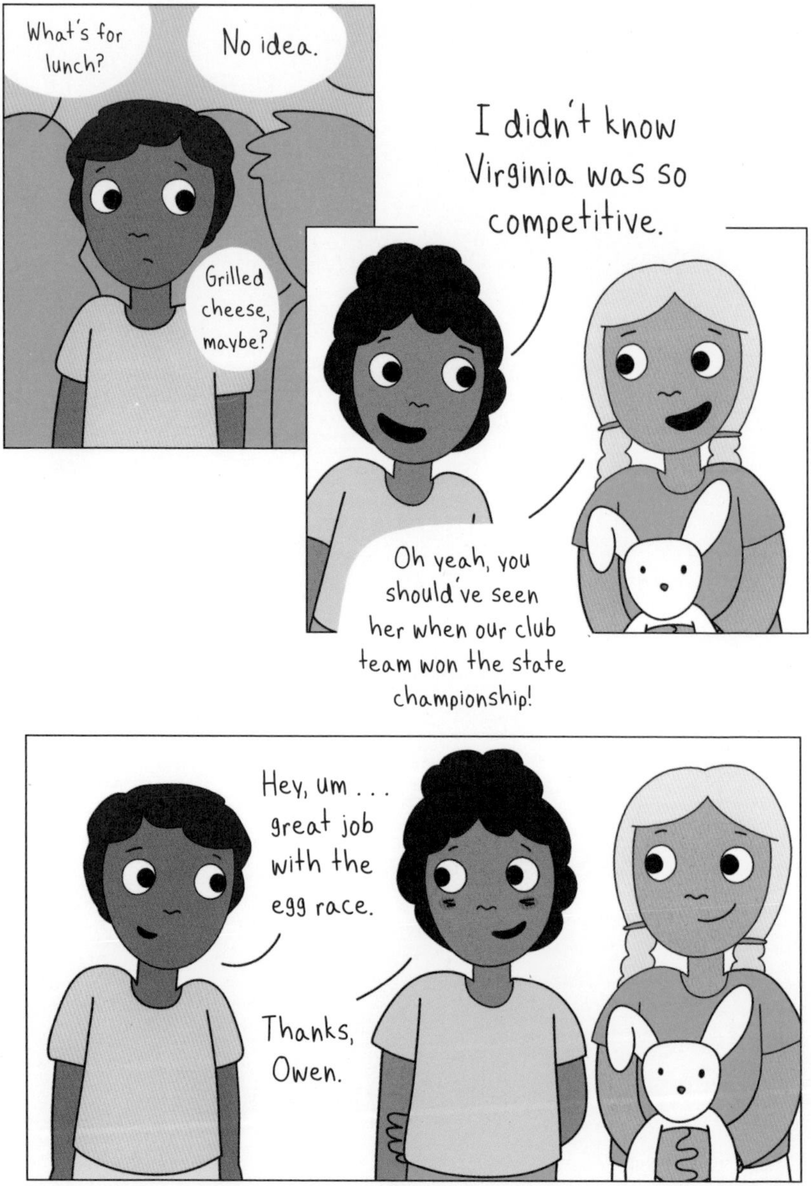
What's for lunch?
No idea.
Grilled cheese, maybe?
I didn't know Virginia was so competitive.
Oh yeah, you should've seen her when our club team won the state championship!
Hey, um . . . great job with the egg race.
Thanks, Owen.

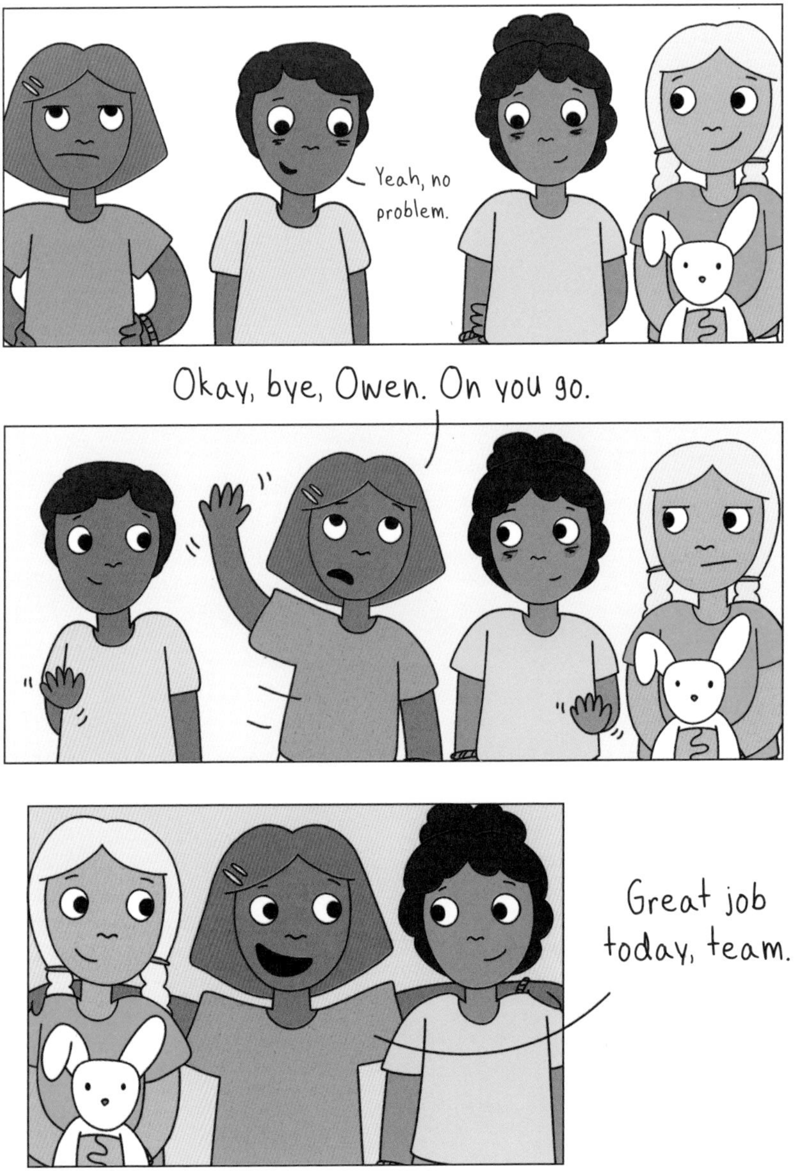
Yeah, no problem.
Okay, bye, Owen. On you go.
Great job today, team.

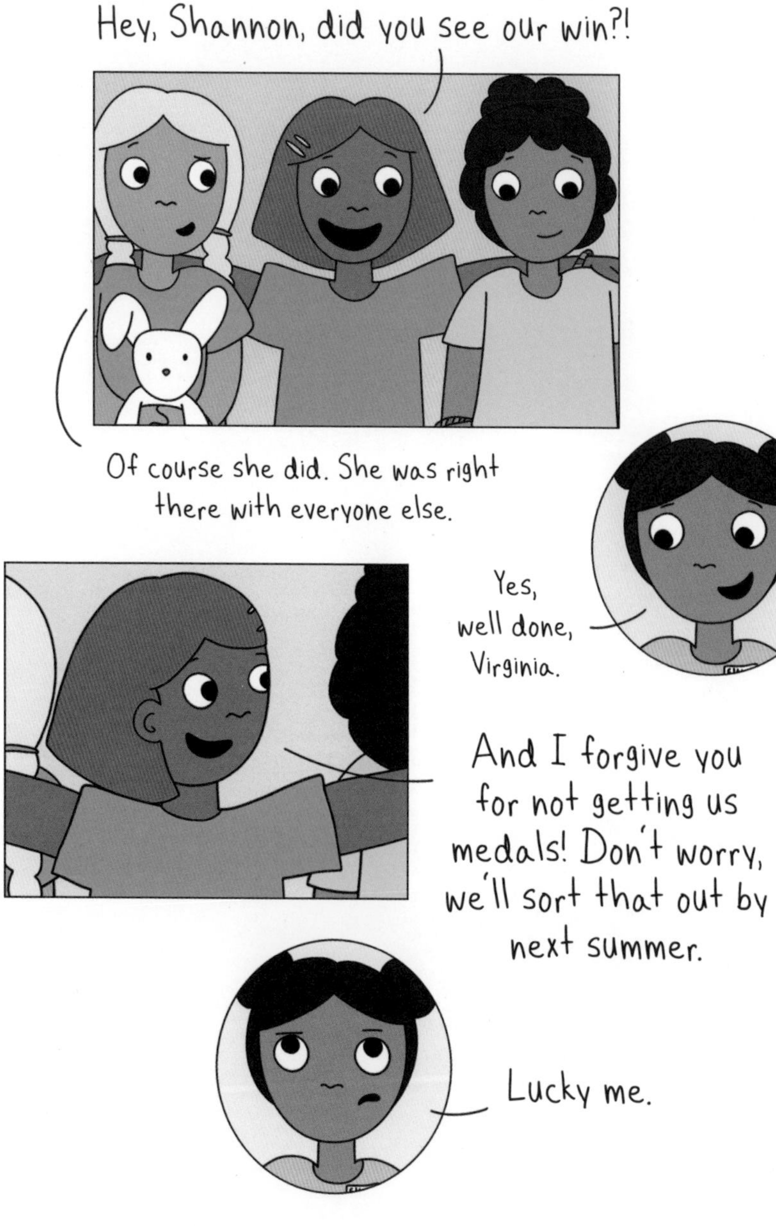
Hey, Shannon, did you see our win?!
Of course she did. She was right there with everyone else.
Yes, well done, Virginia.
And I forgive you for not getting us medals! Don't worry, we'll sort that out by next summer.
Lucky me.

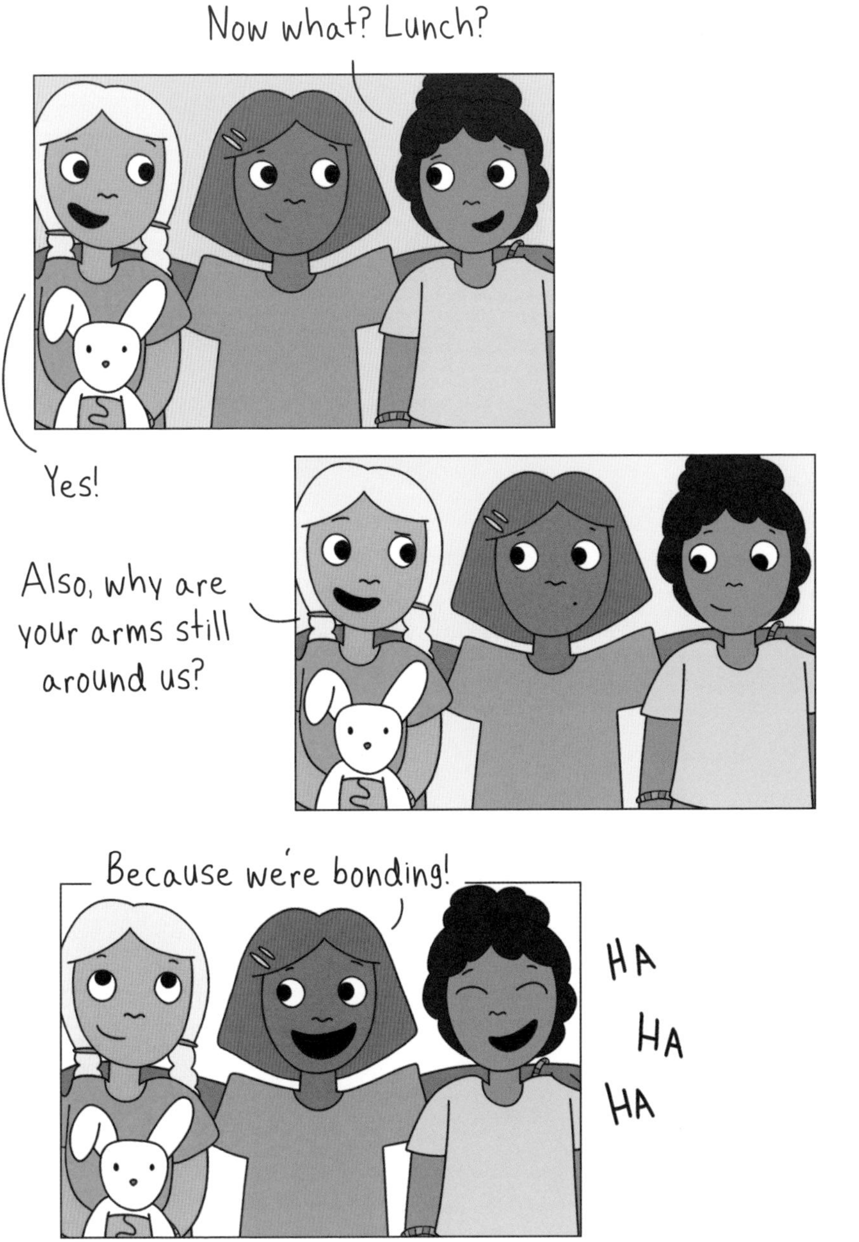
Now what? Lunch?
Yes!
Also, why are your arms still around us?
Because we're bonding!
HA
HA
HA

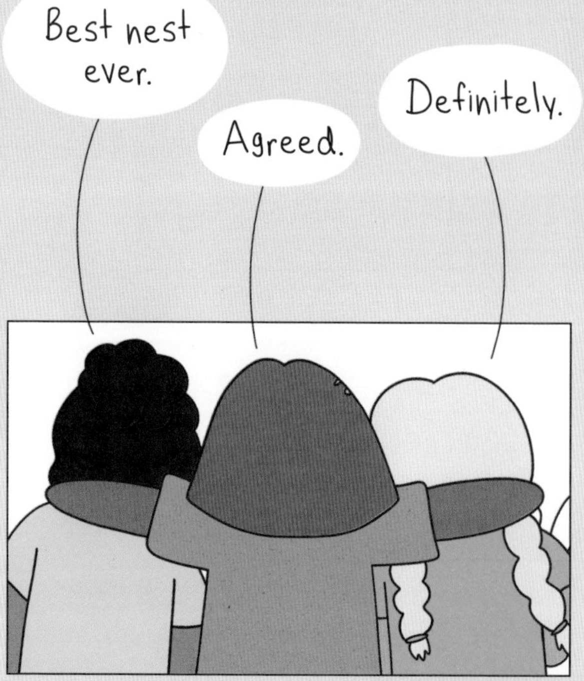
Best nest ever.
Agreed.
Definitely.

THE END
(UNTIL NEXT SUMMER)

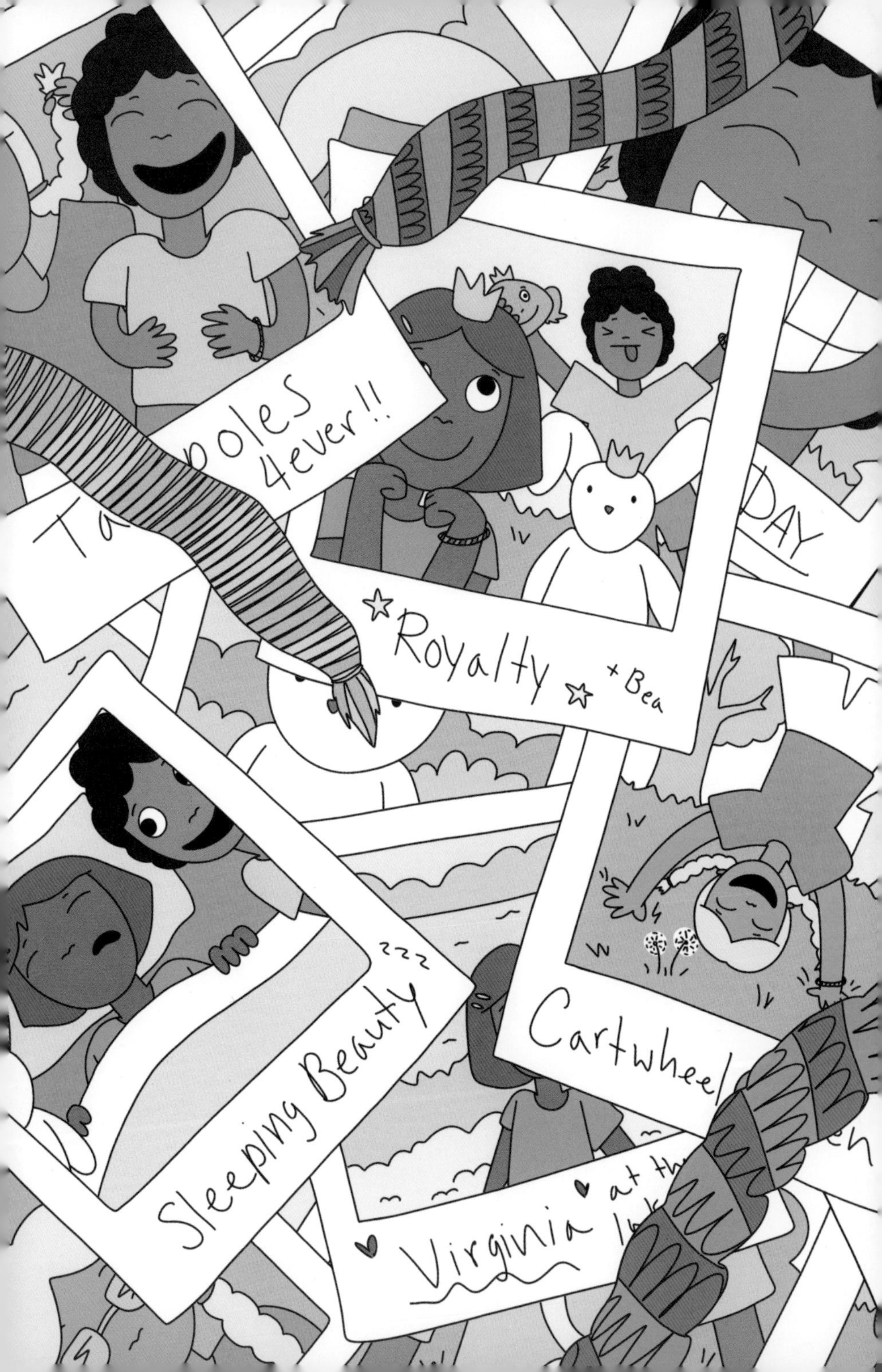
poleS 4ever!!
Royalty
+ Bea
DAY
zzz
Sleeping Beauty
Cartwheel
Virginia

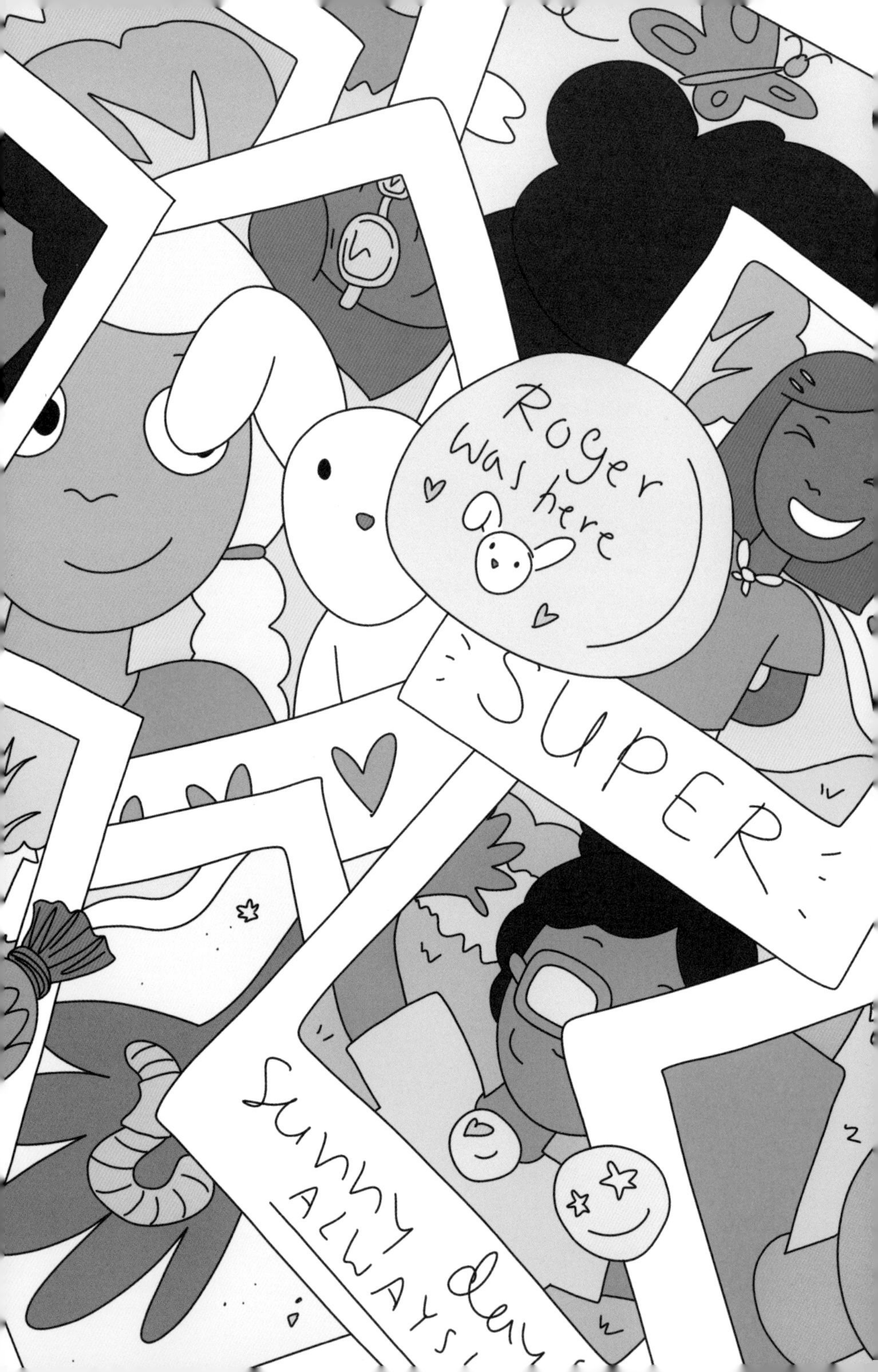
Roger was here
SUPER
Sunny days
ALWAYS

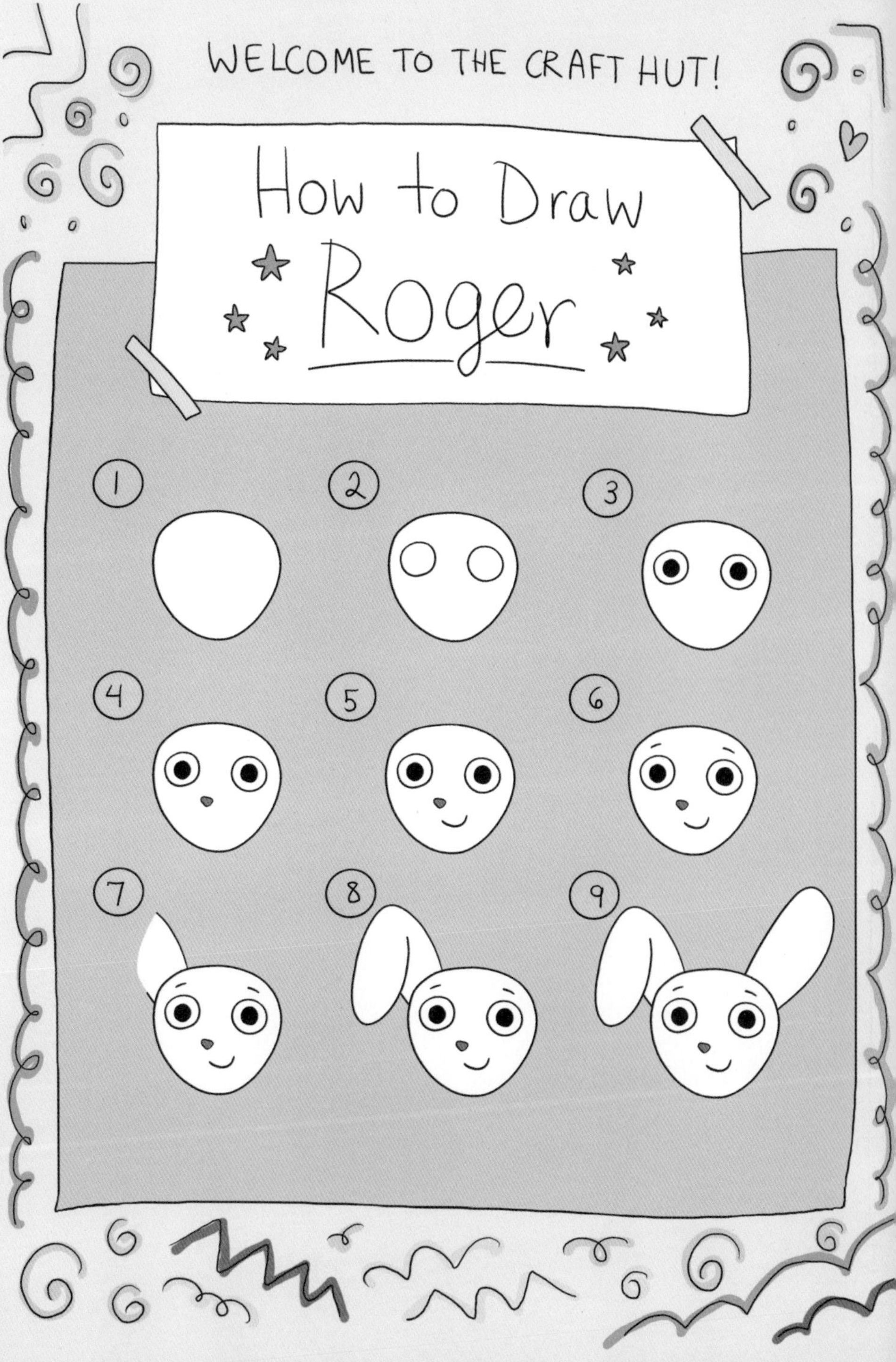
WELCOME TO THE CRAFT HUT!
How to Draw Roger
1
2
3
4
5
6
7
8
9

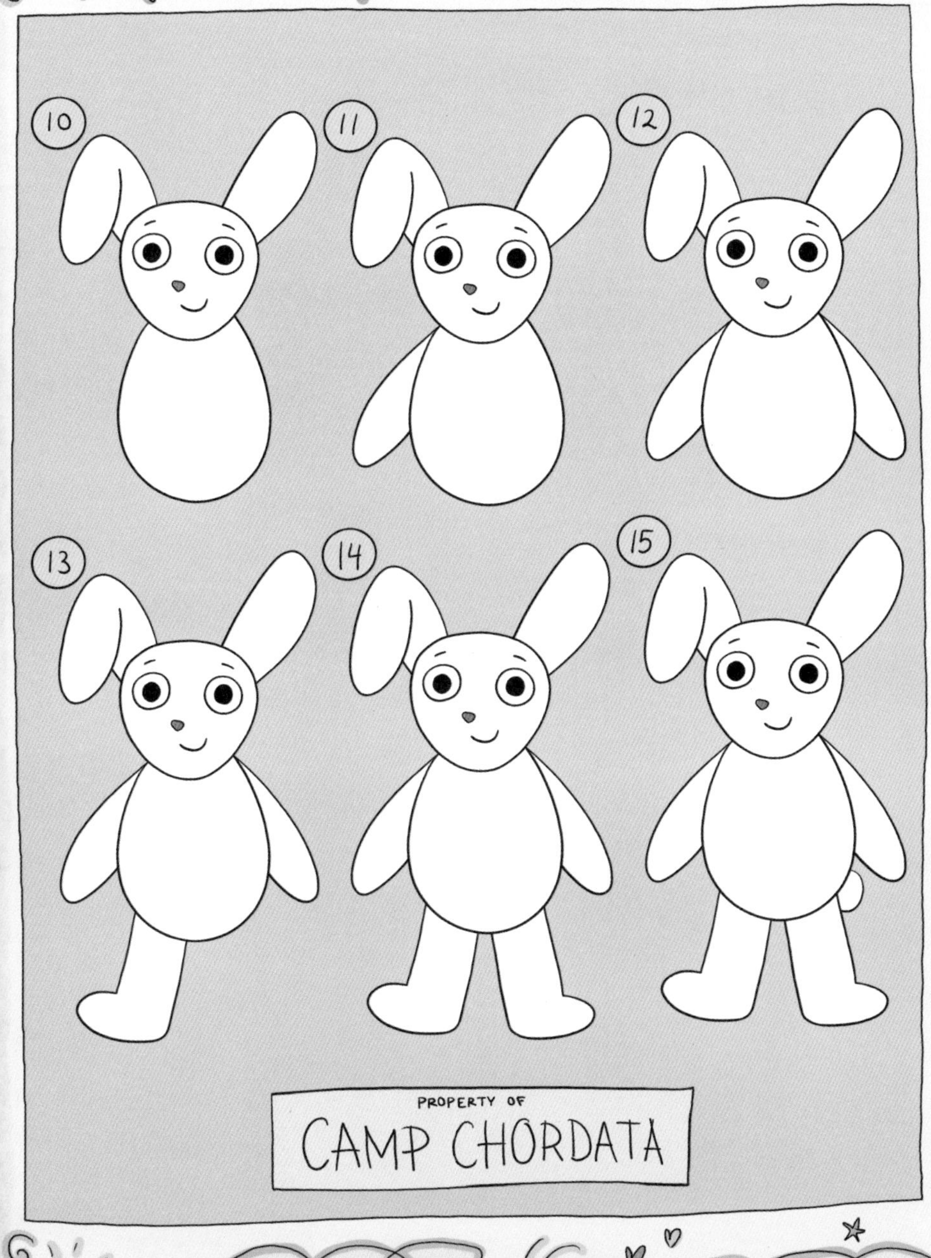
10
11
12
13
14
15
PROPERTY OF
CAMP CHORDATA

ACKNOWLEDGMENTS

Thank you so much to my incredible agent, Wendi, for guiding this story into the perfect hands, and thank you to my amazing editor, Annie Kelley, for believing in me, this book, and these characters. *Camp Frenemies* was incredibly fun to make, and I'm so grateful I got to do it with you! A huge thank-you to Sylvia Bi and Jules Buckley for their awesome design direction and guidance—you both made this book look a thousand times better than it would've otherwise!

I'm forever thankful for my husband, Pat, who patiently listened to me talk about Bea, Virginia, and Roxy like they were real people, and for all the friends and family who were very understanding when I'd take eons to text back.

A special thank-you to all the readers, teachers, and librarians who keep kid lit alive and thriving. I hope this book feels like lying in the sun at the start of the summer season!

Love always,
Liz